More praise for
North of Hope

"Jon Hassler has given us a series of wonderful novels that have earned glowing reviews and a loyal, fervent following among those fortunate enough to have discovered his work.... It will not be surprising if *North of Hope* is the one that makes him the household name he deserves to be."

—*The New York Times Book Review*

"Small town mores, church politics, the law of the reservation— Hassler has tapped every pulse with his pen. This is his sixth novel, and it is great."

—*Detroit Free Press*

"A first-class, four-star, bell-ringing humdinger, and anybody who doesn't like it doesn't like jam on toast ... Hassler is a beautiful writer."

—*Milwaukee Journal*

"Make no mistake about it—Jon Hassler writing at half-speed is a better novelist than most writers writing at the top of their potential."
—*The Washington Post Book World*

"A parable of grace and redemption, it is unquestionably the best book about the Catholic priesthood since Graham Greene's *The Power and the Glory* and Jon Hassler is certainly one of the very best Catholic novelists since Graham Greene."

—ANDREW M. GREELEY

"Hassler is a superb writer. . . . A master storyteller."

—*The San Diego Union*

NORTH OF
HOPE

BY JON HASSLER

NORTH OF HOPE

A Novel

JON HASSLER

BALLANTINE BOOKS · NEW YORK

Copyright © 1990 by Jon Hassler

All rights reserved under International and Pan-American Copyright Conventions. Published in the United States by Ballantine Books, a division of Random House, Inc., New York, and simultaneously in Canada by Random House of Canada Limited, Toronto.

http://www.randomhouse.com

Library of Congress Catalog Card Number: 96-96686

ISBN: 345-41010-6

Manufactured in the United States of America

First Hardcover Edition: October 1990
First Mass Market Edition: November 1991
First Trade Edition: August 1996

10 9 8 7 6 5 4 3 2

For my son Michael

PART ONE

1

Frank first laid eyes on Libby Girard at the Sunday matinee a minute before the lights went down. She and Sylvia Pofford came in together, talking a mile a minute, and took seats two rows in front of Frank and over to his left. His first impulse was to point her out to his friend Danny Ash, who was sitting on his right and talking to somebody in the row behind them, but a second impulse told him not to share her with anybody for the time being, not to draw attention to her beauty before he had time to fully appreciate it in the privacy of his heart.

For Frank was stunned by Libby Girard's beauty. She had large, happy eyes and dark hair. She smiled broadly as she spoke. She had a pretty neck. Unable to take his eyes from her as the theater gradually darkened, he considered it something of a miracle that a girl so dazzling should come to live in a town so dull. Sylvia Pofford had told him there was a new girl in Linden Falls and that she was their age, a junior-to-be, but had withheld the fact that she was a knockout. Which was understandable because ever since the primary grades Sylvia Pofford, unchallenged as the class brain, had been regarding herself as the class beauty— a major case of self-deception, in Frank's opinion, Sylvia having a bumpy forehead and an unpleasant way of squinting when a thought crossed her mind.

The newsreel began and Libby and Sylvia continued talking while a woman with polio, who had been taken from her iron lung to give birth to a baby, exchanged smiles with her nervous-looking husband; while the city of Dresden, four years after the war, was shown to be rebuilding itself; and while Ingrid Bergman announced at a press conference that she was leaving her husband and giving up films to marry Roberto Rossellini and retire to private life. Finally a man sitting in front of the girls turned around and told them to pipe down.

The feature was *A Portrait of Jennie*. It was the first movie in at least ten years to make Frank cry. Watching Jennifer Jones come back from the dead and run across the beach and fall into Joseph Cotten's arms, Frank was shocked to realize his cheeks were wet. He wiped them with his fingers, glancing left and right to see if anyone noticed. He was puzzled—frightened even—to find his emotions so far out of control. This hadn't happened at a movie since he was five and wailed so loud at the terrible things happening to Pinnochio that his mother had had to take him home before it was over. Now, at sixteen, he was weeping for his mother. He was shedding tears more profusely, in fact, than at any time since her funeral. Ever since he and his father and brothers turned away from the open grave and headed across the snowy cemetery to their car, Frank had been strict with himself, never allowing himself to stray from what he took to be the straight and narrow path to manhood. He almost never cried or even felt like it. As a movie addict he had sat dry-eyed through any number of sad farewells, death scenes, lovers pulled apart. Why was he crying now?

Jennifer Jones couldn't stay among the living, even though Joseph Cotten loved her. She told him she had to return to her spiritual realm, wherever that was. She didn't get emotional about it. Her smile remained serene and superior, as if Joseph Cotten's desperate pleading struck her as childish. Frank's heart ached for the man because Jennifer Jones was a real dish, the kind of dark-eyed brunette he had always been crazy about. As she released herself from Joseph Cotten's embrace, Frank silently urged him to implore her one more time. Which he did. He sounded as if he might cry. "It's you I want, Jennie, not just a dream of you." She smiled wisely and advised, "There is no life until you find love, Eben. Then life cannot be lost."

Was this true? Surely it was nonsense. Frank had loved his mother, then lost her. His father had loved her—he lost her. His brothers had loved her—they lost her. Frank recognized the words on the sound track as the sort of whipped cream screenwriters were always coming up with in the concluding scenes in their attempt to make the language as impressive as the music. No, he didn't believe a word of it, and yet as the waves came crashing in and the violins came up, Frank's heart pounded as if he'd just been told some wonderful news. He shook with weeping and he bolted from the theater before the lights came on so no one would see his tears.

It was raining. He stood under the marquee composing himself and waiting for Danny Ash. He saw Libby and Sylvia in the crowd coming out. Libby glanced at him, looked away, and glanced again. Frank watched the two girls hurry off in the drizzle, and it was then that he first heard the voice.

She's the one, Frank. That's why you cried.

Nonsense, he thought, setting off down the street with Danny Ash. Why should the sight of a pretty girl make anyone cry?

But the voice persisted all the way home.

She's the one.

2

"Sylvia, does Frank Healy have a girlfriend?"

"Are you kidding?"

"I wonder if he'd be a good boyfriend for me."

Sylvia made a sound like spitting. "Boys our age are such children."

The two girls, drinking Orange Crush on Sylvia Pofford's front porch, were planning Libby's debut as the new girl in the junior class. It was evening. The rain had stopped. Their conversation was broken by long silences, for neither girl was yet quite free of the spell cast over them by *A Portrait of Jennie*. Across the street the slow-moving Badbattle River was purple and pink. A short way upstream a rapids produced an endless gurgling sound. The voice of Fred Allen drifted out from the radio in the living room, where Sylvia's parents were sitting with books in their laps.

"But he's smart, you said." Coming out of the matinee, she had asked Sylvia about the tall, dark-haired, bleary-eyed boy standing under the marquee.

"A's and B's," said Sylvia. "Mostly B's."

"And he's out for football."

"Second team."

"And he's handsome," said Libby.

"For a child. He's only sixteen."

"Well, we're sixteen."

"But he's such a mama's boy. You've got to date seniors, Libby. Or older. Boys our age are so dull. Bob's got a cousin coming through next weekend on his way east to college. He'd be a good one for you." Bob was Sylvia's boyfriend—Bob Templeton, senior-class president, first-string quarterback, the only son of the only doctor in town. Libby had been introduced to Bob and thought it a superb match, both he and Sylvia being humorless and immensely impressed with themselves.

"What good's a boyfriend in the East?" Libby asked.

"You'd have him to write to. You'd be the only one in our class writing to a guy in college, except me."

"No, I need a boyfriend close by."

"Next year Bob's going to Cornell."

"Next year I'll be married."

"Libby!" Sylvia was shocked. It was Sylvia's frequently declared opinion, handed down by her mother, that the only girls who married before graduation were either pregnant or mentally handicapped or both.

Libby added, for effect, "I'm giving the boys of Linden Falls one year, then I'm choosing." She loved shocking Sylvia. In the city a statement like this had had no shock value, because there she'd had no girlfriends like Sylvia. Her crowd in Minneapolis had come from families much like her own, except that very few of the other fathers drank as much as Libby's father. There hadn't been one college degree in the entire set of parents. Sylvia was the daughter of an attorney and a librarian. She was a pianist, an honor student, and a snob. She had five new dresses in her closet ready for the first five days of school. She had everything Libby lacked, except looks.

From the moment they met, Sylvia had assumed the role of Libby's sponsor or patron or whatever you'd call someone as knowledgeable and possessive and bossy as Sylvia. Libby was lucky, and knew it. She'd been hoping for just such a friend to be her confidante, her rumor monger, her partner on double dates; someone smart, sophisticated, and not as attractive as her-

self. Libby was not duped by this instant friendship. She was
well aware that Sylvia had befriended her for her looks, aware
that Sylvia believed—didn't everyone?—that the next best thing
to being beautiful yourself was going into partnership with
beauty.

Libby drained her bottle of Orange Crush, wiped her mouth,
and tossed off another one, for effect: "If I don't have a baby
before I'm nineteen, I'll feel like I've wasted my life."

"Libby! You talk like a farm girl. The farm girls around here
have babies like that."

"My mother says have your kids early and grow up with
them." Actually these had been the words not of Libby's mother
but of a friend's mother in the city. Libby's mother, a downcast
woman occasionally beaten by Libby's father, refrained from
making general statements about life.

"Bob and I are having two babies when he's out of medical
school and I'm out of law school."

This was followed by a long, respectful silence before Libby
spoke up. "Frank lives in a nice house."

They could see the front of the Healy house from where they
sat. It was half a block downstream, a high old house with bal-
usters missing from the porch rail.

"It's nothing special inside."

"You've been in it?"

"Birthday parties when we were little."

At that moment, the Healys' front door opened and a woman
wearing a broad-brimmed hat and a white dress emerged. She
was accompanied by a man in black.

"That's Father Lawrence and his housekeeper Eunice Pfeiffer.
They eat supper at the Healys' a lot. Eunice cooks."

"Is she a widow?"

"Eunice? Are you kidding? She was born an old maid."

"Oh, no," said Libby sadly. She hated hearing about people
who never got themselves matched up with anybody, and that
was why at sixteen she'd already had seven or eight boyfriends
and would have as many more as it took to find the right one
to marry. Despite the unhappy example of her parents, the single

life was her idea of hell on earth. "Doesn't it break your heart to think she'll never have a family?"

"She's got one," said Sylvia. "She's mother hen to Frank. When Mrs. Healy died, Eunice Pfeiffer sort of took over both their lives, Frank's and his dad's. My mother says it's her age. Her mothering instinct is real strong. It's really tragic."

"Why tragic? It sounds nice for Frank."

"No, that's what's tragic about it. She's trying to make Frank"—she paused, carefully choosing the word—"perfect."

"And is he?"

"Yeah, he's the kind of boy every girl's mother points to and says, 'I'd like to see you get interested in him—he's the perfect boy for you.'"

"So what's wrong with perfect?"

"Who wants a perfect boy when there's real boys around? I mean you'll never catch Frank Healy dancing or necking or anything. All he ever does is make model airplanes and work at the egghouse. He wouldn't go to the Loomis Ballroom if you paid his way."

"What's the egghouse?"

"Schultenovers' Egghouse. They do something to eggs. Eunice Pfeiffer got him the job. He started out the summer cutting grass, but everybody's lawn dried up."

"Is that his dad?" A tall man was following the priest and the old maid out to the street, where they paused to talk.

"Yeah, Martin C. Healy. You know what? He practically lives in the basement."

"How come?"

"Who knows? Frank says there's rooms they haven't used for years."

Father Lawrence and Eunice Pfeiffer strolled off down the street, and Martin Healy went back inside. The priest's black suit blended into the twilight, but Libby was able to keep the white dress in sight for a long time.

"When did his mother die?"

"Years ago. Frank's been strange ever since."

"Strange? How?"

Sylvia pointed to her forehead, indicating a mental case.

Libby knew this wasn't true. The eyes of Frank Healy, as seen this afternoon under the marquee, were deep and steady and wise.

Again the girls fell silent. The white dress turned a far corner. The rapids burbled. Dusk grew dense. Then a screen door slammed and they saw Frank, in swimming trunks, cross his front lawn and cross the street and wade into the river. He was carrying a football. He went in slowly, up to his waist, then stopped and stood still, facing downstream, as though in a trance. He kept moving his right hand back and forth, palm down, over the surface of the water.

"What's he doing, Sylvia?"

"Who knows?"

He turned and threw the ball upstream. It was a remarkably long throw, and the ball splashed in the water nearly opposite Sylvia's house. Waiting for it to float down to him, he lowered himself into the river until nothing but the top of his head was visible. Then he stood up again. He did this a number of times, dipping down and standing up. Was he bathing? Evading mosquitoes?

Again and again he threw the ball. An ingenious method for a boy alone to play catch, thought Libby. Again and again, waiting for the ball, he went through his dunking routine. Then he threw the ball up onto the bank and walked upstream, where the water was deeper. By the time he reached a point opposite Sylvia's house, he was in up to his neck, and he stopped walking. He went under. He stayed under so long Libby became frightened. She stood up and said, "He's drowning."

"He's not drowning," Sylvia scoffed. "He practically lives in the river."

"But he isn't coming up!" Libby ran across the lawn and stopped at the street. Still he didn't appear. She ran to the river, slipped off her shoes, and waded in. The water was up over the hem of her skirt when she saw him surface downstream. It was nearly dark now, and he didn't notice her. He was facing away, standing trancelike again, in the same place as before, moving both hands around and around over the water. Libby, too, stood still, the current pressing around her legs, mosquitoes whining around her hair. She wanted to call to him, but didn't because he seemed involved in a ceremony of some kind. After a while he turned and splashed quickly to shore, picked up the football, and ran to his house.

Libby stepped out of the water and onto the grass. She called good night to Sylvia and walked home carrying her shoes and wishing she had spoken to Frank in the water. She wanted to know why he just stood there and what he was thinking. And why there were tears in his eyes after the movie. And what it felt like to have only one parent. And how you could be a mama's boy if your mother was dead.

3

On Friday of that week, the last week of summer vacation, Frank saw Libby for the second time. He had just returned from his afternoon malt break and was standing at the front window of Schultenovers' Egghouse tying on his apron when he saw her climb the steps to the loading dock of the grain elevator and disappear into its shadowy interior.

The elevator and the egghouse faced each other across the railroad end of Main Street. The egghouse, a small, cubelike building of flaking gray stucco, was hidden all day from the sun by the enormous red elevator, which produced an endless undertone of machinery at work—pulsating hums and growls that Frank found vaguely soothing as he candled eggs. Candling was his primary duty, although since he'd turned sixteen and acquired a driver's license, the Schultenovers, Herb and Selma, sometimes allowed him to take out the panel truck and deliver eggs to the bakery, the two restaurants, and the three grocery stores of Linden Falls and to their dozen other accounts in neighboring villages.

Selma Schultenover came over and joined him at the window, saying, "That must be the Girard girl." Selma, partner to her husband in the egg business, was a fat, chattering woman.

She kept the books, visited with the clientele, and directed Frank and her husband through their day's work. She wore thick makeup in bright shades of purple and all her clothes were too tight. She was about forty-five. "They're living in the Radditz house on Pincherry Street," she said.

Frank pictured the Radditz house—a drab duplex built low to the ground, its rain gutters hanging crooked, and renters continually moving in and out.

"Herb," she called to her husband, "come here and see the Girard girl."

"Yo," said Herb from the back room. Newcomers being a rarity in Linden Falls, he came forward eagerly and stood obediently at his wife's elbow waiting for Libby to reappear. Herb Schultenover was a twitchy, fretful hypochondriac who put a lot of his meager energy into hating the grain elevator. It was Herb's fondest dream that between mismanagement locally and bungled trade regulations in the Truman administration, Linden Falls Feed and Seed would go bankrupt. Frank wondered why, since eggs were the Schultenovers' livelihood and the elevator didn't deal in eggs, Herb felt such a fierce sense of competition. He had a hunch it was envy.

And envy (Frank concluded years later when he thought back to his first employers) of a vaguely sexual nature. In those postwar years there was a militant code of behavior among the men and boys of Linden Falls: males did masculine things and avoided doing feminine things. Men drove cars, they did not ride in cars with women at the wheel. Men did not talk about beauty, illness, or babies. In their early teens boys abandoned all sissified activities such as reading books for pleasure and taking piano lessons and went out for sports. Yet, here was poor Herb, dealing in eggs. On every farm the henhouse was the province of the farmer's wife, and the term "egg money" meant the odd dollar set aside for needlepoint or hairpins or some other frivolity. While the farmer unloaded his oats or barley or wheat at the elevator, his wife came across the street with her three or six or ten dozen eggs and chatted with Selma while waiting for them to be candled; or if his wife was too busy to come to town, the farmer ducked in with the eggs and slipped quickly away. As men made for the door, Herb would call out some remark about crops or the weather, desperate for male conversation, but there was no detaining them. The Schultenovers might have been operating a beauty shop, the place made men that nervous. They came back later to pick up the empty crate and the egg money.

And it wasn't just eggs. It was Selma, too. Selma was overpowering. You couldn't talk to Herb without Selma interrupting and telling you what Herb would have said if she'd given him the chance. She was a good-natured woman, but her talk was loud and fast and her laugh hurt your ears. Men avoided her. It wasn't masculine to carry on, in public, a prolonged conversation with a woman, especially a woman so overtly female, so brightly painted, so breasty.

That summer, however, Frank shared neither the farmers' unease nor Herb's feeling of confinement. Herb, gazing at the elevator from the front window, looked like a small boy wanting to go out, while Frank, without knowing quite why, was secretly pleased to be an egghouse employee. He wasn't fully aware then (as he would be later, looking back) that working with eggs in the presence of Selma day after day would have a very soothing effect on any motherless, sisterless boy.

After a few moments they saw Libby step out onto the sunlit loading dock, accompanied by a man Frank had never seen before, apparently her father. He wore the green twill of an elevator employee, and his wrinkled brow and dapper mustache put Frank in mind of Clark Gable. He took a coin from his pocket and handed it to Libby, exchanged a few words with her, and bent to receive her peck on his cheek.

"Is that her dad?" asked Frank.

Selma nodded. "Started work yesterday."

So that was what a drunk looked like, thought Frank, drawing his long apron strings around and tying them in front. Sylvia Pofford had told him that Libby's father was an incurable alcoholic. Whiskey, said Sylvia, had made him unemployable in Minneapolis, where the Girards, a family of four, had been living until the previous Friday, and his last hope for a job was with his distant relative who operated Linden Falls Feed and Seed. The fourth member of the family, Libby's twenty-year-old brother, Roy, had found work on a farm.

Frank, a movie addict, was struck by Mr. Girard's swarthy, photogenic handsomeness. He was clearly miscast in a job that consisted mostly of wheeling bags of grain onto the dock on a two-wheeled cart. He belonged on the silver screen. His squint was more troubled than Clark Gable's, his mustache grayer, and he was perhaps a little too scrawny to be a star, but sit him on a horse and he might serve very nicely as Hopalong Cassidy's sidekick, or dress him in a suit and he could play a secondary creep in a mobster film.

Herb Schultenover spoke with a momentary sparkle of optimism in his eyes. "Bad idea, hiring a relative. Relatives can bleed you down to poor."

Frank's eyes followed Libby as she jumped down off the dock and strode away. She was wearing black slacks and a man's white shirt with the tails out and the sleeves rolled up. Her dark hair bounced. He felt like running after her in order to keep her face in view. He loved her face. She had Ingrid Bergman's cheekbones.

"Well, boys, let's get to work," said Selma, and Frank followed Herb into the back room. Herb, complaining of arthritis in his shoulder, carried several dozen eggs out the alley door and drove away in the egg truck, leaving Frank alone at the candling table. The back room, kept as dark as possible to make candling easier, smelled of musty cardboard, bad eggs, and dust blown in from the alley. Now and then Frank could hear a dim scrabbling in the walls as the bats shifted in their daytime sleep. An old tennis racket hung on a nail beside the candling table for the purpose of bringing down the occasional bat that came fluttering through the room. Once a day it was Frank's job to check the mousetraps.

But to Frank, fairly new on the job, it had not yet become a depressing place to work. There was something comforting, almost mesmerizing, about holding dozens and dozens of eggs, one by one, up to the funneled light to make sure they weren't bloody, fertilized, or cracked; something sensually rewarding about the vague, floating shapes of their illumined yolks and their various shades of shell—white, cream, tan, brown. He fell into periods of deep reverie at the egg table, eggs triggering his fantasies the way the rosary triggered his prayers in those years. As one by one, like oversized beads, the eggs passed through his fingers, he entered into a lengthy daydream, the same daydream over and over, a kind of never-ending film to which he had attached the title *The Life of Frank Healy*.

Mostly fact, but fiction at certain critical points, *The Life of Frank Healy* was subject to constant editing. There was a version in which his father continued to take an interest in him. There was another version in which his brothers were near his own age, and still another in which he had a sister. There were several versions concerning his mother. In one, his mother died giving birth to him, so he never knew her. In another she was perpetually on view in her coffin, having died only yesterday, and her funeral was yet to be endured. In a third she was not yet dead, but her doctor gave her only a month to six weeks. In a fourth she was destined to live to be old.

In this last version her case of leukemia was abroad in the world but missed its connection with his mother and attached itself to somebody else. The victim kept changing. His favorite version was that in which the illness attached itself to a stranger. And of course there was the version in which Frank himself was the victim—not (strange to say) his worst version. His worst version was what actually happened. Her leukemia was diagnosed in early November, a few days before his eleventh birthday, and she died six weeks later, at nine o'clock on Christmas morning.

Early that Christmas morning he had accompanied Father Lawrence to Basswood and served Mass with three Indian boys, Our Lady's on the Basswood Reservation being a mission church attached to St. Ann's in Linden Falls, Father Lawrence being pastor to both parishes, and Frank (an altar boy at St. Ann's since the age of seven) being very fond of the pastor and accompanying him on errands whenever possible, liturgical and otherwise.

At the conclusion of the Mass, Father Lawrence and the boys came off the altar to find the Basswood postmistress, a non-Catholic, waiting for them in the sacristy. Hers being one of the few telephones on the reservation, Mr. Healy had called her with the message that Mrs. Healy was sinking fast.

Frank struggled out of his twenty-two-button cassock, Father Lawrence threw off his vestments, and they grabbed their coats and sped home. It was a snowy morning, dark enough for headlights at 10:00 A.M. Along the streets of Linden Falls, Christmas lights burned in most of the windows they passed. When they reached his house, Frank's fear turned suddenly to lassitude, a state almost like sleepiness, and he didn't want to get out of the car. Staring across his front yard at the lights of the Christmas tree glimmering in the living-room window, he begged Father Lawrence to let him remain in the car. Death had been lurking in the house for six weeks and he was sick of it.

But of course he had to go in. In the dining room, which had been converted into his mother's sickroom so that she could be downstairs, he found Eunice Pfeiffer at the bedside. Eunice was holding his mother's hand. His father stood at a window looking out at the snow piling down. His brother Peter, six years older than Frank, was upstairs with his door shut.

His mother, he realized, was dead.

The priest drew a small book from his pocket and read some prayers while Frank and his father and Eunice Pfeiffer looked on. Judging by the look on his mother's face, death wasn't as peaceful as Frank had been led to believe. She looked tense.

After Father Lawrence left the house and the body was removed by the undertaker, Martin C. Healy went out walking in the snow and Eunice Pfeiffer went to the kitchen to prepare a snack. Peter came downstairs at her bidding and she served both boys toast and cocoa and urged them to open their presents. Peter did so eagerly. He got a jackknife from Frank, an expandable watchband mailed from an army PX by their brother Joe, a shaving kit from Father Lawrence, handkerchiefs from Eunice, money from his father, and a hand-knit sweater with a sleeve missing from his mother. The sweater was light green with a wide white band across the chest. Eunice said that she would finish knitting the sleeve.

Frank didn't want to open his presents, but Eunice insisted, saying, "Your mother would be so disappointed," and he couldn't disobey her. He opened them silently and unhappily, convinced that the momentous and horrible event that had taken place in the next room ought to be marked by something like penance and self-denial and not by tearing the ribbons and paper from his pen and pencil set (Joe), his handkerchiefs (Eunice), his marble chessmen (Father Lawrence), his crisp five-dollar bill (his father), and his storybook *Augustus Helps the Marines* (Peter). His gift from his mother he refused to open in front of the others but took upstairs to his room. This, too, was a hand-knit sweater, but more beautiful by far than Peter's. It was light blue with a snowflake design on the chest and upper sleeves—and it was finished. So overjoyed was Frank to think that his mother had knit his sweater first that he buried his face in it and cried and cried, drying his tears only when Eunice came upstairs to have a talk with him. She began with holy and consoling platitudes that Frank found hard to concentrate on, but then she shocked him to attention with a statement that would ring in his memory every day of his life.

"Your mother's dying words were about you, Frank. She said, 'I want Frank to be a priest.'"

Frank, candling eggs in the dim back room, pondered the changes his mother's death had wrought on the family. After the funeral, Frank's father fell into a permanent state of self-absorption. Forsaking the living room where he and his wife had spent nearly every evening of their marriage, Martin C. Healy had enlisted Peter and Frank to help him carry his easy chair and books into the basement, and there he rebuilt his life around his workbench.

Peter was a senior in high school that year. Joe was overseas, an artilleryman fighting Rommel in North Africa, and did not get home for the funeral. Of the three Healy boys, Peter had the remote, preoccupied nature most resembling his father's. After high school, Peter followed his brother into the army, and was scarcely out of boot camp when the war ended. After his discharge, he attended business college in Minneapolis and eventually became a tax accountant with a firm in St. Paul. He seldom returned to Linden Falls. Frank and his father would see him only for a day or two at Christmas. One Fourth of July Peter surprised them by showing up with a girlfriend named Bernice and offering to take Frank fishing on the river. They used a neighbor's boat and caught some sunfish. Frank and Bernice, a giggler, hit it off. She promised she'd make Peter answer Frank's letters, but she dropped out of Peter's life soon after that and Frank's letters went unanswered.

Joe never wrote letters either, but he had a friendlier nature than Peter's when you saw him in person. The trouble was that you never saw him, for upon his discharge Joe followed an army buddy to his home town in Montana, got a job with the highway department, and married a girl from Helena named Darla. Joe and Darla asked Frank out for a visit the summer he was fourteen. He made the trip alone on the train and stayed two weeks. He didn't tell them how homesick he was and how glad he was to board the train back to Minnesota.

But it was Frank's father who, after the funeral, moved farthest away. Was it a morbid kind of fidelity to his wife that forced him to follow her underground? Actually the basement wasn't an uncomfortable place to be. It was cool in summer and warm in winter. On a typical evening, after coming home from his job as chief loan officer at Linden Falls Security Bank, he would help Frank clear off a corner of the kitchen table and they would eat sandwiches and ice cream, a butter knife and two spoons their only silver, a prayer their only formality. When the plates and bowls were washed and the butter put away, Frank would remain at the table, taking up his work on a model airplane, while his father descended into the basement and stayed there until long after Frank was asleep. His father's easy chair was tucked between the workbench and the furnace, and near at hand were a lot of papers, magazines, and books. He read about banking, baseball, and woodworking. He fashioned benches and tables and knickknacks out of hardwood, lawn ornaments out of pine. Every few weeks he swept up the shavings and sawdust, but it was never very tidy in the basement.

And then there was that evening once or twice a week when Father Lawrence and Eunice Pfeiffer either joined them for dinner or invited them to the rectory. Frank was eager for these evenings, particularly in his early teen years, for he was doted upon by both the priest, who paid him much more attention than his father did, and by the housekeeper, who by having been his mother's closest friend somehow kept him in touch with her. His father, however, was bored by these lengthy meals. He was polite and gracious enough, but Frank could tell he wished he were down in his basement turning out a chair leg on his expensive new lathe.

Was his father truly oblivious to Eunice's poorly disguised infatuation with him, Frank wondered, or was he only pretending not to notice? Eunice was in her late forties, tall and angular, plain of face, straightforward in speech, fervent in the belief that God smiled on the just and sent transgressors straight to hell. She had a small nose, a small thin-lipped mouth, and the lines around her earnest, green eyes seemed to indicate that everyday life was worrisome and slightly painful. She and her two brothers had been reared on a farm between Linden Falls and Loomis, and none of the three had married. Was Martin C. Healy never aware, as Frank was, that something very piquant began cooking in Eunice the moment he came to the table? Her eyes brightened, her voice rose half a pitch, and throughout the meal it was "Martin, can I warm your soup?" and "Martin, can I warm your coffee?" and "Martin, what's the news uptown?" There was nothing remarkable in the news she pried out of him — somebody had an auction, somebody had pneumonia — but she might have been listening to music, so deeply stirred she seemed. She gazed at him lovingly, but her gaze was not returned. She hung on his words, but he uttered as few as possible and let her drop. Again and again Frank witnessed her reaching across the corner of the table and touching the sleeve of his father's suitcoat (he was always dressed like a banker; even at his workbench he wore a tie under his apron), but not once did his father put his hand out to her.

Martin C. Healy was some five years older than Eunice, a tall man with thick glasses resting on his large nose and a scalp of hypertensive pink showing through his thin gray hair. A little overweight, a little self-conscious when he spoke, and always a little bored aboveground, he impressed Frank as a man whose fire had gone out. Only once had he known his father to act impulsively, and whenever he came to this episode in his reverie in the back room of Schultenovers' Egghouse, he was amazed all over again.

It was on an afternoon in the spring of his freshman year that his father came to the high school and called him out of class to announce that his mother was with God. It astonished Frank that Martin C. Healy, woodworker and loan officer, should do anything so unguarded and mystical as to knock on Mrs. Lindberg's door in the middle of algebra and request that Frank step out into the hallway and there tell him, "Your mother's in heaven, Frank, it just came to me five minutes ago in the bank." He looked perhaps a little more earnest than usual, more serious, but there was nothing else in his expression—no wild-eyed ecstasy—to indicate that he had just heard from the other side of the grave. "So she's okay," his father added.

And Frank, on the instant, believed him. Who was less given to wild imaginings than his father? Who was steadier, more logical, more respectful of the truth? Was it so surprising, considering all the prayers the two of them had sent up on his mother's behalf, that God should send down a personal reply?

"I thought you should know right away," his father continued. "She's been with God for some time. Her stop-off in purgatory is over, and we can quit praying for her soul. We can start praying directly to her for ourselves. It came to me right after lunch, like a message on the phone." His father, moving off down the hallway, spoke over his shoulder: "I've got to get back to work. We'll talk about it later."

But they never did.

———

By the time Herb Schultenover returned from his deliveries and interrupted Frank's reverie with complaints of sciatica and indigestion, it was closing time, and a warm, steady rain was falling. Frank walked home from the egghouse barefoot, carrying his shoes and socks and relishing the cooling rain soaking his hair and clothes and running down his face and arms. He was feeling particularly buoyant because tonight after the movie he and Danny Ash were to make their first visit to the Loomis Ballroom. This major and long-awaited step toward adulthood was to be made possible by Bob Templeton, who had the use of his parents' car.

Frank took a bath and put on his second-best shirt and pants. His best would have fit the occasion, but he didn't want to arouse his father's curiosity. Not that his father was likely to object to his riding with Bob Templeton to Loomis, but his father might carelessly tell Eunice Pfeiffer, and Eunice was certain to disapprove. The ballroom came up now and then in gossipy tales of illicit love and fistfights, and his father's sense of what to tell Eunice was not as highly developed as Frank's.

After supper Martin C. Healy disappeared into the basement to turn out another chair leg on his lathe and Frank ran along the puddled alley to Danny Ash's house and found the Ashes still at dinner.

"Pull up a chair and have some pie," said Danny's father, pointing to a sturdy wastebasket with a lid because there were no more chairs. Danny's father, a livestock trucker, wore nothing over his undershirt. He had blurry blue tattoos on his hairy forearms and a small red scorpion burned into the hairy hollow of his throat. Below the scorpion and suspended on a silvery chain hung a small coinlike medal with the figure of the Blessed Virgin on one side and the head of Christ on the other.

"Maybe you'd like some spaghetti and vegetables," said Danny's mother, a husky woman with a round, dimpled face. "I'm afraid you don't eat right at your house. Tell me honest now, what did you and your dad have for supper?"

"Fish with all the trimmings," Frank assured her, pulling the wastebasket up to the table. The fish had been tuna fish sandwiches, the trimmings a scoop of ice cream and the remains of last night's popcorn. He sat between Danny and Danny's five-year-old sister, Virginia. Facing him across the table were Danny's two younger brothers—Ronny, whose nose always ran, and Jerry, who stuttered. The pie was apple and delicious. He tried to restrain himself from wolfing it down.

Mr. Ash spoke with his mouth full. "Danny tells me you're going to try out for the backfield this year."

"I am. Coach Pangborn says I've got the hands to be a quarterback." He modestly refrained from quoting the coach in full. The hands and the brains both, he'd said.

"Quarterbacks don't do anything but block."

"Not anymore. Coach Pangborn's running the T this year."

"The T? What's the T?"

"T-formation. It's tricky. The quarterback handles the ball every play. Hands it off or passes it or runs with it."

"It'll never work," said Mr. Ash.

"More pie?" asked his wife.

Frank said no thanks.

"Danny says he wants to be a lineman," said Mr. Ash. "Talk him out of it, will you?"

Danny said, "I like to tackle." Danny was shorter than Frank, but stockier. He had his mother's open, round face, his father's blond hair and freckles. "I like to knock guys' pins out from under them."

"Linemen get no glory," said his father. "They just get their faces kicked in."

Mrs. Ash flinched at this. "Mercy, what do you boys see in football?" Her cheeks quivered as she shook her head vigorously. "I think it's a horrid game."

"It's good fun," explained her husband. "But it's more fun in the backfield, Danny."

Danny beamed. "I like to smear guys," he said. "I like to put my shoulder into their bellies and cut guys in half."

The meal ended with bowed heads and everyone mumbling, "We thank thee Almighty God for thy blessings." On "Amen," Danny and Frank dashed out the door.

———

The movie was a mediocre western, *Four Faces West*. At first Frank felt betrayed by Joel McCrea, who departed from his normally virtuous role and robbed a bank. Then, pursued by the marshall (Charles Bickford) and falling in love with a nurse (Frances Dee), Joel McCrea came clean and his motive was judged virtuous after all, if you didn't put too fine a point on it. McCrea's father, it seemed, was destitute and needed two thousand dollars to pay off the mortgage on his ranch. All of which proved troublesome to Frank, whose habit it was to put fine points on all moral problems, and he left the movie wondering if ends sometimes *did* justify means, and wondering why, movie after movie, Charles Bickford never smiled, and wondering, too, what men saw in Francis Dee, who had no ranking in Frank's pantheon of Hollywood goddesses.

The rain had stopped during the movie, but darkness brought no relief from the heat. They rode the seven miles to Loomis at seventy miles an hour with all the windows of the Templeton Pontiac open and the hot wind blowing in their faces. Carl Barkus rode in front with Bob Templeton. Frank and Danny, sitting in back, leaned forward to hear the two older boys discuss women.

"I'm only half a man without Sylvia," Bob lamented.

What a sappy confession coming from the first-string quarterback, thought Frank. Bob was the player Frank wanted to be. He threw the ball fifty yards and ran like a rabbit. Coach Pangborn had been grooming him to direct the team this fall to what everyone hoped would be the Rockets' first victory in three years. At the end of last season their losing streak had attracted the embarrassing attention of daily newspapers in Rookery, Berrington, and Duluth.

"When she's out of town, I miss her something terrible."

Carl Barkus, smoking a Lucky, responded to this with a grunt. Carl was a classmate of Bob's—a senior-to-be—but their friendship struck Frank as odd. Carl, a pock-cheeked, bug-eyed little cynic, was not an athlete and never attended games. He mostly smoked and read novels.

"This is the three-month anniversary of the day I first got my hand on Sylvia's tits," Bob rhapsodized. "I taught myself to

drive like this so I can get my arm around her." He demon-
strated—one hand on the wheel, the other around Carl's neck.

"Watch it," muttered Carl, sliding close against the door.

Bob went on to explain that every weekend since June he
and Sylvia had danced at the Loomis Ballroom, and now with
Sylvia gone on a shopping trip to Minneapolis with her mother,
he was going to Loomis for sentimental reasons and taking
friends along to stave off loneliness. "Without Sylvia," he repeated, "I'm only half a man."

Carl Barkus sat silent for half a minute, his cigarette burning
bright in the wind, then said, "I don't think you and Sylvia make
a very good pair."

"Hey!" Bob was offended. "Everybody says we're a great
couple."

"Not me. I don't say that."

"Hey, what do you know? You wouldn't know a great girlfriend if one hit you in the face. You've never had a girlfriend."

"Sylvia's a dud."

"A dud! Hey, you're nuts. Sylvia's full of fun."

"Fun, Jesus." Carl Barkus turned to the backseat. "Does Sylvia Pofford look like fun to you guys?"

"Sylvia's not bad," said Danny Ash. "Good build on her."

Bob Templeton nodded happily at this, his eyes on the road,
both hands on the wheel. "See?"

"What about you, Frank?"

"Yeah," said Frank, seeing Sylvia in his mind's eye. She was
short. She had pretty hair, green eyes, and a pouty lower lip.
She was anything but fun.

"Yeah what?" said Carl.

"Yeah she's built, and yeah she's a dud."

Bob, slowing as he entered Loomis, said, "Okay, you turds,
here we are if you want to check Main Street for women."

The only living things on the dimly lit Main Street of
Loomis, a dying village with a population of two hundred and
ten, were two old men and a cat. Bob followed a dirt street
through town and out the other side, drove half a mile between
cornfields, and turned through an open gate into a sloping,
muddy field where fifty or sixty cars were parked in crooked

rows. Above them, standing at the crest of the slope, was the fabled Loomis Ballroom, a monstrous firetrap of a building that had originally been a dairy barn.

Having heard so many tales about this place—sexual tales, drinking tales, pugilistic tales—Frank was in a state of high anticipation as he and his friends threaded their way uphill between the cars. He was excited by the mingling odors of ripening corn, overheated radiators, and spilled beer. He was enchanted by the dim, eerie glow given off by the pink bug-repellent light bulb high on a post. He was transported by the syrupy music leaking out through the loose siding of the barn—"My Happiness," featuring a muted trombone.

He was somewhat disappointed to find that the entrance to the Loomis Ballroom, his portal to maturity, was a warped sliding door through which cows and bulls had filed for many years. Here they paid a man fifty cents apiece and had the word "paid" stamped on the back of their hands in the sort of purple ink it took a week to wash off. It was hotter inside than out, and nearly as dark. The dance floor, not as vast as he'd expected, was packed with a mass of moving bodies. At one end was a beer bar and two dozen small tables with folding chairs. At the other was a stage where the spotlighted musicians played. According to a banner hanging on the wall behind them, this was Lucky Mudget and his Orchestra. Lined up across the front of the stage were the four horn players—cornet, sax, trombone, clarinet. They were backed by drums and a bass fiddle. Lucky Mudget, waving a silver baton, wore a suit of gray gabardine with lapels of black velvet. When he turned around to smile down on the dancers gliding beneath him, a pink spotlight caught the brilliant jeweled rings on his conducting hand.

"Would you look at Lucky Mudget's hair!" said Danny Ash, referring to its length. In an age of crew cuts, it curled over his ears and hung down over his collar.

"Just like a woman's." Carl Barkus sneered.

Bob Templeton's eyes were glazed with dreaminess. "This is Sylvia's favorite song, she sings it to me in the car."

A girl approached Bob and asked where Sylvia was. This was a Loomis cheerleader—Frank had seen her at basketball and football games. Spotting two more girls approaching, Frank slid along the dark wall, separating himself from the group, afraid of being asked to dance. The girls of Loomis were forward, he'd heard, and often did the asking.

Carl Barkus, apparently seized by the same fear, came and stood at his side. Together they watched the cheerleader take Bob's hand and lead him toward the tables and chairs. They watched Danny Ash pair up with one of the other girls and step out onto the dance floor, saw him place his hand on the small of her back and glide off toward the orchestra, making it look easy. This left the third girl stranded. She kept glancing at Carl and Frank.

"Why not dance with her, Frank? She's not bad."

True—she was no beauty, but not bad. She had a prominent chin and a lot of curly hair.

"I don't know how to dance," Frank confessed.

"Nothing to it. Put your hand on her back and walk around." Carl indicated the couples sliding past them as the orchestra moved without pause into "Nature Boy." "Look at their feet, nobody's doing anything hard."

"Why don't *you* dance with her?"

"Me?" Carl looked astounded. "Why should I?"

"Because, don't you come here to dance?"

"Naw, dancing's dumb."

"Then what do you come for?"

"To see how dumb it is."

The girl with the chin gave up and walked away. Carl and Frank bought Cokes at the bar and pulled chairs up to a wobbly little table. Carl gave Frank a cigarette, which he smoked awkwardly, as though it were his first. It was, in fact, his third.

"Who's that dish dancing with that big stud?" asked Carl.

"Where?"

Carl pointed to a girl passing slowly in front of them, and Frank's heart bumped—it was Libby. Her partner was a tall, heavy young man wearing his pants tucked into his cowboy boots. Frank had seen them a moment earlier and not recognized Libby, for her dark hair was transformed, arranged not in its normal waves but piled high on her head with a long corkscrew curl dangling in front of each ear. In an engraving in last year's history text Marie Antoinette wore her hair like that on her way to the guillotine.

"That's Libby Girard." Saying her name aloud made his heart bump again, and he wondered if this was love at third sight.

"Who's the guy?"

Frank shrugged. "Some farmer, wouldn't you say?"

"Yeah, his nose is peeling." He had the customary farmer sunburn on his nose, ears, and neck, while his forehead, having been shaded by the bill of a cap, was pale.

Watching the two of them move away and circle back, Frank marveled that a newcomer virtually his own age should be so advanced in the rites of the Loomis Ballroom. How long had she been going out with older men? Dancing this close? Wearing her hair like a queen? In the dim light, swaying with her eyes closed and her ear laid tenderly against the farmer's rib cage, she might have been a twenty-five-year-old cover girl. Or in movies.

And what happened next was straight out of Hollywood. The orchestra took a break and Libby Girard left the farmer, made straight for Frank, pulled a chair up beside him, and sat down. "Hi, you're Frank Healy, Sylvia told me. Do you realize our hair is the same color?" She pulled a corkscrew curl across her cheek and gave him a mock-demure smile. "In here it looks black, but it's really brown. How do you like the way it's fixed?"

"I like it a lot," said Frank, without quite looking at it. He had trouble facing her head-on. She was too beautiful.

"My name is Libby."

"I know. This is Carl Barkus."

"Hi, Carl."

Hunched over his Coke with his head down, Carl Barkus grunted.

Frank felt her eyes return to him. "Sylvia says your mother died when you were ten. That's the saddest thing I ever heard."

Startled that she should encroach upon this sacred subject, he risked a glance at her. Her smile was sweet and full of sympathy. "Eleven," he said.

"Oh, that's so sad. When dads or mothers die, it really gets me down. I knew a girl in Minneapolis, her dad died and she seemed to get over it before I did."

"It looks pink," said Carl, who hated it when people got serious. "In here everybody's hair looks pink."

She smiled at Carl but was not deterred. Patting her hair, she continued: "I mean this girl never talked about it much or acted different in school, but I couldn't quit thinking about it. It's very scary to me, the idea of my dad or mother dying." She laid her hand gently on Frank's arm, asking, "How long did it take you to get over it? You never get completely over it, I suppose, but I mean to get over the worst of it."

He was stunned by her touch, amazed by her candor, and momentarily confused by her forcing him to choose between the masculine answer and the truth. Alone with her, he might have described the endlessly haunting effect of his mother's death, and he might even have risked telling her about his tears at last Sunday's matinee, but Carl was listening. He said, "Not long."

"Oh, you boys!" The band struck up "I'm Looking Over a Four-Leaf Clover," and she sprang to her feet. "You boys are all the same," she said, scanning the dance floor. "I never know which it is—if you're lying or if you haven't got hearts."

He wanted desperately to go on talking to her, or rather to have her go on talking to him, he wanted to take her arm and draw her back into her chair, he wanted Carl Barkus to disappear and allow the two of them to delve into the death of parents and the color of their hair. Oh, to have a girlfriend so beautiful. She was wearing a white blouse without sleeves and a light gray skirt. He wanted to touch the silky material of her blouse. He wanted to reach up and touch her hair.

"Who's that stud you were dancing with?" asked Carl, but Libby was already moving onto the floor on the arm of John Emmerling, a former all-conference center on the Loomis basketball team and now a junior in college somewhere. As they danced away, the smile she beamed up at John Emmerling was no more radiant than the smile she had given Frank, and he took consolation from that.

"Let's go upstairs," said Carl.

"What's upstairs?"

"I'll show you."

They drained their Cokes and made their way to a narrow stairway leading to the game room, formerly the hayloft, where a number of men were playing poker at a round table, others stood at pinball machines, and a foursome played pool. Through the thick haze of cigarette smoke stinging his eyes, Frank recognized one of the pool players as Vernon Jessen, a classmate of Bob and Carl's, a husky farm boy with large, blunt features and a sour disposition. Last year, at left tackle, he had been named to the all-conference team despite the Linden Falls losing streak. Vernon Jessen's current girlfriend was one of the two sexy Peach sisters from Loomis, Mary Sue.

"Hey, Vernon, how come you're not dancing?" asked Carl. "You and Mary Sue break up?"

"No, she gave me a few minutes off." Vernon Jessen bent over the table, sighted along his cue, and sank the two ball in the corner. "She went to the can," he added, taking aim at the six, which he sank in the side. He came over and said to Carl, "Got a smoke?"

"Athletes aren't allowed to smoke."

"Who says?"

"Your coach."

"Hell with Pangborn."

Carl gave him a Lucky. Vernon lit it and turned to Frank and said, "What's the matter with you, Healy?"

"Nothing, why?"

"You're crying."

"I'm not crying. Smoke makes my eyes water."

Vernon blew smoke in his face and went back to his game. Frank's reaction to this, instead of anger, was a sudden and overpowering sense of loneliness. He felt like a stranger among aliens. He had heartily disliked Vernon since junior high and he wasn't fond of Carl. He wasn't interested in poker, slot machines, or pool, and his eyes were watering and becoming downright painful. He'd met Libby and that was good, but now she was in somebody else's arms, and he wondered when, if ever, she would speak to him again. He wished he knew how to dance. He wished he had Danny Ash's easy way with girls. He wished he had Carl

Barkus's cynicism or Vernon Jessen's callousness to help him through difficult social occasions like this. Or, better than yearning for the impossible, he wished he'd gone home after the movie and taken up his balsa and glue and added a wing to his newest bomber.

"Jesus, would you look at that!" said Carl Barkus, turning Frank around to face the table of cardplayers. Seated there with the men was the other Peach sister, Rita Lou, the one with the long neck and the sleepy eyes. She held no cards, but seemed to be present as the companion to the cardplayer on her left, a wiry young man with prominent teeth and a low forehead.

"See that?" asked Carl, his eyes directed under the table.

Frank was astounded to see that Rita Lou's wraparound skirt lay open on her lap, and the young man, holding his cards in his left hand, was burying his right hand—marked "paid"—between her bare thighs.

"Who's the guy?" asked Frank, a little breathless.

Carl shrugged and stepped over to the pool table. "Hey, Vernon, who's the guy with his hand in Rita Lou's bush?"

"New guy," said Vernon Jessen, squinting through the smoke rising from his nose. "Roy Girard. He's got a sister named Libby you gotta see to believe."

"We saw her downstairs," Carl told him.

"Ain't she some piece?" Vernon took a drag and again blew smoke in Frank's face.

Practically blinded, Frank moved off toward the stairway, descended four or five steps, and stood below the thickest stratum of smoke. Below him the tightly packed mass of bodies, blurred in his watery vision and moving sensuously to the slow beat of "You're Breaking My Heart," sent up a strong odor of sweat. And he caught a whiff of something even more pungent and repellent—either the barn had not been properly cleaned or somebody had thrown up. As his eyesight cleared, he picked out Danny Ash, who was now dancing with the curly-haired girl with the prominent chin. He saw Bob Templeton swaying in place, holding the Loomis cheerleader at arm's length as he studied his feet. He saw a fight break out in the pink-lit corner of the hall near the orchestra, the sunburned farmer in cowboy boots taking a swing at John Emmerling and missing, and John Emmerling punching the farmer in the stomach. They were apparently fighting over Libby, who stood against the wall with her hands covering her face. Dancers backed away and watched. Lucky Mudget shifted into something speedy and strident. The fighters exchanged words but no more punches. The farmer forced his way through the crowd and out the door. John Emmerling looked around for Libby, found her, and bent down close to her. Was he talking to her or kissing her? It was hard to tell from where Frank was standing. Suddenly the two of them straightened up, pumped their shoulders three or four times as though to catch up with the music, and set off around the floor in a hopping, twirling step that caused other dancers to scatter out of their way.

A few minutes later, Bob Templeton gathered up his passengers and led them out to the car. Riding back to Linden Falls, Danny Ash, who had had to be dragged away from the blonde with the chin, enumerated with glee the various parts of her body he'd managed to get his hands on. Carl Barkus gave an account of what Rita Lou Peach had let Libby Girard's brother get away with under the card table. Bob Templeton then lifted his voice in song, moaning syrupy lyrics in the manner of Buddy Clark. Danny made it a duet: Carl, now safely away from it, allowed himself to be caught up in the spirit of the ballroom and joined in as the rhythm section: pum-pum pa-dum, pum-pum pa-dum. And Frank, pressed into a corner of the backseat, rode along in dejected silence. He had expected to be thrilled by the dance, but he was repelled. If the Loomis Ballroom was a necessary stop on the high road to love and courtship and holy matrimony, why was it so gloomy and foul smelling and why did fights break out? How could Danny Ash so easily overlook the unsavory aspects of the place and boldly take to the dance floor with a stranger, and what was wrong with Frank that he could never imagine doing the same? Was he by nature an alien? Was he somehow unfit for normal relationships? Was he destined to live out his entire life standing apart from the dance?

4

The boys of Linden Falls High School were a great disappointment to Libby. She hadn't expected her choices to be so limited. In Minneapolis there had been one hundred and ninety boys in her class and one hundred and seventy in the class ahead of her, whereas in Linden Falls there were only thirty-nine boys in the junior and senior classes combined. In the city, too, there was always the interesting boy from another school turning up in your life, but out here in the sticks the only other school within twenty miles—Loomis—had fifteen boys per class, and from what she'd seen of them at the Ballroom they were mostly hay-seeds. Not that farm boys were less handsome than city boys—actually they tended to be huskier and sexier looking—but they were impossible to talk to. They couldn't get their words out.

Having been convinced by Sylvia Pofford that only seniors qualified as boyfriends, and then only if they played football, Libby saw only four likely prospects, and Sylvia already had one of them (Bob Templeton) sewed up. That left Nathan Dunnock, Walt Welner, and Vernon Jessen.

The best thing about Nathan Dunnock was his disposition. He was in two of Libby's classes—typing and social—and he was always chuckling and cracking dumb little jokes. ("Did you hear about the constipated mathematician who worked it out with a pencil?") For Libby there was a comfortable familiarity in this vulgar sort of humor because it resembled her father's in those rare moments when her father was feeling lighthearted. Moreover, Sylvia spoke strongly in Nathan's favor, pointing out to Libby that the Dunnocks were well-to-do, Mr. Dunnock being a car dealer, but Libby developed some serious misgivings. For one thing Nathan's constant chatter struck her as girlish, and for another, at five-eight he was scarcely an inch taller than Libby, and it was her policy never to go out with a boy that short. He was, on the other hand, a halfback, and although Libby didn't know a halfback from a goalpost, Sylvia told her it was a crucial position. In the first game of the season, against a powerful team from Owl Brook, Nathan Dunnock scored the Rockets' only touchdown. Owl Brook scored five and won, 32 to 6. Frank Healy played a few minutes in the final quarter and did something Libby missed that made everybody cheer.

Walt Welner was big and strong and played fullback. In the second game, against Gopher Prairie, Walt scored both of Linden Falls' touchdowns and the Rockets lost by only thirteen points. Walt sat near Libby in study hall and they tried to help each other with higher algebra, which didn't come easy to either of them. His drawback as a boyfriend, besides a drooping right eyelid, was his race. He was part Ojibway, and Sylvia said she'd definitely die before she'd double-date with an Indian. Frank Healy, assigned to the same study hall, helped Walt and Libby with their algebra.

Vernon Jessen lived on a farm and drove a brand-new pickup, a green Ford with a row of amber lights across the top of the cab and a squirrel tail tied to the aerial. Vernon Jessen was as big as Walt Welner and better built—broad shoulders, narrow hips, muscular arms. He was a lineman for the Rockets, which meant (as far as Libby could tell) that he continually threw himself on piles of people and came off the field with his uniform filthy. In the third game, against Staggerford, he came off groggy at halftime, having been kicked in the helmet, but recovered in time for the second half, and the Rockets lost by only ten points, 12 to 2.

Getting to know Vernon Jessen, with his black hair, dark shadow of beard, and small insinuating eyes, was like penetrating a mystery. In school he gave Libby long, smoldering looks. One rainy afternoon he gave her a ride home in his pickup, which had a fake leopardskin seat cover and a rearview mirror trimmed with white rabbit fur. He told her that he personally owned three of the cows and seven of the goats on his parents' farm. He showed her the revolver he kept in his glove compartment for shooting birds and rodents. He asked her if she wanted to screw. She said no.

But Libby's first romance in Linden Falls was with none of these boys. It was a sudden, unforeseen relationship, brief and very cool. The boy's name was DeVaughn Smith, and Libby met him at the funeral of Mr. Meyer, her Spanish teacher.

Mr. Meyer was Libby's favorite teacher that year. He was lively, pleasant, and undemanding. At the end of the first marking period he gave Libby a grade equal to Sylvia's, which caused Sylvia, a serious scholar, to have a little tantrum. Libby was not a scholar. Libby had learned as early as the primary grades that if she put on the false face of someone eager for knowledge and smiled and pretended to hang on every word her teacher uttered, the C average on her tests and papers quite often became a B on her report card. Mr. Meyer gave her her first A in two years.

Then he died. He'd gone hunting alone in the wild, hilly country north of town and fallen down the steep wall of a ravine into a pond. This was during a cold spell in October. It had snowed the night before and the water was icy cold. He broke a leg in the fall, and although he was able to drag himself out of the water, he was found dead of exposure three days later halfway up the side of the ravine. Libby took his death hard. Sylvia shed one or two polite tears, but Libby cried one whole Saturday morning, thinking about Mr. Meyer's sweet little wife and his two sweet little babies and the horrors he must have suffered in dying that lonely death.

School was dismissed for the funeral at St. Ann's. Libby, who had never seen a Catholic service before, was intrigued to see the priest sprinkling holy water on everything in sight and stoking up a pungent little fire in a brass pot on a chain. Frank Healy was the chief altar boy, continually at the priest's side, handing him things and responding to his prayers in a foreign tongue. She thought Frank very handsome in his black robe, which was covered by a white, lacy, half-length garment resembling a shorty nightgown. His broad forehead, dark eyebrows, and quick, penetrating eyes put her in mind of Gregory Peck. The other three altar boys were younger and kept yawning and scratching and staring at the congregation, while Frank was obviously concentrating on the ceremony. Concentrating, in fact, more than the priest, for twice she saw him point to a line on the page of a big book when the priest lost his place.

At the cemetery, which was located at the edge of town between a row of grain-storage bins and a sheep farm, Libby whispered to Sylvia, asking who various people were, until Sylvia said "Shush!" loud enough to cause some of the mourners to turn from the grave and look at them. Frank Healy turned and smiled at Libby. It was a wry, chummy smile that seemed to say, Yes, we all know what a pain in the neck Sylvia Pofford can be. It was then and there that Libby first got the idea of having a backup boyfriend. If it was true, as Sylvia insisted, that Frank was too immature to be a serious boyfriend, why not try him out in a minor sort of role? While scouting among seniors for a boyfriend, she had felt the need of another friend besides Sylvia in the junior class, for while Sylvia suited her in many ways, she wore her out as a steady companion. Sylvia was so terribly solemn. One of the things Libby saw in Frank's smile at graveside was the promise of laughter. Another thing she saw was how much he liked her.

Because Mr. Meyer was a veteran of World War II, somebody played taps on a trumpet as soon as the graveside prayers ended. The trumpeter was hidden behind a bush, so that the music seemed to come from on high, and the effect was powerful enough to make Libby cry all over again. When the last note was carried away on the breeze and blended with the bleating of sheep in the adjacent pasture, Sylvia said, "Come on, let's grab a Coke downtown before fourth hour starts." Libby resisted, curious to see who would step out from behind the bush.

It was DeVaughn Smith, a senior she had overlooked as a potential boyfriend because he didn't play football. Sylvia had pointed him out in the band at pep fests. Libby ran up to him and said, with tears in her eyes, "That was the most gorgeous trumpet playing I ever heard in my life, DeVaughn." He thanked her politely and took a step backward, looking a little startled. He was tall and skinny, shy and serious. He had hazel eyes and a line of freckles across the bridge of his nose. "You made me cry," she said, wiping her eyes. He looked very concerned and said he was sorry. Sylvia called from the cemetery gate, telling her to hurry, and Libby asked DeVaughn if he'd like to join them for a Coke.

They went together for a week and a half. As a boyfriend DeVaughn had a serious flaw: he didn't care much for girls. Libby hung on to him through two football Fridays because she liked watching him march under the lights at halftime and then having him come up into the bleachers and sit with her in his uniform. Before that, Libby had been sitting at games with Sylvia and feeling like an old maid.

"DeVaughn, I have to tell you something," said Libby, after the Willowby game, which Linden Falls lost 30 to 0. "You make being a boyfriend look like hard work."

"It *is* hard work, Libby." He was walking her home, briskly, for they were facing a cold night wind. "What makes it especially hard is that everybody tells me how lucky I am to be going with you."

"And you don't see it that way?"

"No offense, Libby, but I'm not crazy about dates. I'd rather stay home and practice my trumpet."

"Then that's what you should do, DeVaughn. You won't hurt my feelings."

"But I'm supposed to want to go on dates. That's what gets me down. Everybody else wants to go on dates."

"What do you care what everybody else wants? If you like music so much, then stay home and play music."

"I've been writing a sonata for trumpet for a year and a half. Maybe when it's finished, I'll like going on dates."

They kissed at Libby's front door on Pincherry Street. She patted him on the cheek and said, "Will you play your sonata for me sometime?"

"Sure. I might be done with it this winter."

"Let me know."

They kissed again, gingerly, and DeVaughn said good night and walked away. Then he stopped and called to Libby as she was stepping inside and shutting the door: "It's got three movements with a coda at the end."

By this time, two months into the school year, Libby had begun to cultivate Frank Healy's friendship, carefully timing her departure from home each morning so as to meet him on the way to school. (Fortunately it was Sylvia Pofford's habit to rise from sleep at the last moment and be driven to school by her father, so there was no danger of her making a threesome out of it.) On the first of these mornings, Frank asked Libby, "Did you study for the history test?"

"I'm so bad." She laughed. "I took the book home and never opened it."

"It'll mostly be the Bill of Rights, so if you can list them in order you'll be fine."

"What's the Bill of Rights?"

"Additions to the Constitution," he said, half expecting her to ask him next what the Constitution was, she was that unschooled.

"How many are there?"

"Ten." He led her through them, and was gratified by her quickness of mind. Within four blocks she had them memorized.

At first Frank assumed it was sheer luck that he should fall into step beside the girl of his dreams, but after meeting for four consecutive days at the corner of Pincherry and Fourth, it dawned on him that Libby was seeking him out as a friend, and this amazed him. Despite his infatuation he'd made no move to follow up on their abbreviated conversation at the Loomis Ballroom because he'd thought himself undeserving—her looks were so stunning, her social life so fast. Any woman that desirable must be, like his mother, out of reach. So why was she being so chummy with him, so confidential? On the fourth morning, for example, what qualified him to learn the words uttered by a pregnant friend of Libby's from the city the moment she'd found herself miscarrying? ("Christ on a crutch, I'm falling apart!" exclaimed the friend.) He wondered if during the opening weeks of school his face had been an open book in which Libby read yearning and adoration. Or had Sylvia perhaps advised her that here was a boy who could help her pass the tests she was too busy to study for, yet timid enough not to ask her for a date? For they were companions only by daylight. Frank never saw her after the sun went down. Her evenings, at this time, were reserved for Vernon Jessen, who carried her off to movies in Berrington, to dances in Loomis, to the secluded pine grove beside the Badbattle.

The sight of Libby and Frank on the way to school every morning made Vernon jealous, but when he confronted Libby and demanded she ride to school in his green pickup, she defied him, reminding him that Frank briefed her for school every morning—Vernon knew she never studied—and that was how she was able to tutor Vernon, who never studied either. They had angry arguments about it, but in the end Libby proved the more stubborn, and Vernon learned to be satisfied to have her in his pickup during the noon hour and on evenings and weekends.

Thus it was against the backdrop of Vernon's jealousy that Frank's companionship took on its highlights and Libby realized how precious to her was that daily fifteen-minute walk, realized with a kind of joyful, sobering shock that she was cultivating far more than a backup boyfriend—she was discovering a soulmate. Which was terribly odd, she thought, because Frank was so different from herself. He'd never had a girlfriend, never dated, never danced, never gone to parties. He was a loner, a scholar, a thinker. And stranger than all that, he was genuinely religious. She'd known boys who went to church before, but never one who seemed to enjoy it. His devotion to Catholicism, which seemed downright obsessive, was strangely attractive to her, she having grown up in a household where the life of the spirit was never acknowledged. And then there was his humor. She'd never before known anyone to be funny in the wry and understated way that Frank was funny. Instead of depending for laughs on jokes and insults and vulgarities the way most boys did, he invented humorous ways of looking at everyday things, and he delivered his lines so quietly you could miss them if you weren't paying attention.

"What church do you go to, Libby?"

"No church," she replied, a little ashamed. "Our relatives are Methodists, but we sleep late on Sundays."

"So I guess that makes you relatively Methodist," he told her.

Frank, as Sylvia had said, was overmothered. This soon became apparent to Libby. In obedience to the priest's housekeeper he was living his life along lines so strict that Libby was both fascinated and horrified. School days he went straight home from football practice and did homework, practiced the piano, and put together model airplanes until his ten o'clock bedtime. He spent every Saturday afternoon and evening working in the egghouse. Sunday mornings he was an altar boy, often at more than one Mass, and Sunday afternoons he accompanied Father Lawrence on his weekly visits to the homes of elderly shut-ins. He was restricted to two movies per week, and then only if the titles appeared on the Legion of Decency's approved list, which hung over Eunice Pfeiffer's kitchen sink.

Hearing so much about Eunice Pfeiffer made Libby very curious about his real mother, and on a mild morning in early November—the sun slanting down through the bare trees along Pincherry Street and melting the frost on the brown grass—she asked, "Was your mother as strict as Eunice, Frank?"

"I can't remember exactly. The thing I remember most is how much she talked." Libby saw a slight, faraway smile cross his face, and they walked nearly a block in silence before he continued. "I don't have very many memories of her anymore, but in the few I've got she's almost always talking. She's talking to me or my dad or my brothers. I see her standing at the ironing board talking to Eunice. They were together all the time, Eunice and my mother." He chuckled with pleasure. "After an hour of visiting they'd go home and call each other up."

Another long silence, then: "You know, for a long time after my mother died I used any excuse I could think of to call Eunice on the telephone or go over to the rectory, I guess because hearing her voice kept me in touch with my mother."

"Was it just too awful for words, Frank, having your mother die like that?"

His answer was a detailed description of the scene—the dark, snowy morning, the Christmas lights, his arrival too late at the deathbed. He described how death had pulled his mother's face into a forbidding expression she had never worn in life. He said that for the rest of that school year he dreaded going home each afternoon because death seemed to be present in all the rooms, and he was always relieved when his father came in from work. He said he liked being near his father, but his father liked being alone.

"At first I was glad I got there too late to see her die, but now that I'm older I wish I'd been there. I mean her last words were about me, and I should have been there to hear them."

"What were they?"

He cleared his throat nervously, and Libby saw a tenseness come into his eyes. "She said, 'I want Frank to be a priest.'"

How horrible! thought Libby. "Who told you, your dad?"

"No, Eunice told me."

"Did you believe her?"

At this, he turned to Libby, nonplussed. "Believe her? Why shouldn't I?"

Libby shrugged. "I just wondered. It's so—you know—such a serious thing. You'd want to be sure she got it right."

"I asked my dad one time if those were her exact words. He said he came over to the bed too late, and all he caught was the last word. It was 'priest' all right."

They drew close to the school and slowed down to avoid a group of classmates who were dawdling along the sidewalk and seemed to be waiting for them to catch up.

Libby asked quietly, "Will you be?"

"Will I be what?"

"You know." The word "priest" was hard for her bring out. It weighed so much.

"Will I be a priest?" He looked troubled. "If it's my decision, it's hard to know what to do." Then he brightened a little. "But if it's my mother's, then it's easy."

Her sense of horror deepened. She'd never heard of placing one's life in the hands of the dead. "Frank, can I tell you something? You're not making sense."

He didn't reply. He looked away.

"Listen, Frank, it's your life, so it's your decision. How could it possibly be anybody else's?"

He faced her, his expression changed from worried to perturbed, as though he thought her stupid. "Well, it's hard not to take a deathbed wish seriously."

"Of course you should take it seriously. But don't take it as your decision."

He said nothing. As they climbed the steps of the school, she said, "Frank, do you want to know what I think?"

"Sure." His flat tone said he didn't.

"Frank, I don't see how anybody could ever want to be a priest."

On the top step they stood aside, letting others pass through the entrance.

"That's because you're not Catholic," he said.

"No, it's because I believe every man should have a woman and every woman should have a man."

"Really?" He looked thoughtful and a little incredulous, as if it required great effort to think of mating as natural. The first-period bell rang and he continued to stand there, looking at her. "Really?" he repeated. He was still standing there, self-absorbed, when Vernon Jessen came lumbering up the steps and put his great muscular arm around Libby's narrow waist, causing her to laugh excitedly, and swept her through the doorway down the corridor to history class, glancing back at Frank with a sinister grin.

———

Vernon Jessen, destined to be Libby's first husband, had already been a giant at the age of fourteen, when he transferred to Linden Falls High from a one-room school in the country. It seemed to Frank, an eighth-grader at the time, that Vernon spent his entire freshman year terrorizing boys younger than himself. Day after day he preyed on the likes of Frank, catching them in the hallways or out on the playground and paralyzing them with a hammerlock or a half nelson and administering a burning knuckle rub to the scalp or an eye-watering nose twist. The pleasure Vernon drew from this mayhem was apparently sublime, for whenever Frank's head was pressed helplessly against Vernon's chest, he could hear him purring.

During his sophomore year Vernon, already the biggest boy in high school, caught the eye of Coach Pangborn as well as the eyes of several girls who were known as easy lays, and overnight he stopped preying on weaklings. Football and romance, he learned, could be as satisfying as terrorism.

It was during his junior year that the coaches voted Vernon a place on the second eleven of the all-conference football team and he began going with Rita Lou Peach. It was said that Vernon would have made the first eleven if the Rockets hadn't suffered through their third consecutive losing season. It was also said that the reason Rita Lou Peach went to live with her aunt in Duluth the following spring was that she was having Vernon's baby.

And now as a senior, he was zeroing in on Libby. Their romance perplexed Frank. What did Libby see in this gargantuan numbskull who obviously loved only two things in life—himself and his green pickup? Frank had once visited the two hundred stony acres that made up the Jessen farm, had gone out there with Doc Gilpatrick to look at a sick cow, and had found Vernon on home ground even more repellent than Vernon in school.

Frank's occasional trips into the countryside with the veterinarian were instigated by Eunice Pfeiffer, for Frank's job at Schultenovers' Egghouse, being part-time, left Eunice with a part-time worry about his idleness. They were pleasant trips for the most part. The doctor, an affable fellow, kept fishing tackle in his trunk and he and Frank seldom crossed a creek without throwing in a line.

Because of the great number of Jessen eggs Frank candled week after week, and because Vernon's pickup was brand new and had custom hubcaps and a radio, he expected to see a prosperous farm like those pictured on butter cartons and the cover of *Country Gentleman*, a farm with industrious hired hands, at least two silos, and grain stretching to the horizon. But after traveling twelve miles on gravel, two miles on dirt, and a mile and a half through mud, Doc Gilpatrick steered his car through a broken-down gate into a farmyard full of chickens and chicken feathers. The open machine shed was full of goats. Behind a rusty barbed-wire fence a small herd of bony cows stood among thistles. Lying on the ground near the barn was Vernon. He was lying on a bed of cardboard under his gleaming green pickup, attaching a new mudguard to the left rear fender.

"Your dad home?" asked Doc Gilpatrick.

"Nope," said Vernon, getting to his feet and brushing dirt from his pants. He glanced at Frank disdainfully, as usual, and said, "I'll show you the cow."

The aisles of the barn were caked with manure. The ailing cow stood among the flies of a fetid stall.

"What's her trouble?" asked the doctor, patting the cow between the ears.

"Off her feed," said Vernon.

Frank climbed up and sat on the top rail of the stall to watch the examination. The doctor looked the cow in the eye, then put his ear to her belly. He handed Vernon a rope with a heavy metal clip attached, and said, "Here, put this in her nose." The clip had a stiff spring, and the cow jerked her head to the side as she felt it bite into the flesh between her nostrils. Her pain made Frank squirm.

"Now twist," said Doc Gilpatrick, and Vernon twisted the rope so tight that the cow's flabby muzzle became twisted as well. Her eyes crossed and her legs stiffened. This pain at the cow's front end was diversionary, allowing the doctor (after removing his shirt) to insert his arm into her rectum. The arm went in, to Frank's astonishment, up to the shoulder. It took him only a moment to feel whatever he was looking for. He withdrew the arm and said, "Tell your dad to sell her before she dies."

Frowning grimly at the doctor, Vernon released the clip. The cow showed no sign of relief. In her lingering pain she remained cross-eyed and rigid.

"I'll need something to wipe my arm," Doc said to Vernon.

"Yeah," said Vernon, his eyes on the excrement running down the doctor's arm, but he made no move to help.

The doctor's suppressed anger intensified his sunburn. He turned to Frank and said, "There's a gunnysack in the trunk." Frank ran to get it.

Wiping his arm with the bristly sack, the doctor said, "I'll need some water."

Vernon pointed to the door leading to the pasture. "Out there's the stock tank."

Under the windmill Doc washed his arm in the slime-covered water of the tank. Then he put on his shirt and Frank followed him through the barn and out to the car.

"Tell your dad he owes me two bucks," Doc called to Vernon, who had crawled back under the pickup.

Vernon mumbled something.

"What's that?" asked Doc.

Vernon looked out from under the exhaust pipe. "Seems like a lot of money."

On the way home the doctor said to Frank, "Two dollars is a ridiculous fee, but if I'd asked for more, I'd never get it. The Jessens are tight as apple skin."

Frank nodded, silently agreeing that two dollars seemed very little, considering how far the doctor had driven, and how far he had put his arm into the cow.

5

On the first Friday in November, a reporter from the Minneapolis *Standard* drove two hundred and fifty miles to cover the Rockets' last game of the season, in which they were certain to set a new state record for consecutive losses. The sportswriter's name was Dennis Hedstrom. He arrived in Linden Falls several hours before the game in order to interview students and towns-people, asking them what it felt like to lose twenty-eight games over four seasons. Libby, sixteen and city-bred, was puzzled by the welcome this man received. He was interviewed by the editor of the Linden Falls *Leader*, he was invited into English classes to lecture on journalism, and when the principal introduced him at the afternoon pep fest, everybody cheered and he had his picture taken with the team. Were small towns so starved for attention, she wondered, that they would assist in their own humiliation? Was dishonor preferable to obscurity? The answer was yes. Never before had a Twin Cities newspaper sent a reporter to Linden Falls, Frank told her in higher algebra, not even to cover the spectacular two-day grain-elevator fire of 1944, or the ten-minute stopover of Harry Truman's campaign train in 1948.

After school, at Dennis Hedstrom's request, the principal rounded up a few students for him to visit with. Sylvia Pofford, an obvious choice because she was editor of the school paper and girlfriend of the starting quarterback, asked Libby to tag along, and so she was among the six or eight juniors and seniors who sat in a classroom answering the reporter's questions and studying him closely, the way villagers inevitably examine strangers. Libby considered him handsome. He was about thirty. He had light blue eyes and a crooked way of smiling. He wore a striped shirt open at the neck and a dark blue cardigan with a button missing. He scribbled the students' remarks in a tattered little notebook. He had a golden mustache.

Throughout the interview he and Libby played eye games, and by the time it was over he had worked her over so thoroughly with his gaze that she felt like a grown woman and wasn't surprised when he asked her to remain behind, claiming he needed an in-depth profile of one particular student. Sylvia, envious, lingered in the doorway until Dennis Hedstrom dismissed her with a scowl. The door swung shut. He closed his notebook, tucked his pen in his pocket, and said, "You're different from the others."

Libby put her eyes to work. Innocence. Amusement. Bewilderment. "What do you mean?"

"I mean you seem more like a city girl."

"How can you tell?" She stood up and went to a window.

He looked her over. "The way your clothes fit."

She was wearing an outfit her mother had made her—pink blouse and straight black skirt. Her mother had been remarking for years about the way clothes hung on her, how ideal she was to sew for.

"What city?" he asked.

"Minneapolis."

"What part?"

"Northeast." She gazed outside. She watched Vernon Jessen's pickup move out of the parking lot across the street and pull up in front of the entrance to the school. Vernon was waiting to drive her home by way of the park where they usually stopped and necked.

"What high school? Don't tell me Edison."

She turned to him and nodded.

"Wow, that's perfect, that's fantastic. Edison is the juggernaut of the City League this year. Nobody's come within twenty points of Edison. They destroyed Central last week and they're probably destroying Washburn this afternoon. It's possible I could get you an article all your own, Libby. Sunday edition. 'Displaced city girl trades winners for losers.'" He opened his notebook and wrote this down. "What did you say your last name was?"

"Girard."

Scribbling, he chuckled and mumbled, "Fan cheers valiantly but in vain for the losingest team of all time." He turned a page and looked at her. "I'll want to sit with you in the bleachers tonight, Libby. Who do you go to games with? You got a boyfriend?"

Detecting a hint of urgency in his voice, she studied him and saw something like desperation in his crooked smile. Apparently he was talking about a game more serious than football. A game she could play, by changing the subject.

"What's a juggernaut?"

"A hell of a football team. You must have a boyfriend—a girl like you."

She turned her back on him. "What if we win tonight—have you thought of that?"

"Never happen."

"But what if?"

"Upset of the year. Great copy either way."

Long moments of silence in the classroom. No sound but the whisper of steam in the radiator. She stared out the window. She heard blasts from Vernon's tailpipe as he gunned his engine, his eyes on the entrance. Then she heard Dennis Hedstrom's chair scrape, heard his approach, felt his hand come to rest lightly on her shoulder, felt bubbles running through her. "Who do you go to games with, Libby?"

She dipped out from under his touch and glided to the door, where she paused and said, "I'll be sitting in the top row of bleachers behind the Linden Falls bench." She slipped out of the room.

She found Sylvia waiting for her on the front steps. At the

curb the pickup was lurching back and forth as Vernon impatiently shifted in and out of all his gears.

Sylvia, squinting in the sun, asked, "Did you tell him I'm Bob's girlfriend?"

"No."

"Why not?"

"Why didn't *you* tell him?"

"I didn't get a chance. I thought I'd be the one he'd profile and I'd tell him then. How come he decided on you? I'm the quarterback's girlfriend, not you. Do you think he got us mixed up?"

"Maybe," said Libby absently. She was still feeling bubbles.

"That's got to be it. He thought you were me. Do you think I should go in and tell him?"

This amused Libby. She giggled and said, "Why don't you."

Sylvia hurried inside. Libby sauntered down the steps and got into the pickup.

Vernon asked, "Did you tell him I made all-conference last year?"

"No."

He gave her his wounded look. "How come?"

She shrugged. "I forgot."

"You forgot! How could you forget something like that? I was the only Rocket on the all-conference team."

"I didn't forget you were all-conference. I just forgot to tell him."

"Coach never told him, you never told him, nobody told him." He switched off the engine. "What do you think—should I go in and tell him?"

She giggled. "Sure, go ahead."

"What's so funny?"

She didn't admit to Vernon that the reporter's hand on her shoulder had transformed her into a woman much older and wiser than her friends, who now seemed like children. "Go ahead," she said again.

Vernon met Sylvia and the reporter coming out the door. The three of them stood on the steps talking. At this little distance Sylvia seemed to Libby almost beautiful, the sun falling on her violet dress and her red-brown hair. Vernon was wearing his football jersey, red with white numerals. It fit tight and showed his superb build. When the reporter found a fresh page in his notebook and wrote something down, Vernon and Sylvia nodded with satisfaction and descended the steps. The reporter, behind their backs, tore the page out of the notebook and held it up for Libby to see, then slowly tore it in half, all the while giving Libby his broadest, crookedest smile. She made a face at him—mock horror—and turned away. The reporter went back inside.

They dropped Sylvia at her house, then Vernon drove Libby two miles west of town to a small picnic area in the forest. There they kissed. Libby was so full of sex she felt like a pressure cooker. She made some very teasing moves, certain that Vernon wouldn't go all the way because it was a game day. Vernon had told her that when Mary Sue Peach was his girlfriend they'd gone at it two or three times a week but never before games. Good Fridays, he called them. As for Libby, she had never gone all the way.

After a few minutes of intense squirming on the fake leopardskin, Vernon panted, "You're asking for it."

Breaking out of his embrace, Libby hung her head out the window and looked up through the pine boughs. "For what?"

"You know damn well. Tonight. After the game."

"No," she said, not meaning it. She felt ready.

"Don't say no, damn it. That's all you ever say is no."

She giggled and said no again. She felt giddy.

"Goddamn it, Libby, you want me to go back to Mary Sue?"

"She wouldn't have you."

"Hell she wouldn't."

She couldn't stop giggling. "Take me home, Vernon. It's my night to make supper."

Halfway through supper her mother announced that she had found herself a cleaning job. Once a week she would do housework for someone named Harry Schwartz. Her father blew his stack. Libby hadn't seen him pound the table and shout since they moved to town, but for the past few days she'd sensed his anger building up, had heard him muttering about his job, had smelled liquor on his breath at supper, and now suddenly their plates were jumping and he was calling his wife a whore. Libby shrank in her chair. Whenever he acted this way, she felt as if she were losing years off her life. She felt about four. She wanted dolls to hold.

"Lay off her, Dad!" said Libby's brother Roy, springing out of his chair and going to the refrigerator for milk. Roy, a wiry, catlike young man of twenty, was always the one most visibly affected by his father's rage, even when it wasn't directed at him. While Libby and her mother reacted by holding their fear and anger and urge to weep in check, Roy broke out in immediate defiance. At the first sign of trouble, he was invariably on his feet and moving lightly around his father in a nervous kind of dance, peppering him with appeals and sometimes with insults in an attempt to deflect the abuse from his mother and sister.

"We're behind at the grocery store," reasoned her mother. "We can use the extra money." From long practice, she, like Libby, had developed the ability to reply to his insane ranting in a matter-of-fact, dispassionate tone.

"Of course we can use the money! But there's other ways of getting money than finding yourself a boyfriend!"

"Who's Harry Schwartz?" asked Libby in a small voice. She was sure her mother had never been unfaithful, so why did her father erupt in a jealous fit whenever she sewed or washed clothes or cleaned house for a man?

He turned to Libby and sourly spat out his words like lemon seeds: "He's a bachelor that works at the bank, and he thinks he's God's gift to women."

"He's not home when I clean," said her mother softly. "He's at work."

"Give you a key, did he? That's handy. Drop in on him day or night, I suppose."

Roy, bobbing around on his toes with his hands around a milk bottle, repeated, "Lay off her, Dad."

"Stay out of this, you parasite!" The eyes he turned on his son reminded Libby of the close-up photo of a hawk in her biology text. The bird's dark feathers had little streaks of white in them like tweed, like her father's hair and mustache, and you could see terrible anger in its smoldering, hooded eyes. "Why aren't *you* paying for groceries, you goddamn parasite? When I was your age, I was doing field work fourteen hours a day."

"Not in November, you weren't." Roy's boldness always amazed Libby. She didn't admire it exactly—it seemed foolhardy—but she marveled at how it sometimes succeeded in distracting her father. As now:

Fist on the table—plates in the air: "I drove a corn picker fourteen hours a day in November."

"That was in Iowa. This is up north, remember? This is as far north as you can go and still be in the United States. Up here there's hardly any corn to pick." Roy's employment as farmhand had ended in mid-October.

"Don't tell me there's no corn up here. We run corn through the elevator every day."

"But not much."

"Enough to pick."

"Not enough to hire help to pick it."

Libby saw her chance to leave the table. She stood up, but took only a step or two before she felt the hawk's eyes turn on her.

"Where you going?"

She smiled at him. "The game."

The smile had no effect. "Who said you could go to the game?"

A hush fell over the kitchen, his wife and two children aware that when he used this tone on Libby, his rage was more intense than usual, and his spell of anger might extend through the evening and into the next day. Ordinarily Libby—his pet—was spared.

She made her voice breezy. "Everybody goes to the games, Dad."

"Sit down."

She returned to her chair, sat, fluffed her hair. She was able to keep her voice light and steady. "I'm going with Sylvia. I told her ages ago I'd be going."

Fist down, plates up: "Answer my question!"

Another hush, filled with the sound of his breathing—alcohol produced a whistle in his nose—and then her brother took over.

"Up north! That's all we heard from you in the city—how great life would be up north. Well, if life is so great up north, how come we can't pay our grocery bill?"

Her father, roaring, lunged at Roy and grabbed a handful of his shirt, her mother sprang between them, crying, "Now stop, now stop!" and Libby ran upstairs, trembling and feeling sick. From her room she could hear Roy continue to needle her father for as long as it took her to change into her gray slacks and white sweater and streak on a little eye shadow and slip downstairs and grab her coat. Drawing the front door closed behind her, she heard her father roar louder, heard the smack of a fist on flesh, heard her brother cry out, heard her mother scream.

She walked around several blocks in the dark, and when her shaking stopped, she went over to Fourth Street to pick up Sylvia. They hurried across town to the floodlit athletic field, climbed into the bleachers behind the team bench, and were immediately joined by the sportswriter. He sat between them with his notebook on his knee. He was wearing a trench coat and scarf. He stirred up a feeling in Libby such as Vernon never caused. It was like being high on beer but without the dizziness. It was like being older than she was, and more experienced. When Sylvia left to buy popcorn, he said, "I know who your boyfriend is, Libby. I saw you in his truck."

She imagined how it must look to a reporter from the *Standard*—city girl keeps company with hick—and she wanted to deny it, but she didn't. She simply smiled, keeping her eyes on the field, and for the rest of the game she trembled with a frightening kind of anticipation.

"I'm staying at Riverside Rest, Libby," he told her at the final gun. "Cabin six. I could make Vernon Jessen all-state."

He squeezed her shoulder and hurried down out of the bleachers and followed the team into the dressing room.

6

Coach Pangborn assured his Rockets after the game that by giving the undefeated Berrington Bears their biggest scare of the season and losing by only seven points, they had made him very proud. Then, taking Frank aside, he designated him as next year's first-string quarterback, which caused Frank, after showering and dressing, to leave the locker room walking on air.

He lingered in the gym, as usual, to look over the dancers at the sock hop, to listen to the records, to drink the syrupy punch concocted by the home-ec class. He knew there was no danger he'd be asked to dance as long as he sat unapproachably high in the bleachers with the dozen or so other boys as socially retarded as himself, and he was about to climb up and join them when Libby appeared at his side, looking edgy. "Frank, is Vernon still in the showers?"

"No, he left."

"Where did he go?"

Frank shrugged. "I'd be the last one he'd tell."

She stamped her foot and said, "Damn." She glanced around at the dancers. "Frank, can I sit with you for a while?"

"Sure, come on." He stared to climb.

"Not up there."

They sat at floor level, elbows on knees, chins in hand.

"Frank, I'm sorry you didn't get into the game."

"But I did."

"You did? I didn't see you."

How could you have seen me? he wanted to say. Every time I looked up in the stands that hotshot from the city was feeding you popcorn a kernel at a time. "I played a little at the end," he told her.

The eyes she turned on Frank were sad. She said, "My family's at war again."

"Aw, I'm sorry." He gave her a timid pat on the shoulder of her woolly white sweater.

She crimped her mouth and nodded grimly. "And now Vernon's all mad because of a little argument we had after school."

"Dear Hearts and Gentle People" gave way to "Mule Train." Libby changed her position, sat slump-shouldered, her arms hanging straight down between her legs. With her right foot tapping out the hectic "Mule Train" beat, she said, "I think he's standing me up."

Frank didn't say he was sorry. Her romance with Vernon Jessen, going into its third week, grieved him. How could she fall for a goon like that? Was it Vernon's size that appealed to her? His gruffness? Frank had been reared to believe that amiability would serve him as a winning virtue through life, but now he wasn't sure. He thought of the day he'd gone out with Doc Gilpatrick to look at the Jessen cow. Vernon, so callous with people, so bullish with cows, had won Libby's heart. Is that what girls liked? A stud? A brute? A slob? True, Bob Templeton's polite, easygoing manner was a lot like Frank's and Bob had Sylvia—but who cared who had Sylvia?

As Frankie Laine's wailing gave way to the Ames Brothers' "Rag Mop," Vernon appeared in the gymnasium doorway, pushing Mary Sue Peach ahead of him onto the dance floor. It was Mary Sue whom Libby had replaced in Vernon's life. She was attractive in a wide-eyed, doll-like way. She had a round, shiny face and hair the color of brass. For his size, Vernon was surprisingly agile on the dance floor. Their jitterbug twirl was designed to show off Mary Sue's legs, her skirt opening like an umbrella every time she spun. Passing near Frank and Libby, Vernon bestowed upon them one of his rare smiles of satisfaction while Mary Sue gave Libby a triumphant smirk.

Libby, shaken, said to Frank, "Will you walk me home?"

They took the long way to Pincherry Street, along the dark river. Ghostly shreds of ground fog hung over the water. Was it Libby's presence at his side, or was it the cold, clear atmosphere of late autumn that made everything so vivid? The stars glittered and flashed as if sending signals to earth. There appeared to be a statement of some importance, too, in what the water was repeating as it churned and gurgled over the rapids. The grass under their feet was crunchy with frost. The ten o'clock curfew sounded and somewhere a dog howled.

The curfew did not apply to youngsters over sixteen and was more or less ignored by everyone over twelve, and yet Frank felt vaguely uneasy being out at this hour. Not that his father was a harsh overseer, but Martin C. Healy had grown accustomed to hearing his son come in within half an hour of the end of football and basketball games or as soon as play practice ended or the first show at the Royal let out, and he would be puzzled tonight when he heard the ten o'clock whistle and looked up from his workbench or his newspaper and realized that Frank was still out. That's all right, Frank told himself, let him puzzle over it, I need a few more minutes to get the girl of my dreams to her front door. Which was all he intended. It never crossed his mind that they might exchange a good-night kiss.

And they didn't. Approaching her front porch, they heard angry voices inside. Libby clutched his arm and veered off across the yard and back to the sidewalk and they walked from one end of town to the other, Frank listening intently as Libby spilled out her troubles. She said her father had raised hell with her mother and her brother at supper and she'd left the house before he got around to her. She said her father was a monster sometimes. She didn't know how her mother managed to stay in his life year after year. If Libby were her mother, she'd have left him by now. Her brother hated him, and as soon as he found a decent job he was moving out and never coming home again. She herself didn't hate her father exactly. She was sometimes scared of him, and on nights like this when he made life hell for everybody she was mad at him, but no, she couldn't really say she hated him. "You can't hate a drunk, can you, Frank? I mean I don't think he knows what he's doing. He's a different person when he's drunk."

"Does he hit you?"

"No, he threatens to. He's put his fist up to my face a few times, but he's never laid a hand on me. He mainly hits my brother."

"Does he hit your mother?"

"Not very often."

"How often?"

"Well, I mean she's had her share of black eyes in her life, but usually he just insults her."

"Does your brother hit him back?"

"No, he just sort of pushes him. My brother always gets the worst of it, and it's like he *wants* to get the worst of it. I mean it's like he doesn't want to hurt my dad for fear of killing him. You can see how much he hates him—his eyes get wild—but even though he's quicker than my dad, he never really lets him have it. But my dad really lets my *brother* have it. See, it's like this. My dad will insult my mother and my brother will step in to defend her and my dad will turn on my brother and really let him have it. It seems like when he goes after my mother, it's really to get at my brother."

"Has your dad been yelling like that ever since supper?"

"No, probably not. He goes to sleep after supper. What we just heard was him probably waking up from his nap. He wakes up at bedtime and can't sleep, so he sits up talking mean for an hour or two and keeps everybody else awake."

The sidewalk gave out at the edge of town. They kept walking. Beyond the glow of the last streetlight they met the Badbattle again near the tourist cabins. RIVERSIDE REST was spelled out in flickering tubes of pink neon. It was colder now. Stones and roots made walking difficult beside the dark river.

"Frank, can I come over to your house for a while?"

"When?"

"Now."

"Now?" He was astonished.

"Just for a while."

An outrageous request. A girl in the house at this hour? At any hour, for that matter. His father would surely disapprove. His father, instead of confronting him, would convey his disapproval through Eunice Pfeiffer, and Eunice would speak to Frank for both of them. She'd give him her set speech about the priesthood, the words he'd been hearing more and more often lately—how proud everyone was of Frank for getting this far through high school without having a girlfriend. It was so foolish to have a girlfriend at Frank's age, so imprudent, so unnecessary, so downright damaging to someone who possessed the precious gift of a religious vocation.

"Please, Frank." They stopped and stood at the edge of the water.

"Jeez, Libby." He was alarmed. It wasn't only his house that was off limits—it was his heart as well. Greater than his infatuation with Libby was his fear that she might penetrate deeper into his solitary life than she already had. What if she asked him to hold her, to console her with kisses? The prospect was terrifying. He wasn't ready to take her in his arms like a lover. He was only now, after knowing her two months, learning to be comfortable with a girl as a daytime companion. He was light-years away from intimacy.

"I don't mean to stay," she said. "I just mean for a little while. I can't go home." She turned away from him, letting go of his hand in order to find a hankie in her pocket. She wiped her eyes as she spoke. "I can't listen to any more of my dad's ranting and raving, Frank. I'm so sick of it I could die. I just want to sit somewhere warm and quiet for half an hour." Gazing down at the thin layer of fog over the dark water, she didn't see that he was backing cautiously away from her. "You could go to bed if you wanted. I'd just like to sit in a chair in your house for a while."

He turned and hurried stealthily toward the glimmering streetlights, leaving her alone in the dark, talking to the river. He was out of sight by the time she realized she was alone. She turned slowly in a circle, holding back a new surge of tears. She looked at the sky. The stars seemed closer and more numerous than she'd ever seen them. They seemed caught in the webs of the bare trees. She stood for a long time at the edge of the water, recalling the evening in August when she'd watched Frank submerge himself in the river in front of his house and wishing she had the courage to do the same—and stay under until she drowned.

But the water, she knew, was frigid, and what she needed was warmth. She climbed the bank and found cabin six of Riverside Rest. There was a dim light in the little window. The door rattled when she knocked. The door opened and Dennis Hedstrom peered out into the night. Seeing that it was Libby, he broke out in his biggest, crookedest smile and said, "Wow, I didn't think you'd come." He was standing there in his pants and undershirt and bare feet and holding a magazine.

She stepped inside and he shut the door. The cabin was furnished with a chair, a bed, and a coat tree. In one corner, curtained off, was a sink and a toilet. In another was a space heater that gave off a strong smell of oil and not much heat. Dennis Hedstrom's suitcase lay open on the floor. Standing in the suitcase was a bottle of liquor with the cap off. He picked it up and said excitedly, "How about a drink, Libby? I've got a bottle of the best."

She said no thanks and took off her coat and stepped out of her shoes. She sat down on the bed and took off her socks and pulled her woolly sweater over her head. She unbuttoned her blouse. She stood up and dropped her slacks.

"Wow," said Dennis Hedstrom.

She got under the blankets to remove her underwear. Dennis Hedstrom turned off the light, climbed into bed, and gave her, with her full and arduous cooperation, more pain than pleasure. She stayed less than half an hour. Walking home through the cold, silent town, she hoped sex would be more fun with other men.

A hope fulfilled the following night, and regularly thereafter, by Vernon Jessen in his pickup.

7

Following his father's example as a sports fan, Frank had begun reading Dennis Hedstrom's column in the Minneapolis *Standard* when he was twelve years old, but after the hatchet job he did on Linden Falls he never read him again.

"You will find the village of Linden Falls lying inert in the valley of the scum-covered Badbattle River," Dennis Hedstrom's article began on the Sunday following the Berrington game, the same issue in which Vernon Jessen was named all-state tackle. After defaming the town and the school, he went on to vilify the team by reporting on only the first twelve minutes of the game (the Rockets fell immediately behind by twenty points) and ignoring the last three quarters, when after a shaky start the Rockets played as they had never played before, making half a dozen goal-line stands and scoring two touchdowns. At the final gun (20 to 13), the sportswriter portrayed the Rockets as "straggling off the field dragging behind them their perfect record of defeat," when actually their spirits had never been higher. He portrayed their coach in the locker room as "obviously embarrassed by his players' ineptitude," when in fact Coach Pangborn had gone around congratulating each boy and speaking effusively about his high hopes for next year. It was obvious to Frank that

Dennis Hedstrom saw only what he came to town expecting to see. The Badbattle, in fact, was spring-fed and clear as glass. Scum was in the eye of the beholder.

Having failed to bring Libby home for the quiet half hour she begged of him, Frank spent the weekend in agony, cursing himself for his timidity and fearing he'd lost her forever.

On Monday morning, however, she turned up at the corner of Pincherry and Fourth smiling her wide smile and telling him about a dream she'd had in which she was wandering the snowy streets of a strange city without being able to open her eyes until Frank led her to a zoo, where she beheld a cage of beautiful birds. Was this the downcast girl he'd left on the riverbank? Today she was laughing and radiating a joyous inner light that warmed him as he fell in step beside her. Fascinated by her skill at bouncing back, he resolved to try to cultivate this same resilience in himself.

Libby made no reference, that morning or ever, to his deserting her on the riverbank. Indeed, from that point on, their attachment grew steadily stronger, more profound, more rewarding, and he speculated that perhaps he'd earned a new and deeper form of Libby's commitment by revealing the limits of his own. In other words, he sensed in Libby as well as himself a kind of liberating relief in realizing that their relationship was not complicated by the threat or promise of romantic intimacy, as though having put romance aside, they were free to explore whatever else was in their hearts.

Dreams were only the beginning. As fall became winter and winter became endless, they went deeper into themselves in search of memories and worries and puzzles and hopes and brought them up one by one to be examined. They exchanged gossip and daydreams and tales from their past. They honored each other's secrets, and the only secret they held back from each other was how they felt about each other.

Libby didn't speak of her fondness for Frank because she didn't know what to call it. In some ways it felt like love; but love, she thought, was what you felt for boys who took you to dances and kissed you. What did you call it when the bond was based almost entirely on talk?

As for Frank, love was a word he never allowed himself to

utter. Almost as powerful as his love for Libby was his fear of being in love. Love was treacherous, uncharted territory. Girls were so mysterious. Romantic attachment was such a risk. On his journey to the priesthood—if that was truly his destination—love was the wild, forbidden mountain range he'd have to find a detour around. Perhaps if he'd grown up with a sister or two, he would have been less skittish around girls, less awed by the otherness of their bodies, less wary of their emotions. A meeting of minds he could handle, for that entailed only talking and listening—his two best skills—but the danger was in advancing from talking and listening to dancing, to touching, to kissing, to any sort of intimacy outside the intellect, for then he was sure to fail. And if by some miracle he failed to fail the physical tests of love, then surely he would sin.

For Frank was a boy with sin on his mind. It had been implanted there by the nuns of St. Ann's Elementary, who honed each student's conscience to a sharp edge and trained him to hold it to the throat of his impulses. Thus by the time Frank and his classmates had left the eighth grade, they were armed and ready for their lifelong battle against evil. Girls that age talked about taking the veil and becoming brides of Christ or, failing that, marrying a virtuous man and having lots of Catholic babies and infusing their households with holiness. Most of the boys planned to become priests.

Then, crossing town and entering the public high school, these Catholic freshmen came face-to-face with the facts of secular life. It surprised Frank how quickly his classmates lightened their metaphysical load, sorting through the nuns' proscriptions and discarding what they didn't need. The girls, learning more about boys and how they felt about boys and how boys felt about them, forgot about the sisterhood, and the boys, watching girls change shape before their very eyes, dropped their plans for the priesthood. Frank, however, didn't make the transition his friends did. With Eunice Pfeiffer keeping watch over him, he never truly passed out of grade eight, and throughout his high school years he was continually shocked and bewildered to see the choices that became available to his friends and not to him. Before the end of his freshman year, for example, Danny Ash was already feeling up girls, and as a sophomore, Sylvia Pofford began going steady with Bob Templeton, while Frank, now a junior, remained locked in the armor of his fears and inhibitions.

Though his movements were restricted, his vision was unimpaired. It was Frank's gift to be vigilantly self-aware, and despite his fear of love he knew he was in it. Months later, even years, he would look back and pinpoint the exact day when his crush on Libby blossomed into love. It was the morning in January when he first opened up on the subject of the long-standing sorrow that followed his mother's death. This was a topic he'd always been ashamed of, his grief springing as it did (he was sure) from some unmanly flaw in his character. "I guess Eunice Pfeiffer figured out how I was feeling," he told Libby, "because she asked if I'd like to spend a night now and then at the rectory, and I did. And I still do. I still sleep there once in a while."

"That's nice," said Libby tenderly. "You've got two homes." They were walking slowly through a thin veil of lightly falling snow.

"And you know something else, Libby?"

"Tell me."

"Swear you'll never tell a soul."

"Swear."

"I was really sad, and what helped me get over it, more than anything else, was how Eunice Pfeiffer would rock me to sleep on her lap." He looked expectantly at Libby, anticipating her laughter. "Can you picture it? Isn't it funny?"

"What's funny? I think it's sweet."

"What's funny is how big I was."

"You were only eleven."

"For a while I was eleven, but then I was twelve. And I was still doing it once in a while when I was thirteen." He laughed with embarrassment, ashamed of admitting to behavior so ridiculously soft and unmasculine. "That's the funny part."

But still Libby didn't laugh, and that was the moment that he knew he loved her.

———

In February Frank had a dream in which his father began paying attention to Eunice Pfeiffer's fond smiles and love pats and then quickly married her. Frank woke up devastated. Describing it to Libby the next morning, he called it a nightmare.

"Oh, Frank, they're made for each other," Libby gushed, enchanted by the thought of a love affair in late middle age. "Your dream is telling you they're made for each other."

"They are not!" he barked, shocked by her reaction.

"Yes they are. You've got to get your dad to propose to Eunice Pfeiffer."

He actually flinched at this. "Good Lord, I see too much of Eunice as it is." The solace Eunice had offered him in his early teens had long since turned oppressive, though he had never given voice to it before.

"But you're only home for another year, and then think how lonesome your dad will be."

"My dad likes being lonesome."

"He *can't* like being lonesome, Frank. Nobody likes being lonesome. You've got to talk sense to him and get him to propose."

"I wouldn't call that sense. Besides, whoever heard of talking sense to a parent?"

"I do it. My mother and I talk sense all the time."

"*My* mother is *dead*!"

Libby, momentarily silenced by his petulance, wondered what caused it. Meeting him on the corner this morning, she'd noticed an altered look in his eye, a murky expression clouding what was ordinarily the most open, most trusting face she'd ever seen on anyone as old as seventeen. But never mind his petulance, this was a topic—matchmaking—that she couldn't let drop.

"Listen, Frank, your dad's happiness is at stake. You should be giving him pep talks about love."

His response to this was a muttered word she didn't catch, and they walked a block in silence. It was a warm day for midwinter, nearly thawing; the deep snow was wet and sticky. Frank packed a snowball icy hard and pitched it at a tree. "I don't mind her cooking supper at our house twice a week, though it makes for a lot of dishes to wash, and I don't even mind it when she signs me up to serve at funerals and weddings without asking me."

He made another snowball and threw it at another tree. "But I *do* mind it when she goes to my teachers on parents' night and acts like she's my mother."

A third snowball. "And I *do* mind it when they have visiting priests at the rectory and she calls me in to provide the entertainment on the piano."

A fourth. "And I *do* mind it the way she tells my dad how to raise me, especially what movies I can't go to. Will I have to be twenty-one before I get to see Jane Russell in *The Outlaw*?"

"I saw it," said Libby. "You're not missing much."

"And worst of all, she's always going through our house making sure everything is just the way my mother would want it. The dishes in the cupboard. The doilies on the sideboard."

"It sounds like she wants to *be* your mother, Frank."

"I know it, and she's not like my mother in the least. My mother was . . ." He found himself suddenly speechless, seized by the desperate need to describe the sort of person his mother had been, and by the horrible suspicion that he hadn't really known her.

Libby tried to help, saying warmly, "I wish I could have known your mother, Frank."

He tried again. "She wasn't at all like Eunice. She was . . . my mother was . . ."

"Your mother was married."

"That's not what I mean."

"But it *is* what you mean. Marriage is what makes a woman a woman."

"Libby, has anyone ever told you you're obsessed?"

"Every girl is, until she's married."

"Sylvia isn't."

"I mean every girl with a heart."

"Were you always like this? I mean were you born with this mating urge or what?"

"I guess so," said Libby, laughing.

8

In an era when you measured the intensity of a girl's love by the amount of a boy's clothing she wore, Frank was mightily dismayed when Libby began wearing Vernon Jessen's letter sweater to school. She also wore Vernon Jessen's class ring and—to Frank's particular disgust—Vernon Jessen's sweat socks. On chilly days she wore Vernon Jessen's stocking cap, and on the morning in April when she turned up at the corner of Pincherry and Fourth wearing Vernon's necktie as the belt of her skirt, Frank was hard-pressed not to cry out in anguish. But at least Libby was still exclusively his on their daily walk to school, he reminded himself, and next year Vernon would be out of the picture entirely, either tending the livestock on the Jessens' scrubby farm in the gully or fighting communists in Korea. For in an era when each generation was given its own particular war, the Korean conflict was erupting on schedule, causing many of the senior boys to talk about enlisting.

Bob Templeton was one of them. Dr. Templeton, a former infantryman and past commander of the Linden Falls American Legion Post, was greatly invigorated by the grim news from Korea. He regaled his son with heroic tales from the trenches, and while he stopped short of ordering Bob off to war, he repeatedly pointed out the wonderful terms of the G.I. Bill, particularly wonderful to someone facing the expense of medical school.

Bob succumbed. Four days after graduation Dr. and Mrs. Templeton drove Bob and Sylvia to Berrington, where Bob was put on the westbound train to boot camp. Waving farewell from the platform, his mother shed tears of apprehension, his father shed tears of patriotic fervor, and Sylvia, tearless, called, "Send me your picture in your uniform right away."

Walt Welner enlisted in the marines and was gone by the Fourth of July. Nathan Dunnock joined the navy and left in August. DeVaughn Smith and Carl Barkus secured draft deferments by enrolling in college, DeVaughn at faraway Antioch, where he would major in music, and Carl fifty miles down the road at Berrington Junior College, where he intended to kill two years reading novels till the war ended. The rest of the graduating boys took jobs—a few on farms, several in the factories of Berrington, two or three in the Twin Cities—and waited for their draft numbers to come up. Vernon Jessen, who had no military or bookish aspirations, stayed home on the farm and continued his moonlight romance with Libby, who got a summer job waiting on tables at the Colonial Café.

Before the summer was over Vernon became sole owner of the farm, his father claiming to be incapacitated by asthma and signing the deed over to his son in an attempt to protect him from the draft. This had been a fairly common ploy during World War II, draft boards declaring agriculture a priority industry and awarding a deferred classification to the last healthy male on each farm, and the Jessens were betting that the regulations of the past war would apply to the present.

This prompted a good deal of skepticism in the egghouse. Farm wives visiting with Selma Schultenover pointed out that Mr. Jessen's asthma, a minor complaint in peacetime, had only worsened when the North Koreans crossed the 38th Parallel. Frank detected more amusement than bitterness in these remarks, and he gathered that the elder Jessens were quite well liked by their neighbors, who considered them rather a pitiable couple, both of them being soft-spoken rustics of a passive, kindly nature who had been answering to the whims and commands of their only child since his infancy.

And then to everyone's suprise, including perhaps his own, Vernon's father, on an oppressively hot and overpollinated day in August, died of asthma. Libby and Sylvia attended the funeral in a small country church. Libby described it to Frank on one of the rare occasions when they happened to meet on the street that summer. She said it was very sad. She said Vernon's mother behaved strangely. She bumped into people in the graveyard and then stood staring at them without seeing them. She seemed half-asleep. Vernon, she said, was rough with her, turning her this way and that and muttering in her ear. Libby said that Vernon, controlled by his grief, just wasn't himself. Vernon *was* himself, thought Frank, but he didn't say so. Frank, without knowing her, felt very sorry for Mrs. Jessen, alone now with the goats and chickens and Vernon.

Though they worked at opposite ends of a rather short Main Street, Libby saw very little of Frank that summer because he had two jobs. Besides spending his afternoons and his Saturdays in the egghouse, he was on St. Ann's payroll five mornings a week, attending to the lawns and various other duties assigned by Father Lawrence and Eunice Pfeiffer. Many of these mornings he spent on the Basswood Reservation, helping a carpenter and a painter refurbish Our Lady's Church.

Though they seemed unremarkable at the time, Frank would look back on these mornings with a sense of happy satisfaction, convinced that they had provided him with some of the most gratifying moments of his youth. They began at 7:25, when Frank left the house and ran down the alley to serve as altar boy at Father Lawrence's daily Mass, after which he joined the priest and Eunice Pfeiffer in the breakfast nook of the rectory for a sumptuous meal of pancakes, sausage, eggs, and sweetbread, and then he and Father Lawrence would set off for Basswood, fol-lowing Highway 2 west through the dewy woodland and then turning north on County Road 13, where it bent around the west shore of Sovereign Lake. This lake was a vast body of water shaped like an hourglass and measuring nearly thirty miles from north to south. The village of Basswood was about halfway up the west shore, a little north of the narrow part of the hour glass. It was nineteen miles from Linden Falls to Basswood in the summertime, eight miles farther than in the winter, when you could cross the mile-wide narrows on the ice.

Our Lady's, a small frame church with three stained-glass windows on each side and a squat steeple over the front door, was being reshingled, rewired, and repainted inside and out; decayed strips of siding were being replaced; the twenty-four pews were being sanded and varnished and new linoleum was being laid in the sanctuary. The carpenter was a young Indian named Duck, and the painter was an elderly Swede named Hanson. With a wet cigarette constantly smoldering at the corner of his mouth, Duck told war stories as he worked. He'd been in the Sea Bees. Saipan, Tarawa, Iwo Jima—you name the hellhole, he'd been there.

Hanson the painter, a gaunt, wrinkled man with a wad of chewing tobacco tucked inside his lower lip, was a slow, silent worker. He paused often in his painting to unroll his paper envelope of tobacco and hold it out for Frank to take a pinch and to take one himself.

What, besides their summer beauty, was so gratifying about these mornings in Basswood? Surely it was the companionship of Duck and Hanson, who in treating Frank so freely to their stories and cigarettes and chewing tobacco were implicitly declaring him a man among men; and it was surely, too, the distance from Schultenovers' Egghouse, which by contrast to the sweeping shoreline of Sovereign Lake had become for Frank, after a full year at the candling table, a confining and dismal place to work. And of course it was the distance as well from Eunice Pfeiffer, whose everlasting watchfulness was becoming steadily more oppressive as Frank edged up on his eighteenth birthday. But more than anything else, it was the pleasure of being in the company of the man he loved like a father, particularly out in the country and away from St. Ann's, where the priest was often too busy to give Frank his full and sustained attention.

The Reverend Adrian Lawrence, forty-four years old that summer, was a short, thin-faced man whose heavy horn-rimmed glasses rode low on his long nose and whose hair was turning white before its time. He didn't talk much, but his reticence, unlike Frank's father's, never had the effect of discouraging conversation. He smiled easily and paid you the compliment of listening intently to what you were telling him. He was awkward in all kinds of physical endeavor—sweeping the floor or buttoning his coat, his every movement was tentative and bumbling—but there was nothing obtuse or clumsy in his relationships. He was continually sought out by parishioners, neighbors, and priestly colleagues for his kindly nature, for his hospitality, for the serenity radiating from deep in his soul.

It wasn't clear to Frank why they made so many trips to Basswood that summer. Duck and Hanson seemed not to require the priest's supervision, and they could easily have found a boy on the reservation as helpful as Frank. Moreover, Father Lawrence was next to no help at all, having no talent for painting or carpentry, and though he tried to make himself useful by picking up scraps of lumber and handing tools up ladders, he was quite often in the way. Occasionally the priest went across the road to the Indian Health Center and visited with the two nurses who were its staff and who belonged to Our Lady's parish. Now and then, word came out of the forest concerning the ill health of some Indian and he went off in the car to the sickbed. It was at 10:30 each morning when the priest made his primary contribution to the refurbishing project, taking from the backseat of the car the pastry of the day sent out by Eunice for their coffee break. Unless it was raining, they ate this midmorning snack in the shade of an oak at the edge of the lake, the four of them sitting in a row in the shoulder-high weeds and looking out over the water as if expecting a performance of some kind.

Like the Swede and the Indian, Father Lawrence was full of stories, and it was here beside the lake that he told them. Growing out of his lifelong interest in the exploration and settling of the north woods, his were mostly tales of local history, with a remarkable number of deaths in them.

"See over there, where the Badbattle comes in, that's were twenty-two people died in a train wreck and a logger died trying to free a logjam. They were unrelated accidents, and they both happened on the same day." The priest capped his thermos of coffee and pointed across the mile-wide narrows to a notch in the tree line where the river entered the lake. They could see the glint of a bridge crossing the river. "There used to be a railroad bridge over there, running alongside the road bridge, and that's where the train slipped off the tracks and three cars plunged into the river and twenty-two people were either crushed or drowned. It happened just about three hours after a bunch of logs jammed up there in the mouth of the river and a logger named Sturdevant tried to get them moving by poking at them with his pike and he fell down between two logs and had his head bashed in. This is about nineteen-five I'm talking about. May or June of nineteen-five or -six."

Duck drained his coffee cup. "There's still pilings over there where the railroad went across." He and Frank lit cigarettes. "Fish bunch up around them pilings in the spring. Good place for spearing."

"My old man worked those lumber camps," said Hanson between licks of his fingers and lips—the pastry today was a caramel ring. "Gone from home the whole winter. Lived in the camps from freeze-up to spring thaw. One winter he had the job of icing the roads for skidding the logs. One misstep and you're buried under tons of trees. Life's easier for the workingman these days, I tell you."

"Easier for the priest as well," said Father Lawrence, unwrapping a cigar and embarking, not for the first time, on the story that perhaps did more than anything else to set the course of Frank's adult life. Like a sublime and tragic song, it was a story that never failed to affect him.

"On Christmas afternoon of 1893, Father Zell set out from this very spot to cross the lake on foot, and he never made it." Father Lawrence tossed the cigar wrapper into the weeds and struck a wooden match. "He was the first priest through here, serving the Indians and the white settlers, you probably heard of him."

"Heard my grandma talk about him," said Duck.

"A great man, Father Zell, one of the true saints of the church. His parish was practically the whole northern tier of counties, and he'd think nothing of walking fifty miles to marry

or baptize or bless a fresh grave." Father Lawrence touched the
flame to the cigar and sucked and puffed until it crackled like
burning leaves. "Well, that Christmas Eve he spent the night in
John Pipe's house, which stood about where the Health Center
is, and on Christmas morning he celebrated Mass in John Pipe's
living room—this was twenty-five years or so before Our Lady's
was built—and then he started out across the ice to celebrate a
second Mass over there on the far shore. In those days there was
another clan of Indians living over there—you can still see their
burial mounds if you know where to look." The priest pointed
his cigar once again at the spot where the river came in. "Now,
of course he'd had nothing to eat since midnight because he had
that second Mass to celebrate, and so he was already weak from
lack of nourishment when a sudden wind sprang up and picked
the snow off the ice and obscured his vision. He walked and
walked and never found land. At one point the Indians waiting
on the far shore caught a glimpse of him in the blowing snow
and a party of men set out to guide him, but they, too, were
baffled by the wind, and when they finally came upon his body,
his heart had already stopped and his arms and legs were frozen
so they couldn't bend them. The nearest weather station in those
days was Minneapolis, two hundred and fifty miles south of here,
and they had a temperature of twenty-two below zero that
Christmas Day."

So enthralled was Frank by the Father Zell story (perhaps,
in part, because his own mother had died on Christmas Day),
that he'd made it his business to read every book and pamphlet
Father Lawrence could find for him on the early priests of the
north woods. And he'd found quite a few, for now at midcentury
most of the parishes of northern Minnesota were celebrating their
golden jubilees by going to press with the minutiae culled from
pastors' journals and the sketchy memories of old people. Poring
over the inflated, pietistic prose of these booklets, Frank was
tempted to transfer his worship from certain baseball players
(Ted Williams, Johnny Mize, and Bob Feller were his holy trin-
ity) to the team of frostbitten, mosquito-bitten, God-bitten men
who suffered incredible hardships to bring Christ to the frontier.
They were a small team—nine priests in all of northern Minnesota in the late 1800's—and because of the vast distances be-

tween settlements they seldom saw one another, each going his
solitary way on foot and horseback, by sleigh and railroad, by
canoe and lumber wagon, carrying the sacraments across the
prairies and into the forests and leaving behind in every hamlet
and tent and sod hut the solace of Christ's redemption. Wherever
they went, all nine were respected by the faithful and faithless
alike, but only Father Zell (Frank learned from his reading) was
spoken of with admiration bordering on love. God's Pathfinder,
the Indians called him. Whites and Indians alike traveled in car-
avans to Berrington, the seat of the diocese, following his body
to its grave.

"How old were you when you heard the call?"

"The call?" Father Lawrence, at the wheel of his boxlike blue
Kaiser, looked puzzled. It was a cloudy noon in August and they
were returning home from the reservation. "What call is that,
my boy?"

"To the priesthood."

"Oh, that. Oh, I guess I was your age. Younger maybe."

"What was it like?" There was urgency in Frank's tone. Having been taught by the high-school faculty to think of himself
as college material, and by Eunice Pfeiffer and the nuns of St.
Ann's and any number of clerical visitors to the rectory to think
of himself as priest material, he felt himself drawn to Aquinas
College, a rural campus near Berrington, where it was possible
to be both an undergraduate and a seminarian at the same time.
To follow such a course, however, required a number of preliminary steps, and though he still had a year of high school left,
it was not too early to apply to the college registrar and to meet
with the diocesan vocational director and to be interviewed by
the seminary rector and to appeal—in person—to the venerable
and imperious Walbert Swayles, Bishop of Berrington, for his
sponsorship. But first, there was the mysterious matter of the
call. "Was it God actually talking in your ear?" he asked.

Father Lawrence broke out in a little smile. "I guess I thought
so at the time. It sounded a lot like God. But it was really my
uncle."

"Your uncle?"

"My uncle Charles was a priest, my mother's brother. On many a Sunday afternoon he came to our farm and helped my parents figure out what each of us children should do with our lives. He said my sister Margaret should marry a farmer and she married a farmer, he said my sister Philomena should become a nun and she became a nun, he said my brother Henry should take over the farm when my parents retired and he took over the farm, he said my brother Cornelius, who drank, should get lost and he left home and was never heard of again, and he said I should be the priest. Not *a* priest, mind you—*the* priest, as if every family had to have one. 'Elizabeth,' I can hear him saying to my mother, 'Adrian will be the priest.'"

"And that's it? That was your call?"

"I'm afraid the call, as a means of communication, is largely overrated. The voice doesn't come from above so much as from within." Though many were urging Frank toward ordination, his pastor was not one of them. It wasn't in his nature to tell people what to do. "What is your head telling you, my boy?"

"It's saying opposite things."

"Of course. Most people's do that."

"Does yours?"

"No, not often."

Frank knew this to be true. Adrian Lawrence, a contented, uncomplicated man, seemed never to suffer the torments of indecision or regret. "So how do I decide?"

"There'll be a sign."

"What kind of sign?"

The priest shrugged. "There's no describing a sign till you see it."

"Where do I look for it?"

"You don't look for signs. They look for you."

"When your uncle said that—did you have a sign?"

"Not that I recall. I didn't need one."

"How come?"

"I was never undecided."

Frank pondered this for a mile and a half, then concluded, "Maybe that was your sign."

9

What was God's purpose concerning the egg? After more than a year at the candling table, the monotony was becoming torturous, and Frank tried all sorts of tricks—even theological speculation—to divert himself. Did God intend the egg to be eaten or hatched? Nourishment or procreation? Did Frank's throwing away a fertilized egg make any difference in the divine plan for chickens? How many chickens, nationwide, were being aborted today by candlers? Why weren't all these eggs fertilized instead of only a very few? Were roosters holding back?

And growing weary of chicken-egg philosophy, he wove athletic fantasies, imagining each game of the coming football season, each forward pass, each goal-line stand, each victory. He indulged in military fantasies as well, for as an alternative to the seminary Frank was considering the infantry, having received two letters from Bob Templeton, the first telling him that the army was hell, and the second, written in triumphant terms after boot camp was over, urging Frank to enlist and get in on the wonderful privilege of being a soldier in the worldwide struggle against the rotten communists. Since Frank had no mental picture of Korea and no clear impression of what a North Korean communist looked like, he went back a war and substituted the landscapes and enemies of World War II, imagining himself doing heroic things against the Nazis at Anzio and Normandy and against the Japs in the Philippines. He imagined himself home on leave wearing the dress uniform Bob had on in the photo he'd sent with his second letter. Wouldn't Libby be impressed?

His most rewarding fantasies, by far, were those in which Libby played a role. Throughout the summer, deprived of her daily companionship on the walk to school, Frank had been seeing a great deal of her in *The Life of Frank Healy*. He'd invented several new episodes in which he stepped out of his role as backup boyfriend and became her one and only. In the pivotal episode, Libby had had a serious fight with Vernon Jessen, and she turned to Frank for solace. He imagined this happening at the Loomis Ballroom with hundreds of dancers looking on. By some miracle his handkerchief, when he pulled it out of his pocket to dry her tears, was fresh and clean. By another, he knew how to dance. After a very few steps on the dance floor, Libby laid her head on his shoulder, and Lucky Mudget, looking down and sensing the poignancy of the occasion, shifted from something fast to the soothing and languishing strains of "So Tired," his brasses muted the way Russ Morgan played it on the radio. "Let's get away from everybody," Libby implored, looking up at Frank through her tears, "let's be alone for a while," and immediately they were parked in the woods beside the Badbattle. Parked in what? The Healys had no car. In the egg truck, what else? The full moon shone on the glassy river, an owl hooted in the distance, and Libby told Frank she loved him. "I know," he said, trying out the self-confident manner of Robert Ryan, "you've loved me all along." Which he quickly tempered by adding softly, in the style of Van Johnson, "I love you, too, Libby, I'm yours forevermore." All this while candling eggs.

And then, incredibly, while *not* candling eggs.

On the Saturday night before school started, during a lull in the egg trade, Frank prevailed upon Selma and Herb Schultenover to release him for a few minutes so that he could go down the block to the Royal and watch the conclusion of *Kiss of Death*. On Saturday nights the ticket taker let Frank in without paying, his egghouse apron being the sign that he couldn't stay long.

Kiss of Death was Richard Widmark's first movie, in which he played a psychotic murderer. Frank and Danny had gone to it the night before and Frank was strangely charmed by the way Richard Widmark cackled as he killed. Frank went in and found a seat near the back, on the aisle, and was taking his ease in the dusky light reflected off Victor Mature's undershirt when suddenly—miraculously—Libby appeared at his shoulder and whispered, "Move over."

He was stunned. Could this be real life, or was he hallucinating? He moved over. Libby sat down and took his hand in both of her own.

"Hi," he whispered. "What's going on? Where's Vernon?" Saturday nights, after depositing his eggs at the egghouse, Vernon customarily took Libby dancing.

Her answer was her lovely dark-eyed smile and perhaps the most beautiful phrase he'd ever heard her utter: "That stupid crumb." Frank's ribs ached with pleasure. His fantasy was coming true.

They watched the last few minutes of the movie, and when the newsreel took its place on the screen (Harry Truman addressing the camera with his hat on), Libby said, "Let's go dancing."

"Dancing?" He imagined the customers crowding into the egghouse now that the first show was over, the egg crates piling up in the back room, Herb Schultenover candling alone, Selma growing impatient.

"Loomis," said Libby, drawing him out of his seat and up the aisle to the crowded lobby, where in the brighter light he saw that her skirt was lavender and her sleeveless blouse was cream and her hair was combed in a new style that covered part of her right eye. She was ravishing.

"Loomis it is," he blurted, and took her hand and led her back into the theater and down the aisle toward the fire exit. If it was boldness Libby wanted in a man, then Frank would be bold. They crossed under the screen (Bob Feller whiffing Yankees) and he led her out the door leading to the alley. They hurried to the panel truck parked behind the egghouse, where

Libby, as if reading Frank's mind, went straight to the passenger side and got in.

"Be right with you," he said, removing the radiator cap and wondering what he would use for engine coolant. After standing idle for several hours, the leaky radiator would surely need filling. There was a sink and a pail in the back room, but Herb was no doubt in there candling. Frank then remembered the jug of vinegar in the back of the truck. On one of his delivery rounds, Herb had bought vinegar and dill and cucumbers for Selma, who spent all her late-summer Sundays canning. Frank emptied the jug into the radiator and got in behind the wheel. The key, as usual, was in the ignition.

They had covered only a mile in the moonlight when Frank came to understand why Detroit recommended water. The pungency of hot vinegar made their eyes burn, made them put their heads out the window for fresh air, made them laugh so hard they nearly went in the ditch, and when they parked in the sloping, dark pasture below the Loomis Ballroom and switched off the engine, they heard a girl in the next car say to her necking partner, "I smell pickles."

At the sliding door their hands were stamped for a dollar, and inside the ballroom they were met by the amazed stares of friends and strangers alike, stares caused (Frank imagined) by the captivating figure they cut as a couple, but caused in fact (Libby told him with a giggle) by his egghouse apron. He untied the apron, threw it aside, and they made their way to the dance floor, where he suddenly lost his nerve because he didn't know how to dance. He confessed this to Libby.

"So what, I'll teach you," she said. "I taught Vernon. I've taught lots of guys."

Holding each other in a loose embrace—which seemed to Frank a kind of sacred act, his right hand laid reverently on the small of her holy back—they circled the floor to the strains of "Sentimental Journey," stumbling and gliding by turns. This was followed by "Smoke Gets in Your Eyes" and "Harbor Lights," and Frank began to get the hang of it.

"You learn fast," said Libby, holding him tighter.

He was also tiring fast. He hadn't realized that being graceful required so many leg muscles. With "Baby Face," Lucky Mudget picked up the tempo, and they left the dance floor and merged into the crowd of drinkers at the bar, where Libby, though years underage, bought two bottles of beer and handed one to Frank. They saw Sylvia Pofford standing at the end of the bar chatting with a girl from Loomis, and they went over and joined her. The Loomis girl had a snub nose and a sweaty brow. Sylvia, as always, looked cool. The three girls did all the talking—new boys at the dance, new clothes for school—and Frank, standing nearby in a state of transcendent happiness, felt privileged to be listening to them, felt privileged to be swigging beer, felt privileged to have danced. The world was a storehouse of privileges, he told himself, recalling Bob Templeton's statement about the privileges of soldiering and recalling Eunice Pfeiffer's insistent reminders of the privileges of the priesthood and basking in the exquisite privilege of being out with Libby for the evening. Dear God, he said inwardly and dizzily, I never realized that the life you gave me contained so many privileges.

After a few minutes of chatter, Libby asked casually, "Have you seen Vernon?"

The Loomis girl said she hadn't.

Sylvia said, "He's bound to show up."

Frank, to be amusing, said, "Vernon who?"

Whereupon Libby and Sylvia and the girl from Loomis turned to him with expressions of such profound seriousness that he wondered if he had offended them with his innocent little joke. Where had he seen this same look not so long ago, this expression of abject pity? In *The Asphalt Jungle*? Yes—Louis Calhern regarding some poor sucker of an underling, some dolt who was serving, unaware, as the decoy in a larceny plot.

Then Roy Girard, Libby's brother, came down the steps from the game room gripping the necks of six empty beer bottles between his fingers and carrying his hand of cards in his shirt pocket. "I just seen Vernon," he said as he brushed past his sister. "He's looking for you."

"Vernon who?" Frank said again, beaming, but Roy, shoving his way forward to the bar, apparently didn't hear him.

"Come on," said Libby, taking Frank's beer from him and

setting it with her own on a table strangers were sitting at. She led him back to the music. The beat was syncopated and Frank moved clumsily and Libby did nothing to help him to be graceful. He saw her eyes darting along the walls until they fell on Vernon, who was standing near the bandstand, alone, his hands in his pockets, his head thrust hungrily forward, his eyes riveted on Libby. Instantly upon seeing him, she pressed herself against Frank and put both arms around him, forcing him almost to a complete stop, and they swayed in a tight embrace, Frank speechless with joy. This was what the leading man and woman did in movies when in mid-dance they became oblivious to all but their overwhelming love for one another. He closed his eyes, buried his face in her hair, and asked himself, Is this the sign I've been waiting for? Is God calling off my mother's deathbed wish, letting me off the hook, telling me there's to be a woman in my life?

After moving about in this trancelike hug for a minute, Frank opened his eyes to discover that they had drawn near Vernon. "Libby," Vernon was calling in a husky, desperate voice. Libby seemed not to hear him, or care, for at the sound of her name Frank felt no reflex in the nerves along her spine. She pressed herself closer, and Frank felt the heat of her body from his thigh to his ear. He glanced again at Vernon and thought he looked pitiful. Did Vernon realize that justice was being served, that he was deprived of Libby by his own foul nature, that now she belonged to the better man?

When the piece ended, Libby suggested they go outside, and Frank gave her money for two more beers. They carried the bottles out into the fresh night air and sauntered down between the cars to where the egg truck stood over its puddle of vinegar. Vernon was following them, though Frank didn't know it until he spoke in the darkness, breathing heavily into Frank's right ear, "Let go of her, asshole."

Frank spun around, startled. Libby turned slowly, apparently having sensed Vernon's presence all along.

"Who are you calling an asshole?" Frank asked.

Vernon, ignoring him, said to Libby, "The pickup's over that way."

Libby closed her eyes and said, "Oh Vernon," making at least four syllables out of his name, making it ring on the quiet night air like a song. She took her hand from Frank and gave it to Vernon, and the two of them walked off toward his truck. She got in on the driver's side and so did Vernon. They slammed the door and Vernon turned on his headlights and his fog lights and the amber lights over his cab and spun his wheels all the way out to the road, fouling the air with dirt and exhaust.

"You're the asshole!" Frank screamed, trembling and sweating and weeping. "You're a goddamn draft-dodging chickenshit asshole!"

The pickup rounded a bend and was gone. Frank shook with rage. Then he wept a little more. Then, when his shaking stopped, he poured his beer into the radiator and drove back to Linden Falls. Passing under the lights of Main Street, he looked at his watch and saw that he had won and lost Libby and learned to dance in a mere forty minutes.

In the back room Herb Schultenover said, "Where the hell have you been?" He didn't answer. He put on a fresh apron and Herb left him alone at the candling table. There were a dozen or more crates of eggs to examine. Between crates he brought the hem of his apron up to his face and wiped his eyes.

He came to the Jessens' crate. He threw out two eggs that were fertilized and eight others that weren't, and when he carried the empty crate out of the back room, he found Vernon standing at the counter waiting for it. He was grinning. Avoiding his eyes, Frank set the crate on the counter and told Selma, "Four dozen and two."

"What?" said Vernon, his complexion suddenly inflamed with anger. "I brought in five."

"Minus ten bad ones," said Frank.

"Now wait a minute," Vernon growled, narrowing his eyes the way he used to as the playground bully. "Let me see them."

"I threw them out."

"It's the hot weather," said Selma. "Eggs rot."

"Not ten," Vernon insisted haughtily and bitterly, as if they were ten blemishes on his family honor. "I never had ten eggs rot on me, ever."

"Some were cracked," explained Frank.

Selma was counting out Vernon's payment into his hand and Frank had turned to go back to work, when Vernon said, "Have the boy take the crate out for me, would you? I have to go to the hardware store." He left.

"Frank," said Selma pushing the crate down the counter in his direction.

Enraged, Frank seized the crate and carried it outside, intending to stomp it to kindling on the sidewalk. But there, sitting in the pickup, was Libby. Larger than his grief and anger and envy was his love for Libby, and he restrained himself. She was sitting closer to the driver's door than the passenger's, with her left arm resting on the back of the seat, so that even without Vernon at the wheel, she seemed molded to his body. Approaching the truck, Frank tried to smile without malice. He wanted his smile to say that his hate was entirely for Vernon, none of it for her, and that if she had to make him the ploy in her plot, well, that's what backup boyfriends were for, and anyway, he probably had it coming for the way he'd abandoned her that night on the riverbank. A noble smile, in other words. But he couldn't dissemble. It was all he could do to control the shuddering sob that was working its way up from his breast, and he avoided her eyes as he placed the crate in the back of the truck.

"Frank," she said, leaning out the window.

He retreated a short way before he turned and looked at her.

"Thanks," she said.

For what exactly? For carrying out the egg crate? For delivering her to Loomis and into Vernon's arms? For walking her to school a hundred mornings?

"Thanks for everything," she said, and she threw him a kiss.

Brokenhearted in the back room, he candled carelessly, cracking eggs left and right. When the egghouse closed, he looked at his watch and calculated that the second show had a reel or so to run. He returned to the theater and watched it, but this time the homicidal cackling of Richard Widmark failed to move him.

10

On the following Tuesday morning, the first day of his senior year, Frank arrived at the corner of Pincherry and Fourth determined to overlook Libby's betrayal and eager to tell her of his latest dream. He had dreamed that he was preparing to travel the Badbattle from Linden Falls north to Hudson Bay in a one-man canoe, and although he had the encouragement of his mother and the assurances of his father, who were both helping him pack his clothing and provisions into the sort of duffel bags that soldiers used, he was secretly afraid to embark.

The morning was foggy and cold, unlike the warm and sunny atmosphere of his dream, and he shivered as he waited on the corner. He waited until the last minute before concluding that Libby was ill or skipping school for the day—last year her attendance record had been less than exemplary—and he set off alone, suppressing the heartache he'd been suffering since Saturday night and trying to convince himself that Vernon, tied to his farm, was certain to fade quickly out of Libby's life.

Hearing his name called, he turned and saw Sylvia Pofford hurrying to catch up with him. So unusual was the sight of Sylvia Pofford on foot instead of riding to school in her parents' luxurious car that Frank wondered if the laws of nature had undergone a transformation. They had, and Sylvia confirmed it. Sidling up to him in a new pink dress and carrying a new pink notebook and a new black purse and looking at Frank in a new, fond way, she said, "From now on it's you and me, Frank. Libby quit school to marry Vernon."

He recoiled with horror, both from the message and from the messenger. Putting off the more shocking and tragic half of her announcement, he considered the first half first. What did she mean, you and me? Was she speaking of this walk to school or proposing a relationship? The latter, he decided as she took his arm—a display of affection that left him cold. Over the years as classmates and neighbors Frank and Sylvia had developed between them a mild cordiality, a bond warmer than tolerance yet cooler than friendship. What she wanted, Frank guessed, was a temporary fill-in for Bob Templeton, whose last letter came from a troop ship on the high seas and whose ring she still wore. Beginning the next morning, Frank successfully evaded her by taking various other routes to school. Sylvia was smart and comely and mature and they had their academic ambitions in common, but she had one great failing. She wasn't Libby.

Libby and Vernon were married within the week. Their hurry, Sylvia explained in the hallways of the school, was caused not by pregnancy, as many supposed, but by the Berrington County Draft Board. Farms were no longer the sanctuaries they had been. Selective service priorities had changed and young men were now seeking refuge in matrimony rather than agriculture. This was Berrington County's first indication that a new age of armed conflict had dawned. A few months earlier, at the first news of American troops in Korea, the citizens of Linden Falls had begun—reflexively and as one—to peel the tinfoil from their gum wrappers and to save tin cans for scrap-metal drives and to put aside coins for the purchase of defense stamps, but now they were coming to realize that this was a war of indefinite purpose and halfhearted measures, and although the men struck down in battle were just as dead as the casualties of Hitler's war, nobody on the home front would be expected to do anything so patriotic as to drive thirty-five miles an hour on bald tires or go without sugar, bananas, or nylons. No scrap-metal drives this time. No food-ration booklets. No songs on the Hit Parade by Irving Berlin.

Frank was not invited to Libby's wedding, a brief ceremony in the country church where Vernon's father was buried. Sylvia went with her mother and reported to Frank that Libby wore a white homemade dress with accordian pleats and that Vernon's pants and suitcoat didn't match. "My mother says it won't last," said Sylvia. "She says Libby's too fast to be stuck on a chicken farm. She says the war will be over any day and so will the marriage."

But the war went on and so did the marriage. By the time MacArthur put his troops ashore at Inchon and began driving north toward the Yalu, Libby had assumed most of the duties of the farmer's wife. On Saturday nights she shopped for the Jessen groceries and brought the Jessen eggs into the egghouse while Vernon went around the corner to Kruger's Pool Hall and drank beer. Sylvia reported to Frank that they were never seen at the Loomis Ballroom anymore. But Sylvia was. With Danny Ash.

Frank and Libby, each time she came into the egghouse, tried to recover their old familiarity, but they had trouble talking to each other. Though roughened a little by farm work and no longer very attentive to her makeup and hair, she was no less attractive to Frank and her smile came as easily as ever to her pretty lips. Indeed she seemed to grow even more beautiful as she grew large with child. But so utterly changed was her station in life that they groped for topics of common interest without finding them, and their conversations were stilted and never took flight. Libby, it was clear, had very little interest in what was happening at school, and Frank knew next to nothing about farming. Though absent from the bleachers, Libby was the imagined audience Frank performed for on the football field, and yet on the Saturday evening in November when he reviewed for her the Rockets' triumphant season—three wins and four losses and Frank and Danny named to the all-conference team—she listened to him with only half her attention, the other half directed at the chalkboard behind the counter where Selma Schultenover wrote the daily egg prices. Sensing the effort she was making to hear him out, he gave up on football and asked about the Jessens' harvest of corn. She said the Jessens didn't raise corn. So they fell back on the two subjects about which they could always manage at least a few remarks no matter how tedious—the weather and Sylvia.

The one topic that would certainly have captured her interest—his undiminished love for her—he kept hidden in his heart, for how did you tell another man's wife that you couldn't get over loving her, and that the pain caused by her marriage was equal to the pain caused by your mother's death? Speaking of his wound to no one and nursing it alone in the dark privacy of the candling room, he thought how much like his father he had become.

In the spring, on the day General MacArthur was relieved of his command by President Truman, Libby became a mother. Sylvia reported to Frank that the baby was a full-term, seven-pound girl, and he calculated that Libby had been pregnant the night he drove her to Loomis in the egg truck. They named the baby Verna.

And then one Saturday night about three weeks after the baby was born, their egghouse conversation became spirited again, and Frank learned that no wound lasts forever—either it heals or you die of it. On this Saturday they were able to pass beyond the spring rains and the unstable price of eggs and Frank told her about the alternating moods of joy and regret in his series of letters from Bob Templeton. Bob's letter of last summer, written from the Pacific in the agony of seasickness and full of regret over enlisting, was followed in the fall by a letter written in a pup tent on a hilltop in Korea claiming that the military made men out of boys and Frank must hurry and join up. But now Bob had written from a hospital in Seoul telling Frank to apply for a student deferment and enroll in college—anything to avoid the draft. Bob's feet had been frozen and he was in danger of losing his toes. Libby, hearing this, looked deeply grieved. Frank told her that Sylvia, receiving this same news, had written to Bob immediately to ask if he could still dance. Libby laughed. Frank was gratified to find that she could be sad for Bob and laugh at Sylvia's obtuseness, but still there was something missing from their conversation, a certain level of excitement they hadn't quite managed to recover from their talks as juniors in high school.

Well, speaking of toes, said Libby, did Frank know that Vernon's mother had six toes on her left foot? Libby, making this announcement, hooted with laughter, startling Selma Schultenover and making Frank suspect she was kidding, but no, Mrs. Jessen, as Libby went on to describe her, was a spooky, meddling woman with eleven toes. She had rigid opinions about babies and Libby got into lots of arguments with her about diapers and the baby's sleeping habits and formula. "Come out to the truck and see the baby," said Libby, her eyes dancing with maternal pride.

Frank, carrying her empty egg crate, accompanied her to the pickup, where Vernon sat behind the wheel holding the baby in a yellow blanket. Vernon looked oddly benign, cowed even, like a man who'd been listening to a great many unpleasant arguments about diapers and the baby's formula. Libby climbed into the cab and took the baby from him and lifted a corner of the blanket. The baby had a wisp of white hair and a red face and reminded Frank of the small pet monkey in *Tarzan of the Apes.* "So that's Verna," he said, attempting a tone of admiration.

"Isn't she darling?" Libby brushed the baby's forehead with a kiss. "Isn't she beautiful?"

"You bet," said Frank.

He placed the crate in the back of the truck as Vernon started the engine. Libby threw him a kiss as they backed away from the curb, and Frank called, "Thank you, come again."

He returned to the candling table, and as he presented egg after egg to the aperture of light, it dawned on him that what had been missing from their conversation was love. True, they had recovered something of the lilt and spontaneity of the old days, but he had not sensed in their exchange the exhilarating undertone of love. Indeed, it seemed to have been this very lack of emotion that permitted them to put their stilted ways behind them and enter into the amiable sort of chatter he'd been taught to foster with all the farmers' wives who presented him with their eggs. "Thank you, come again" was what he said to every last one of them.

And with this realization came a sudden and wonderful sense of liberation. He was no longer the slave of his love for Libby Girard Jessen. Surely this was a sign.

11

Arrangements were quickly made, with the help of Father Lawrence and Bishop Swayles. According to his letter from the rector of Aquinas Seminary, he was to be given an exploratory tour of the campus at 4:00 P.M., Sunday, May 20; he was to be interviewed by the rector at five; and he would join the student body for supper at six and for vespers at seven.

Father Lawrence drove him there in the Kaiser. It was a warm, blustery afternoon, the sky bright as aluminum, the ponds and lakes dotted with floes of dissolving ice. It was an hour's drive to Berrington and another fifteen minutes beyond, for St. Thomas Aquinas College and Seminary was sequestered in a wooded valley and connected to the highway by several miles of unpaved road. Along this road, they saw an eagle, a porcupine, and a skunk. A deer put its head out of a thicket and watched them go by. When they came to the clearing of shrub-lined walks and buildings of stone, they sat for a minute in the car, taking it in. A group of boys younger than Frank were playing catch with a football and a pair of college-age men strolled across the grass carrying books. Under a red maple a priest sat on a bench smoking a pipe and reading a newspaper.

Father Lawrence said, "Well, my boy, does this look like a place where you could spend eight years of your life?"

"Eight years is a long time," said Frank, apprehensive at the prospect of entering this secluded, self-contained world of strangers. He felt he wouldn't transplant easily, wouldn't be quick to make friends. "Did you spend eight years here?"

"Only four. I took my undergraduate work elsewhere."

"Did you like it here?"

"Very much."

"Wasn't it strange, never seeing women?"

"Visitors come on Sundays. Mothers. Sisters." Then, as though realizing too late that he was speaking to someone with neither mother nor sister, the priest hastily pointed his cigar at two small buildings in the distance. "Some spend twelve years here. There's the prep school." He shifted his cigar, aiming it at the broad three-story building directly in front of them, the largest on campus. "That's Christopher Hall, where you'll take your classes and have your meals. And of course that's the church next door."

The Church of St. Thomas, standing beside Christopher Hall and connected to it by a covered walkway, seemed to Frank no bigger than Our Lady's on the reservation. "It's sort of small," he said.

"Holds about three hundred souls, and that's everybody. Forty or fifty preps, a hundred and fifty undergraduates, maybe sixty or so divinity students in the major seminary."

"And the faculty?"

"I'd guess there are twenty-five or thirty on the faculty. Some of them have rooms in the student dormitories and the rest live in that house over there on the left." There were three stone houses standing back against the woods, two very large ones and the other much smaller. Each had a screened porch across the front.

"Who lives next door?"

"The help. Groundskeepers, cooks, painters, suchlike. The rest of the help live in Berrington—those with families."

"And the little house?"

"That's the bishop's house."

"I thought the bishop lived in Berrington."

"He does, but this is for when he visits. Ordination time."

"A whole house for one man once a year?"

"Or if some other dignitary happens by."

"Why can't the bishop stay in the faculty house?"

"Then you couldn't tell him from the faculty."

Frank recalled his interview with Bishop Swayles in the chancery office in Berrington, his autocratic manner, his affected way of speaking, the vigilant servitude of his underlings. "The bishop has the big head, doesn't he?"

Father Lawrence peered at Frank through the smoke of his cigar. "You'll learn not to say things like that about your boss, my boy. You'll only think them."

Frank's tour guide was an undergraduate named Rick, a lanky, beetle-browed basketball player on his way to being a priest of the St. Cloud diocese. After touring the classrooms, library, and refectory of Christopher Hall, they walked down a long slope to view the gymnasium and playing fields, which Frank had not seen from the car. On the softball diamond a prep-school game was just breaking up, and the man who had been acting as umpire and was directing certain boys to pick up bats wore a black cassock and a baseball cap. On the baseball diamond another priest was hitting grounders to an infield of six or seven boys and flies to an outfield of seven or eight. A few boys were scrimmaging under an outdoor basket. Two were playing tennis. Frank inquired about football and was sorry to learn that Aquinas College had had to give it up a few seasons ago, the equipment being too expensive, but the basketball team (Rick told him with pride) had defeated Rookery State College and certain other large schools this past winter, and the baseball team was doing the same this spring.

"Are you a pitcher by any chance?" Rick asked him.

"I pitch for Linden Falls," said Frank, "but I'm no Bob Feller. Football's my sport."

"We'll need pitching next year. Both of our best pitchers graduate."

From the gym, they followed a winding road to the floor of the valley and came to an ivied two-story building facing away from the campus. This was the seminary. Its front lawn sloped down to a swift-running stream, and Frank was gladdened beyond reason to learn that this was his beloved Badbattle. Standing at the front door, over which the words *In Omnia Gloria Dei* were carved in the lintel, Rick pointed out the footbridge leading across the river to a garden hewn out of the woods. At the center of the garden, he said, was a grotto he found conducive to prayer. He then pulled open the heavy door and said, "Father Sparks is waiting for you. He's in the first room on your left. Don't be shocked by his looks. He lost it fighting the Japs. Supper's at six, I'll meet you back at Christopher Hall."

"Lost what?"

"You'll see."

Frank stepped into a broad hallway smelling of pipe tobacco. The rector's door stood open. Father Sparks, a high-strung, youngish man, invited Frank into his book-lined sitting room for what turned out to be less an interview than a lecture. Father Sparks was a study in black and white. The ghostly pallor of his face and hands matched his white shirt and contrasted sharply with his black shoes and black pants and the black patch over his right eye. "Very pleased to have you aboard," he said, shaking Frank's hand and indicating the straight-backed chair he wanted Frank to sit in.

Facing him in a high-backed rocker and stoking and lighting his black, curve-stemmed pipe, the rector took Frank through a typical day in the life of a seminarian—class hours, study hours, prayer hours, supervised recreation hours, free hours. Rocking vigorously, he enumerated the many rules and restrictions Frank would face if he matriculated. Except for vacations there would be no unsupervised absence from campus. No grade below C would besmirch the seminarian's transcript. No lights in the rooms after 11:00 P.M. No cars on campus, no liquor, no girls. There would be no socializing with people "from the outside" except upon authorized occasions such as the bishop's annual tea and the Daughters of Isabella's annual ice-cream social and certain Sundays devoted to family visitation and of course any number of interscholastic events such as basketball and baseball games, tennis matches, and debate meets. Seminarians, he said, were men apart. They must despise and spurn the world for a time as they prepared themselves to reenter it as priests of God. "So tell me, Mr. Healy, do you think you have the fortitude to live the sort of life we lead in this valley?"

"Yes," was Frank's immediate and unequivocal reply. The circumscribed days outlined by the rector did not discourage him. Having grown up directionless in his father's house, he hungered for exactly this sort of purposeful and ordered existence. He was resentful, it was true, of being directed along the straight and narrow by Eunice Pfeiffer, but it was one thing to have a priest's housekeeper leading you by the nose and quite another to be taken into a male community dedicated to the honor and glory of God. Where better to make up your mind about the priestly vocation than here in this beautiful valley with its faculty of clergymen and its winning athletic teams and the Badbattle bubbling beneath your window? "Yes," he repeated, gazing steadily into the rector's only eye.

Father Sparks stopped rocking and asked in a lowered, confidential voice, "Are you sure you're priest material, Mr. Healy?"

Frank hesitated. Must he decide this minute? If he revealed his misgivings, would he be denied entrance? "I have my doubts," he said, unable to lie.

"Ah." The priest looked relieved. "Plenty of time to resolve your doubts, Mr. Healy. It's men coming in wearing blinders that I worry about."

His next inquiry might have been the most urgent of all, for he leaned forward in his rocker and lowered his voice even further, almost to a confessional whisper.

"As you may know, Mr. Healy, we're developing quite a reputation on the baseball diamond."

"So I've heard."

"We'll be strong in the infield next year, and we have a few good hitters coming back."

Frank said he was glad.

"What I'm wondering—can you pitch by any chance?"

"Yes," said Frank solemnly.

The rector sat back, smiling and rocking and puffing on his pipe. "Swell," he said.

After supper in the refectory (sausage and fried potatoes) the community filed into the church, where the evening sun falling through the great window behind the altar suffused everything in a rose-gold light, and where the prayers were chanted in Latin. A book was put into his hands, and Frank, though he knew very little Latin and next to nothing about Gregorian chant, joined in with a zeal that amazed him, as if he couldn't keep his mouth shut if he wanted to, as if this choric, measured monotone echoing eerily off the vaulted ceiling was the form of prayer he'd been trying to master all his life without knowing it existed. To think this was one of the alternatives a man might choose: to plan your day around prayers like this, to live your hidden life of the spirit in this beautiful valley apart from the world. He thought of the many times he'd washed away his sadness or loneliness or boredom by jumping into the Badbattle and wading upstream. Time after time, summer after summer, he'd been drawn through the water against the current without knowing why, retracing his steps so often that his feet memorized every rock and stone and hump of sand in the riverbed. Well, now he knew why. He'd been trying to reach this valley, this campus, this life of pure peace. He closed his eyes and listened as the voices around him swelled, repeating the phrase of a psalm over and over, a phrase of incomprehensible and beautiful Latin that seemed to be saying "Will you join us, Frank Healy, will you join us?"

12

And so he joined them. He settled effortlessly into the
routine of the valley, studying and praying and pitching Aquinas
College into the baseball playoffs in the spring of both his freshman and sophomore years. By the spring of his junior year, when
besides playing for the college team he was helping to coach the
prep-school team, his contentment had grown so complete that
he couldn't imagine ever leaving the valley. This contentment
he took as a sign that he must remain for the entire eight years
required for ordination.

One day in the spring of his junior year, Frank's roommate
came back from lunch and announced, "There's a dame in a truck
asking for you, Healy."

Frank, sitting at his desk, looked up from his book—*Exploring Metaphysics*—and rubbed his eyes. "A dame?" He shook
his head to clear it of drowsiness and philosophy.

"In a truck," repeated his roommate, David Schwartz, a grocer's son from Milner, North Dakota, who then closed the door
and uttered a resounding belch. Dropping onto his rumpled bed,
David Schwartz extracted from the sheets a tattered paperback
copy of *Absalom, Absalom*. Like Frank he was a third-year seminarian, but unlike Frank he was highly susceptible to spring fever

and had been devoting all of April and early May to William Faulkner and naps.

"Did she tell you her name?"

"Nope."

"What does she look like?" Frank closed his text on a lacy bookmark crocheted by Eunice Pfeiffer. In his mind's eye he was picturing Selma Schultenover in the egg truck.

"Chapped lips. Nice eyes." David lowered his book and studied Frank. "You aren't sick, are you?"

"I'm fine."

"Sparks asked me if you were sick."

"And you told him I'm too busy to eat?"

His roommate hesitated before answering. "Something like that." He returned to his novel.

"Schwartz, what did you tell him?"

"Too holy to eat."

"Damn it, Schwartz, now he'll want to have a talk with me." Frank, passing through an acute phase of asceticism, had quit smoking, had given up movies and newspapers, and was experimenting with food, trying to function on as few meals as Father Zell did in the last year of his abstemious life among the Indians. Father Sparks, fearing for Frank's health, disapproved of this experimentation, and so did Father Borelli, the baseball coach, who claimed Frank's fastball was losing its smoke.

"She's down there with her motor running," said David Schwartz.

Frank put on his jacket and went downstairs to the front entryway, hurrying past the rector's open door so as not to be called in and lectured about his caloric intake. He stepped outside and examined the sky. A pink and blue thunderhead building up over the south end of the valley appeared to be moving away to the east—no threat to the doubleheader against Rookery State scheduled to begin at 2:30. A pair of fat ducks waddled slowly and comically down the lawn to the river. The Badbattle, swollen with spring runoff, had flooded the garden beyond the footbridge and was lapping at the stone feet of Mary in her grotto. The team bus from Rookery pulled into the clearing and made its way along the winding road to the gymnasium. The wind was chilly. Frank massaged his right shoulder, still a little stiff from Wednesday's game against St. Wendelin's. He would need extra warm-up time today before he faced the first batter.

Stepping around the corner of the seminary, he saw the pickup standing in the drive, but did not immediately recognize it as Vernon Jessen's. The years had dulled the truck's green finish, crumpled a fender, and shattered a headlight. Nor did he instantly recognize the driver. Because of the sun glinting off the windshield, he was standing at her open window before he saw that it was Libby.

"God, Frank, you're thin."

Her smile was not the wide-open display of delight that used to light up her entire face and lift his heart. This was a limited smile. It did not extend as far as her eyes, which were slightly puffy and surrounded by lines of worry or exhaustion. Nice eyes, David Schwartz had said, but what did David Schwartz know of the sixteen-year-old Libby Girard who had hit town like a cover girl and whose beauty had caused fistfights at the Loomis Ballroom? David Schwartz was right about the lips, however. They were chapped. And so were the hands that tightly gripped the top of the steering wheel. Obviously being Mrs. Vernon Jessen wasn't an easy life. He was moved to pity when he noticed how threadbare her blue poplin jacket was.

"Aren't you eating right, Frank? Should I be sending you food in the mail?" This was delivered with her customary undertone of laughter and he was heartened to hear it.

"I'm fine," he told her, trying to disguise his unease. That she was stirring up in his breast an uncomfortable mix of nostalgia and pity was only part of it. Another part was her invading the campus on a nonvisiting day. He imagined the rector, whose single eye missed very little of what went on in his seminarians' lives, peering out a window and formulating an inquiry. "That young woman, Frank, on Saturday afternoon. Not a sister? Not a cousin? Not an emergency? Not a baseball fan? What then?"

"It's beautiful here," said Libby, taking her eyes off Frank and casting them along the tree line across the swirling river. "But it took me forever to find the place. Why aren't there signs?"

"I guess they like it secluded."

She took in the lawns, the walkways, the buildings of stone. "But isn't it boring?"

"I guess . . . it's not so bad." He was tongue-tied with apprehension, fearing that she might renew in him the love that had been so hard to get over. Standing stiff-armed, his hands deep in his pockets, he looked down at his shoes and said, "How's the baby."

"Verna? She's not a baby anymore. She's three, believe it or not."

"Three. Imagine that. Time does fly." He might have been speaking to any egghouse customer.

"She's my best friend, Frank."

He looked at her. She didn't appear to be joking, and this baffled him and increased his unease. He turned away and looked at the sky, unable to imagine circumstances so dire that a three-year-old would be your best friend. "How's Vernon?" he asked.

Her voice deadened. "The same."

Still uncivil? Frank wondered. Still a bully? He saw that the thunderhead was advancing up the valley after all, and boiling as it came. A rain-out would not disappoint him. Facing arch-rival Rookery State gave him the jitters, particularly on only two days' rest. He could put the time to better use preparing for Monday's philosophy test.

"Frank, could we go somewhere and talk? Into Berrington maybe?"

He grimaced, feigning regret. "We've got a baseball game coming up in a few minutes." In an hour, actually, but he was shy of admitting to her that trips off campus had to be applied for and approved. Not until this instant had he ever in his three years as a seminarian felt unduly restricted.

"Someplace here then? Have you got a coffee shop or something?"

The refectory was locked between meals and the snack bar was open for only an hour each evening. He said, "I guess right here's as good a place as any," and he went around and got in on the passenger side. The seat was no longer covered with imitation leopardskin. It was a black synthetic material and Frank's half of it was very dusty—did she and her husband never go anywhere together? The border of rabbit fur had been removed from the mirror. On the dashboard were a broken rattle and the melted remains of a chocolate bar. On the seat between them were jeans and a sweatshirt, neatly folded, and on the floor a pair of woman-sized boots, prompting Frank to wonder if she had changed on the way, perhaps to deceive Vernon. "Maybe you could drive down there," he told her, pointing to where the road wound through a small orchard near the river. It made him nervous to be sitting directly under the rector's window.

The apple trees, standing in rows, were small and gnarled and putting forth tiny leaves the color of celery. Libby parked facing the water and stared at it for a moment before she turned off the ignition. She said, "I'm leaving Vernon."

Frank nearly said he was sorry before common sense prevented him. He said, "I'm not surprised."

"But I suppose you *were* surprised when I married him."

"Very."

She continued to gaze at the water. "I was pregnant."

"I guess that's a good enough reason."

"I thought so," she said, nodding. Then she shook her head. "But it's not. It never is."

The thunderhead, advancing swiftly across the sky, put out the sun and let down veils of rain over the far end of the valley. The apple boughs tossed stiffly in the wind.

"I'm twenty-one years old, Frank, and I feel like an old woman."

Frank said "Hmmmm," drawing it out, trying to make it convey his sympathy.

"Can you imagine what life is like on that awful farm, Frank?" She turned to him. "I feed the chickens and feed the goats and milk the cows, and Vernon feeds the cows and milks the goats and butchers the chickens, and his mother gathers the eggs and cooks the chickens and herds the cows. How did this happen, Frank? How did I get trapped in this kind of life? We're like the peasants in that world history book in school, remember? Did your God play a great big joke on me?"

He repeated, "Hmmmm," and added, "Well." If this encounter

was a preview of pastoral work—and he suspected it might very well be—he felt miserably unequipped for it.

"Do you know anything about goats, Frank? Have you spent time around goats?"

"No."

"They stink."

They were silent for a time, watching the rain advance over the forest. When she spoke, her tone was softer. She sounded sleepy.

"I don't know what it is, Frank, it's been years since we saw each other, but I've been feeling drawn to you more and more until I just had to talk to you. I told myself, He's studying to be a priest and you're only asking for trouble if you go and see him, but it's like I couldn't help it. It's like if I didn't talk to you, I'd die." A faint smile appeared on her lips. "Remember how we used to talk, Frank?"

"Yes."

"I never had talks like that with anybody else in my whole life."

"Not even Sylvia?"

"Are you kidding?"

"How's Sylvia doing?"

"Who cares."

"I wonder if she found a replacement for Bob." Bob Templeton had disqualified himself by returning home with only eight toes and a slight but permanent limp.

"No doubt," said Libby.

Rain was now pouring onto the playing fields and across the lawns. A windblown sheet of rain swept over the pickup, turning the windshield opaque.

"I need to know if there's a chance we could ever get together, Frank. I mean, you know . . . I'm so lonesome for you. It's like nothing I ever felt before, and I'm wondering if it's love." There was a quaver in her voice, confusion in her eyes. "I'm beginning to think I've never really been in love, Frank, and I'm wondering if you can tell me what love feels like."

"No, not me," he said, aware that he was lying. He did indeed recognize what she was talking about. It was the same yearning he had felt so intensely for her from the time he first saw her at the Sunday matinee until that spring evening nearly two years later when she became merely one more farmer's wife supplying eggs to the egghouse. It was—as she suspected and he knew—love. Dear God, protect me from falling back into all that.

"I couldn't stand it anymore, not talking to you, so I went to the bank and asked your dad when you were coming home on vacation, and he said you might be staying here."

"It's true. They're putting me on their maintenance crew for the summer."

"Why, what did you do wrong?"

He laughed. "It's a job you apply for. I've been applying for three years and finally got it."

"Why would you apply for it?" She looked puzzled and sounded as if she might cry. "Aren't you ever coming home anymore?"

"I love it here, Libby." He spoke gently, like a priest to someone bereaved. "You have to understand that this is my home now. This place feels more like home to me than my real home ever did."

Now she looked hurt as well as puzzled, as though his summer on campus were a kind of betrayal. "Are you going to be a priest for sure?"

"Probably."

A glimmer of hope flashed in her eyes. "Not for sure?"

The wind blew stronger, keening through the apple boughs and causing the pickup to bounce on its springs. He said, "Probably for sure."

"So in other words . . . there's no chance of us being . . . you know . . ."

When he saw her eyes fill with tears, he was visited with a momentary vision of their riding off in the pickup together, his priestly resolve thrown aside and Libby smiling the gleeful smile that used to greet him every morning at the corner of Pincherry and Fourth. Driving along a tunnellike road in the forest, she would spill out four years' worth of farm stories and he would counter with three years' worth of seminary stories, and then they would come out on a wide plain and she would floor the gas pedal and they would speed away laughing and never looking back.

"You know what I'm asking, Frank?"

He nodded, the vision fading.

"You're saying there's no chance?"

He nodded again.

They silently regarded one another for several seconds before she suddenly threw her arms around him and buried her face in his neck. Her hair smelled faintly of a scented shampoo. He felt her shoulders quake with sobbing, felt tears on his neck. He patted her hair and said, "Where will you go, Libby?"

"Home to my mother," she murmured.

"She's still in town?"

He felt her nod.

"Will it be okay? With your dad, I mean?"

It was half a minute before she drew away from him and wiped her eyes with the frayed cuffs of her jacket. She looked out her side window, watching a cassock-clad priest and a young man in a suit crossing the campus together under a single umbrella. "My dad's gone," she said, "but that's a whole other story."

"You'll take the baby with you?"

She turned to him with a forceful sigh of impatience. "She's not a baby anymore. Her name is Verna."

"Okay. What I mean is, Vernon will let you have her?"

"What does Vernon care? He wanted a boy."

She started the engine, gunned it twice, and drove uphill, scattering a flock of waddling ducks. Stopping beside the seminary, she said, "I'm not asking you to love me or anything like that, Frank. I'm not asking you to not be a priest if that's what you want to be." The careworn lines around her eyes became more pronounced. "And I won't even ask you to see me. Seeing me makes you very nervous, I can tell." The anguish in her eyes intensified, appealed for mercy. "But, please, Frank, can we just talk on the phone once in a while?"

Again he was embarrassed to admit to the restricted life he was leading—the rector discouraged phone conversations. "It's hard to talk on the phone," he said. "There's just one phone on each floor and it's out in the hall and everybody listens."

With a sigh she sank into herself, deflated.

"We could write," he suggested.

She shook her head. "I never write letters. Writing isn't the same."

"Well . . ." He gripped the door handle, eager to be dismissed, and feeling guilty for his eagerness.

"I can't believe how nervous I make you," she said, looking away, her voice even deader than before. "Why can't you talk to me, Frank? What's changed you?" She appeared to be asking the ducks on the grass.

"I don't know, Libby. I guess we've just been leading such different lives. . . ."

"I know," she droned, "but can't two people do that and still be friends?"

"Well . . ." The vision of their riding away in the pickup returned to him, this time accompanied by a pang of longing so sharp and sudden that he reflexively opened the door and got out. Safely at arm's length from her, he said, "Sure, we can be friends." Rain soaked his hair and the shoulders of his jacket. He reached in and took her hand and kissed it and patted it, attracting her sad gaze, a gaze so bereft and grief-stricken that he had to avert his eyes. "Write to me," he said, and closed the door.

He backed against the building, and there, sheltered from the driving rain, he watched the pickup move slowly along the winding drive and around to the front of Christopher Hall and along the tree-lined gravel road leading to the world outside the valley. When it was out of sight, he went around to the front and climbed the steps to the broad oak door, half expecting a voice to tell him—as a voice had told him five years before—*She's the one*. But he heard no such voice. He heard only the rain spattering on the concrete steps and the groan and squeak of the iron hinges as he pulled open the door. He was relieved not to hear the voice, yet his apprehension remained. How could he be certain that she wouldn't keep turning up in his life?

He hurried past the rector's open door and up the stairs to his room, where David lay snoring on his bed. He took off his jacket and dried his hair and sat down at his desk. He opened *Exploring Metaphysics* and felt exceedingly hungry. He looked at his watch, wondering how he could possibly wait until supper at six. Well, at least there would be no baseball game. If there were, he'd surely collapse on the mound. Trembling with hunger, he lifted the crocheted bookmark off the page and without comprehension read a long paragraph, his mind filling up instead with all the things he'd tell Libby in the pickup as they sped off across the farmland to some distant and uncertain destination. He lay down to nap, but he could not rid his brain of the vision. Dear God, he pleaded, please keep her out of my life.

And God did, for twenty-three years.

PART TWO

13

It was midnight and six below zero when the stove blew up. Awakened by the huffing of an overfed fire, Frank Healy had shed his sleeping bag and was crossing the cold tile in his bare feet to adjust the oil flow when the lid blew open and flames roared up out of the firepot and licked at the wall. He ran back to his cot and slipped into his shoes, ran to the door and flung it open on the frigid moonlight, ran to the stove and kicked it loose from the copper tubing that fed it, kicked it across the floor and out over the doorsill. It toppled down the steps and sank, sizzling, into a snowbank.

He felt for the light switch and turned it on. The light, fluorescent and too bright for a room so small, hurt his eyes. He saw oil streaming from the severed tube and inching across the uneven floor in two directions—toward the sleeping bag hanging off the side of his cot and toward the tall oak bureau containing vestments, candles, cruets, and chalices. He lifted his black overcoat from the coat tree, draped it over his shoulders, and carefully descended the icy wooden stairs. Stepping around the steaming stove (the dying fire had shrunk to small blue tongues), he waded through the snow to the back of the church. "Dear God, do you laugh?" he said aloud to the moon as he turned off the oil flow at the tank. "I know I'm not the priest you called to your service—if indeed that was you calling—but I'll get it right yet. Please stay amused as long as possible." The moon, nearly full and straight overhead, was surrounded by a hazy, yellowish ring.

Silently he continued to address God: My brother the tax accountant makes fifty thousand a year and owns a house in St. Paul with four wonderfully warm bedrooms. My brother out west earns twelve dollars an hour mixing tar to repair highways and sleeps with a comely wife who loves him. Why wasn't I satisfied with normal aspirations?

Back inside, he soaked up the oil with the small rag rug beside his cot, imagining as he did so the bemused, fatherly look Monsignor Lawrence would turn on him tomorrow when he learned about the stove. He could hear the old man's quiet, reproving words: "Frank, Frank, how many times have I advised you not to sleep in the sacristy of that godforsaken church out there?" Three times was the answer—once a week since they'd become housemates—but Frank would politely refrain from saying so.

"That oil burner is a piece of junk, didn't I tell you that, Frank? All you have to do is go across the road and present yourself to the Pearsalls and they'll give you a warm meal and a warm bed to sleep in." Monsignor Lawrence, near sleep, would be tipped back in his soft mechanical chair, the Sunday paper scattered around him on the carpet, and Mrs. Tatzig would be making noises in the kitchen—dishwashing noises, bronchial noises—while Frank explained all over again that by spending the night in the mission church rather than a private home he was more readily available to his flock. And Monsignor Lawrence, turning his deaf left ear on this argument, would no doubt call Mrs. Tatzig in from the kitchen and tell her about the fire in Our Lady's sacristy; whereupon Mrs. Tatzig, an asthmatic widow built like a bulldog and fiercely devoted to the upkeep of the rectory and the care and feeding of her monsignor, would remind Frank that the Basswood Reservation was no place for a white man. It was Mrs. Tatzig's conviction that God had put Indians on reservations to prevent the mixture of races.

Throwing the oily rug outside and shutting the door, Frank began to tremble. In less than a minute the room had been drained of all its heat and so had he. He crossed the room and fanned the door to the sanctuary open and shut, hoping to draw warmth in from the large oil burner standing near the back row of pews, but that fire, too, would soon expire, he realized, because he had closed the valve at the tank.

He returned to the cot, sat down, and dug the caked snow out of his shoes. Then he rubbed his feet briskly, attempting to draw feeling back into his toes. What he brought back was icy pain. He tried blowing on them but they were too far away— he was not as bendable as he used to be, not as thin in the middle. Frank's middle, in fact, was becoming something of an embarrassment to him. For many years he had cultivated the ascetic, caved-in look he thought suitable to the priesthood, but last spring when Aquinas Academy closed—along with the college and the seminary—he'd given up caring what he looked like. He'd stopped exercising and begun eating between meals. He'd increased his consumption of rum. He'd brooded. At the urging of his bishop, he'd gone to a therapist who defined his problem as short-term depression and asked, "What are you feeding with all those calories, Father Healy?" "My big leak," was Frank's reply. "I've sprung a very big leak, and my spirit is draining away."

He switched off the light and crawled into his sleeping bag with his coat on. Lying on his back, he realized that he was still panting from exertion. His heart was beating in his ears. He calculated the months since he'd last exercised. More than half a year. He recalled the exact day—Friday of the first week in June. On Tuesday of that week, after defeating the Evanstown Rangers by seven runs, his Fighting Knights had hung up their spikes and uniforms for the final time, ending Frank's career as a prep-school coach. On Thursday of that week the Academy held its sixty-fifth and final graduation ceremony on the lawn in front of Christopher Hall, ending his nearly two decades as a prep-school teacher. Frank, headmaster and the students' choice, delivered the commencement address. It was a stifling, muggy afternoon. His talk was once interrupted by applause and twice by people fainting and falling off their folding chairs. The next day he played his last game of basketball, a pickup game with five students who were waiting for their parents to come and get them. Shivering now in the frigid sacristy, he recalled standing in his T-shirt and tennis shorts under the outdoor basket, the basketball under his arm, sweat pouring down his brow, and as he waved farewell to the last carload—the Scanlon brothers from Duluth—he was visited by a sudden and frightening revelation: My God, now I have no one to play with!

He lay in the dark, listening to what sounded like a sheet whipping on a distant clothesline. It was the fire in the big oil burner guttering and dying. Then there was silence. Then a barking dog. A gust of wind pressing on the north side of the church. An answering bark. The boom of ice shifting on Sovereign Lake. A car driving by. A third dog barking. Silence again. What a lot of dogs lived on the reservation—nervous little mongrels with dull coats and hungry eyes. Was it true, as Mrs. Tatzig claimed, that Indians ate dogs?

Frank's feet kept him awake. He seemed to be turning to ice from the feet up. Finally, when his trembling grew to shuddering, he gave up. He slipped into his frozen shoes, gathered up his clothes, dropped his alarm clock into his overnight bag, and let himself out the front door of the church.

He paused on the step, looking left and right along County Road 13, the north–south artery running through the heart of the reservation. He'd intended to go next door to the Pipes' and request the use of their couch, but seeing no light in the windows of their trailer house and no pickup parked in the yard, he knew they weren't yet home from the Homestead. Across the road he saw a dim light showing through the front window of the Indian Health Center. He didn't want to impose on strangers, but what choice did he have? The searing wind felt like needles on his face.

Two miles south of the church a bearded man named Roger Upward stood in the middle of County Road 13 and shouted at the woman who had broken free of his grip.

"Goddamn it, Verna, you go back in there and I'm done with you forever."

Verna, a slim young woman in cowboy boots, stopped running long enough to spin around and spit in his direction, her eyes and bracelets flashing in the moonlight. Then she darted between the parked cars to the door of the tavern, and there under the red neon she turned to him a second time and spat on the stoop. Then she pulled open the heavy door and wiggled her hips at the night before slipping inside.

"Verna!" he called, watching the door swing shut on her long blond hair and her tight blue jeans and her red flannel shirt. *His* red flannel shirt. Turning and teetering drunkenly in the road, he lifted his teary eyes and his runny nose to the moon and howled a broken cry of anguish and anger that formed a little cloud of steam above his head. Falling silent, he heard his cry echo in the woods. Judging by the icy ring around the moon, he guessed it was ten below zero. Where had he parked his pickup? It took him a minute to remember. He walked stumpily along the line of cars parked at the side of the road, talking to himself, vowing that he would not relent this time, would not take her in (as he had done twice before) if she came to his door saying she was sorry, nor would he go groveling after her (as he had done once before) and talk her into coming back. He simply couldn't risk another of her betrayals. The pain was more than he could stand.

The instant he touched the door handle of his pickup he realized that he'd left his gloves in the booth. He'd left his jacket, too. He began to shiver. He turned and looked at the neon lettering over the door—THE HOMESTEAD—and decided not to go back inside. He'd return for the jacket and gloves tomorrow, when Verna wasn't there. But she *would* be there. She'd be there day and night until she got tired of Judge Bigelow again, goddamn her. Well, he'd stay indoors all day tomorrow, close to the fire. He'd ask his sister Millie or somebody to go pick up his jacket and gloves.

The pickup wouldn't start. He ground the starter until the icy key stung his fingers like fire. He changed hands and ground it until the battery died. He got out and slammed the door. It sprang open. He kicked it shut, but it sprang open again, its latch frozen. He turned and gazed at the Homestead. He stood with his hands clamped in his armpits and his beard freezing stiff around his mouth. Should he go back inside? He heard, or rather felt like a pulse, the bass beat of the jukebox. Willie Nelson. You could get mighty sick of Willie Nelson. He heard a woman shriek. Verna. You could get fed up with Verna drinking herself into a shrieking jag.

Through the partially frosted windows he saw the movement of a few couples dancing, saw the yellow lights over the bar, saw the silhouette of a very large man mixing a drink. Judge Bigelow. You could murder that son of a bitch and the world would be better off. He saw the figure of a young woman move around to help out behind the bar. Verna. You could die.

He was tempted to go in and plead with her once again. Or go in and ignore her while he collected his jacket and gloves and sat for a while sobering up for the walk home. Or go in and put his boot through the glass face of the jukebox and pretend it was the Judge's face. But he didn't go in. He turned and walked north along 13. It was over a mile to his house. If he didn't want to freeze to death, he'd have to keep moving.

But why, he asked himself as he weaved from one side of the road to the other, didn't he want to freeze to death? Why, without Verna, would a man want to live?

14

A light came on in the entryway, and Frank peered through the lace-curtained glass in the door. He saw a small man in a Chicago Bears sweatshirt approach with a can of beer in one hand and a *TV Guide* in the other. The porch light came on overhead and the man peered out at him for a moment or two before he opened the door.

Frank, shivering, introduced himself: "Frank Healy, the priest." Then, laughing, he opened his coat to reveal his pajamas of blue and white stripes. "I'm in need of a bed—my stove blew up."

"My God, a priest in his pj's," said Dr. Pearsall. "Get in here where it's warm."

Frank, pushing the door shut behind him, said, "Thanks."

"I'll get some booze into you right away," said the doctor, leading Frank down a hallway that smelled of rubbing alcohol. Half the house served as the Pearsalls' living quarters, the other half was a clinic. "My wife'll be down in a minute. As soon as she heard your knock, she ran upstairs to get decent, thinking you were a wounded Indian in need of stitches or something." Entering the living room, a long, low-lit room furnished in maple and chintz, he added sternly, "We were enjoying a little foreplay on the couch."

Frank said he was sorry and decided the doctor was drunk.

"Wait till you see her, you'll be sorrier yet. Have a chair. What do you drink?"

Frank chose a rocking chair near a radiator and set his bag down beside him. "Do you have some rum?"

"Of course I have some rum." The doctor looked offended. "What with?"

"Coke."

"The last priest drank scotch," said the doctor on his way to the kitchen. "Sucked it down like mother's milk."

In his absence, Frank gazed at the television set, watching John Wayne lead a platoon of marines across *The Sands of Iwo Jima*. The picture was snowy. He moved the chair closer to the heat and hugged himself for warmth.

The doctor, still wearing an expression of irritation, returned from the kitchen and handed Frank a tumblerful of rum and Coke, saying, "Welcome to the goddamn boondocks."

"Thanks."

"Libby," he called at the top of his small voice, "come and see the new priest in his pj's." Then he crossed the room and sat down facing the television, his back to Frank. "Can you hear this all right?" he asked over his shoulder.

Frank said he could.

They watched a few minutes of the movie before the doctor's wife, a dark-haired, attractive woman, opened the hallway door and Frank stood up, straightening his pajama collar and buttoning his overcoat. She took two or three steps into the room, then stopped and cocked her head, recognizing him before he recognized her. "Frank!" she shrieked, and sprang at him and clung to him and kissed him. And still he might not have recognized her in the half darkness had her husband's summoning call, "Libby," not been ringing in his mind.

He stepped back and beheld her. The hair, short and straight, was gray at the temples, and the eyes weren't the eyes he remembered. But the nose was the same nose—thin and slightly turned up at the end—and the brow was the same wide, smooth brow upon which he used to dream about planting kisses, and the smile was the same wide, gleeful smile he'd fallen in love with at sixteen. She was wearing a robe and furry slippers, and under the robe a floor-length flannel nightgown covered with a pattern of strawberries.

"Libby," he said, feeling awkward as he volunteered another brief embrace, uncertain how much affection to show, how much she expected, how much would be tolerated by her testy husband, who was on his feet and gaping at them, puzzled. Stepping back from her once again, Frank was captivated by the change in her eyes. They were more expressive eyes than ever, but darker somehow, inward looking, careworn. Instead of reflecting the light the way they used to, they seemed to absorb it. They absorbed Frank.

"Tom, this is Frank Healy, my . . ." She shook her head, smiling yet frowning, a catch in her throat.

"Your what?" said Tom, coming forward, holding his can of beer to his heart.

"My dearest friend from high school."

Her husband said, "You never went to high school."

"I went to high school, Tom." She laughed breezily.

"You said you never went."

"I said I never finished."

Frank took a swallow of rum and grimaced—fire all the way down.

"Here, sit down," she said, unfastening a button of his coat and patting the arm of the rocker, "and tell us everything you've done since I saw you last."

He resisted her attempt to take his coat, giving her an embarrassed laugh and a glimpse of his pajamas. He explained about the stove.

"I didn't hear any explosion," she said.

"Actually it was more of a whoosh."

"Whoosh, bullshit," said her husband, scowling at Frank. "You had a nightmare. You were being chased through the snow by an Indian, and he had you in the sights of his rifle and was about to blow your ass off the face of the earth, and that's why you're sitting here in your pj's with your knees knocking, Father Frank Healy."

Frank smiled weakly, recalling Father DeSmet's claim, when they'd exchanged positions three weeks ago, that Dr. Pearsall of the Basswood Health Center drank more beer than anyone DeSmet had ever known, that he could swill a twelve-pack in one sitting. DeSmet also reported that a skiing accident many years ago had left the doctor's spine slightly deformed, and that his stoop made him look older than his age.

"Get the good father a blanket," said Tom. "He's shaking like a leaf."

"I'll be fine," said Frank, sitting down in the rocker.

"Get him a blanket," Tom insisted.

Libby picked a cocktail glass off a table and raised it high. "To Frank," she said happily. "My long-lost friend." She wasn't as inebriated as her husband, but her smile was slightly glazed, her words thick on her tongue.

Tom raised his can of beer and growled, "Get him a blanket."

"No, really, I'll be fine," said Frank, trembling.

"A blanket," Tom repeated.

"He said he doesn't want one, Tom."

The Pearsalls stood facing each other in a silent contest of wills that lasted several seconds and ended in a draw. Simultaneously they turned away and sat down, Tom on the couch across the room, where he could keep an eye on television, Libby on a stool next to Frank.

"You smell funny," she said, giggling.

Frank put his hand to his nose. "Fuel oil."

She reached for his hand and sniffed it. She made a face. "You'll want a shower. I'll get you towels. Tom, would you turn that off?"

Tom, who had fallen asleep the instant he sat down, snapped his eyes open and said, "I'm watching."

"Well, turn it down then."

"I'm listening," he said, his eyes closing, his head dropping to his chest.

Libby turned a bright-eyed look on Frank as if to say, What can you do with a drunk as funny and charming as my husband?

An unconvincing look, thought Frank—it contained too much pain to be as merry as she intended. Was Tom the pain? "The guest room's ready for you," she said, gripping Frank's wrist.

"Just this once," he told her.

"Oh, come on. Why in God's name would you want to sleep over there in that little cubicle behind the altar. I've seen it. Gene DeSmet showed it to me. It's musty and depressing."

"I have this plan—possibly foolish—that Our Lady's can be rejuvenated if the priest is available overnight instead of just for an hour on Sunday morning."

"Available for what?"

"Confessions. Counseling. Conversation."

"But Gene DeSmet was out here overnight and he didn't inspire any Great Awakening. Face it, Frank, you won't find any spiritual cravings on the rezz."

"Gene came out for your hospitality—he told me. It was a night away from home."

Voices blared from the TV. Libby pointed to her husband and said, "You'll have to excuse him, he's had a hard day at the office." She laughed and sipped her drink. "Two patients. This morning Mrs. Pipe came in with hives, and this afternoon one of the Upward brothers needed his ear sewn up. Do you know the Upward family?"

Her husband opened his eyes and called out, "The Upwards are maniacs."

"There was a Millie Upward in our class," said Frank.

"Now she's Millie LaBonte," said Libby. "We're treating her for anxiety."

"The Upwards are maniacs," Tom repeated.

"They're fond of guns," Libby explained. "The older Upward was shooting at a mouse and hit his brother in the earlobe."

"The whole family's in love with guns," said Tom, suddenly alert and sitting erect on the edge of the couch. "They sleep with guns. They're married to guns."

Frank said he'd never heard of hunting mice with guns.

"It wasn't exactly hunting. It happened in their kitchen." Libby chuckled. "A mouse ran across the floor while they were eating breakfast and he shot from his place at the table and his brother got in the way."

"What about *Roger* Upward?" Tom shouted, getting to his feet. "As long as we're on the Upward family, let's figure out what to do about dear Roger."

Libby turned to him and raised her voice: "What's to figure out!" It wasn't a question. It was more of a challenge.

"Because he's a goddamn loser and he's making a loser out of Verna!" His voice dropped: "Give the good father a drink!"

"He has one."

"Give him two!"

Libby tipped her head, laid it sideways on her palm, smiled at Frank, and said, "Are you forty-four yet?"

"Just."

"Me too."

"I know," he said. "December tenth."

"You remember. How sweet."

"Goddamn it, Libby, don't ignore me! Did I or did I not tell you to get the good father a drink?"

Frank caught a moment's interruption in Libby's smile, a flash of bewilderment or misery. But her voice was light as she repeated, "He's already got a drink, Tom."

The quick return of her smile reminded Frank of how resilient she'd been as a girl. Morning after morning at sixteen she'd emerged from what must have been a very dispiriting household, and yet by the time she'd met Frank down the street her spirit had been so high that it lifted his along with it. He'd thought of her often over the years, and what impressed him most in retrospect was her ability, despite a downcast mother and an abusive father, to be so dependably buoyant.

Her husband came stooping toward them once again, his straw-colored hair hanging in his eyes, his can of beer held to his heart. "I said get him a drink."

"Don't be silly, he's not half done with what you gave him." She straightened up on the stool, her hands on her knees, her head tipping back as Tom advanced and stood over her with a menacing scowl.

Frank, recalling that her father, too, had been menacing when he drank, got to his feet, prepared to step between them and protect Libby, whose expression had become intensely sad. He laid his hand on Tom's shoulder and spoke firmly: "Listen, it's past my bedtime. Show me where to sleep and I'll be out like a light."

There was a long silence as Tom made the effort to transfer his drunken gaze from his wife to his guest—a slow turning first of the head, next of the crooked torso, and finally when the eyes were aimed correctly, they were a long time focusing. And when they were focused, they were no longer menacing. Frank read in them—to his amazement—fear. And then, after a few blinks and another woozy transformation—friendliness.

"Frank Healy, we're living in a goddamn foreign country out here. We're aliens, Frank Healy. Did you notice the street-light is out?"

"Yes, I did."

"Frank Healy, tell me . . ." He reached up and hooked his hand over Frank's shoulder. "Do you want anything to drink?"

"I'm fine, Tom."

"Frank Healy, do you know why the streetlight is out?"

"No."

"Because the Upward brothers shot it out."

"I see."

"They always shoot it out. The highway department will send out two men in a truck and they'll put in a new light and the Upward brothers'll shoot it out again. It's been going on ever since we came here. Nothing anybody can do. Not even Caesar Pipe. Don't go to bed, Frank Healy."

"Really, I have to."

"Libby." He turned to the stool and seemed perplexed not to see his wife sitting there. "Libby!"

"What?" She was at Tom's other side, linking arms with him, the sadness gone from her face.

"Libby." His voice was tender. "What's to eat?"

"Pizza. Shall I put a pizza in the oven?" She was asking Frank.

"Not for me, thanks."

"Put a pizza in the oven, Libby."

Watching her step over to the television and turn down the

sound and then cross to the kitchen, Frank was suddenly as tired as he claimed to be—the warm room, the rum.

"Frank Healy, do you know how much gunfire there is out here during any given week?" Fear was returning to Tom's eyes. "Do you know how much, Frank Healy?"

"No, how much?"

His answer was delayed by a long silent belch.

"A lot."

"Is that so?"

"Indians shoot deer, they shoot streetlights, they shoot mice, they shoot themselves. Do you know Caesar Pipe?"

"He's one of my trustees," said Frank, allowing himself to be steered to the couch, where he sat and stared at a rock band performing silently on the screen. The lead guitar player was a pink-haired boy in red leather.

Tom settled close by his side. "Caesar Pipe's the tribal leader, you know."

"Yes. A good one, I'm told."

"He tries to keep rowdiness under control by firing his revolver over the heads of rowdies. I've seen him do it. He'll pull out his revolver and fire right over their heads. The Upward brothers are the most fired-over people on the reservation."

"I'll bet."

"And do you know who's absolutely terrified by that, Frank Healy?"

"Not the Upward brothers apparently."

"Me."

"You?"

"I am the most terrified person on this reservation, Frank Healy." He raised his right hand. "I swear to God, I am terrified by guns." Another belch. "Libby!"

She looked in from the kitchen.

"Libby, what the hell's happened to the TV, I can't hear it."

"Turn it up if you want to hear it."

"Libby!"

"Yes?"

"Bring the good father a drink."

Frank finished his drink and accepted another. Soon there

was pizza. Then ice cream and coffee. Then Tom watched an old movie—James Stewart and Walter Brennan—on a channel that kept fading out, while Frank and Libby matched high-school memories. When the movie ended, Frank sensed something like desperation in the Pearsalls' urging him not to go to bed. He could imagine Father DeSmet enjoying their company immensely. Father DeSmet, a convivial young man, had obviously misrepresented the Pearsalls to Monsignor Lawrence, who had never met them and spoke of them in sedate terms. ("Lovely people, the Pearsalls, Frank. Devoted people. Think of it, dedicating themselves to the Indians like that. You really ought to let them put you up in their house.")

Over the sound of TV, they heard the ice of Sovereign Lake rumble and crack. Tom's eyes grew large with fear—feigned or genuine, Frank couldn't tell. "Why does the lake do that, Frank Healy?"

"Ice expands and contracts with the temperature. It opens up long cracks."

"Jesus, and people drive on it."

"They aren't wide cracks. They're only an inch or two and they freeze shut right away."

Libby asked, "Do you drive on the lake, Frank?"

He nodded. "It cuts off nine miles to town."

"Jesus." Tom sighed in disbelief. "Just the other day it was water."

"It hasn't been water for a month," said Frank. "The ice is a foot thick."

"But there's thin spots," warned Tom, his eyes large, his fear apparently genuine.

"Only one," Frank told him. "Over near the far shore where the river comes in. It's marked off with oil drums and the road goes around it."

Libby beamed happily. "I told you it was safe, Tom. Let's start driving on it."

Again the ice thundered.

"Jesus," Tom repeated, falling asleep.

Frank asked about Libby's daughter, and the expression of bewilderment and misery returned to her face.

"Mental problems," she said.

"Where is she?"

Tom, suddenly awake, looked at his watch and said angrily, "She's probably at the Homestead."

"She lives with you then?"

"She came here with us from Chicago," said Libby. "But we hardly ever see her. She's gone native."

"Native American," Tom seethed.

Roger Upward, trembling convulsively from the cold, had covered more than a mile of County Road 13 before he slipped on an icy rut and came down on the back of his head. He didn't lose consciousness, but lay stunned for a minute or more, unable to move. Then, struggling to his feet, he felt a sudden, blinding pain running front to back across the top of his head. Had he cracked his skull? His head felt lopsided, as though his brain had come loose. The moonlight, dim as it was, hurt his eyes. Then the pain of his freezing feet and thighs and shoulders returned with a ferocious bite that distracted him from his head injury. His hands were the only painless parts of his body now—they were frozen numb.

He no longer felt drunk. His inebriation having been knocked or frozen out of him, he was now seized by a fear for his life as strong as any fear he'd felt as a squad leader in Vietnam. When he rounded the last bend in the forest and knew he would make it safely home, his fear reversed itself. Instead of dying, it was living that scared him. Living without Verna.

If my fire is out, I won't light it, he told himself. If there's an ember in the stove, I'll throw in some paper and kindling and thaw myself out and live another forty years and miss Verna every day till I die, but if there isn't any fire, I won't go to the trouble. I'll lie down on the bed and never wake up.

He went around to the side of his one-room house and reached into the doghouse for the key on the nail. Chances are there won't be a fire, he thought, steeling himself for death. He and Verna had been gone all afternoon and evening. Twelve hours usually put a fire completely out.

The little dog cowering in the doghouse wasn't his. Roger no longer owned a dog. Roger's dog, the color of a fawn, had disappeared in the early fall, most likely shot in the forest by a hunter who mistook it for a deer. This dog, a stray, was much smaller. It whined at the back of the doghouse as Roger groped for the key on the nail. He couldn't feel the key with his frozen fingers. He couldn't feel the nail. He gave up and went to the door of the house and hurled himself against it until the latch gave way and he stumbled in past the bed and the chair and came to a halt in front of the wood stove. Clamping the handle between his two hands, he opened the cast-iron door of the stove and peered in. The fire was out.

He looked for matches—to hell with dying. The box of wooden matches over the range was empty. He searched the house for a matchbook, knocking things off shelves and upsetting the table by the bed. He found a matchbook in a shirt of Verna's. It took him forever to open it, and when it was open he couldn't bring his thumb and finger together to tear off a match. He tore one off with his teeth. He worked at striking it for a minute or more, but he couldn't hold it tightly enough and couldn't co-ordinate his trembling hands. He tore out others with his teeth, but he couldn't strike a spark with any of them, and by the time the matchbook was empty his arms and legs were numb and the terrible pain was returning to his head.

It was Roger Upward's policy never to ask for help—his brothers Johnny and Pock were forever bothering him for help and he resented it—but now if he'd had a phone he would have used it. He would have called his sister Millie and asked her to get out of bed and drive over and start a fire for him and bring her purse along. Millie would have done it. She was never any-thing but good to him. She would have been glad—though she wouldn't say so—to find Verna gone. She would have started his fire and fixed him something hot to drink and found him a pill of some kind to take away the pain in his head. Her purse was a regular pharmacy. But he had no phone. His household accounts had been in disarray ever since Verna took over the checkbook, and the phone had been disconnected months ago.

He lay down on the bed. He tried burrowing under the covers

but the pain in his head made him helplessly dizzy and he gave up. Every movement required enormous concentration and increased his pain. He lay on his back and strained to keep himself awake by concentrating on a series of disconnected thoughts. Death by freezing, he'd heard, began with sleep.

He regretted never writing a letter of condolence to the wife of his buddy Corporal John Vincennes of Pittsburgh, Pennsylvania. John stepped on a mine eight years ago last spring and lived for two days cut in half.

He wondered if he ought to cut more wood, or if the pile behind the house would last till spring.

He wondered, if he died tonight, who would find him. He hoped it wouldn't be Millie and her daughter Elaine, who often stopped by on their way home from Sunday Mass. Millie was fretful and emotional and she ought to be told the bad news by somebody gentle. The new priest maybe. Millie liked the new priest. They'd been classmates in high school, she'd said.

He thought about Verna. He remembered the night he first saw her. She was dancing at the Homestead. The sweet face, the long light hair, the slim, exciting body. She and Roger's brother Johnny were dancing to something by Emmylou Harris. She wore white jeans and a black shirt and every time she passed Roger's booth she gave him the eye.

He remembered the night she first went home with him. She wouldn't let him out of bed in the morning. They lay entangled till noon.

He remembered the first time she stayed all night with Judge Bigelow at the Homestead. Roger thought his heart would break. He pleaded with her the next day, sitting in his pickup at the front door of the Homestead, Verna standing on the stoop looking very sexy with no bra under her T-shirt, the Judge standing in the shadows behind the screen door and listening to everything they said, not realizing that Roger had seen him cross the dance floor and take up a position he thought was invisible. Roger said things to bait him, but the Judge never came out of the shadows, not even when Verna hopped into the pickup and he took her home. Her home by that time was no longer the Indian Health Center where her mother was the reservation nurse and her stepfather was the doctor. Her home was Roger's little house in the woods.

He remembered the day Dr. Pearsall came looking for her and she hid in the woods behind the house, saying she never wanted to see that son of a bitch again. Roger stood in the doorway and swore she wasn't anywhere around, and the doctor knew he was lying and Roger knew he knew, but he stood his ground and the doctor finally gave up and roared away in his BMW, but not before calling Roger a broken-down drunken Indian and Roger calling the doctor a broken-down drunken doctor.

The next day Verna's mother came looking for her. That day it was true that Verna was gone. That was the day she disappeared and stayed away for nearly a week, and when she came back she refused to tell Roger where she'd been. But later, one night when she was high, she let it be known that she'd spent the week in Chicago with her stepfather. It was supposed to look like a trip back to the city to see her shrink, she said, but really it was so her stepfather could pick up a fresh supply of pharmaceuticals.

Drugs for his medical practice, Roger assumed at the time, but tonight, not more than an hour ago, as Roger watched Toad Majerus peddling dope and pills at the Homestead, it dawned on him that the supplier was Dr. Pearsall. No wonder there was so much more pot smoking and pill popping around Basswood than there used to be. That twisted shrimp of a doctor was a pusher. And another suspicion occurred to Roger tonight in the Homestead. If the trip to Chicago was only for pharmaceuticals, why did Verna need to go along? He'd asked her point-blank tonight, and that's what set her off. "Verna," he'd said, high on booze and a couple of pills, "have you ever been in bed with your mother's husband?" Verna answered him with spit.

Roger, frozen beyond pain, began to mumble what he'd tell John Vincennes' widow if he lived to write the letter. He'd tell her John was the best friend he'd ever had and a hell of a brave soldier besides. He mumbled what he'd tell Caesar Pipe if he lived to see him again. He'd tell Caesar where the dope and pills were coming from. Then he took up Verna's name, mumbling it over and over until he lost consciousness.

At 2:00 A.M., when Frank pleaded for sleep, Tom seemed to be getting his second wind and Libby discovered that she had drunk too many martinis. "Come, I'll show you your room," she said, weaving out into the chilly hallway and over to the staircase. The men followed, Tom giving Frank an account of three violent deaths he'd encountered during his seven months on the reservation. A highway accident. A hunting accident. A suicide. "This living among Indians is spooky, Frank Healy, and what I want to know is, what's your story? What are you doing here?"

"I'm a priest," said Frank, wearily climbing the stairs.

Libby, tightly gripping Frank's arm, steered him into the guest room, then she continued along the hallway to the linen closet. Frank sat heavily on the bed, dropped his overnight bag between his feet, and sighed with fatigue. The guest room was freshly papered—stylized tulips—and smelled of spice. The bedside lamp had a frilly shade.

Tom came in and stood over him, a beer in one hand and his shoes in the other. "I know you're a priest, but you're no dumbbell and you're no spring chicken. You're nothing like that fuzzy-faced boy-priest you replaced. So what's in it for you?"

Frank raised his eyes to Tom, liking him, a little, for his forthrightness and thinking, For all I know he's a good match for Libby, but I'd have to see him sober sometime to decide.

"What's your story, Frank?"

Did he want the material answer or the spiritual answer? Frank had learned long ago that almost everyone expressing curiosity about the priesthood was either a fervent cynic or a fervent believer, seldom lukewarm, and it was no use trying to explain spirituality to the cynic or worldly rewards to the believer. Tell a believer you were in it for the free ride—Mother Church promised you food, clothes, shelter, and spending money till the end of your days—and the believer laughed politely at what he assumed was your failed attempt at humor. Tell a cynic you'd been called by God to work among his people, and the reaction was about the same, except the cynic's laugh was usually accompanied by the sort of jaded leer no believer would have been capable of: *Who you trying to kid, Father?*

Or was Tom Pearsall the in-between sort of questioner—Frank had met a few—who rejected both the material and the spiritual answers in favor of the psychological answer? He played a hunch.

"It fulfills my needs."

The right choice apparently, for something quickened in Tom's eyes. "Ah, needs. What needs?"

"Not now, Tom. I'd have to take you back to my childhood."

"I don't mind. I'll go down and get us drinks."

"It's 2:30, Tom. Don't you ever sleep?"

"Not much. My back. I've had back pain ever since I left Chicago. I've got a chiropractor in Chicago. I go back for treatments."

Libby came in with towels—three or four of them—and announced, "I'm dizzy, you guys." She had gone pale and aged a few years. She dropped the towels in Frank's lap.

"Libby, you know why Frank Healy's a priest?"

"I think I might pass out." She made for the door and stopped there, leaning against the doorframe. She turned slowly to look at the men and said, "Why?"

"Because it fulfills his needs. Which he will tell us about in the morning. That okay, Frank Healy? We go over your needs in the morning?"

"If you're up."

"I'll be up. My back gets me up."

Libby darted to the bed, bent to Frank, and planted her lips so hard on his mouth that he nearly tipped over backward. Then she hurried out the door, her robe flying.

"Needs," said her husband, pointing after her. "What a bundle of needs." He crossed the room and paused in the doorway to smile at Frank. Or was he smirking? "She's not growing, you see. She's got no identity except in relation to me. She's my wife. She's my nurse. She's nothing on her own. You get my meaning?"

Frank, dead tired, nodded vigorously, but this did not forestall an explanation.

"She's got no spirit, no push. Last summer she showed a little initiative—she started taking a health survey of Indians—but it came to nothing. She talks about painting landscapes, but the only landscape she ever looks at is the scrubby woods out these windows and she never opens her paintbox. She used to dote on her daughter, but not anymore. She's outlived her hopes for Verna—she'll tell you that herself."

Tom waited for a response, but Frank, sitting with his eyes closed, said nothing. Tom stepped into the hallway and summed up his diagnosis as he pulled the door shut: "She's a case of arrested development."

Me too, thought Frank, opening his eyes, relieved to be alone. He shifted his eyes to the floor-length mirror beside the door and saw that he still wore his overcoat. He felt too tired to stand and take it off. Falling back on the bed, he went immediately to sleep, but was soon awakened by a voice.

She's the one.

No, he answered, removing his overcoat and crawling into bed. If I'd chosen the married state, she might have been the one, but I didn't.

She's the one, the voice repeated.

15

"What's up, Padre?"

The enormous Caesar Pipe—elected leader of the Basswood band of Ojibway Indians—stood in the doorway of his purple and cream trailer house, bellying out into the winter dawn. His T-shirt said LINDEN FALLS REDI-MIX. His pajama bottoms, several sizes too short, exposed a length of hairless ankle above his slippers.

"We've got trouble in church, Caesar. Sorry to get you out of bed."

A grunt. "Wiring?"

"This time it's fuel oil. The stove blew up last night. The small one."

A frown. "Hurcha?"

"No, I'm fine."

A grin. "You don't look it."

"Short of sleep," Frank explained, turning up his collar against the wind. "I disconnected the stove. It's outside, by the back door."

"C'mon." Coatless and apparently unfazed by the cold, Caesar Pipe led Frank around the hitch end of his trailer house to a large toolshed in the backyard, where he pawed through a clutter of assorted hardware.

Frank, waiting, stepped back from the shed and studied the north wall of Our Lady's Church. White paint peeling. Stone foundation cracked. Poor insulation apparently—no snow on the roof. Either by a miracle or by Caesar Pipe's watchfulness, the three leaded windows on this side had been spared from gunshot and stoning. (Two of the three windows on the south side were boarded up.) In the belfry over the door, instead of a bell, was the nest of some very large bird. Rising crookedly from the tip of the steeple was a TV antenna, which was connected by a black cable to the Pipes' trailer house. Comparing its present appearance to what he remembered of its fresh-looking renewal in the summer of 1950, Frank rehearsed an observation—*Caesar, this is the shabbiest-looking church in the diocese and your antenna is the shabbiest thing about it*—but he decided to keep his mouth shut lest he alienate one of the few members of this dwindling congregation.

Three weeks ago Bishop Baker, acceding to Frank's request and transferring him from the cathedral in Berrington to St. Ann's in Linden Falls, had warned him that the co-parish on the Basswood Reservation was edging toward extinction. "Be prepared to oversee its demise, Frank—Indians aren't as Catholic as they used to be. It's a trend going back a decade or two, so don't blame yourself when it happens."

Frank, dismayed to imagine himself last in the long line of priests to the Indians, had uttered no protest in the bishop's office, but had secretly vowed to revitalize the Basswood parish, recalling how his boyhood drift toward the priesthood had picked up irresistible momentum on that summer morning of 1950 when he sat in the long grass with Duck the carpenter and Hanson the painter and listened to Father Lawrence (not yet Monsignor Lawrence in those days) tell the story of Father Zell's martyrdom. And now, standing under Our Lady's belfry in the frigid December wind, he was struck by an intuitive feeling that his success or failure as a priest would be closely tied to the survival of this old frame church in the wilderness. He stepped around Caesar Pipe's shed and looked beyond the church at the snow-covered lake. The sky, preparing for sunrise, was flooding the earth with nearly enough light to cast shadows, and the far shore—a mile distant—was just now coming into view. He thought of Father Zell wandering around in the baffling snowfall of that long-ago Christmas and falling dead on the ice.

"Got a flanging tool somewhere in this mess," said Caesar Pipe.

Frank turned from the lake and looked into the shed. Caesar was bent over a large, mouse-nibbled carton. Against the back wall, covered with a sheet of clear plastic, stood a yellow snowmobile.

"Caesar, we'll have a lot of repair work to do, come spring."

The Indian straightened up and gave Frank a half-amused look. Often, in facing Frank, Caesar Pipe looked like a man suppressing laughter. Was it all white men he found entertaining, Frank wondered, or only all clergy? Or simply himself? He must ask Father DeSmet next time they met if he recalled this wry little smile returning again and again to this wide, coppery face.

"A paint job," said Frank, "and the foundation needs patching."

The Indian nodded.

"And there's a bird's nest in the belfry."

"No." Caesar shook his head. "Squirrels."

"Have you got a ladder? If it's squirrels, they ought to be removed before they chew their way into the church."

"Had a ladder. Borrowed it out and never got it back."

"Maybe we should buy one."

"Maybe we should."

"We'll need one for painting in the spring. How much would a ladder cost?"

"Ten dollars."

"No, I mean a good one. Aluminum."

"Ten dollars. The ladder I lent to Carl Butcher is aluminum. He'll sell it for ten dollars." Caesar Pipe resumed his tool search.

"If it's your ladder, why would you buy it?"

"Because I borrowed it from the Upwards."

"You said it was yours."

"It was mine for a while. Then I lent it out."

"So can't you borrow it back?"

"Could, I guess."

"Do it. Borrow it back."

"I'll do it if you say so, but I'd rather buy it."

"Why buy it? It doesn't belong to Carl Butcher."

"Balance of trade."

Drop it, Frank advised himself. Conversations with Caesar Pipe often ran crooked like this and led to dead ends. But he was curious, and squirrels could be damaging. "What do you mean, balance of trade?"

Caesar Pipe moved deeper into his shed and spoke from the shadows. "The stores in Linden Falls get all our money. Why not bring a little white money back on the reservation for a change?"

Frank took out his billfold, which contained two tens and a five. He reached into the shed, handing Caesar Pipe one of the tens. "Buy it, Caesar. And remember it's parish property."

Caesar, looking at the ten, scratched the back of his head. "We probably should buy it from the Upwards, too, since it was theirs to start with."

Frank held out both tens.

"Okay, that ought to do it, but I got no pocket. Leave them in the sacristy, will you?"

Returning the tens to his billfold, Frank felt he'd now earned the right to criticize.

"Caesar, your antenna on the steeple."

"Yeah?"

"It looks like hell."

The Indian stepped out of the shed with a pliers in one hand and a hacksaw and a flanging tool in the other. He peered up at the steeple. "Wind sort of bent it over, I guess. We get ourselves that ladder, I can straighten it."

"No, Caesar. Straight or crooked, it's an eyesore."

"Best place for reception. Pulls in Fargo."

"Put it on your own roof."

"Could, I guess."

"Do it. Put it on your roof."

"I'll do it if you say so, but the wife won't like it. Wrestling comes out of Fargo."

"Then maybe I should talk to her."

"'Preciate it."

"I'll talk to her after Mass."

Caesar Pipe looked delighted. "Whyn't you do it now? Go in where it's warm, Father. I'll kick her out of bed and have her make you some coffee."

"No, don't bother."

"Church'll be cold. No use the two of us freezing."

"No, that's all right, I'm staying with the Pearsalls."

Caesar Pipe nodded, vastly amused.

"You're sure I can't help with the oil burner?"

Caesar Pipe laughed.

Frank crossed the road with his mind on Father Zell, God's Pathfinder. As a seminarian Frank had been shocked to come across the sort of theologian who could dismiss Father Zell as stupid for observing the holy fast that Christmas Day. "Setting off across the lake on an empty stomach—and dehydrated besides—was the next thing to suicide," said Father Schmittbauer, professor of moral theology. "He was only forty-five—think of the years of work he cut himself off from by being so fastidious."

Outraged, Frank came to the man's defense, pointing out that Father Zell had many times said an early Mass in Basswood and a later Mass on the far shore of Sovereign Lake, and that under normal conditions it was less than an hour's walk across the ice—Frank had walked it himself. (He didn't mention that he had done it experimentally, on an empty stomach.) Frank's voice rang in the classroom: "He couldn't have foreseen the wind coming up. Is it suicide to be caught in a blizzard?"

Fool or martyr? The class was split, and Father Zell became the subject of several term papers and turned up in Father Schmittbauer's final exam. *Three hundred words on the moral implications of Father Zell's fasting unto death.*

Fool or martyr? To this day Frank held fast to his conviction (Father Schmittbauer had called it wrongheaded mysticism) that Father Zell's holiest act was his final and total obedience to what he took to be God's orders—no food or drink between midnight and the consecration of the Sacrament—and held fast to the belief that as a priest of the nineteenth century, Father Zell should not be judged by the pragmatic standards of the twentieth.

Frank let himself into the hallway and followed the aroma of coffee to the kitchen. Libby in her robe—not so fresh-faced as last night—sat at the window sipping from a steaming cup. She smiled weakly and said, "Up so early?"

"Up and out. I've got Caesar working on the oil burner."

She crossed to the stove, poured him a cup of coffee, set it before him. "Beauty is so rare out here, Frank, you have to take it where you find it." Frank guessed she was referring to the sunrise. She returned to her place at the window and gazed out at a flat area of hazelbrush and snow enclosed by a wall of jack-pines. The sun was struggling up out of the trees. A minute passed before she continued.

"You can't tell me the human spirit was created with much of a tolerance for jackpines. I do a little oil painting. In order to get jackpine green you have to mix in a lot of black, which is made from charred animal bones." She turned to him and smiled, but not with her eyes. "Charred animal bones. Imagine."

"What animals, do you suppose?"

"I've always supposed rabbits," she said. "You're not drink-ing your coffee."

"Not before Mass, thanks."

"Fasting?"

He nodded. "For a couple of hours."

"I thought fasting went out with fish on Friday."

"It did."

"And women wearing hats to church."

"I'm not all that strict about it," he said, wondering if he could have resisted if offered a Bloody Mary. Probably not.

"Imagine spending your life looking at jackpines," she said. "No wonder Indians don't have much pep."

He knew what she meant, having spent most of his forty-four years in the shadow of one jackpine or another. It was a contorted, sinewy tree. Its battle for life in poor soil was evident in every inch of its shapeless boughs and scabby bark. In good soil it refused to grow at all.

"The Basswood Reservation is eight hundred square miles, Frank, and do you know how many Indians are living on those eight hundred square miles?"

"Not very many."

"Eight hundred."

He nodded. He would have guessed four hundred. Their houses were hard to see in the trees.

"Isn't that the single loneliest fact you've ever heard in your life? A square mile of swamp and forest for every man, woman, and child in the tribe?"

He nodded again.

"And isn't it crazy, Frank, you and I and Tom being on a reservation?"

The sun was making him squint, making him warm. He took off his coat and moved his chair to the right, putting himself in her shadow. "I wouldn't say crazy. We're here with a mission, aren't we?"

"Mission?" She looked perplexed. "What's yours?"

"Christ's command to go forth, et cetera."

She nodded slowly. She said, "In our case it was a judge that said go forth. Tom got himself into trouble in Chicago. It was either prison or a year's service to minorities."

So Frank had heard. It was rumored in Linden Falls that the reservation doctor had come north trailing trouble. Mrs. Tatzig, St. Ann's housekeeper, had hinted at drugs. "I'm sorry," he said.

"Thanks." Libby smiled. "So are we. Drug-related, as they say."

Accustomed to sad confessions, Frank lowered his eyes in a discreet, priestly manner and waited to hear more. But she was silent.

"Dealing?" he asked, in case she needed an opening.

"Sort of. He wrote prescriptions for addicts. He's on probation and forbidden to write prescriptions for a year. He has to call Dr. Clayton in Linden Falls to write them." At the sound of steps on the staircase, she lowered her voice. "We were given our choice of locations—there's dozens of reservations needing doctors—but Verna more or less made the decision for us. A lot was made in therapy about her separation from her father. She kept insisting that she needed to come back here and live near him, and her therapist agreed."

"Vernon Jessen? He's still around?"

She nodded. "Still on the farm where I left him. Still there with his mother."

"Do you see him?"

"I saw him once."

"Verna sees him?"

"Once."

Tom Pearsall came into the kitchen coughing, his face stiff from sleep. He sat at the table and rubbed his eyes with the heel of his hands as Libby set coffee before him. His response to Frank's greeting was a sullen grunt.

"You know what I'm thinking, Tom?" Libby's words came out slurred—she was nervously biting her cheek. "Verna might talk to Frank."

Tom shook his head. "Nobody like that wants to talk to a priest."

"I mean maybe he could at least get a sense of her condition."

"If she won't listen to you or me, what the hell makes you think she'll listen to a priest?" Tom turned from his wife and squinted at Frank. "You want a drink?"

"No, thanks."

"Well, isn't that odd."

Libby spoke quickly, to cover the insult: "Verna's been living with an Indian, Frank."

"Yes, I gathered that."

"And a couple of blacks and a few whites and a hophead from Barcelona," said her husband.

"Tom, stop it!"

"Sorry." He didn't look sorry. He looked disgusted.

"I think we should arrange for you to meet her, Frank."

"She'd make hamburger out of Frank."

"Would you be willing?"

Frank said, "Sure."

"She'll grind him up and press him into a patty."

Frank stood up and put on his coat. "Why don't you two work this out, whatever it is."

"Hey, sit down." said Tom. "I thought we were going over your needs this morning." Now suddenly he was looking friendly.

"I've got a Mass at 8:30."

"Come back after. We'll go over your needs."

"Sorry, after Mass I meet with the parish council, then I'm due back in town for the late Mass there."

Tom's expression transformed itself into a pout. He dismissed Frank with a wave of his hand and a disapproving shake of his head.

Libby accompanied Frank to the front door. "You have to ignore him. Religion sets him off sometimes."

"Me too, sometimes. Thanks for the room."

"Your hands are cold." She was holding both of them. Hers were warm. "You'll come back and see us?"

"Well, sure." Why did this feel like the wrong answer?

"Next Saturday we'll be gone, and the two Saturdays after that. Please use the house."

"I'll see. I'll let you know."

"Don't let us know, just do it. The Pipes will have the key. We're going to Chicago for Christmas. My mother's there, in a home, and Tom has treatments on his back."

He sensed the kiss coming before she made the move. It was a hard smack, like the one last night in the bedroom.

16

Wearing purple for Advent, Frank celebrated Mass for fifty people in Our Lady's cold church. This number, according to parish records, was about twenty percent of the Catholics living on the reservation, but it was twice the number Monsignor Lawrence had led him to expect. "Converting the Indian was a glorious enterprise for Father Zell and the rest of the early missionaries," Monsignor Lawrence had said yesterday as Frank was heading out the door with his overnight bag, "but the Indian's faith is falling off, and why shouldn't it—the faith is falling off across the entire United States." Not that Monsignor Lawrence was upset by this. Having somehow aged to a state of absolute serenity, the old priest spoke of the falling off of the faith in the same gentle, resigned way he spoke of the falling snow and the rising price of fuel oil. "Go out there and say your Mass for the two dozen souls who want to hear it, Frank, and then say a prayer for the hundreds who stay away week after week. It won't be long before you can stay here and say a prayer for all of them without leaving the house—the bishop's told me Our Lady's days are numbered."

As Frank, at the altar, recited the opening prayers for the second Sunday of Advent, his breath was visible as frosty vapor.

He looked at each of his parishioners and thought he saw, written on their faces, the entire history of the rigors and wrongs suffered by the Ojibway nation. The eyes of the old drooped sadly, and their faces were deeply seamed. He read pain in their wrinkled brows and the tight way they held their mouths. At the gospel everyone, even the children, stood at stiff attention and appeared to concentrate on every phrase as though the Word of God were grim and sobering news. When he began his homily, the entire congregation, making slits of their eyes, might have been peering into a snow squall.

Frank knew some of them by name. He knew Carl Butcher, the man now in possession of the ladder Caesar Pipe had borrowed from the Upward brothers. Carl Butcher was slouched in a rear pew between two watchful women. The thin woman was his wife, the heavy one his daughter Bernadine. The three of them had lingered after Mass last week to sell Frank several fillets of walleyed pike from Sovereign Lake. Mrs. Butcher and Bernadine were employed at the Basswood Museum, a cement block tepee standing at the intersection of County Road 13 and U.S. 2 at the south edge of the reservation. Less a museum than a gift shop, the tepee was open for business only during the tourist season. Winters, Bernadine and her mother painted wooden duck decoys and wove baskets in their home while Carl Butcher netted fish out of the fifty-yard stretch of ice-free water where the Badbattle River flowed swiftly into Sovereign Lake.

There were several little boys and girls sitting in pews with their mothers or grandmothers. One of these women, Millie Upward, Frank recognized from his student days in Linden Falls High, where youngsters from the reservation used to be bused to school. (Now the Indians had their own school, K through 12, a red-brick windowless structure standing like a fortress on a hill overlooking the lake.) Millie Upward—now Millie La-Bonte, according to Libby—had been Frank's classmate until she dropped out at sixteen. Her dropping out was a relief to the faculty, for she was emotionally unstable and blew her stack every so often. More than once, coming to the end of her patience with math problems, Millie stood up and raged at the teacher. She had a phobia about darkness and closed rooms, and one day when the history teacher—a meek, ineffectual man named Englehart—showed a movie, she erupted in some kind of fit, and when he tried to remove her from the room, she clawed at his face and drew blood. To this day Frank remembered the movie, a tedious flicker of grainy battlefield scenes interspersed with inappropriate shots of Ike and Churchill and Omar Bradley looking jolly. He remembered, in contrast to the gray film, the bright blood running down Mr. Englehart's cheek when the lights went on. Today Millie LaBonte was the picture of decorum. Her pewmates were twin girls about six years old, a boy about eight and an older girl in her teens. Her husband, according to Caesar Pipe, worked as a welder in the coal fields of Wyoming. Did she remember Frank? Coming up to Communion last week, she had given him a little smile that seemed to mean that she did.

He made the homily short. He spoke of the healing power of the Sacraments, and as he concluded with the story of Father Zell dying on Sovereign Lake in the service of his Savior, he felt once again the same old priestly zeal that had carried him through the seminary to ordination. It warmed him. It actually made his spine tingle. He hadn't felt this sure of himself for a long time. For a few moments thereafter, crossing from the pulpit to the altar and there reciting the offertory prayers, he felt that Our Lady's Church in Basswood, dusty and cold and half-empty, was exactly where he belonged at this time in his life. He felt that by allying himself with this small band of Indians in this tiny clearing in the woods, he might somehow come to understand his destiny. Here something would happen, he didn't know what, to justify his life as a priest.

But Frank's experience with a murky spirit had taught him not to trust this ray of light. All summer and fall, he'd been fighting to keep his big leak from reopening, and sure enough, soon after today's Consecration he felt his optimism draining away, his ardor, his sense of himself as a worthy priest of God. By the *Our Father* he was struggling to keep his soul inflated—he pictured a punctured football—and by Communion time he was asking himself cynical questions about his desire to imitate Father Zell. Was it truly a longing to be of service to God and humankind? Couldn't it just as likely be a death wish?

After Communion Frank made two announcements. He reminded his flock that he was available in the sacristy on Saturday evenings, not only for confessions but also for get-acquainted visits. He then asked the members of the parish council to come into the sacristy and talk about church maintenance. "The Mass is ended, go in peace," he said.

"Where are the others?" he asked the Pipes, who stood in the sacristy watching him divest.

"What others?" Caesar Pipe was now wearing a tweed sportcoat over his Redi-mix T-shirt.

"The parish council."

"That's us. Joy and me."

Joy Pipe, a square-faced woman wearing her black hair in bangs and her black jacket zipped tight to her throat, said, "The way the council works, Father, you tell me and Caesar what to do and we do it."

Frank shut the closet on his vestments, glanced at the indoor thermometer—fifty-one—and slipped into his overcoat. "The rules call for a parish council of at least seven members."

"What rules?" asked Caesar.

"Diocesan rules."

The smile again. "Two's plenty."

His wife said, "There's special rules for Indians, Father."

"I see," said Frank dubiously. "I wasn't told."

"There's reservation rules," she explained, "and there's rules for the world at large."

"But, Mrs. Pipe," Frank argued, "in the eyes of the Church the world is one."

"The world was one before the white man came. Now the world is two."

"I see," he said again. And did. Since the white man had assigned the Indian a special place to live—special and worthless—why shouldn't special rules pertain?

"About the ladder," said Caesar. "I talked to Mel Green. He can't let it go for less than fifteen dollars."

"Buy it from Carl Butcher for ten."

"Butcher sold it to Green."

"The ladder he borrowed from you?"

"It's a good ladder."

Frank opened his billfold and gave him a ten and a five.

"And ten for the Upwards," said Caesar.

He handed him the remaining ten. Caesar took the money and handed it to his wife.

"I wanted to talk to the parish council about repairs and cleaning and redecorating."

Caesar stepped over to the oil burner and played with the dial. "Guess this is working okay."

"It is. Thanks for fixing it." Frank carried the water cruet to the door and emptied it into the snow. "We need a team of men and women to clean the church."

"Copper tubing's bent pretty bad. 'Fraid it might leak."

"Replace it then. We can't be risking another fire." Frank wiped out the cruet and placed it in the cupboard. He put the half bottle of wine into his overnight bag. "The church is dirty."

"Copper tubing's funny stuff, Father. Got to work with it warm, otherwise it cracks."

"Next time you're in town, pick some up—charge it to St. Ann's." He turned to Mrs. Pipe, who was straightening his sleeping bag on the cot. "You'd agree, wouldn't you, the church needs cleaning?"

She nodded. "Lots of mouse turds."

"Didn't Father DeSmet put together a cleaning team?"

"The way it works, Joy cleans on her own," Caesar explained. "No team."

"No team," his wife repeated, shaking out his pillow.

"Five dollars an hour," said Caesar.

"All right," Frank conceded, although his sense of parish-as-community was offended. From his childhood he recalled the appointed day each spring and fall when dozens of men and women, clergy and nuns included, went to work on St. Ann's, waxing floors, polishing pews, repairing kneeling pads, puttying windows, taking up old stair treads and laying down new, cleaning the furnace, washing and ironing the cassocks and altar linens, and sitting down, finally, to a festive potluck supper in the basement. Certain children also took part each year; they ran for tools, beat rugs, watered plants, scraped old paint, sorted music in the choir loft. Frank was the most industrious and obedient of these children. Whereas other children appeared at whim and disappeared when the fun gave out (and it gave out pretty fast if you were scraping paint), Frank hung around till the last crumb was swept up and the last light switched off, a deliriously happy member of this expanded family whose chatter and energy and warmth were so lacking in his own incomplete family. Motherless, he was mothered every cleaning day by all the women of St. Ann's.

The Pipes followed him out to his car. While Frank scraped the frost from his windshield, Caesar cleared the back window by pressing his hands flat to the glass.

"Aren't you going to ask him?" said Mrs. Pipe. She stood hunched over, her back to the cutting wind, her hands jammed into the pockets of her black jacket. She was nudging her husband with her elbow.

"Okay." Caesar stepped around the car. "Padre, the wife and I were wondering. We got this grandson in Minneapolis. Hell of a nice kid."

"Billy," said his wife.

"Bad place, Minneapolis. Trouble, you know. The kid lives there with his mother. We're thinking of asking him to come back up here and live with us."

"He likes to hunt and fish," said Mrs. Pipe.

"Yeah, he lived up here till he was ten or so, and if he wasn't out on the lake fishing, you'd find him clear to hell and gone back in the woods."

"Hunting," said his wife.

"But see, what's holding us back is there's no jobs or anything. His mother, she's all for the move, but what does a kid do once he gets here?" Caesar looked to his wife to help him explain. Which she did.

"He can't just sit on his ass."

"How old is he?" asked Frank.

"Fifteen, sixteen—how old is he, Joy?"

"Seventeen."

"Yeah, seventeen. Here, give me your keys and I'll start her up."

Frank took out his keys. "Is he in school?"

"Off and on, I guess. Is he in school, Joy?"

"Off and on."

Caesar got in and started Monsignor Lawrence's car, a red and white Oldsmobile—eight cylinders, enormous horsepower. *It'll do a hundred in nothing flat*, the monsignor was fond of telling visitors, while looking to Frank for verification. *It'll do sixty, that's all I can vouch for*, was Frank's reply. Caesar raced the engine—wind swept the pungent, blue-black exhaust this way and that—and then he got out and held the door open for Frank.

"Thanks, Caesar." He got in.

Mrs. Pipe sidled up to her husband and gave him the elbow again. "Ask him."

"Well, Padre, what we wondered was, could the boy work for you?"

Frank had seen this coming. "Doing what?" he asked.

"Odd jobs around the church, for something to do."

"For spending money," added his wife.

"I don't know. We can't paint and fix up till spring."

"Not just here. Maybe at the church in town."

"Well, I could check with the monsignor."

"'Preciate it," said the Indian, turning to his wife for confirmation that his duty was done. Apparently it was, for she was loping across the snow toward her house. Free of her, Caesar relaxed; the look of amusement returned to his face. "It would mean a lot to Joy."

"The boy's been in trouble, you say?"

"Nothing bad. Skipping school, and like that. Got in with the wrong crowd, you know how kids are." Caesar gripped the door, ready to shut Frank inside. "You'd probably like him." He chuckled. "He's got a religious streak."

"I'd have to talk to him, Caesar."

"That can be arranged."

"I've got to run, Caesar—I've got a Mass at eleven. Thanks for fixing the stove."

"I'll straighten the antenna, maybe you'll like it better."

"I doubt it."

Caesar laughed and slammed the door.

Backing into the street, Frank gave the Olds too much gas, skidded in an arc, and came to a stop with the back bumper against the front steps of the church and his eyes on the front porch of the Pearsalls' house. He saw movement in a window above the porch. It was Libby pulling the drapes aside and waving good-bye.

Raising his hand to her, he straightened the car and set off slowly south along 13. A few Mass goers lingered beside their cars, visiting. He came upon Millie LaBonte sitting at the wheel of an old bronze Chrysler. She was calling out the window to her eight-year-old boy, who was playing with a dog on the other side of the road. He saw the teenage girl in the front seat and the twin girls in back. Millie waved at Frank as he passed.

Thirteen curved along the shoreline for a mile, then it left the lake and snaked through the forest. The trees stood deep in a blanket of snow. Birch and aspen and jackpine—white and gray and dead green. Here and there a tributary road led to a clearing where a small house stood under its cloud of chimney smoke. Most of these clearings contained, at their edges, a few snow-covered cars and pickups with flat tires or no tires at all, rusting beaters bought from used-car dealers in Linden Falls and Berrington and driven only a few miles before they died.

Another mile and the lake was visible once again. He passed a rusty blue pickup standing at the side of the road with its door half open, and then he came to the Homestead, where he left 13 to follow the plowed trail down to the lake. He let the car idle its way down the slope, examining the facade of the tavern as he went by—log—and read the lighted beer signs in the windows—Bud, Miller, Pabst. Parked beside the Homestead was a red and black Bronco, a brand-new, boxy vehicle with a snow-plow attached to the front bumper. Behind the Homestead was a small yellow Datsun. It was old and dented and parked next to a trash pile.

Frank guided the Oldsmobile slowly over the bump at the base of the slope, then stepped on the gas and moved off across the lake at high speed.

"Lanny, Lanny! Let that dog alone!" called Millie LaBonte to her little boy, who was struggling to wrench a stick from the jaws of a playful short-haired mutt.

Turning to tell his mother to cool it, Lanny let go of the stick, and so did the dog. As Lanny bent to retrieve it, the dog snatched it up in its teeth. Lanny gripped it and pulled. The dog pulled harder and Lanny skidded off down the road.

"Lanny, you hear me?"

When honking failed to separate her son from the dog, Millie LaBonte put the car in gear, made a U-turn in front of the church, and laid on the horn two feet from his ear. Lanny, momentarily stunned, let go of the stick. So did the dog. Lanny and the dog picked it up together. The twins opened the back door and hopped out to join their brother and attach themselves to the dog, one hugging it around the neck, the other pulling on its tail. Millie LaBonte looked at her daughter Elaine in the seat beside her and said, "Make them stop that." Elaine, a slight, agile young woman of sixteen, hopped out, crossed the road and gripped Lanny by an arm and a leg, and dragged him back to the car. The dog and the two girls were dragged along with him. The dog she frightened off with a swat on the nose and the children she tossed into the backseat. She got in beside her mother and coughed. They drove off.

They had gone about half a mile south on 13 when Lanny said, "He likes me, he wants to come home with me." Millie looked in the mirror and saw the dog chasing the car. She floored it until the dog gave up. Then she slowed down, way down, and they moved through the forest scarcely faster than a walker's pace, all five of them scanning the underbrush for deer, scanning the road for deer signs.

They were approaching the turnoff to her brother's house when Millie LaBonte spotted a deer standing under a white pine not twenty feet from the road. She stepped on the brake and they sat for a minute or more, staring out the windows, all four children looking as hungry and reverential as their mother. They salivated, imagining fresh venison. The deer returned their gaze. It cocked its head and twitched an ear, listening to the engine idle.

"A doe," said Lanny.

"A big doe," whispered his mother. "A hundred and fifty pounds, maybe more."

"Where's the gun?" asked Lanny. "Didn't you bring the gun?"

"No," said Millie, "we'll get Roger's."

"Jesus, Ma, how come you never brought the gun?"

"Don't swear."

"But how come you never brought it? We always bring it."

"Your uncle Johnny came and took it yesterday. We'll get Roger's."

The deer turned and leaped over a fallen tree and bounded up a brushy hillside. They lost sight of it for a few seconds, then saw it come to a stop at the crest of the hill. They saw another deer, a buck, step out from behind a spruce and stand at the doe's side. Both animals kept their eyes on the car, watching it move slowly along the trail to Roger Upward's house.

Millie was vaguely alarmed the moment she got out of the car and smelled none of the tang of woodsmoke that ordinarily filled Roger's clearing. Roger's pickup was gone. Roger and Verna weren't the type to stay overnight at other people's houses. At least Roger wasn't. Verna herself spent lots of nights where she didn't belong. Millie looked up and saw the smokeless chimney. Then she saw the shattered door. "What's going on?" she asked aloud, approaching the house slowly, fearfully. Her little girls formed a line behind her, following stealthily. Elaine and Lanny remained standing beside the car, their eyes on the deer.

Millie LaBonte's brother lay on his back on the bed, the toes of his boots pointing straight up, one of his forearms standing up from the elbow, the thumb and two fingers of that hand curled as though gripping a baseball. His mouth was open and his eyes were closed.

Millie and the girls stopped a little distance from the bed and studied him.

Lanny came in. Not realizing that he was looking at death, he joked, "He looks dead."

One of the smaller girls stepped up and put her hand out to touch the man's beard, but held back when her twin, suspecting the awful answer, asked, "Is he asleep?"

Elaine came in and said, "The place is messier than usual," before she saw her uncle on the bed.

Millie moved closer. She stood over her brother a long time, gathering the courage to lay her hand on his forehead. It was stone cold. She felt dizzy.

Elaine turned away.

Millie LaBonte squatted down and collected her little ones in a brief, tight embrace; then she sent them out to the car and told Elaine to go and get Dr. Pearsall and Caesar Pipe and to use somebody's phone to call Father Healy.

She watched the car swerve out of the icy yard and move slowly off along the narrow trail between the trees. Then she started a fire in the stove. She stared at the flames for a few minutes, then turned and stared at her dead brother. She felt herself building up to a case of the shakes. Her tranquilizers were in her purse and her purse was in the car. She felt in the pockets of her jacket for loose pills and found two, a white one and a blue one. She put the white one in her mouth and went to the pail in the sink for water. The water was ice. She went outside and swallowed the pill with a mouthful of snow.

17

There was confusion in the front entryway as Tom searched the drawer of the hall stand for a lost glove, Libby asked the coughing girl for directions to her uncle's place, and three little children streamed indoors and tried going deeper into the house. Thus a minute or more passed before the girl gave her uncle a name. Roger Upward.

"Christ, where's Verna?" asked Tom, wheeling around and staring at the girl, his face gone suddenly white.

She shrugged. "We didn't see her." She was a slight, fine-featured girl wearing a coat too big for her and a pair of small silvery combs in her hair. Libby recognized her from an office visit months ago. She remembered her problem—bronchitis—but not her name.

"Elaine LaBonte," the girl said when asked. "My mother's waiting at Uncle Roger's house. There wasn't any fire in the stove, like nobody'd been there all night."

"Was he shot?" asked Tom.

She shrugged again. "He's lying on the bed, like he just laid down and froze to death."

"We'll follow you," Tom said, hurrying out the door with

one glove. He was across the porch and down the steps before he checked himself and came back. "Libby, aren't you coming?"

"I told you I'm through chasing after her." Libby was afraid to go, but she didn't say so. She felt her stomach cramping in the knot her daughter had been tying there for years. What if Verna were somehow responsible for the man's death? What if they found Verna dead, too?

"You'd better come," said her husband flatly. "She might need you."

She capitulated. Libby always lost her volition the moment someone told her she was needed. "All right," she murmured. She put on her hooded, fleece-lined jean jacket and sat down on the deacon's bench to pull on her boots. Tom knows best, she told herself. I'll try once again to convince her to come home. Not that she'll be convinced, but you can't give up talking sense to a fool, not even if she's twenty-six years old and bent on destroying herself. You have to keep hoping for the day when she'll stop acting crazy and fall back on all the sensible advice she's been ignoring since she was fourteen.

Elaine LaBonte said, "Mrs. Pearsall, my mother asked me to call the rectory in Linden Falls. She wants a priest to see him."

"I'll call for you." Libby stood up and allowed the twin girls to finish zipping her boots.

"She wants Father Healy, not the old one."

"Call the ambulance while you're at it," said Tom.

Libby opened the door to the waiting room—the nearest phone—and the children followed her in. While she summoned the ambulance from the Linden Falls Hospital, the boy named Lanny walked across the seats of a row of folding chairs, causing his two little sisters to laugh with admiration. Libby gave the dispatcher directions to Roger Upward's house, and then she called St. Ann's.

We won't find Verna at Roger Upward's house, thought Libby as she waited for her call to be answered at the rectory. At least not alive. It isn't Verna's style to hang around a cold shack with the fire out and a body on the bed. Verna has the instincts of a survivor. At this very moment she's probably in the warm bed of the next man she thinks will shield her from trouble but who will only compound her problems.

She got Monsignor Lawrence on the line, a man she'd never met but for whom she'd learned from Father DeSmet to have very little respect. He told her Father Healy was saying Mass and would be finished soon. "A death, you say? Shall I come myself?" The old man's voice was soft and melodious.

"No," Libby told him, "they're asking specifically for Father Healy."

"All right, my dear, I'll tell him the minute I see him. Where will he go?"

"Roger Upward's place. Tell him to turn right off 13 a mile north of the Homestead Tavern. He'll see the name 'Upward' on a mailbox."

"Ah, yes, I know the very road. I was the Basswood priest myself many years ago. Thirteen was a treacherous road in those years, mud holes up to your hubcaps. I suppose it's all paved over now."

"No, not paved. It's still gravel."

"Well, count your blessings, my dear. Gravel's better than mud."

"Thanks for conveying the message, Father."

"Glad to be of help. My condolences to the bereaved."

Elaine LaBonte, herding the little ones out of the waiting room, said, "It's awful, seeing him dead." Earlier, speaking in the hallway, the girl had seemed not the least distraught, but now Libby detected a crack in her voice. Or was it a cough coming on?

"You're sure he's dead?" Tom asked.

"He's dead," said the girl, beginning to weep. Her tears arrested the little ones on their way outside. They gazed up with astonishment at their sister's wet cheeks.

"Then I won't do you much good, will I?" said Tom. "You'll want the coroner."

"But won't you come?" she implored.

"Yes, I'll come. And Caesar Pipe better come, too."

"He already left. I told him first."

Libby followed the others outside. Tom went around the

corner of the house and unlocked the door of the garage he'd had built last summer for his BMW. Libby, waiting for him to back it out, watched Elaine LaBonte and one of the little girls cross the road and climb into the enormous old car parked in front of the church. Elaine had to sit forward on the edge of the seat in order to touch the pedals and see over the steering wheel. "Come on, you kids," she called to the other twin and Lanny, who remained at Libby's side.

The twin, pulling at Libby's skirt, said, "His hand's sticking up in the air."

"Whose hand?" Libby asked.

"Uncle Roger's."

"And his mouth is open," said Lanny.

"Come on, you kids," Elaine LaBonte called again, wiping her eyes.

Libby saw Mrs. Pipe watching from a window of her house trailer.

Meanwhile Frank finished reading the gospel ("There was a man named John sent from God. . . .") and looked out over the congregation that nearly filled St. Ann's, the beautiful brick and stained-glass church of his childhood. Although St. Ann's was twenty degrees warmer than Our Lady's, he still shivered a little from the chill he'd carried home from the reservation.

"This is the word of the Lord," he said, lifting the open book to his lips, then closing it, then clearing his throat a number of times, stalling, searching his mind for the homily he'd delivered from this altar at yesterday's five o'clock Mass. He'd intended to deliver that same message on the reservation this morning, but the Father Zell story had intruded and now he couldn't remember what it had replaced. Nor could he remember what he'd said in Basswood that had led up to the Father Zell story. He sensed, with a sinking heart, that he was having another homiletic blackout.

This had happened to Frank three times last summer. Facing his congregation in the Berrington cathedral, he'd stood in the pulpit dumb as a post. Terribly embarrassing. Worse than embarrassing—frightening. His first sign of the big leak. Following the second blackout, he'd gone, at Bishop Baker's urging, to see a therapist, a pretty woman who wore a long flowered skirt and sat in a windowless office and listened attentively to his life story. She gave him no advice but asked him a few interesting questions. "Have you ever wondered what your congregation might say to you, Father Healy, if they could address you from the pulpit?" ("Yes, constantly.") "Was your father a forceful man, did he tell people what to do?" ("No, hardly ever.") "Do you feel emasculated when you dress up in Mass vestments?" ("No.") "Did your mother resemble your vision of Mother Church?" ("?")

He described for this woman his helpless feeling the first time he was struck dumb. He'd intended to preach about the Sacraments, he told her, beginning with the old catechism definition—*outward signs instituted by Christ to give grace*—when he went absolutely blank. Which, said the therapist, was an outward sign instituted by his unconscious to give warning. Warning of what? he asked. Most likely faulty signals between his head and his heart, she told him. Whereupon an alarm clock sounded, signaling the end of his fifty minutes, and she said the fee would be only seventy-five dollars—clergy discount.

When on Labor Day weekend it happened for the third time, Frank could sense the alarm running through his cathedral audience. The first lapse had been easy to forgive and forget, the second lapse at least forgivable, but by summer's end the whole congregation was aware—as Frank himself was—of a gradual decline in his articulateness, a deadening of his wit. The church was filled with unease as he opened his mouth to speak and nothing came out. He didn't prolong the anxiety, his or theirs. He silently blessed them, went back to the altar, and took up the Mass where he'd left off.

The next day he considered phoning the therapist for another appointment, but decided against it because he had felt very uneasy throughout the first session, uneasy sitting in a small room discussing his state of mind with a woman. Would he have been more comfortable with a man? Yes, without a doubt. Sequestered all those years in the all-male society of Aquinas Academy,

Frank had lost touch with the female half of the human race. How did you talk to a woman without feeling defensive and flustered? How did you ignore the scents women wore and the spangles that hung from their ears? How did you know what they were thinking behind all the little tricks they played with their eyes?

Thus, instead of relying on the therapist in the flowered skirt to help him seal his big leak, Frank had called upon his intuitive sense (which his experience had taught him to trust, and which was advising him to back up to square one) and asked to be reassigned. And it had worked, more or less. The blackouts had not followed him to Linden Falls. Here, living in the same house with his beloved Adrian Lawrence and meeting familiar faces whenever he stepped out the door and reading familiar names in the weekly *Leader* and watching the sun's course through the sky from the same spot on earth he'd grown up on, he felt his psyche gradually repairing itself. There was a lot to be said for going home.

And so this morning's congregation, unaware of his homiletic blackouts or his big leak or his alienation from women or any other tribulation a priest might fall heir to in his middle forties, waited patiently for Frank to say something wise. Frank was waiting, too. Three times he opened his mouth to speak and shut it again, all the while letting his eyes rove over the faces before him. Near the baptismal font sat Sally Milowski, home from the city for the weekend with her big new husband and her small new baby. Sally was the daughter of Frank's classmate Sylvia Pofford. Sally's baby appeared remarkably strong and belligerent for its age, striking its mother with its fist and intermittently bawling something that sounded like "Worms!" Sylvia Pofford, now Sylvia Dunnock, was a senior partner in Linden Falls' only law office. Meeting Frank on the street these days, Sylvia was polite and chilly, dismissing him with a reference to how busy she was and a vague promise to host a party of old schoolmates someday. Apparently Sylvia didn't go to church anymore.

Think, Frank ordered himself as his eyes fell upon Danny Ash sitting under the Sacred Heart window with four of his half-dozen children. *Talk about Advent.* Danny Ash, Frank's closest friend in high school, had gone to work at the bank, and there, tutored by Frank's father, he had learned the lending business, and upon Martin C. Healy's death had risen to the position of chief loan officer. Danny and his wife Audrey (a former Loomis cheerleader) had been well into their thirties before they began producing children, and Frank thought there was something pathetic about a pair of harried, gray-haired, forty-four-year-old parents trying to cope with six kids between two and twelve. The Ash house was a mess indoors and out. The neighbors put up fences.

And now, after nearly a minute of silence, Frank sensed a ripple of unrest running through St. Ann's—the straightening of scarves and collars, the crossing of legs, an outbreak of little coughs and throat clearings. In desperation he went fishing for something, anything, that might be swimming around in his unconscious, and he blurted before he quite knew it:

"God is elusive."

His audience settled back, relieved, their throats clear, their scarves and collars adjusted, their hands resting easily on their laps. Frank's voice made them feel good. They liked having a hometown boy back home, particularly this hometown boy who made such a handsome priest, who last week had said something wise and witty, and whose career as a teacher had been so distinguished at the diocesan boarding school, an institution which very few of their boys had attended but many of their dollars had gone to support. They were ready now for Frank to lead them with his customary grace from his enigmatic opening— "God is elusive"—to some holy and heartwarming conclusion. Which he did, speaking of the faithful as pilgrims and of the lifelong process of searching out this elusive God, catching glimpses of Him in this life, and seeing Him plain in the next. His congregation was pleased by his brevity (eight minutes) and he himself was pleased with this latest triumph over depression. Another little skirmish won. Another setback for the lethargy, muteness, and malaise that had dogged him through the summer and fall. "God bless us," he said, signing off and returning to the table of sacrifice and the formula he could speak by rote.

"Maybe now she'll come to her senses," said Tom. "Maybe she'll go back to college."

Strapped into the BMW and following the old bronze Chrysler out of the village of Basswood—past the tarpaper house, past the two stucco houses, past the three new federally funded ranch-style houses, past the out-of-business general store with its 7-Up poster fading in its cracked front window—Libby ignored what Tom was saying about Verna and put her mind through its daily exercise of trying to see how their being in Basswood was good for Tom and good for Verna and good for herself and good for the Indians. Day after day she went through this routine, struggling to cheer herself up.

Obviously the move to Basswood hadn't done Verna any good. How simple-minded they had been, Libby and Tom, to think that Verna would reform in a rural setting. True, Verna hadn't been hospitalized since leaving Chicago, but for the past several weeks Libby felt sure that her daughter was building up to a manic episode of dangerous proportions. Mixing her meds with booze the way she did, it was only a matter of time. And now a dead man in her bed.

Libby knew the man, had seen him three times. One afternoon last summer she and Tom had stopped at the Homestead on their way back from Linden Falls, ostensibly to buy a twelve-pack but actually to check on Verna, who hung out there, and Verna had introduced him. "I want you to meet Roger, Mom. Roger, this is my mother and this is Tom." Roger was a quiet, good-looking man with sad eyes and a beard. Weren't Indians generally beardless? He must have been a mixed blood. He stood up from his barstool and said something brief and polite. Verna told them he worked sometimes as a carpenter with his brothers and sometimes as a fishing guide on his own, but right now he was between jobs. Libby said she was happy to meet him and shook his hand. Tom turned away from him without speaking.

The second time was the day last fall when Libby went to Roger's house looking for Verna. For many days before this

Verna had dropped out of sight, and now people were saying she was back. Late September, Libby recalled. A day of great beauty in the forest. Sunshine glinting down through yellowing aspens. Leaves spilling to earth. The lake glittering through the forest. She was driving Gene DeSmet's car because early that morning Tom had abruptly left the house with the BMW and not said where he was going. The crisp leaves were noisy underfoot as she walked up to the open door of the tiny house and called Verna's name. Roger came around the corner of the house carrying an armload of wood. He was polite. Verna was gone, he said. Where? she asked. He didn't know. When? This morning. Libby went home puzzled. In the evening Tom phoned from Chicago to say he was taking Verna to a week-long series of meetings with her therapist.

"Look at the way she fishtails," said Tom, his eyes on the car ahead. "She shouldn't be driving, she's only a child."

"It's an emergency," said Libby.

A light snowfall began to sift down through the bare trees as the two cars left 13 and moved slowly along the icy trail to Roger's house.

"You can bet she drives all the time—the law doesn't mean crap to Indians." Tom, too, was fishtailing, the souped-up BMW too impulsive for slippery roads. "She can't be more than twelve."

"I think she's fifteen. She came in with bronchitis, remember?"

"She did?"

"Two or three months ago."

"They all look alike."

Libby turned to her husband in disbelief—twelve years married and he could still astonish her with his cruel remarks. He was looking straight ahead, scowling out from under the bill of his flat tweed cap. His chin was buried in his tartan scarf. Strings of unwashed hair hung over his ears. Without taking his eyes off the car ahead, he asked, "Why are you looking at me like that?"

"You need a haircut."

"I don't have time."

He had idle hours every day. What he didn't have was the ambition to drive to the barber in Linden Falls.

"I'll cut it." Her customary offer. She liked cutting hair. As a girl she'd cut her father's.

Tom's customary refusal: "Hmmph."

She turned away, uncertain whether life on the reservation was doing Tom any good. For some reason he'd grown more solicitous of Verna, and that was a good thing. Verna had been fourteen when Libby married Tom, and for a long time he paid very little attention to her. Then, finishing his internship and settling into his comfortable practice at the Silver Park Clinic in Chicago, he began to devote time to Verna, grew fond of her. Then he disliked her. That pattern continued throughout Verna's late teens and early twenties. He'd go along for six months or more trying to help her overcome her volatile tendencies—getting her to the best therapists, researching the pharmacology of mental illness—and then overnight he'd grow resentful of the trouble she was causing and shut her out of his life.

Libby had never seen Tom look so shocked as just now, in the hallway, when he learned the dead man's name. "Where's Verna?" he'd blurted, the way Libby herself used to blurt it when she was told bad news about the crowd Verna hung around with in the city—a car accident, a drug bust. In those days Tom seldom displayed much concern. Cool, he was, and constantly reassuring, calming her down, explaining her fears away. ("Verna always lands on her feet, Libby. Smart people learn from their mistakes, and Verna is smart.")

Lands on her back is more like it, thought Libby, who after six months in the woods had finally trained herself no longer to be shocked by the number of men whose beds her daughter got into. Verna was simply incorrigible. It was a relief, finally, to accept the fact that your daughter was beyond help. For years Libby had agonized over Verna because she assumed she could be brought back from the perilous edge of self-destruction, but now she no longer deceived herself about that. Moving from the city to the woods, Verna hadn't missed a beat. For sleeping partners she'd switched from blacks to Indians—and occasionally the horrible man they called the Judge who ran the Homestead. For her daily high she'd switched from drugs to alcohol. If she were ever to be reclaimed, rehabilitated, redeemed, it would take more than her mother's solicitude. It would take a miracle.

"She must not be here," said Tom as they rounded the last bend and came upon Caesar Pipe's mustard yellow pickup parked in the clearing, but not Roger's. "Drive over to the Homestead and see if she's there while I go in and look at the body."

"No," said Libby.

"What do you mean, no?"

She didn't answer. She wasn't sure what she meant. She was experiencing a moment of unusual vision or insight, and it was filling her with a calamitous sense of futility. She was seeing herself from a distance, watching herself struggle year after year to straighten out her life and never get it right. Tears of self-pity pressed for release.

"Don't give me that line about not chasing after her anymore," said Tom in the high-handed tone that rankled her. "You'll be chasing after Verna all your life, and you know it."

She looked out her side window and said nothing. This was another change since their move to the woods—Tom's hectoring tone, his condescension. More and more often he behaved toward his wife like a wise father on the verge of losing patience with his slow-learning child. Gone was the chatty relationship Libby had loved in the early years of their marriage. Nowadays when she expressed an opinion opposed to his own, he responded with a reprimand or, worse, with a silent, long-suffering smirk. Often when she told him how she was feeling, he informed her that she only *thought* she was feeling that way. "You're actually depressed," he told her when she was angry. "You're actually frightened," he told her when she was depressed. Last night in bed, when she'd said that seeing Frank Healy had made her happy, he told her she was incapable of happiness. "You're not happy," he'd insisted. "You're afraid of being happy. You're drunk."

The door of the one-room house opened and Caesar Pipe filled the doorway. Advancing through the snow, which was falling more thickly now, Caesar spoke first to Elaine LaBonte: "Your ma says you kids stay in the car where it's warm," but the little ones were already piling out to play in the snow. He turned next to the Pearsalls: "You better have a look at his head."

A fire crackled in the stove, but the tiny house was not yet warm. Libby could see Millie LaBonte's breath as she described coming in and finding her brother on the bed. "Ever since he was a boy I knew something like this would happen," she said. "Don't ask me how I knew, I just knew." Millie LaBonte resembled her daughter in the eyes and in the tilt of her head, thought Libby, but her face was much broader than the girl's and her brow was checked with creases that made her look very old.

"Are you okay?" asked Libby, taking her hand.

The woman shrugged, withdrawing her hand. Her face was impassive. "I took my pill, if that's what you mean." Her medicine had been recommended by Tom's predecessors, and she had come to the Pearsalls when one of her prescriptions ran out. Tom and Libby had spent an hour studying her purseful of bottles and trying to convince her she was overmedicated.

Libby stole a look at the body on the bed and felt tears spring instantly to her eyes. She had no emotional reserve these days. She'd become inured to the sight of the human corpse years ago, practically before she'd finished nurse's training, but lately she'd been haunted by a childish abhorrence of death. She'd wept for days in October after watching a woman die as she was pulled from her mangled car at the intersection of 13 and U.S. 2. And one snowy evening in November when she and Tom guided the coroner to the Cashman house at the north edge of the reservation and there saw the body of the sixteen-year-old Cashman boy, who had taken his own life with a revolver, she'd lost control of herself. She'd had to leave the house and weep alone at the edge of the woods in the dark.

Caesar Pipe rolled the partially frozen body onto its side and held it there while Tom examined the back of the head, parting the dark hair with his fingers and feeling for bumps or a fracture. A little blood had congealed in the hair, and there was a rosy spot on the gray blanket where the head had lain—not the red of blood, it seemed to Libby, but the delicate pink of the wild roses that had bloomed along the reservation roads last summer.

Turning away, she met Millie LaBonte's eyes again—level, expressionless, unnerving.

What was the woman thinking? Was she speculating about Verna's part in this disaster? Did she suspect Verna of treachery? Of murder? Do *I* suspect her? No, I do not, thought Libby. Verna is incapable of killing. She's incapable of caring enough to kill.

"Hell of a conk on the head," pronounced Tom, easing the dead man onto his back.

"Guess I better ask a few questions," said Caesar Pipe, who as tribal leader had been deputized as the reservation arm of the Berrington County Sheriff's Department. He glanced from Libby to Tom and back to Libby. "Your daughter at your house?"

Tom said she wasn't.

"How long since you seen her?"

"Three weeks or so," said Tom. He turned to his wife and asked, "How long, Libby?"

"Thanksgiving."

"Thanksgiving," Tom repeated.

Libby looked out at the falling snow and recalled their disastrous Thanksgiving. They had invited Verna to come to dinner with Roger Upward at two o'clock. She showed up at nine in the evening to apologize and ask for money. Tom, drunk by then, blew up. Then he relented and gave her money. Verna, smiling serenely, said "Bye-bye" and drifted out the door. Waiting for her out in front was a man in a car Libby didn't recognize.

Caesar Pipe patted the dead man on the knee and went to the door. "Millie, stay here till I get back, will you? I'm going over to the Olivers' and telephone the sheriff."

Millie LaBonte gave him an absent, medicated nod.

Caesar turned to Libby. "If you see your daughter, will you tell her to look me up?"

"Yes," said Libby, now fully realizing with a touch of terror that Verna, innocent or not, was in grave trouble. She was notorious as Roger Upward's reckless, on-again, off-again companion. She'd be the first one investigated.

Caesar Pipe left. Millie LaBonte opened the stove and poked at the fire.

"You *called* the ambulance, didn't you?" Tom asked peevishly.

Libby nodded, understanding that Tom was feeling overlooked and undervalued, Caesar having left only the women with instructions. Again she felt tears welling up. She went to the window. Caesar Pipe was lifting the little boy out of the back of his pickup as the twin girls tried to climb in over the tailgate. Elaine LaBonte got out of her bronze car and corraled the three of them so that Caesar could drive away. Snow was falling so heavily now that Libby lost sight of the yellow truck before it rounded the bend in the road. She turned to Millie LaBonte and said she had called the priest. She said more, trying to draw her out, but the woman, apparently having said all she wanted to say, pulled up a chair and sat staring into the stove.

Libby slipped outside. She pulled her hood over her head and tied it under her chin. She joined Elaine LaBonte, who stood at the edge of the clearing watching her little brother and sisters steal off into the woods. Lanny was in the lead, carrying a long stick and pretending to stalk a deer. The twin girls took big steps, trying to plant their feet in his prints.

"You ought to have something on your head," said Libby.

"That's okay, I always go around with my head bare." Elaine wore a veil of snow on her black hair and across her shoulders.

"Bronchitis can lead to pneumonia. You have to be careful."

Elaine called to the children: "You kids, come back, you'll get lost."

One of the twins started back. Lanny forged ahead. The twin in the middle stopped, undecided.

"What did he die of?" asked Elaine.

"The medical examiner will have to tell us. Possibly a blow to the head."

"Shit."

"I'm sorry. Were you close to him?"

She shrugged, looking off. "Sort of." She paused. "Sort of not." Then with feeling: "It's just that there's so many bad people who could use a blow to the head, it isn't fair when somebody who isn't bad gets killed."

"I know. I met him. He seemed nice."

The girl turned probing eyes on Libby. No tears now. Seriousness. Maturity. Libby, looking into the girl's clear, coffee-colored eyes, lost control of herself. "Oooooh," she wailed, suddenly engulfed in tears, shuddering with despair, dropping her head on the girl's snowy shoulder and repeating, "Oh, oooooh."

"I don't mean Verna's one of the bad people. You didn't think I meant that, did you?"

"Noooo," Libby wailed.

"When I talk about bad people, I mean real assholes. I mean like Judge Bigelow. Verna was probably not good for Uncle Roger, but she's not really bad in her heart. I don't think Verna can help what she does, do you?"

"No," Libby agreed, sobbing. "She can't help what she does." She raised her head and turned in a circle, facing the forest on all sides, and knew she wasn't crying for Verna alone. She was crying for this little cluster of humanity awaiting the ambulance. She was crying for Roger Upward. She was crying for Elaine LaBonte and her cough and her slightness of body and her inability to control the monstrous car she drove. She was crying for Millie LaBonte and her nervous condition. She was crying for the three little children thigh-deep in the snow ("Caw, caw," they called, peering up at a crow flapping high in a tree), beautiful little children already reconciled at six and eight to becoming the next generation of this furtive, aimless band of Indians forever skulking around in the forest they'd been banished to. And most of all she was crying for herself, banished like the rest of them to this wilderness of lost hope in the forty-fourth year of her life.

The snowy silence was suddenly broken by the siren they'd been waiting to hear. First the red flashing lights emerged from the curtains of snow, and the ice white headlights, and then the garish orange and blue ambulance itself. It skidded to a stop at the door of the house. Two men got out wearing black leather jackets and white pants. The three children came running. A third man got out, a man in his late middle age—the coroner. Glancing at Libby, he seemed not to remember her from the night of the Cashman suicide. He wore a cashmere coat and a hat with a small green feather in the band. He followed the other two men into the house.

"Do you want to go in?" asked Libby.

"No," said the girl.

"Let's sit in the car, it's cold."

"No, I'm fine." The girl was pressing her tennis shoes into the snow and examining the prints.

"I'm sorry for falling apart," said Libby. "I'm such a baby these days."

The girl didn't respond, but edged away and returned, side-stepping, her eyes on her feet.

Libby got into the BMW and found Kleenex in her purse. Soon Caesar Pipe returned in his mustard pickup and was followed a few minutes later by a patrol car with the sheriff's insignia painted on the door. She remained in the car until the body was carried out of the house. She stood with the LaBontes, watching the stretcher slide into the ambulance. None of the family betrayed emotion. When the ambulance pulled away, the three little children chased after it and Elaine coughed and her mother turned to her and brushed the snow from her hair.

Tom stood at the BMW, jingling his keys. "Come on, Libby."

"What did the coroner say?"

"Autopsy. Come on, get in."

She didn't get in. She was stalling, hoping Frank would show up. "What can we do for you?" she asked the LaBontes.

Millie LaBonte looked from Libby to Tom. "Nothing," she said. Libby sensed that if it weren't for Tom, she'd have said more. Indian faces took on a particular expression when their eyes fell on Tom. A closed-up, wary look. Libby had seen it again and again when the two of them made house calls last summer. Often she'd gone alone, her goal being to survey the health needs of every household on the reservation, but now and then Tom went with her. She knew it had been boredom, not dedication, that stirred Tom out of the house, but whatever his motive, she was glad to have him at her side. He took the fear out of exploring nearly impassable roads far back in the forest and knocking on the doors of strangers. But he also made it harder to gain entrance. At best she was turned away from nearly half the houses with a wordless shake of the head, and with Tom along her rate of failure was three out of four. ("Hi, I'm Libby Pearsall and this is my husband Tom. We're your new medical staff, and we just want to say you're welcome at the clinic anytime, day or night, and we want to inquire if there are any medical problems in your household you'd like to tell us about.") Because it was summer and the houses were hot, no doors were shut in their faces, but the Indian face, Libby soon learned, had a door of its own. Was there some vast, uncrossable gulf between races, she wondered, or why when the Ojibway face shut down did she feel as she had felt when she first saw the ocean from a headland in Oregon—that limitless watery waste with nothing to focus on.

"I called Father Healy," Libby assured Millie LaBonte. "He should be here soon."

"We're all right." Millie LaBonte's tone told the Pearsalls they were dismissed.

"Please call us for help of any kind," said Libby, getting into the car.

Tom gunned the engine and kicked up a spray of snow as he sped away. Rounding each curve in the narrow road, Libby expected to meet Frank.

Tom said, "We are not well loved by Native Americans, Libby."

"I know," she said, going back in memory to her ill-fated health survey. She and Tom had tried everything. They had tried dressing up, after dressing down didn't work. They had tried breaking the ice with phone calls, but half the houses had no phones. One day they had gone around in Caesar Pipe's pickup, in case it was the BMW that repelled the Indians. They had hoped word of mouth would eventually go on ahead of them opening doors, but it was a rare face that flickered with recognition. "Let's leave the poor devils alone," Tom had groaned after being turned away three times in succession on his last day out. "But they need us," Libby insisted. To which Tom replied, "You've got that wrong, Libby. You need to think they need us."

Well, of course she needed to think that. If she didn't think she was needed here, she'd die of despair. It was the last place in the world she wanted to be. She'd never liked the rural north. As a girl of sixteen moving from Minneapolis to Linden Falls (population 2,002) with its stodgy little school (graduating class: 44) and its two blocks of businesses (one movie, no department store), she had felt lost and very lonely. Then, as now, the north seemed so empty, so excruciatingly cold in winter, so dull in summer, so hopelessly removed from whatever nourishment had fed her spirit in the city.

"Verna's probably at the Homestead," said Tom, turning south on 13. "Let's have a look."

18

"Ah, Frank my boy, I was just getting your lunch. You must be famished." The old monsignor shut the refrigerator with a swing of his rump and carried a plate of cold chicken across the vast kitchen to the breakfast nook.

"Famished is right," called Frank from the back entryway, wiping his feet on the scatter rug as carefully as if Mrs. Tatzig were watching. In an hour or so Mrs. Tatzig would return from Sunday brunch at her sister's and examine the kitchen floor for tracked-in dirt. He hung his black coat in the closet that had been the pantry when he was a boy and had the run of the house. The pastor then, as now, had been Adrian Lawrence, for this was the old man's second tour of duty in Linden Falls. Briskly rubbing his cold hands, Frank crossed the kitchen to the liquor cupboard.

Monsignor Lawrence set down the plate of chicken and looked at his watch. "A short Mass."

"The longer I'm a priest the less I can think of to preach about, Adrian." Frank drew out a bottle of rum.

"Preach on charity, my boy, that's what I always do."

"I know." Frank stirred his drink and regarded the small, baby-faced old man in red suspenders gazing at the busy bird-feeder outside the breakfast-nook window. Whatever strength

Monsignor Lawrence had drawn upon in his long term as chancellor of the diocese of Berrington, the job he'd held between his two appointments at St. Ann's, none of that strength was apparent in his childlike, vulnerable, wonder-filled eyes.

"I daresay I've made a reputation for myself, Frank, preaching on charity."

"You have for a fact, Adrian."

Putting his first drink of the day to his lips, Frank wondered if it was denseness or holy innocence that kept Monsignor Lawrence unaware of his true reputation. How could a man reach the age of seventy-one without knowing that his nickname was Loving Kindness (the phrase recurred in all his sermons) and that it was uttered with disdain by most of the priests of the diocese? During his years as chancellor, the monsignor had had no idea how bitterly he was scorned and despaired of by his troops. He was too soft to be the bishop's right-hand man, they said, and too humble to be in his right mind.

And how many times in recent weeks had Frank been offered the condolences of his colleagues? ("Sorry to hear about your new assignment, Frank. It'll be the pits living under the same roof with Loving Kindness.") Frank hadn't bothered explaining that the assignment had been made at his own request. Only Bishop Baker knew of Frank's desire to return to Linden Falls and live for a time with his boyhood idol. ("It's nice to know Loving Kindness has finally found the state he's ideally suited for, Frank—semiretirement. Too bad you end up being his lackey.") To this Frank had replied that both he and the monsignor were the lackeys of Mrs. Tatzig. No one but the bishop knew that Frank was making a last-ditch attempt to recover the equilibrium and priestly zeal he had lost when the Academy closed.

The old man, turning from the window, repeated, "Preach on charity, Frank my boy." He returned to the refrigerator and poked his head in, searching for something more to please his boy. He took out a jar of herring.

"No thanks, Adrian."

Next he tried Jell-O—orange, with a big scoop gone from the middle.

"No, chicken's plenty."

The old man moved to the breadbox, fumbled with the latch, and took out a sack of bread. "Bread?"

"Sure."

Frank sat down to his meal of chicken and rum, and as he waited for the monsignor to join him—he had gone back to the refrigerator for cottage cheese—he recalled the Sunday dinners of his adolescence when Eunice Pfeiffer would carry a platter of chicken or roast beef to the dining-room table the moment Frank and Father Lawrence came in from church, and no matter who the guests might be (trustees, visiting clergy, Frank's father) the chair at Adrian Lawrence's right hand was always reserved for Frank, who invariably served late Mass and sometimes early Mass as well. "Frank my boy" was a carryover from those years.

Then he brought to mind his countless Sunday dinners at the Academy. They were festive, particularly after Frank became headmaster and arranged for the preps to eat separately from the college students and seminarians and declared the second and fourth Sunday of every month visitors' day. The bright, high-ceilinged dining room was crowded with guests who lingered on into the afternoon visiting with the faculty about their boys. ("How are John's grades, Father, do you think he's premed material?" "Jerry's so tight-lipped at home, Betty and I can't believe you got him to try out for a play.") In good weather many of the visitors, before leaving for home, would fan out through the woods, following various trails along the Badbattle to the hidden little lake that was always too cold during the school year for swimming but pretty enough in any season—birch and pine crowding the shoreline—for picture taking.

Frank had foreseen the end. For several years he'd watched enrollment drop and expenses rise. Bishop Baker, soon after he took over from Bishop Swayles, had warned that Aquinas College and Academy must either close or force the diocese into bankruptcy. Thus Frank and his colleagues had overseen, efficiently and stoically, every stage of its demise, and at the very end, when the chapel was dismantled, the registrar's files hauled off to storage, and the keys turned over to the three men in business suits representing Berrington Vocational Institute (the

Aquinas valley was to become its new campus), Frank went into an emotional tailspin.

It was a vocational crisis. He went to his bishop for advice, suspecting—fearing—that while happily devoting himself to the formation of young minds he'd misplaced his desire to do the things priests were meant to do. "What things?" the bishop wanted to know. "Things like bringing hope to the hopeless," was Frank's reply. "Consolation to the sad. Love to the unloved."

Bishop Baker insisted that Frank had been doing those things at the Academy all along, but Frank said, "No, the Academy was a place apart from real life. The boys were mostly gifted. They were mostly from well-to-do families. They were gone out of our hands long before they had to face the harsher realities of life, long before they had any real need of a priest. I've worked there all these years without ever being in touch with real life myself." The bishop remained unconvinced, and Frank gave up trying to explain, except to add, "In all this time I haven't once felt that I've moved anyone's soul closer to God, my own included."

This meeting had taken place in the bishop's sunny parlor last spring. Although Bishop Baker had been two years in office by this time, he and Frank were not well acquainted. Frank had resisted confiding in the man, and for good reason: until the Academy closed he didn't know he had anything to confide. And for a poor reason: after serving Bishop Swayles all those years— a holy and hidebound old tyrant—he found it disconcerting to be working for a bishop no older than himself who played the trumpet in a jazz band.

When at this meeting the bishop inquired about his background, Frank had described himself at the age of eleven—a motherless boy feeling hopeless and sad and unloved until he was comforted and restored to spiritual health by the pastor and housekeeper and nuns of St. Ann's. They had guided him through his adolescence, and at seventeen, deciding it was his turn, his calling, to come to the aid of others, he had gone from high school straight into Aquinas Seminary. (Why, he wondered after leaving the bishop, had he said nothing about his mother's deathbed wish?) Eight years later he went straight from ordination back into the high-school classroom—hardly a typical move for a priest, but old Bishop Swayles, a shrewd judge of his troops, knew that Frank was a born teacher even before Frank knew it, and Frank assumed that he could carry out his pastoral mission at Aquinas Academy as well as in a parish. For seventeen years he assumed that. Then, with the dissolution of the school, he looked back on his career, prepared to see himself bringing up the end of a long line of distinguished teacher-priests and discovered that he had scarcely been a priest at all.

Bishop Baker urged him not to be so hard on himself. "I happen to know you were the quintessential teacher, and that's a noble thing to be." No, Frank objected, he was not so much the quintessential teacher as the quintessential baseball coach.

The bishop concluded the interview by asking Frank to join the cathedral staff in Berrington, where he would be one of two associate pastors and learn how parishes worked. Frank complied, and endured five months of great unhappiness before asking to be transferred to his old home parish to assist his friend and mentor, Adrian Lawrence, whom the bishop a year earlier had replaced in the chancery. Call it intuition or the voice of God, Frank felt certain that if he was to recover his balance and cross the divide between the classroom and parish work, he'd never do it in the bishop's rather opulent house or at the high altar of the magnificent cathedral; he'd have to do it in the co-parishes of Linden Falls and Basswood, where he'd first heard the call to the priesthood. Coincidentally—luckily—word had been going around that Father DeSmet was suffocating up there in the northern end of the diocese and yearning to be replaced.

"Frank, do you read Shelley?" Monsignor Lawrence fit himself stiffly into the breakfast nook opposite Frank. Along with a plastic container of cottage cheese, he'd brought a small red book to the table.

"Years ago," replied Frank.

Thank God for Shelley, he thought. Father DeSmet claimed to have been read to—endlessly—from the early fathers. ("With Loving Kindness it's St. Jerome for breakfast and St. Augustine for lunch, Frank. For dinner it's either St. Gregory the Great or

Walter Cronkite, depending what time Mrs. Tatzig dishes it up.")

The old man opened the book, cleared his throat, and adjusted his glasses as though to begin; but then he raised his eyes and said, "Mrs. Graham's having an awful time with her kidneys." Health as preface.

"Poor woman," said Frank.

"It's related to her heart."

Mrs. Graham was one of the lonely shut-ins Monsignor Lawrence visited every Sunday. When Frank arrived three weeks ago and the monsignor took him around to reintroduce him, he'd been shocked to find these five invalids and near invalids shrunken to husks of the people he remembered from his boyhood. He found Mrs. Graham, widow of the town's first undertaker, closed up in an overheated house that smelled of illness and onions. She'd grown bitter. Listening to her whine about her neglectful children and the high price of medicine and her nosy neighbors and her incompetent doctor, Frank had gone back in memory to his mother's funeral and recalled how solicitous Mrs. Graham had been, how gracious. She had straightened his hair and kissed him on the cheek as he started down the aisle behind the coffin. "Be a little man," she had whispered.

The monsignor examined the page of poetry, cleared his throat again, then stalled again: "Frank, what can I get you for Christmas?"

"Well, let's see, I have enough handkerchiefs." A request for rum would have been vetoed by Mrs. Tatzig, who did the monsignor's shopping. Father DeSmet claimed to have acquired twelve handkerchiefs during his eleven months here—four each on his birthday, Christmas, and Easter. "I could use socks." Black surely. Mrs. Tatzig would see to that.

The old man nodded and turned to the window. Frowning at the half-dozen sparrows at the feeder, he seemed to be working up to something difficult. Finally he blurted, "Shelley's good with love, you know."

"Yes, I remember."

"Not as good as Shakespeare maybe, but good."

"Go ahead, Adrian, read."

Out came a quatrain in one quavering breath: "'Oh, lift me from the grass! I die! I faint! I fail! Let thy love in kisses rain on my lips and eyelids pale.'"

This caught Frank in midbite. He put down his drumstick, amazed.

Timidly the monsignor looked up, saw Frank's surprise, and quickly closed the book. He wore an expression of shame.

"That's not so hot, Adrian. Shelley must have done better than that."

"Yes, he must have." The old man squeezed his eyes shut and gritted his teeth.

"Adrian, what is it?"

A long silence. All but one of the sparrows flew away.

"We'll need fuel oil one of these days."

"Adrian, what is it?"

"I checked the gauge. It's below the quarter mark."

Frank, wiping his fingers on his napkin, sat back and waited.

"Frank, I'm having lewd thoughts lately." The monsignor, his eye on the remaining sparrow, spoke softly. "Sometimes it happens to old men, you know. There's a woman appears and disappears in my head saying intimate things. First time in years. Fifty years. It's all so vivid." He stole a look at Frank. "What's that smile mean? Are you laughing at me? My confessor says pray and the thoughts will pass. Dr. Clayton says don't pray, just enjoy them."

"I'm with the doctor."

"Frank, be serious, think what could happen."

"What could happen?"

"I'm playing with fire."

"No, you're not."

"I could go to hell."

"No, you couldn't."

A long pause. Frank picked up the drumstick. The sparrow continued its meal at the feeder.

"It's the same woman each time, Frank. I don't see her so much as hear her. She sounds like Jo Stafford."

Frank chuckled.

"Quite a voice, Jo Stafford's. Remember 'Tree in the Meadow,' Frank?"

Frank couldn't stop chuckling at this facet of the man he'd never known—the pop charts.

"Please, Frank, don't laugh." But the monsignor was chuckling, too, the stress of confession behind him.

Frank quit laughing but continued to beam at the old man, marveling at his childlike expression. Childlike his faith as well. And childlike his lack of self-understanding. To this day Adrian assumed he'd been a fine chancellor, while even Frank, one of his few loyalists, had to admit that his term in office had been undistinguished if not an outright failure. Unfortunately Bishop Swayles had given him credit for shrewdness he didn't possess and consulted him about pastoral assignments, with the result that dozens of priests were posted to parishes they were unsuited for, farm boys to cities and city boys to villages. Pastors were mismatched with assistants, setting off smoldering grudges in several rectories. Adrian, solicitous to a fault, deferred to the demands of certain self-seeking clergy, spoiling them nearly to the point of uselessness, and on top of everything else his chancery staff mishandled money. Frank agreed with his colleagues that all of this was regretful and true, but he stopped short of believing the man a boob. What Frank understood, and what so many of his colleagues were blind to, was that while Adrian Lawrence was never the businessman or politician or warlord that people expected their chancellor to be, he was, at least, a saint.

"'Tree in the Meadow,'" said Frank. "Wasn't that Margaret Whiting?"

The monsignor cocked his head. "Maybe it was."

The phone rang.

"I wonder what's become of Jo Stafford," said Frank, leaving the breakfast nook.

"Don't you still hear her?"

"No. Haven't for ages."

The old man gazed out the window at the bird. "Well, I do."

———

Libby stood at the pay phone, her back to the men at the bar and the pool table, her hand over her ear, shutting out the thud and twang of the jukebox.

"St. Ann's."

"Frank?"

"Yes."

"This is Libby."

"Hi."

"Did you get my message?"

"No."

"There was a man found dead out here this morning. I talked to the monsignor."

"Oh, dear, he forgets."

"It's Millie LaBonte's brother. She wanted you to come."

"I'll be right out."

"Well, the body's gone now. They took it to town for an autopsy."

"But I should see Millie."

Libby had hoped for this. "I'll show you the way."

"Give me twenty minutes."

"I'm at the Homestead."

"I wondered. I hear Tom T. Hall."

"We're here looking for Verna. It was the man she'd been living with." She paused. "And now it looks like she's living with Judge Bigelow."

"Who's that?"

"The proprietor of the Homestead." She turned from the wall and described him to Frank, her hand cupped over her mouth and the mouthpiece. "He's fat and repulsive. At the moment he's leering at me while serving Tom his beer. He's giving me this big, stupid smile. Have you ever been in here, Frank?"

"No, is it anything like the old Loomis Ballroom?"

"Smaller, but on that order. Dismal."

She looked around the dark, cavernous room. She looked at the three small windows across the front wall. Bud, Miller, Pabst—the tubes of garish neon seemed to obstruct what little light might have spilled in from the snow-laden sky. It was this lack of light in particular that took her back to the dances of her youth at the Loomis Ballroom—the sensation of being lost in murk the moment she stepped through the door, of being enclosed in a shadowy netherworld where she could curse or kiss or chugalug beer and nobody cared. And this place even smelled like the Loomis Ballroom—the same searing odors of stale smoke, spilled beer, and toilet disinfectant.

"I remember dancing with you, Frank. I think it was the first time you danced."

"And the last," he said.

"You're kidding."

"Swear to God, the only dance of my life."

"Frank! You priests."

"I'm just thankful it was with you."

She did not reply to this, but drank it in slowly, like wine, allowing it to warm her. Last night and this morning she'd waited for Frank to betray some vestige of the love he once felt for her, a word or embrace or even a lingering look to indicate he'd not forgotten their bond as teenagers, but he'd shown her nothing, not even when she kissed him. He'd remained so guarded, so relentlessly clerical. Or, worse, so indifferent. *I'm just thankful it was with you.* At last a tender word.

"Libby? Are you still on the line?"

"Yes. I'm trying to outstare Judge Bigelow. He has the most repellent face I've ever seen. Come and look at it."

"I'm on my way."

"Be careful, it's snowing."

She replaced the receiver and returned to her stool at the bar.

"I talked to Frank."

Tom, sitting on her right, showed no sign of interest, did not take his sleepy eyes from the TV on a shelf over the cash register. Football. The three men on stools beyond Tom were watching, too, with the same vacant stares. A one-sided game apparently, for the fans on the screen looked scarcely more interested than the Homestead audience.

She lifted her glass carefully so as not to wet her sleeve on the sloppy bar. Judge Bigelow's style of serving tap beer was to slam down the glass and watch the foam spill over the brim.

"Your money's no good here," said the Judge, drawing Tom

another beer. "These are on the house while you wait." He picked up Tom's five-dollar bill, reached across the bar, and stuffed it into the collar of Tom's down vest. "She'll be a while yet, if I know Verna." He fixed a smile on his face. "She never likes anybody to see her not made up." He turned the smile on Libby, expanded it a little, and said, "You know that better than anybody, being her mother."

Libby's stomach turned over at the thought of her daughter attaching herself to this large, fleshy man well over fifty whose hair was died jet black and whose small hands were sickly white. Hearing him speak, you suspected that the gravelly voice was not his own, but that of somebody tough he was trying to imitate. Libby had heard from Joy Pipe and others that Judge Bigelow made lots of money getting Indians drunk and keeping them that way. According to rumor, he also sold drugs and pot. How had Elaine LaBonte put it? He was bad in the heart?

Libby knew that this wasn't Verna's first time with the Judge. Between her other alliances of longer duration, it was usually here to the Homestead that Verna retreated. Free room and board and booze—the Judge's offer was open to Verna in all seasons. Was her companionship worth all that? Between her tantrums and her sprees and her periods of despondency, were there times when Verna could be responsive and lovable?

Libby was startled by a voice on her left: "Hi, Mrs. Pearsall, my name is Toad Majerus."

She turned to see a tiny man climbing onto the stool beside her. He had a meaty, underslung jaw and the bug eyes of a glandular malfunction. His severely bowed legs were as short as a six-year-old's; sitting, he could barely touch his boots to the top rung of his barstool. He smiled broadly at Libby, revealing toothless gums. "Toad isn't my real name. My real name is Myron, but it's been years since anybody called me Myron, and it's a name I never cared for. I'm the cop here at the Homestead." He uttered a high-pitched laugh. "Years ago when the Judge hired me, he started calling me Toad and the name stuck. I worked in a greenhouse and I worked for a plumber and I been with a carnival, but this is the first job I ever had where I felt like I

belonged. You never know how good it feels to belong someplace unless you spend most of your life belonging no place."

"I think I know what you mean," said Libby.

She had seen this tiny man twice before, on previous visits
to the Homestead. The first time he had been standing waist-
high to a group of men at the pool table. The other time he had
waddled across the dance floor carrying a pail and a mop.

"I just happened to come back here at the right time. I was
getting drunk sitting on this very same stool after my ma's funeral, and the Judge happened to be looking for a handyman and
I took the job and been at it ever since. It doesn't hurt business
to have a good-natured midget around, I know that as well as
the Judge. People like having a midget to look at now and then,
same as they like to look at elephants or skyscrapers or newborn
babies or anything else that's not normal size. My ma always
prayed I wouldn't make my living as a freak, and I think me
going with the carnival was what killed her, but with this job
it's not only my size that counts, it's my ability to keep the place
clean and orderly. The Judge is a stickler for cleanness and or-
derliness, ain't I right, Judge?" His thick face broke out in an
expression of supreme glee. He laughed his screechy laugh again.

"Don't bother the lady," growled the Judge. "Go out and
shovel the front step."

Tom leaned forward and cast a dispirited eye around his wife
at the midget, who beamed at him and said, "Hi, Doc."

"You ever had anybody test you for thyroid problems?"
Tom asked.

"Nope."

Tom drained his glass and slid it toward the Judge for a refill.
He retrieved the wet five from inside his down vest and laid it
on the bar again, turning his attention back to the game.

Toad Majerus said, "That hubby of yours is a swell doctor,
let me tell you. I've heard people say so."

"Thank you," said Libby.

Tom burped.

"And you're a swell nurse. I've heard that, too."

She doubted the truth of this, but thanked him again.

"Hey, Doc, you ever see a rash like this?" Tugging on the collar of his sweatshirt, Toad Majerus dropped down off his stool and went around to the other side of Tom, who bent to examine him. Libby caught sight of a small piece of paper as it passed from the midget's hand to Tom's. Something to do with drugs, she supposed, turning away. Whatever Tom was up to with drugs—and he was doubtless up to something—she didn't want to know about it.

"Wash it," said Tom, dismissing the midget. "You itch because you're dirty."

"It's too bad my ma didn't live to see me in this job," said the midget, returning to the stool on Libby's left. "I left home at fifteen and never saw her again, except laid out in the funeral home, but we kept in touch by mail. Birthdays I used to get a card from her, and under the verse she wrote the same thing every year: 'Another birthday, my how time flies, promise you won't be a freak.' I still got all seventeen or eighteen cards in my trunk, all with them words on. I could show you."

"No thanks," said Libby absently, her eyes on the door at the back of the room, behind which Verna was supposedly preparing for her entrance. Judge Bigelow had gone to that door to summon her when he saw Libby and Tom come in. "You got company," she'd heard the Judge call. "Your mother and the doctor." He'd returned to the bar and told them Verna was changing her clothes and would be right out. That was twenty minutes ago.

"It's okay, I understand," said the midget. "Birthday cards don't mean much if it's not your birthday."

She nodded, wondering if Verna had left by another door. She'd been evading her mother for years.

"And if they're not your cards," he added.

Libby nodded again. Neither she nor Tom had said a word to the Judge about Roger Upward's death. Caesar Pipe was likely to turn up any minute and break the news, but so far nobody here had heard. So if Verna was giving them the slip, thought

Libby, it would not be guilt or fear concerning Roger that drove her away. It would no doubt be her loathing for her mother.

"I'm cleanup man along with being cop, Mrs. Pearsall. In the mornings I sweep out the place and haul the garbage to the dump—the Judge put hand controls on his Bronco because my feet don't reach the pedals—and in the afternoons I sort beer bottles and check the rat traps and more or less watch over the place, and then in the evenings I try to keep the crowd under control by kicking out fighters and steering passing-out drunks into the booths at the back of the room, but that part of my job's mostly all in fun. I mean look at me, I'm too small to be a cop. When drinkers are good-natured, they pat me on the head and laugh and buy me a beer, and when they're drunk, they sometimes take me out behind and throw me in the lake. If it's summer, that is. It's all in fun. It's a fun-loving crowd."

Or it might be her loathing for Tom, thought Libby. Verna's hostility toward her stepfather was intermittent. There had been periods, particularly in her teens, when Verna had been Tom's best pal, running errands for him, mixing his drinks, laughing hysterically at his little jokes. There had been other times when she backed off, when his requests for a drink or an errand were met with a sulky sort of refusal and his jokes fell flat and Verna couldn't seem to look him in the eye. At times like that Tom would seem to be studying Verna in a way that made Libby nervous. Libby had once seen, in a zoo, a mouse in a tiger's cell. It was a concrete cell from which the mouse could find no escape, though it moved busily about, looking for one. In the opposite corner the tiger, having just eaten its meal of raw, red meat, reclined with its head on its front paws, watching the mouse and waiting. Waiting for what? For hunger to return? For the mouse to wear out and lie still? In the tiger's eyes Libby saw patience, a touch of boredom, and most striking of all, mastery. The tiger's eyes were like Tom's when he fixed them on Verna.

And then there was rage, of course. It was at mealtime that Verna typically blew up at Tom, and the blowup almost always took Libby by surprise. One minute there was peace and the next there was war. This was in contrast to the storms Verna un-leashed on her mother—dark clouds and hot winds building up for days, followed by a sprinkling of irritations and tears and culminating in a long, steady rain of curses and threats and moans of despair. But an attack on Tom could be as unexpected as a crack of thunder on a sunny afternoon. ("Verna, would you pass the butter?" "Fuck you, okay?")

Something happened on TV to make the four watchers at the bar perk up, and Judge Bigelow turned around to look.

"Ain't the Judge some specimen?" said Toad. "Biggest man around. Weighs two-thirty, two-forty. He ain't a real judge, but he used to be, before they changed the court system. Justice of the peace. Some states still got them, but there ain't a single justice of the peace left in Minnesota. He treats me right. I get room and board and beer and a little spending money. He's hard-boiled, I'm not denying it, but you won't hear me say a word against him. The Judge is my shepherd, I shall not want." He tittered and looked at Libby to see if she caught the allusion. She smiled and he nodded happily. "When the doctor in Linden Falls thought I had skin cancer and done some cutting—see these scars on my face?—the Judge picked up the tab. When I had my teeth out, he picked up the tab for that, too, and he says if the day ever comes when he doesn't get a kick out of looking at my toothless face, he'll buy me a set of plates. Ain't that right, Judge?"

Bigelow turned from the TV and ordered, "Get off your dead ass and quit bothering the lady."

"Ain't I right, Judge—you might buy me a set of teeth some-day?"

"I said go out and shovel."

Toad dropped to the floor, saying, "I'll be right back, Mrs. Pearsall," and hurried across the room to the door, where he met Frank coming in.

"Hey"—the midget laughed—"we can start the services, the father is here. Hi, Father, I'm Toad Majerus."

"Happy to know you." Frank bent to the little man and gripped his stunted fingers. "I'm Frank Healy."

"Yeah, I know, the Judge pointed you out this morning, going by in that two-tone Olds."

"Sideways, no doubt. It's no good on ice."

"You're a swell priest, you know that? Word's going around that you're a swell priest."

"Thanks. It's news to me."

"I had religion for a while when I was in Missouri."

"Rubbed off, did it?"

"Yup, it rubbed off coming up through Iowa." Laughing, Toad pulled a stocking cap from his back pocket and drew it down over his ears; then he picked up the shovel standing beside the door and went outside.

Frank stepped over to Libby's stool, took her hand, and said "Hi."

"Could we wait here a little bit?" she asked. "I'd like you to meet Verna."

"Sure," he said. "Hi, Tom."

The doctor held up his beer glass in salute.

Libby suggested they sit at a table.

Tom, carrying his glass and muttering something about stupid referees, accompanied Libby and Frank to the farthest table from the jukebox and the pool players. "You're too late," he said, sitting down. "The dead man's gone."

"I'm going to drop in on the family," said Frank.

"Good luck—they're maniacs."

The jukebox went silent. "Oh, to hear Lucky Mudget's musicians again, Libby. 'These Foolish Things,' remember?" She nodded, smiling, feeling her spirits rise. Frank did that to her. His smile shone in his eyes. It lit up her soul, lit up the Homestead, the gray afternoon.

"Lucky Mudget and His Orchestra," Frank explained to Tom. "They played 'These Foolish Things,' while your wife taught me to dance." He tipped his head slightly to the left as he spoke, the way she remembered from his boyhood when he was caught up in telling a story or concentrating on classroom instruction. His face had changed a great deal since the day she drove away and left him at the door of the seminary. His chin had grown fleshy, his mouth lippier, fuller, less animated as he spoke. His hair had turned gray at the temples. There was a little dent or hollow in each cheek, under the eye. But the voice was the voice of years ago—low, deliberate, furry. And the eyes of course. The gentle blue eyes.

Tom covered his mouth and burped.

Judge Bigelow shouted from behind the bar, "Hey, what'll it be, fella—you in the black coat." The three men on stools turned to hear the answer. So did the pool players.

"Rum and Coke," said Frank.

The Judge mixed it and slid it down the bar. "You'll have to come and get it, my waitress is off duty."

Frank stepped up to the bar, recalling suddenly that he had no money. "How much?"

"A dollar." The Judge was leaning forward, his hands spread on the lid of the beer cooler behind the bar, supporting his great weight on all fours.

Frank showed him his empty billfold. "Can I pay you next time? I spent my last dollar on a ladder."

"Put it on my tab," called Tom.

The Judge flashed a smile at the Pearsalls.

Frank returned to the table. The Judge lumbered off into shadows beyond the dance floor and entered his private quarters.

Tom looked darkly at Frank. "Roger Upward was probably murdered."

"Really?" Frank looked at Libby.

"Who knows?" she said, shrugging and looking pained.

The front door opened and Caesar Pipe came in, followed by the midget with the shovel on his shoulder. Caesar, removing his gloves and stuffing them into the baggy pockets of his sportcoat, stopped to greet the three men on stools and consult with them about the football game; then he came over to the table, pulled up a fourth chair, and sat down. The midget stood beside him, snow melting off his shovel and dripping down the back of his sweatshirt.

"Your daughter here?" asked Caesar.

Libby nodded. "We're waiting for her to come out."

"You looking for Verna?" asked Toad Majerus. "Why didn't you say you were looking for Verna?"

Everyone turned to him.

"I saw Verna take off in the Judge's car."

Libby slumped in her chair and sighed, "Well . . . hell." She turned to Frank. "Let's go."

Caesar looked from Tom to Libby. "Does the Judge know about Roger?"

"We didn't tell him," she said.

"What about Roger?" asked the midget.

"Nothing," said Caesar.

Judge Bigelow came out from his private quarters and said, "Verna's gone." He fit himself between Libby and Tom, leaning heavily on the table. "Took my Datsun. Maybe she drove over to Roger's place to get her things. She's always talking about breaking up with Roger. Maybe she's finally doing it."

"I bet she's finally doing it," echoed the midget. "She's figured out Roger's not her type, and she's finally doing it."

"She shouldn't have taken the Datsun," said the Judge. "The Bronco goes better in snow."

"Roger's a real dull guy," the midget explained to Frank.

"You can't blame her," the Judge told Libby. "Roger's never going anywhere in life. A girl like Verna needs somebody who's going somewhere."

"Some guys when they get drunk, they come to life," the midget continued. "They rip and roar and laugh and joke, but Roger gets drunk and just clams up."

The Judge leaned close to Libby's face, smiling his repellent smile. "You haven't got a worry in the world, Mrs. Pearsall. Verna's got a home here with me as long as she wants it."

"A real serious guy," said the midget. "I can't see where booze does Roger the least bit of good."

The Judge, elaborating on his pledge to provide a home for her daughter, pulled a chair up beside Libby and lowered his weight onto it. He told her that Verna was one girl in a million, that never in all his years at the Homestead had he known a girl so classy. "Classy's the word for your daughter, Mrs. Pearsall, and smart as a whip. So what if she gets a little high-strung now and then? I can handle her. Tell me, Mrs. Pearsall, honest to God, who else can handle Verna the way I can?"

Tom said, "I can."

Maybe, maybe not, said the Judge's raised eyebrows.

"Verna's a swell dancer," said Toad Majerus.

One of the men at the bar called for a beer, and the Judge went back to work.

Libby got to her feet, telling Tom, "I'm going to show Frank the way to Roger's house."

Caesar Pipe, standing, said, "I'll be in touch."

Tom said, "I'll be home later."

Frank followed Libby to the door.

"The Judge is a swell dancer, too," piped Toad Majerus, trailing after them with his shovel. "You ought to see him and Verna together on the dance floor."

Caesar Pipe hung his sportcoat over his chair and went to the jukebox to read its offerings.

Judge Bigelow called, "You take care now, Mrs. Pearsall. Verna will be sorry you couldn't wait."

"The man was murdered?"

"Possibly," said Libby. "He'd been hit on the head. They're doing a postmortem."

It was slow going on 13, the snow deeper now, and continuing to fall. Frank kept his wheels in the ruts of a vehicle that had gone before.

"She's just like she was in Chicago, Frank. Why did I think moving here would change her?"

"Hope dies hard."

"I'll tell you what I was banking on. I thought seeing her father again would help to settle her down. In therapy she was talking about her father all the time, saying how deprived she felt, and I thought if she came back here and got a good look at what her father was really like and how little she means to him, she might come to terms with that particular hang-up."

"What's he like these days?"

"He's rotting away on that chicken farm."

"Has she gone out there?"

"Last summer she called him up right after we moved here and said she'd like to stay with him for a week or so. He said he had no objections, so I drove her to the farm. Her grandmother served us coffee in the kitchen and talked about her garden. She's got the shakes, like Parkinson's. I think her mind is okay, but she needed a bath and her dress was filthy. Vernon just sat there drinking coffee and smoking and making it clear he didn't have anything to say to me. He did make an effort to be nice to Verna, but you could tell he didn't know what in the world to talk to her about. He and his mother live in a time warp out there, Frank. The house hasn't changed since the day I moved in as Vernon's bride, except now it's all worn out. Nothing's been replaced or remodeled or even painted. The wallpaper in the kitchen had the same old pink flowers, only now they're gray. They're still cooking on a wood range. Verna took enough clothes with her to stay a week, but when I got up to leave, so did she. 'I thought you were staying,' said Vernon, and Verna said, 'Well, you see, I have these allergies,' and she hurried out to the car and shut herself inside. Driving home, I said, 'You don't have any allergies,' and she said it was the smell she couldn't stand. I told her farms smell like that and she'd get used to it. 'I'll never get used to goat shit,' she said. 'At least the reservation doesn't smell like goat shit.'"

Frank asked, "How long did it take *you* to get used to it?"

Libby leaned into Frank, touched her ear to his shoulder, and laughed. "I never got used to it. I didn't tell her that." She straightened up and stopped laughing. She gazed ahead in silence until they came to Roger Upward's road. "Here's where we turn."

Swerving and spinning his wheels, Frank turned onto the narrow trail.

"When I left Vernon, she was three. I stayed in Linden Falls with my mother for six months, and he never made any effort to see her. So when I went back to the city, I didn't feel any obligation to stay in touch with him. I should have known better.

I shouldn't have let the connection go completely dead. It's got to be part of her trouble. . . ."

Libby paused, then put her hand on Frank's sleeve. "What does this remind you of—my carrying on like this?"

"The walk to school."

"God, yes—weren't we the pals, though?"

"The best."

"Did you ever think of me after you were a priest?"

"Of course."

"And did you think of the day I came to the seminary to see you?"

"Yes, often."

"That was the all-time saddest day of my life. I drove away from there very depressed. I think I would have taken my own life . . . if it weren't for Verna."

Frank, looking pained, said, "It was that bad?"

"I don't know what I'd been hoping for. I knew it was foolish to think you'd leave the seminary and marry me. But I'd never felt so close to anyone as I did to you, Frank. All those days of confiding in each other on the way to school, all the trust we'd built up in one another. Why did all that have to be thrown away?"

He didn't reply. He was recalling the fallout from that meeting in the orchard below the seminary. Father Sparks, chronically suspicious of female intentions, had reported what he'd witnessed to Frank's home parish. Father Lawrence, no alarmist, passed it along to Eunice Pfeiffer as an item of idle chitchat that Frank and a young woman had spent a half hour parked under the apple trees. Eunice Pfeiffer, ever the guardian of purity and God's plan for humankind, confronted Frank when he next came home. Who was the girl and what was that half hour in the orchard all about? She was the old girlfriend of a fellow seminarian, Frank had lied. She couldn't seem to give the fellow up, and she'd come to question Frank about the fellow's sincerity. Eunice Pfeiffer believed this story, but the lie took its toll. For months Frank hated himself for telling it—not because he had deceived Eunice Pfeiffer (it was none of her business), but because, through a hastily invented falsehood, he had dismissed Libby from his life, and all she had meant to him.

"Over the years," said Libby, staring ahead at the thick snowfall, "did you ever wonder if you did the right thing?"

"Yes," Frank said. He didn't tell her that he was wondering now.

19

Tom left the Homestead and set off for Linden Falls, driving cautiously despite his eagerness, for although the snowfall had thinned and the sky was growing bright in the west, the road was snow-packed and slippery. It took him half an hour to arrive at the motel at the edge of Linden Falls. The red neon said simply MOTEL, as did Verna's penciled scrawl on the scrap of paper the midget had given him. He parked in front of number four, next to the Judge's little Datsun. He locked the BMW, cast a satisfied look around the nearly empty parking lot, and knocked on the door. Verna, giggling and wearing nothing but a silver ring on her little finger, flung the door open and raced back to bed. He lunged at her, catching her before she could burrow under the covers, rolled her over on her back, and pressed himself down upon her. His cold vest made her shriek and tremble. He kissed her roughly and said, "What the hell's going on?"

"I need it." She laughed. "What took you so long?"

"I mean what's going on with Roger?"

"That jerk. Come on, get in bed." She struggled to free herself, but Tom held her down, asking, "When did you see him last?"

"Last night. Why, is he looking for me?"

Satisfied that she was unaware of Roger's death, he rolled off her and watched her slip quickly under the covers, a lithe animal of blond hair and porcelain flesh. Unzipping his vest and unbuttoning his shirt, he changed the subject lest the news short-circuit her libido. He said, "Do you realize how long it's been since we did this?"

"Since our trip to Chicago." Verna was sitting against the vinyl headboard with the blankets pulled up to her chin. Above her on the wall hung a framed print of Times Square. She asked, "Has Roger been calling your place?"

"No." Tom removed his shoes and took off his pants and underwear. Stepping across the room to lay his watch on the bureau, he looked at Verna in the mirror. That face—the expectant lift of the dark eyebrows, the tousled taffy-colored hair, the alluring purity of the smile. Primed for sex, she was always at her prettiest. And under the blanket—that body. The body of a girl, changed very little by the ten or eleven years that had passed since their first intimacy. It was her youth that had aroused him then, and it aroused him now. Despite all the makeup, she still looked sixteen and innocent. His wife, except on rare occasions growing rarer by the year, had lost the power to arouse him. His wife blamed his drinking, but that, of course, was the sort of claim you expected from a woman in her forties. Anyhow, didn't sex get stale for all husbands and wives? After twelve years of marriage wasn't it the piece you got on the side that reminded you you were still alive?

When he turned from the mirror, Verna, seeing his tumescence, thrust out her arms and cried, "Yes, yes, bring it to me, bring it to me," and he cupped it in his hand and carried it to the bed.

Afterward, he told her about Roger and she cried. He was both amazed and perturbed that she should cry. He hadn't realized that Roger had meant that much to her. He'd assumed Roger's house was like the Homestead, simply one of her safe harbors between adventures and skirmishes with other men.

When he got up and dressed, her crying grew hysterical and he had to shout to quiet her down. She begged him to stay, but he couldn't. Given the ice and snow, Libby would grow alarmed if he didn't get home soon.

"Please!" Verna cried. "Please stay!"

"I can't," he said, facing the mirror. It was pathetic and disgusting, her kneeling naked on the bed like that, pleading with him.

"Please stay, Tom! Roger's dead!" Her voice rose to a wail. "Who have I got except you?"

"Judge Bigelow." He spoke with resentment. The Judge was his rival. Every man Verna looked at was a rival.

"No, not the Judge. He's a slob. He won't understand."

Tom sat on the bed to tie his shoes. "Won't understand what?"

Sitting back against the headboard and shaking her head in despair, she wiped her eyes. "How I'm feeling. I treated Roger like shit. He was good to me and I treated him like shit. Without Roger who have I got except you?"

"Your mother. Come home."

Another wail: "I can't come home."

"Why not?" He returned to the mirror and combed his hair.

"I can't be in the same house with you, are you too dumb to understand that?"

"Why's that?" Buckling the strap of his watch and closing the zipper of his down vest, he only half listened to her lengthy and fanatical reply—platitudes she'd picked up in therapy about guilt and self-hate and sexual addiction and anger and depression. His mind was on his refrigerator. Did he have enough beer at home to last till Tuesday? The Homestead was closed Mondays.

Meanwhile Frank, using the Pearsalls' phone, was calling all of the LaBontes and Upwards in the book. Having found the old bronze Chrysler gone from Roger Upward's yard, Libby had directed him to Millie LaBonte's house, which was a mile or so west of the lake. There, too, they had found no one, and so they had made their way to Basswood at a crawl, the

Oldsmobile plowing snow with its bumper and heating up and trailing steam from under its hood.

Frank reached Millie LaBonte on the fifth call, and he had trouble putting the slow, soft voice on the phone together with the shrill, nervous Millie Upward he remembered from high school. He offered to help with the funeral arrangements, to preside if she wished, in Our Lady's Church or elsewhere. Millie LaBonte turned away from the phone for a few moments, consulting with someone, then said, "That would be good, but my brother quit going to church."

"Never mind that," said Frank. "We can bring him to church one last time, if you think he'd have wanted it that way."

"I want it that way," said Millie. "And I guess his brothers haven't got nothing against it. Roger, I don't think he'd mind."

"Fine. What day?"

"Tuesday, I guess. I'll call you."

He gave her his phone number.

"But, Father, I thought the church wouldn't bury fallen-aways."

"What church is that, Millie?"

"The Catholic Church."

"Never mind, Millie. This is the Basswood Church."

He came away from the phone explaining to Libby that he had to hurry home with the Oldsmobile so that the monsignor could visit his shut-ins, but Libby insisted that he remove his coat and sit at the kitchen table for at least one drink. The kitchen, she said, was the warmest and therefore her favorite room in the house. After he had been settled at the table for a while, relaxed and sipping rum and reminiscing, Libby asked him suddenly and bluntly, "What do you think of Tom?"

He looked at her. She was sitting close at his side and wearing a level, unsmiling expression that seemed to ask for candor.

"I'd guess he's unhappy," said Frank.

"Obviously. But what do you think of him? Do you like him?"

He groped for a gracious fib, then decided not to dissemble. "Not much," he said.

"Nobody does, at first. But you might, with time. He gets less abrasive the longer he knows a person."

"Do *you* like him, Libby?"

"Tom grew up in poverty," she said evasively. "He worked his way out of a poor family in a wretched neighborhood and graduated from medical school near the top of his class. Then he discovered he didn't like being a doctor. That's why he's so frustrated. Examinations, case histories—it's all drudgery to Tom because he's indifferent to people. He's got a very low level of compassion."

"He should have gone into research."

"He hates research."

"Then why medical school?"

"Because nobody else he knew was capable of being a doctor. The degree itself was the goal, not the practice of medicine. But he did practice, and he did all right—till the drugs messed us up. He wasn't the most popular physician in the Silver Park Clinic, but he had his faithful patients. In his standoffish way he appealed to the snobbish element in that neighborhood. They took his disdain for professional reserve. And of course he's sardonic, and there'll always be people who relate to that, even when they're sick. *Especially* when they're sick."

Libby sipped her wine and went on, speaking in the same headlong, unhesitating manner he recalled from their high-school days. "At first he didn't know he was in the wrong profession. He blamed his patients. He kept saying they were rich and fastidious and shallow and treating them was thankless work. We took a lot of vacations. We flew to Africa, to the Caribbean, to South America. Tom talked about doctoring in the Third World, where he'd be appreciated, so we'd go and look over the possibilities. We spent two weeks in Tanzania and two weeks in Peru and the squalor reminded him of his own upbringing, and we hightailed it back to the Silver Park Clinic in Chicago."

"You worked there, too?"

She nodded.

"Would that have appealed to you—the Third World?"

"I thought so at the time. I thought I could nurse anywhere

and be happy. But now in Basswood . . ." She gave Frank a sidewise, puzzled smile. "Where have my noble instincts gone?"

"The Third World plus jackpines—a deadly combination." He regretted his facetiousness when instead of responding with amusement, she cast her eyes out the window and spoke in a low, disconsolate tone.

"Ironic, isn't it, that just about the time he got over his missionary illusions we were sent here?" Without looking at Frank, she touched his cheek, unconsciously it seemed, the way a child will reach out to make sure a parent is in place, or a lover will reach out to her beloved. The touch made him suddenly warm and nervous. Dear God, this is it. This is where I get off. My heart is kicking with something I'm afraid is love. I've got enough trouble putting my vocation back together without a woman stealing my heart.

He finished his drink and put on his coat. In the front entryway Libby put out her hand as before and touched his cheek. He took the hand and kissed it and went out the door in a state of agitation. The snowfall had stopped. The clouds overhead were wispy and sunshine came slanting through the trees from the west. He drove south to the Homestead, where he surveyed the lake and saw that several cars had beaten a trail through the fresh snow to the far shore. Easing the Olds down the bank and speeding across the lake, he felt less agitated the farther he left Libby behind. Across the lake, up off the ice and traveling the road to Linden Falls between meadows and pastures, his agitation changed to elation. Dear God, am I not the happiest man in the world and doesn't life make perfect sense? Libby is Tom's wife and my bond with her has nothing to do with sex because it's a pure mingling of souls. Are we not lucky to have run across each other at this precarious midpoint of our lives, and will we not go on in this perfectly sensible and gratifying manner, satisfied to do nothing more than make one another a discreet part of our weekends? And isn't this a gorgeous afternoon—the sun slanting across the fresh snow and the tattered snow clouds trailing away to the east and, dear God, look there, those handsome horses grazing in that snowy pasture, their rough winter coats tawny in the sunlight.

With the shadow of the Oldsmobile traveling the edge of the pasture, Frank honked his horn and the horses lifted their heads and turned in his direction, blinking and breathing steam at the low, gold sun.

20

Needing to be near the door in case the children mis-behaved, Elaine LaBonte didn't join her relatives at the front of the church. She led her little brother and her little twin sisters into a rear pew, and from there she surveyed the congregation. She was surprised by their number, more than on Sundays. She hoped her uncle Roger somehow knew this and was pleased. She saw the Pipes and the Butchers, the Cashmans and the Greens. Her uncle Johnny and uncle Pock were pallbearers. So were Cae-sar Pipe and Mel Green and Carl Butcher. The sixth pallbearer was a man Elaine didn't know, an Upward from Minneapolis. She wished her father had come home for the funeral, but the coal fields of Wyoming were too far away.

She saw that her uncle Johnny had taken the bandage off his ear for the funeral. His face, with half his right earlobe missing, looked lopsided. He'd lost it playing with the big dog that was always hanging around the house Pock and Johnny lived in. Johnny and the dog were rolling around in the snow when the dog got its claw caught in Johnny's earring and ripped open his earlobe. Knowing how Dr. Pearsall hated guns, Johnny told him his brother had accidently shot him while aiming at a mouse in their kitchen. They told Elaine about it later, laughing like idiots, but Elaine didn't think it was funny.

Father Healy, vested in white, emerged from the sacristy, blessed the coffin, and was saying the opening prayers of the Mass when Elaine saw Mrs. Pearsall come in and slip into a pew across the aisle from her. She wore a burgundy coat with a collar of fur. Her hair was combed back severely from her face. Elaine was fascinated by Mrs. Pearsall, partly because she wanted to be a nurse herself someday, and partly because she had seen two different sides of the woman on Sunday afternoon—the efficient side when she was phoning for the priest and ambulance at the Health Center, and the vulnerable side when she stood weeping in the snow outside Roger's house. She kept an eye on Mrs. Pearsall throughout the ceremony and noticed that she never took her eyes off the priest. Was there something going on between them? Whenever Father Healy's eyes fell upon Mrs. Pearsall, she responded with a sad little smile.

Toward the end of Mass, Elaine's coughing attracted Mrs. Pearsall's attention, and she turned her smile on Elaine and the children. On the strength of this smile, Elaine resolved to work up the nerve to ask Mrs. Pearsall for a job at the Health Center. It was Elaine's ambition to get her nursing degree and come back to Basswood and try to make the reservation a healthier place to live. She admired Mrs. Pearsall for what she had tried—and more or less failed—to do last summer. She'd gone door-to-door, trying to take stock of everyone's health. Elaine, three-fourths Ojibway herself, could succeed where the Pearsalls failed.

Some of the congregation walked while others rode the half mile to the cemetery. Elaine didn't want to go, but her mother, weepy and drugged, was in no shape to drive. What possible good, Elaine wondered, could result from watching somebody be buried? It was scarcely two months since she had watched with horror as Tim Cashman's coffin was lowered into the ground. Tim Cashman had been Elaine's boyfriend four years earlier, in junior high. She had liked him, despite everyone insisting he was strange. His death had been a terrible shock. Nobody had thought him strange enough to kill himself. There ought to be a limit (she thought as she steered the bronze Chrysler through the cemetery gate) on the number of open graves you had to look down into in any given lifetime.

When Father Healy finished his graveside prayers, Elaine watched him turn to her mother and embrace her, causing her mother to lose her fragile composure and weep in his arms. Then he turned and embraced whoever else looked like they might stand still for a hug, including Elaine herself. Then he invited everybody back to church for a snack.

He had brought a big coffeemaker from Linden Falls, and Joy Pipe and Mrs. Butcher furnished cold cuts and bread and cookies. The throng stood visiting in the aisles, sat visiting in pews. Elaine, moving among them, heard from Carl Butcher the theory that Verna had murdered Roger by hitting him on the head and leaving him to freeze to death. But that didn't make sense, said Joy Pipe, because why would Roger's house be all torn apart and the door busted off its hinges if it was Verna? There was also the theory, according to Uncle Johnny, that a burglar who thought Roger was at the Homestead had broken into the house, and when he found Roger home, he knocked him out and Roger froze to death. But Joy Pipe, quoting Caesar, said that didn't make sense either, because no burglar would pick up a man he'd knocked unconscious and lay him out straight and neat on his bed. And besides, said Joy, what did Roger ever have that was worth burgling?

Elaine's mother, now becalmed somewhat by another pill, expressed the opinion that Roger had cracked his head by falling down after he left the Homestead, and by the time he walked home he was already half-frozen to death and couldn't start a fire and just lay down and died. That was more or less Caesar's opinion, said Joy.

Then the Butchers' fat daughter Bernadine spoke up and said word was out that Verna was shacking up with the Judge and maybe Caesar should go to the Homestead and question her. At this, Caesar spoke up and said he'd done so. He'd gone to the Homestead Sunday afternoon and was told Verna had been there and left, so he sat there until nine o'clock at night, and finally she'd come back, driving Judge Bigelow's Datsun, and he'd questioned her for a half hour or more. "Verna's not involved in Roger's death," said Caesar. "She was real broke up over it."

Bernadine then whispered in Elaine's ear that Billy Annunciation was going to move back to the reservation. This excited Elaine. She had liked Billy Annunciation when they were little. She asked Joy Pipe if this was true, and Joy said maybe. Billy hated the city and she hated having any grandson of hers turning into a city Indian, and so he might move back up north.

Elaine's excitement was compounded when she moved from the coffee urn to the vestibule and stopped Mrs. Pearsall as she was leaving and asked her about a job at the Health Center and was told yes, she and the doctor could find things for her to do after school and on Saturday mornings. The job would start after New Year's, when the Pearsalls returned from their three-week vacation in Chicago.

At this point Father Healy hurried into the vestibule to say good-bye to Mrs. Pearsall, and Elaine, backing away, saw them exchange a little kiss.

PART THREE

21

January. The first Sunday of the new year. Overcast and very cold. Attendance at all Masses diminished by flu.

After lunch, because the monsignor wasn't feeling well, Frank went out into the gray and frigid afternoon to call on the monsignor's shut-ins. First he visited the Hallorans, Bert and Trisha, an ancient couple living unharmoniously in a small apartment over a furniture store. Bert, a frog-shaped man with a shaggy mustache, was ninety-one. Trisha, a bent gray woman whose eyes sparkled with a kind of mad vitality, was eighty-nine. Both were immobilized by maladies of the limbs—arthritis, sciatica, corns, and hammertoes—but their hearts were beating strong and their minds were said to be as good as ever, by which it was understood that Trisha's mind was less good than Bert's, as proven by her artistic interests.

Artistic, dreamy, undependable—that was Trisha's reputation. She'd given music lessons for forty years, and Frank had been one of her pupils. To this day he recalled his dislike of the impressionistic pieces she'd forced upon him. He'd spent the sixteenth year of his life obediently perfecting "Clair de Lune" for recital, and he wondered now, looking back, why he had persisted. Who was he obeying? His dead mother, most likely, for he assumed as a boy that she would want him to continue lessons. Did anyone alive speak louder than the dead?

Trisha Halloran greeted Frank by limping over to the door and taking his face in her gnarled hands and rising on tiptoe to give him a kiss on the lips, while her husband, standing at his walker across the room, muttered, "Stop that, you hussy, the man's a priest."

After taking Communion, Bert clumped into the kitchen to make cocoa, and Trisha sat next to Frank on the couch, ran a cold, crooked finger around the inside of his Roman collar, and asked if he'd like to take it off and get comfortable. No, he said, he had to visit certain parishioners this afternoon who disliked seeing a priest out of uniform.

"I'm one of them," Bert called angrily from the kitchen.

Their topic, over cocoa, was death: death at a distance as reported on television—Lebanon, Ulster, Nicaragua—and death locally as reported in the Linden Falls *Leader*. What about the man found frozen in his bed on the reservation last month, and the sheriff's ongoing plea for information—did Frank know anything about that?

Yes, he told them, Roger Upward was last seen leaving the Homestead late on a Saturday night. Examination of the body indicated a fractured skull and a very high level of alcohol in the blood together with a drug of some kind. He died of hypothermia. The sheriff and Caesar Pipe had questioned dozens of people including Roger Upward's woman friend, but no suspects had been charged, nor had any motives suggested themselves. The blow to the head may have been caused by an assailant, though there was no clear proof that it hadn't been accidental, as in a fall.

"We understand the woman friend is the daughter of the reservation doctor." Frank could tell by Trisha's tone how proud she was to have this fact up her sleeve—news not from the newspaper.

"And she's white," said Bert, making his mouth small to indicate distaste. "What do white women see in Indian bucks?"

"Not the doctor's daughter," Frank corrected. "His wife's

daughter. His wife was Libby Girard, remember? She lived in Linden Falls for a year or so when she was in high school."

"What class?" asked Trisha, whose favorite reading to this day was the high-school annual.

"My own," said Frank. "She had this daughter by her first husband, Vernon Jessen."

Both Hallorans, after straining their prodigious memories, appeared at once crestfallen at not being able to recall a Libby Girard and exultant at having another fact in their possession. Frank knew they'd be sharing it with friends on the phone as soon as he left.

He also knew that in the commerce of old age, a business like any other, gossip was coin of the realm, and so he provided the Hallorans with enough information to trade on for days to come. He said that Libby and her husband were contributing a year of their lives to the cause of better health on the reservation. At present they were off on a three-week Christmas break, visiting Chicago, but they would be back on the job this week. As soon as it was out of his mouth, he regretted saying that their daughter had a history of mental illness and that she was currently living with the man nàmed Bigelow who ran the Homestead. He'd momentarily forgotten about the stigma attached to mental illness.

"A loony!" both Hallorans cackled in unison.

And the scandal attached to cohabitation.

"Shacking up?" they screeched, Trisha's eyes widening in wonder, Bert's narrowing in disgust.

Frank stood up, urging the old couple to remain seated, but both of them struggled to their feet to see him off. On each wrist Trisha wore four or five metal bracelets that rang in Frank's ear when, in the doorway, she put her arms around his neck and kissed him again on the lips.

"Let go of him!" Bert growled angrily, jabbing at the carpet with his walker. "The man's a priest."

In her white Colonial overlooking the Badbattle, Mrs. Graham, the undertaker's widow, kept Frank in his chair for nearly an hour, pouring out the tedious history of her skirmishes with certain dolts who had sold her a defective car in 1951 and certain other dolts of more recent memory who had sold her a defective television and a defective health insurance policy. Assenting politely to her accusations and complaints, but giving her only half his attention, Frank contemplated—and was saddened by—the vast difference between this woman and the woman she had been. Sitting here in her soiled dressing gown, her hair wild, her hand shaking and spilling her brandy, she seemed to be energized by very little in life except her bitterest memories. Each time Frank tried to change the subject—the weather, the neighbors, the plans for a new water tower—her eyes glazed and she coughed in his face. But at the mention of a person or a streak of luck that had turned against her, her eyes quickened, her voice grew sure and strong, and her coughing went away. Many years ago she had been kind and gracious and pretty. How many times in those three days between his mother's death and the funeral had Frank sought this woman out and laid his head on her breast? "Be a little man," she had told him.

When at last Frank was taking his leave of the Widow Graham, she said, "You had an Indian funeral last month."

"Yes, a man named Upward."

"My husband buried too many Indians."

"Yes, they die untimely deaths out there."

"I don't mean that. I mean he buried more Indians than he got paid for. I told him not to bury Indians, but he'd always go ahead and do it. He'd always say it's racial prejudice to turn away Indians and I'd always say it's not racial prejudice to turn away deadbeats. We had a lifelong standoff about Indians, he and I. I'll bet you weren't given a nickel by the Upward people."

"I was given fish and wild rice."

"I'll bet the rice was seconds. All crumbs."

"We'd have to ask Mrs. Tatzig. It tasted good."

"And the fish was pike, I suppose."

"Yes."

"I hate pike."

How does Adrian do it? Frank asked himself as he drove away from the Widow Graham's house and headed for the Widow Schultenover's. The monsignor was a superb listener. Making the rounds with him that first Sunday, Frank had witnessed the monsignor's patient manner with these five woolgatherers, marveled at his willingness to sit through endless, pointless, patternless monologues and never cease to look attentive. In one of these houses, in fact, Frank had seen the listener outlast the speaker. It was Widow Schultenover who put herself to sleep with a memory about her late husband's pleurisy while Frank, following the monsignor's example, sipped his coffee and sat quietly waiting for her to wake up, which she did eventually, resuming her story not where she had left off but ten minutes closer to the beginning.

Several years ago, upon retiring, the Schultenovers had converted their egghouse into their living quarters, and it was in this square box of a building at the industrial end of Main Street that Frank gave Communion to the eggman's widow.

Mrs. Schultenover was no longer the husky dynamo who had energized the egg business. She was shorter and smaller than she used to be, compressed and eroded by osteoporosis and a stomach ailment. After taking the Sacrament, she served Frank a big slice of cake, and sitting in the living room with its front-window view of the grain elevator across the street and its side-window view of a used-car lot, they spoke at length of farmers who had supplied their enterprise with eggs during Frank's time on the job. The Ripleys. The Christiansons. The Kludts. A dozen others.

By the time Frank left the Widow Schultenover, carrying with him a square of foil-wrapped cake for the monsignor, an early twilight had fallen across the town. Driving along Main Street, he read the flashing numbers on the marquee over Security State Bank; it was 3:32 and 18 below zero; CDs earned 7 percent compounded quarterly. He followed Main Street to the edge of town and beyond, his final call taking him five miles out into the country, where Eunice Pfeiffer lived in two rooms at the back of her brothers' farmhouse.

Eunice Pfeiffer, the woman who had devoted seven or eight years of her life to directing Frank through his adolescence, would turn eighty this year. The two bachelor brothers she lived with—one younger, one older—were uncommunicative men who kept to their separate parts of the house, Kelvin upstairs and Raymond in the front rooms. Kelvin was interested in mechanics, and although the Pfeiffers had retired from farming years ago and rented their land to others, he spent his days tinkering in the machine shed. Every afternoon he started up the tractor and drove to the end of the driveway to fetch the mail. Raymond, who had never cared for mechanics—or farming, for that matter—passed his time reading, playing solitaire, and napping. These large, inscrutable men hardly ever spoke to one another, nor to their sister, whose respiratory system was such that she could not breathe cold air without nearly suffocating, and so she passed the winter confined to the house, praying the rosary, paging through seed catalogs, and watching game shows on the small black-and-white TV that stood on her dresser.

It was apparent to Frank the moment he entered the farmhouse and was kissed and fondled and led by her jittery hand to her rooms at the back—as it was apparent to all who knew Eunice Pfeiffer—that he was her life's work. After leaving the service of the Church (Father Lawrence's successor at St. Ann's had been intolerably lax and liberal in matters of worship, and she had quit in protest), Eunice had held a succession of short-term jobs around town, including that of bookkeeper at the grain elevator and clerk at the five-and-dime, before gravitating home to the farm, where life with her brothers was far from happy, but what did her personal happiness matter (she was fond of saying) as long as she had helped to create a priest of God?

She was still tall and angular, and now in her old age her skin was pale as paper and deeply wrinkled. She wore fur-lined boots and three sweaters (her rooms were drafty) and her white hair was pulled back in a knot. The years had done nothing to diminish the hint of anxiety in her small, green eyes. On her nightstand, tied with red ribbons, were the letters Frank had written to her over the past quarter century, and on the wall, together with the Sacred Heart, the Blessed Virgin, and John F. Kennedy, hung two enlarged photographs of Frank. In one he wore his high-school cap and gown. The other had been taken on ordination day.

They made a little ceremony out of Communion; then Eunice went to the kitchen and brought in tea and apple pie. Frank sat where he was told to sit, in the rocking chair by the window, and he looked where she pointed to the snowdrifts as she described the garden she would plant in the spring; zinnias here, cosmos there, and hollyhocks along the sunny side of the barn. When he finished his pie, he read the articles she had clipped for him from periodicals both secular and religious—the pope in South America, Minnesotans in St. Peter's Square, ethics (or the lack thereof) in government. He listened—and didn't listen—as she spun out memories of his mother: the recipes and dress patterns they shared; his mother's taste in music, radio programs, and china. "Theresa was the best friend I ever had, a living saint, and a light went out of my life when she died."

"I know," said Frank sympathetically. But, strange to say, he did not recall Eunice being the important element in his mother's life that she claimed to be. It was only after Christmas Day of his eleventh year that his memory, possibly faulty, brought Eunice out of obscurity and gave her a leading role in his household.

"January is endless," she said, crossing the room to warm his tea. "It's only Epiphany and it seems like ages since Christmas." She was sure-handed with the teapot and her strong, sensual voice was that of a much younger woman. "Did you have a nice Christmas, Father?" She'd stopped calling him "Frank" the moment he was ordained.

"It was all right. The Vogels had us to dinner."

Actually, it had been supremely tedious. The Vogels, old friends of the monsignor's, were unable to converse for long if money wasn't the topic. A certain Christmas record had repeated itself endlessly on the stereo while Frank and the monsignor listened patiently to Mr. Vogel's advice about investments and Mrs. Vogel's assessment of neighborhood property values. Round yon virgin mother and child and it was hard to find a CD yielding 8 percent. There was a time when a fifty-foot lot sold for twelve thousand dollars, glory to the newborn king, but the market was soft and the neighborhood, following yonder star, wasn't what it used to be. On the way home the monsignor had told Frank how much he'd enjoyed the outing. "Lovely people, the Vogels. I hope you get to know them better as time goes on, Frank." Exactly what was so enjoyable? Frank asked. "Their friendliness, my boy. You have to like people who'll take in a couple of lonesome priests on Christmas Day and feed them food that good." Frank confessed to his boredom: "I guess I'm too fussy, Adrian. I'd like the conversation to move away from finance now and then." "Finance?" said the monsignor, as if he hadn't heard a word all afternoon.

Frank, rocking slowly, stifled a yawn and stole a look at his watch. He told Eunice Pfeiffer that he was getting to the age when a long nap was an essential part of his Christmas Day, what with Masses at midnight and all morning long.

"And hours and hours of confessions beforehand," she said.

"Not so many confessions anymore, Eunice. Confession is scarcely more popular than flagellation these days."

"Well, it's the Church's own fault. It's the modern system of confessing that keeps sinners like my brothers away. They can't abide the face-to-face method."

"But we offer a choice—the curtain or face-to-face. Either way, Adrian and I sit there by the hour with our ears cocked for evil, but few come to tell us of any."

"It's a godless time."

"So it seems."

"It will pass."

"Let's hope. And how was your Christmas, Eunice?"

The old lady rolled her eyes and brought them to rest on the door separating herself from her brothers. "Raymond spent the day reading a book about Frank Sinatra, and Kelvin was in bed with a cold. I wasn't feeling so wonderful myself—a touch of the flu."

"I'm sorry."

"There's very little joy in this house, Father."

"Is that so?" He knew it was so.

"Are your Christmases clouded by the memory of your mother's death the way mine are?"

"No, it was so long ago."

"I dwell on it every Christmas. I dwell on her words." Her eyes moved from Frank to the photo of Frank's mother standing on the dresser. Curly dark hair, happy eyes, left hand fingering her blouse collar. Next to it, and somewhat larger, was a photo of his father. Small eyes behind wire-rim glasses, long face, long ears, a quizzical lift to his eyebrow, as if he were about to ask a question.

"I didn't think she was conscious," said Eunice. "She was mumbling nonsense and her eyes were fluttering—and then suddenly she took a deep breath and looked me straight in the eye and told me what she hoped for you. It was a whisper but it was as clear as anything. 'I want Frank to be a priest,' she said."

Frank nodded, looking into his tea. How many times had he heard this account of his mother's last words? It was invariably followed by a reverential silence, which Frank, rocking and staring out at the barn, found particularly unsettling this afternoon because Libby, due back from Chicago tonight or tomorrow, was much on his mind today. It was impossible for him to hold Eunice and Libby in his mind at the same time and not feel tension.

He stopped rocking and set down his cup and saucer. "I really must go, Eunice. The monsignor's car starts hard when it's this cold."

"Kelvin can start it," she said, then added, to delay his departure, "Did you hear from your brothers at Christmas?"

"From their wives. Joe's wife wrote a note. Peter's wife just signed their names to a card."

Eunice shook her head. "It's such a tragedy when families lose touch. I'm sure your poor father was grieved that your brothers hardly ever came home." Her eyes returned to the two photos on the dresser.

"It may have been his example that made us lose touch." Even as Frank said this, he knew it would cause her to bristle.

"How can you say that, Father?" She pierced him with a hurt

look. "How can you even think it? Martin was a dear man who loved his wife and loved his three boys and he didn't deserve to live out his life grieving as he did."

"Are you sure it was grieving, Eunice?"

"What else?" Irritation brought two points of color to her cheeks.

Frank said softly, "He simply turned in on himself." He didn't want to argue.

Stridently she said, "Yes, but it was his grief that turned him in." Then she changed her tone and said with fondness: "And how quietly he endured it. Martin had the patience of a saint."

Or if not the patience, the self-absorption, thought Frank as he got to his feet and thanked her for the tea. He took his leave in stages, stopping in the kitchen and again in the front hallway to hear her out. She was eulogizing his father, whose long years of unhappiness, she said, were not unlike her own, and his stoical endurance was an example she had learned to follow. She stood well away from the cold that fell through the front door when he opened it and stepped out into the rosy twilight. "Pray for me, Father," she called in farewell, "as I pray for you."

Walking to his car, he felt the old lady's eyes on him and he didn't need to turn and look at them to understand what they were saying: Be a better priest than you already are, Father Healy. Be perfect. I am already as proud of you as any priest's mother can possibly be, but make me prouder still.

22

Libby and Tom had set out from Chicago before dawn on this first Sunday of the new year. They were halfway between Minneapolis and Berrington when Tom announced that he was out of beer.

"How could you be out of beer?" said Libby. "You bought gallons."

"I'm out of beer."

"Well, we're almost home."

"No, we're not."

"Less than a hundred miles to go."

"Jesus."

They had been on the road ten hours with Libby at the wheel for most of that time because Tom had opened his first beer at nine in the morning. They had stopped twice for meals and six times for Tom to relieve himself, which he had done beside the highway. At each stop he had stood hunched against the frigid wind for what seemed to Libby a very long time, his head bent low as if he were reading a message in the snow he was yellowing.

"Libby, I'm out of beer," he repeated. He had been silently inebriated for most of the day, dozing and waking and staring at the road. Or silently drugged—Libby couldn't always tell the difference. Now, with less than two hours of road ahead of them, he sounded playful. "Oh, Libby, this is so *boring*. Aren't you bored out of your mind?"

"It was your idea not to fly, Tom."

"How could we fly, for God's sake? We can't have people snooping in our luggage."

"I know."

They had gone to Chicago not only seeking respite from the wilderness and to visit Libby's mother and Tom's chiropractor, but also to pick up a suitcase of prescription drugs, which Tom didn't want to take on a plane. As a doctor he might have convinced airport authority—as he had convinced Libby—that the drugs were a vital part of his mission of mercy to the Indians, but there was always the chance of happening upon a distrustful security guard who would run a check and discover the prohibition placed on him by the court and the board of medical examiners. Hands off drugs for a year, the board had ruled. No prescriptions. No handouts, not even samples from pharmaceutical firms. Besides, in today's load he was carrying pot as well as pills.

"Libby, I'm out of beer."

"Please, Tom, I'm exhausted."

"That's why I'm telling you. Talk to you, keep you awake."

"I'm not sleepy, just exhausted."

They traveled a mile in silence then. Jackpines and bare aspens. A frozen swamp. A barn at the crest of a hill. More jackpines. There was a blood spot in the southern sky where the sun was going down.

"How about if I sing, Libby? Would you like me to sing?"

She didn't reply.

"Or poems. I could recite you a poem."

Preoccupied with her thoughts, she was scarcely conscious of his words as he recited himself to sleep. She was looking back to the day last June when they had first driven to Basswood. She'd been at the wheel most of that day. Her spirits had been foolishly high, for she imagined a happy reunion between Verna and her father, and she imagined Verna and Tom and herself rejuvenated in the pure country air. She knew at the time that she was being naive—as though the city of Chicago had been founded to thwart their happiness, as though their chances of fulfillment increased with every mile they put behind them—but naive or not (she had reasoned) why not allow herself one full day of extravagant hope before reality came shambling back into their lives? The sky had been so incredibly blue that day, the air so brisk and fresh smelling.

Today was one of the coldest days on record—eighteen below at noon and falling, said the radio—and she was heading north bereft of the hopes of last June. And yet she was not downhearted. She had a new reason for returning to the wilderness, and that reason was Frank. During these three weeks in Chicago she had missed Frank acutely. Frank had touched, without trying, a part of her that had lain dormant for a long time, had taken her back to her girlhood when things were simpler and warmer. She'd phoned him four times from the hotel in Chicago and felt a little giddy each time he answered the phone. By the fourth call she'd found it impossible to conceal her emotion. She told him that if it weren't for his presence in Linden Falls, she didn't think she'd have the heart to return to the reservation and that she was counting the days till she saw him again. She stopped short of saying that she was investing in Frank all her hopes for happiness. Devalued hopes, surely, but her spirit wasn't entirely spent. There had been times this fall and winter when she'd feared her spirit was bankrupt, one or two awful days and nights, in fact, when suicide seemed as reasonable as staying alive, but that was before Frank had turned up.

Tom, waking from a hundred-mile sleep, said, "We'll stop for some beer."

"We've got beer at home, Tom."

"You sure?"

"Cases."

Twilight had dissolved into night. There were stars overhead and a small piece of moon in the west. Ahead, they could see the neon light of the Homestead casting a dim red glow over County Road 13.

"We'll stop anyway. See Verna."

"I'm not up to seeing Verna tonight."

"That's okay, I'll run in and see her."

"Tom, I'm dead."

"Just for a minute."

"We can call her," said Libby. But she slowed down, undecided. Five or six cars were parked beside the tavern. Roger Upward's snow-covered pickup remained at the side of the road where its battery had died nearly a month ago. Twice they had phoned Verna from Chicago. She said she was tending bar for the Judge by night and watching soaps by day.

"Just for a minute, Libby."

"No," she decided suddenly, stomping on the gas and causing the car to lurch forward. She was fed up with Tom's whining. She lacked the energy to face her daughter.

Tom expressed no objection. "Okay," he mumbled, slumping down in his seat and gazing out his side window at the dark trees speeding past.

At home Tom went straight from the garage to the kitchen, where he opened a beer. Libby carried in her overnight bag and the suitcase containing her clothes.

"You should have let me bring those in, Libby."

She dropped the suitcase in the hallway and climbed the stairs with the overnight bag. "Would you bring that up when you come? I'm going to bed."

"How about calling Verna?"

"I'll call from the bedroom after I shower."

"I'll get on the phone down here. I've got meds for her."

Libby paused in her undressing to dial St. Ann's rectory. She was told by Mrs. Tatzig that Frank was out on a sick call.

"This is Libby Pearsall. Please tell him we're back."

"You been to Chicago I hear."

"Yes."

"Heard they had lots of snow in Chicago."

"Yes, a week or so ago."

"My sister spent a weekend in Chicago during the war. Her husband was stationed there. It's by a big lake."

"A Great Lake."

"He wasn't her husband then yet. They got married after the war. I'll give Father Healy your message."

Libby showered, put on her flannel nightgown, and went to the head of the stairs. "Tom, I'm calling, if you want to get on the phone."

No reply. He was either asleep or engrossed in TV.

She went back to bed and dialed.

"Homestead." It was Judge Bigelow.

"I'm calling for Verna."

"Who wants her?"

"Her mother."

Unctuously: "Ha, Mrs. Pearsall, I didn't know your voice. Are you home from Chicago?"

"Yes, could I speak to Verna, please?"

"I tried getting ahold of you, Mrs. Pearsall. Verna's in the hospital."

Libby flinched as if slapped. She imagined a car accident first, Verna with head injuries and broken limbs. Then she imagined a beating at the hands of Judge Bigelow, her nose broken, bruises around the eyes. Then she pictured a psychotic episode. Which the Judge confirmed.

"She got to acting real funny, Mrs. Pearsall."

Libby closed her eyes. She asked, "What hospital?" There was no hospital in Linden Falls.

"Berrington. There wasn't nothing to do but call Caesar Pipe. We tried to calm her down but she wouldn't calm down."

Libby could picture it. Verna flying. People very likely amused at first, then alarmed, then terrified. Time and space distorted for Verna, everything speeding up, the center not holding, Verna flying apart, people confused by her confusion, backing away, looking away in embarrassment, looking desperately for someone to step forward and take over, bring her down, turn her off. Who took over this time? Who in that dark tavern of strangers laid soothing hands on Verna? Surely not the Judge. You knew at a glance that the Judge was incapable of succoring the afflicted. Who then? It was silly, she knew, to be so hung up on who helped Verna, but each time it was the same for Libby—she had to know the identity of the person who came to her daughter's aid.

"You there, Mrs. Pearsall?"

"Yes, I'm here. When was she admitted?"

"Last night. One, two in the morning."

"Who came to her aid, Mr. Bigelow?"

"Caesar Pipe and his wife. I called Caesar right away."

"I mean before that."

"I don't get you, Mrs. Pearsall."

"Didn't somebody help her?"

"I helped her. I called Caesar."

"I don't mean who called the Pipes. I mean didn't anybody hold her hand? Talk to her?"

"Might have been some Indians doing that."

"Might have been?"

"Yeah. I made her stay back in the corner of the dance floor, and there was a couple of Indians sort of hanging around her."

Of course, thought Libby. Who were gentler than the Ojibway? Who were better prepared, through adversity, to offer consolation? "Who were they, Mr. Bigelow?"

"Couple of Indians, like I say."

"What were their names?"

The Judge's voice turned brisk, indicating that he was eager to get off the phone. "I got a number here for the Berrington Hospital, if you want to write it down. They said the family should get in touch."

Libby wrote down the number, then suddenly sat up straight, her eyes wide with delayed intuition. "Mr. Bigelow, did you touch my daughter during her episode?"

"Did I what?"

"Did you get physical with her? You made her stay in the corner of the dance floor. How did you make her stay there?"

Heatedly: "I *told* her to stay there." He paused, then reverted to his conciliatory voice; he even made it laugh a little. "Your daughter's always been one to do what the Judge tells her, Mrs. Pearsall. No need for you to worry about your daughter when she's with the Judge. No need to ask a question like that, either." Another little laugh, like a snarl. "You could hurt a man's feelings, asking a question like that."

Libby wanted to slam down the phone, but had learned the hard way never to alienate a friend of Verna's lest she lose track of her. More than once, in Chicago, it had been a friend Libby found especially repellent who was best able to put her in touch with her daughter.

"Thank you, Mr. Bigelow. I'll call the hospital."

"Tell her to hurry home, Mrs. Pearsall. The Homestead's not the same without her."

"Good-bye."

"Let me have a word with your husband, would you, please? I got a boil on my back I want to ask him about."

She laid the receiver on her pillow and went downstairs.

Tom sat atilt on the couch, asleep. She switched off the TV and put her hand on his brow. "Tom, the telephone."

He groaned in his sleep, slipping sideways, and lay flat on the couch.

"Tom, Verna's in the hospital."

He opened his eyes, but did not lift them to Libby. They were trained on the dead TV screen. They looked pained. More than pained. Anxious. It was the look he had flashed at Elaine LaBonte three Sundays ago when she came to tell them that Verna's lover was dead.

"She's in Berrington, and Judge Bigelow wants to talk to you."

He raised his hand to her, open, palm up. A loving gesture, she thought, and took the hand in her own, but he shook free and pointed to the phone on the end table. She handed him the phone and went upstairs.

He was off the phone by the time she picked the receiver off her pillow. She dialed the Berrington Hospital and asked for her daughter.

"I'll connect you to the Hope Unit," said the operator, and as Libby waited for the next voice on the line, she recalled the series of euphemisms attached to the psychiatric wards Verna had occupied. In the nine years since she was seventeen, Verna had checked into six hospitals—the Grace Unit, the Aurora Unit, the Share and Care Unit, the Tomorrow Unit, the Growth Unit, and the Harriet Y. Ammermann Memorial Mental Wellness Unit.

A woman said, "Hope."

"I'm Verna Highsmith's mother."

"Yes?"

"What's her condition, please? I've just found out where she is."

"Verna's been transferred to our Special Care section, Mrs. Highsmith. I can give you a nurse over there."

"Please."

Libby waited, picturing a locked inner chamber for the intensely disturbed. Three times in her six previous confinements, Verna had been lodged in such a place. Three times she had not.

"Special Care, this is Jaimie." The voice was a man's.

"I'm Verna Highsmith's mother. Can you tell me how she is?"

"She's been pretty distraught since I came on at four. Especially the last hour or so. Is evening generally a bad time for her, Mrs. Highsmith?"

"I can't say. She hasn't been living at home lately. Actually, my name isn't Highsmith. It's Pearsall."

"Well, we get some in here that are more distraught in the evening, and we get others that are more distraught in the morning."

"How is she distraught?"

"Bad vibes. Crying. Temper. You're her mother, you say?"

"I am."

"Then you know what I'm talking about. I'm not talking off-the-wall, I'm talking manic behavior alternating with down-in-the-dumps."

"What's she like right now?"

"Down in the dumps. She's slouched down in front of the TV."

"Is her talk coherent?"

"Yeah, pretty much, when she talks."

Libby was relieved. Verna's deepest plunges were often marked by gibberish.

"Who's her doctor?"

"Let's see." Jaimie's voice became faint as he turned away from the phone. "Darin, who's Verna Highsmith's doctor?"

It took half a minute to produce the answer. Besides paper

shuffling, Libby heard a scream, a shout, and a song—whether on TV or in real life it was impossible to tell.

"Dr. Pella checked her in by phone, Mrs. Highsmith. There's no doctors here on Sundays."

"He'll be in tomorrow?"

"Yeah, can you come in? I'm sure he'll want to talk to you about meds. We don't have a history for Verna."

"I'll be there. What time?"

"Ten or so. I'll let him know you're coming."

"Now can I talk to Verna?"

Faintly: "Darin, can Verna's mother talk to her?"

Another half minute. A violin. A wail. A deep, hacking cough.

"Hello?" A new voice, not Jaimie's.

"Verna?"

"Mom, it's just awful."

"Verna, your voice sounds so different." It was a slowed-down voice, deeper than normal.

"Mom, it's just awful here. Will you come and see?"

"What's awful?"

"My room, Mom. My roommate. The creeps in charge. The toilet paper. Everything."

"Are you on medication, Verna?"

"Yeah. It's awful."

"How are you feeling?"

"Awful. Come and see. You and Tom . . ." The voice trailed off. A moan. A slamming door. A sneeze. The voice returned. "Or just Tom, if you don't want to."

"I want to, Verna. I'm coming in the morning."

"Can I talk to Tom?"

"He's sleeping."

"Jesus Christ, can't you wake him up?" The voice was suddenly higher, faster. "Is he passed out or what? Doesn't he care enough about me to even talk to me?"

Libby weighed whether to go downstairs and implore Tom to talk to Verna. If he refused, Verna would be hurt. Better to use the excuse Verna was asking for.

"He's passed out. He's been drinking all day."

"Will he come with you tomorrow?"

"The Health Center's open tomorrow."

"He can come anyway, can't he? God, your Health Center is such a joke. You're like two little kids playing doctor and nurse."

This was followed by weeping. "Mom," "Tom," and "God" were some of the words uttered between gasps. The weeping went on and on.

"Verna, what is it?"

"You've got to come, Mom." A flood of tears. "Tonight. I've got to see you tonight."

"I'm exhausted. I've just driven seven hundred miles."

"You've always come in the past. I need you."

"Tomorrow, Verna. I'm coming tomorrow. Early."

"Tomorrow! I could be dead tomorrow. I *will* be dead tomorrow, I've just decided."

"Verna, I'm saying good night now." Suicide, the old threat, had lost its effect. "I'll see you at ten in the morning."

"You'll see me dead."

"Good night, Verna."

Libby hung up, switched off her lamp, and lay in the dark with her eyes open, paralyzed. Seven hundred miles of highway. Ten years of Verna's mood swings. Twelve years of Tom's drinking. Seven months of jackpines. Eighteen below and falling.

One thing was coming clear to her: her love for Tom was wearing thin. What had been only shadowy misgivings over the past year or more had come to light this afternoon somewhere between Chicago and Basswood: the qualities she had loved about her husband—his work with the sick and suffering (including Verna), his sense of humor (cleverly perverse), and his man-of-the-world self-confidence—were qualities he no longer possessed. He was seldom solicitous of others anymore; only of himself. His joking had crossed from cleverness into a stale and predictable kind of bitterness. What she had interpreted as self-confidence was a blustery cover for a serious lack of self-regard, and beneath that, fear.

Should she leave him? She put the question out of her mind. She wouldn't consider it now, not while they lived in Basswood.

It was she and Verna who had led him to spend his probationary year in this godforsaken wasteland, so she could not very well abandon him to it. The year was better than half over. She would see it through, suppress the impulse to flee. Come spring she'd consider it.

Having made this determination, she was suddenly sleepy. She curled in a ball, pulled the covers up to her ear, and wondered if Frank would go with her to Berrington. She would stop at the rectory tomorrow and ask him.

23

The next morning Monsignor Adrian Lawrence, who began each day with prayers in his room, stood up from his prie-dieu and felt a familiar pain in his chest, a severe stabbing sensation located a little below where he imagined his heart to be. He dropped into the chair at the foot of his bed and tried to ignore it by mumbling a couple of psalms from memory and next by picking up his prayerbook and returning to the meditations for Epiphany week. Rereading Monday's and then going ahead to Tuesday's, he felt the pain subside. He read Wednesday's and Thursday's as well, and then it was gone. He thanked God for this as he shaved; then he dressed and went down to the kitchen, where his attention was divided between the news in the paper, the birds in the feeder, and the morning thoughts of Mrs. Tatzig.

"There's only nine of your socks in the wash this morning, Father."

"Is that so?"

"You aren't changing them every day."

"I thought I was." He spread out the paper before him in the breakfast nook. The movement frightened off the sparrows.

"And how come nine? Where's the other one gone to?" Mrs.

Tatzig bobbed across the kitchen from the sink to the stove and back again. Heavy and long-legged, she walked with the mincing steps of a much smaller woman and caused the floor to bounce slightly. She was a brusque, swarthy woman fond of corduroy, cardigans, and cats. Her hair was dyed a deep shade of orange.

"I'll look under my bed," said the monsignor.

"I looked under your bed."

"Then I don't know, Marcella. It will turn up."

In this Victorian house of five bedrooms and countless crannies and closets and gables, Mrs. Tatzig was its most obtuse fixture. She had moved in twenty years ago, shortly after Mr. Tatzig, a railroad worker, was killed in a highway accident. She was less religious than her predecessor Eunice Pfeiffer, less introspective, less deferential toward the clergymen entrusted to her care.

"This house needs new insulation, Father."

"It does, I agree."

"Mornings like this it's drafty."

"It is indeed."

"Cat'll be up on the furniture all day."

"That's not good."

"Can't blame the cat when the floor's cold."

Adrian Lawrence lifted his cup off the newspaper, turned a page, and studied the weather map. A bit warmer today, thank God. Near zero, perhaps, by afternoon. One by one, the sparrows fluttered back to the feeder.

"It's a new one, Father."

"A new what, Marcella?"

"A new sock."

"Ah."

"One of your new ones from Christmas."

"Maybe the cat dragged it off."

"The cat never does that." She ripped open a box of cake mix and poured it into a bowl. "By the way, a woman called for Father Healy last night. That Pearsall woman from the reservation."

"Lovely people, the Pearsalls."

"I left him a note. Did he call her?"

"I don't know. He got in very late."

She cracked two eggs into the bowl. "He's an odd duck, isn't he?"

"Who?"

"Father Healy."

He turned to look at her. "Why do you say that, Marcella?"

She measured milk in a cup. "He isn't your normal assistant. He doesn't play golf."

"Marcella, it's January."

"But I mean he doesn't even own any clubs. And he never has priest friends in."

"He likes his privacy, Marcella. He spent all those years at the Academy."

"And he drinks a lot."

"Mmmmm."

"Father?"

"Yes?"

"I say he drinks a lot of rum."

"More than he should, perhaps."

"And you never know what he's thinking. He's too quiet."

"Not all priests are like Father DeSmet, Marcella."

"Oi," exclaimed Mrs. Tatzig, gladdened by the memory of Frank's predecessor. "That live wire. He's missed around here."

"He talked too much, Marcella. I used to turn off my hearing aid."

"Oh, go on."

"Give me Frank Healy any day over Gene DeSmet."

She jammed the blades of the Mixmaster into their sockets and lowered them into the bowl. "I'm the opposite, Father. Give me a live wire instead of a spook." She switched on the mixer, and it whined and snarled in a painfully high register. The monsignor turned off his hearing aid.

When Frank came in from the schoolchildren's Mass, it was customary for the two priests to plan their day's work over breakfast. They did this in the living room because the monsignor liked to catch at least the last few minutes of a certain morning program on TV, being very fond of the anchorwoman. He liked to see what she was wearing and whether she appeared to have had a restful night's sleep. On mornings as cold as this one, Frank built a fire in the fireplace.

"How many this morning, Frank?" The monsignor was referring to voluntary Mass goers as opposed to schoolchildren, who were coerced.

"Four." Frank, kneeling, struck a match.

"Down from Saturday."

"Yes, it's the weather. Fifteen below when I got up."

"Inhuman. But warmer this afternoon."

"Lester Fredricks died last night, Adrian."

"The poor man—it was only a matter of time. How's his missus?"

"Worn out. She'll need a long rest. She'd like you to take the funeral."

"Glad to. When?"

"Wednesday."

"Do I have anything else going on Wednesday?"

"Not that I know of," said Frank.

The paper flared, the kindling caught. Frank carefully placed two sticks of pine on the flames and then picked his coffee and toast off the mantel and carried them to the couch. The living room was large and somber, redecoration having been carried out by a parish committee at a time when paneling the color of mud was on sale. The carpet was rusty shag. The fireplace was too far away for warmth, and Frank covered his knees with an afghan. The monsignor was tipped back in his adjustable chair, his oatmeal, toast, grapefruit, and coffee on the lamp table beside him.

"How many on the reservation yesterday, Frank? I forgot to ask."

"Fifty."

"Down from last week."

"By five."

"Mrs. Pearsall called for you last night."

"I saw the note. I got in too late to call back."

"A lovely couple, the Pearsalls. I'm so glad you're staying overnight in their house."

Frank had done so now for four Saturdays, three in their absence as a favor, making sure the furnace was working and the windows and doors secure. As much as he relished the warmth and comfort of their guest room, he was determined, now that they were back, to return to his cot in Our Lady's sacristy. A few of his Basswood parishioners were warming up to him, seeking him out on Saturday nights with their problems—not in droves, but one or two each week. That was one reason. The other was that each time Libby phoned from Chicago she'd tripped a switch in his heart and words came spilling out of him the way they had done in high school, heartfelt words such as he uttered to no one else, man or woman. Amazing, a talking jag like that while you were cold sober. And dangerous probably—a priest liking a woman that much.

A handsome man on TV smiled smugly at the two priests while putting on his clothes. At the mention of a certain brand of shaving lotion, a pretty brunette appeared at the man's side and put her nose into his ear. The pine in the fireplace crackled and spat. The clock on the mantel struck the quarter hour.

"What time do you have, Frank?"

He looked at his watch. "Five to nine."

The old man cranked his chair erect and trudged through the shag to the clock. He snapped open the hinged glass over its face and moved the minute hand ahead. "It's never been right since the move." He inserted a key and cranked. "Clocks like to settle into a place and stay put. I should have left it in Berrington."

The clock, like the man winding it, had been retired from the chancery, where it had stood on a shelf in the reception room and told the approximate time to visitors as far back as Father Zell and his contemporaries before the turn of the century. Its toneless, businesslike chime (bonk bonk) and its hollow, deliberate tick (thock thock) were so dear to the old man's heart that he had asked, upon being replaced, if he might take it with him to Linden Falls—surely the only time in his simple life (Frank supposed) that Adrian Lawrence had requested anything for himself. Bishop Baker, eager to sweep out the chancery's trappings along with its personnel, bestowed upon the monsignor not only the clock but also the chancery Oldsmobile and the chancery cat.

The cat, foggy green in color, black in disposition, was passing its late middle age brooding like a watchdog on the deep windowsill behind the couch and snarling when people came to the door. Frank could hear it there now, behind him. Its purr was a kind of suppressed growl.

The monsignor returned to his chair and gave his attention back to the man on TV, who was now tying his necktie and saying, "Give me an after-shave with a bite." At this, the pretty brunette bit his earlobe. This was followed by a brief news report, and then the anchorwoman appeared on the screen. Frank saw the monsignor's face soften, saw him break into a little smile.

"She looks nice in red, Frank."

"She does."

"Why doesn't she wear red more often?"

"I wonder."

The doorbell rang. They heard Mrs. Tatzig open the back door and welcome her sister into the kitchen.

Frank asked, "How's your cold, Adrian?"

"Better, much better."

"Will you go to the meeting tonight, or will I?" Last time the monsignor had sent Frank to the parish council in his place.

"If you can see your way to attend, you'd be doing me a great favor, my boy."

"I can."

"Good." Adrian spoke with his eyes fastened on the screen. "I'm useless on committees."

"Kindergarten will come up. What shall I tell them?"

"Whatever you think."

"But they'll want the pastor's opinion."

"I don't have one, my boy. You're the educator."

St. Ann's school was becoming a perilous drain on the parish resources, teachers' salaries being the fastest-growing item in the budget. Two years ago the parish council had eliminated grades seven and eight, and now they were debating the necessity of kindergarten.

"I don't know a thing about five-year-olds," said Frank.

"I don't either." It was nearly a minute before the woman in red was replaced by the weatherman and Adrian Lawrence drew his eyes away from TV and leveled them at Frank. "They aren't very big, are they?"

"What aren't?"

"Kindergartners."

"No. Very small."

"I never went to kindergarten, Frank. Never missed it."

"I think kindergarten's a good thing."

"Isn't it mostly naps and finger painting?"

"Plus a little reading and counting and learning to be supervised."

"You went yourself?"

"Right here at St. Ann's."

"That was before my time."

"I think I'll go to bat for kindergarten."

"Lovely."

Frank, a former smoker, smelled cigarette fumes wafting in from the kitchen, where Mrs. Tatzig and her sister were visiting loudly. Her sister, a chain-smoker named Charlotte Johnson, dropped in at the rectory nearly every morning but seldom advanced beyond the kitchen. Mrs. Tatzig claimed that the reason her sister couldn't look a priest in the eye was that she suffered the guilt of the fallen-away. She hadn't been to church for many years—not since the day her husband, Alfred Johnson, a lifelong grocery clerk, had been driven from the confessional unabsolved. This had happened in 1966 during the brief residency of Father Xavier Edwards, an eccentric, elderly man later committed to a mental hospital. In his eight months in Linden Falls Father Edwards refused absolution to well over one hundred penitents, and the sin that customarily set him off was the venial matter of a careless prayer life. Adultery, theft, and false witness he readily forgave, but skipping grace at meals enraged him. "Get out and make room for a worthy Christian!" he had shouted at Alfred Johnson. "Without prayer you're lost, get out!" Alfred Johnson went straight home from the confessional and told his wife it was a relief to be lost. As a convert from Lutheranism, he'd thought confession a wacky affair from the start, he said, and he urged her to be lost along with him, and she complied.

Frank sipped his coffee and said, "I'll need the office between two and four, Adrian. I've got some appointments."

"Fine."

"And there's that survey from the chancery."

"Would you fill that out and mail it in, Frank?"

"There's a page where it asks for the pastor's recommendations."

"Put down whatever. I'll stand behind it. Chancery affairs are so bothersome, Frank. So incredibly boring."

"Did you think that while you were chancellor?"

"Of course not. I thought it was all so important then. I thought the Church needed my talents as an administrator, and maybe it did, but now that I'm a pastor again, I see what being a priest is all about. A man's talents are best put to use in parish work, Frank. And do you know what parish work consists of? What it comes down to? What our job really is?"

"What?"

"Being nice to people."

"That's all?"

"Loving-kindness. Nothing more or less."

"Isn't that oversimplifying it, Adrian?"

"Nothing simple about it." The old man squinted at Frank. His smile faded. "You went out to see the shut-ins yesterday."

Frank nodded.

"And you were nice to them."

"Sure."

"And was it simple?"

"Well . . ."

"Was it simple being nice to the Hallorans?"

"I wouldn't call it complicated."

"But it's not simple, Frank. It's hard work sitting there with that dizzy Halloran woman sitting on one side of you and her unfriendly husband sitting on the other and listening to their spats. And how about Mrs. Graham—have you ever known such a foul-natured woman?"

"But you keep going back."

"Of course. They depend on it."

"But every week, Adrian? No priest is obliged to make home visits every week."

"My own fault. When I moved back to town, I went each week because they begged me to, and because there weren't all that many people from the old days around here I could talk to. But now I'm wondering, my boy, if you'd care to take over the Sunday visits yourself."

The doorbell sounded again—the front door apparently, for the cat was standing on the windowsill hissing. Neither priest went to the door because Mrs. Tatzig, who made it her business to confront all visitors, came bouncing through the room at high speed. There were a few words and a cold draft from the entryway before she returned, announcing that someone wanted to see Frank.

"Come on in, it's cold by the door," she said into the entryway. "The living room's not much warmer, but the fire's pretty to look at."

Libby stepped into the room and said, "Hi."

"Libby." Frank sprang from the couch and went to her. He put out his hand and then awkwardly drew it back before touching her. "Libby, I want you to meet my housemates. This is Mrs. Tatzig."

"Hi."

"This is Libby Pearsall, Mrs. Tatzig. She's the nurse in Basswood."

"Quite the outfit," said Mrs. Tatzig. "You didn't buy them duds in Basswood."

"No, Chicago." Libby wore a gray tam tilted over one ear. It matched her gray jacket. Her heavy plaid skirt was pleated and long. On her face, Frank noticed, she wore a pinched look not entirely concealed by her smile.

Frank beckoned her over to the recliner that the monsignor was struggling to climb out of. "Adrian, here's Libby Pearsall at last."

"Lovely," said the old man, attempting to stand. "Lovely. Just lovely." In his haste to get out of his chair he had not moved it to its upright position, and he kept slipping back into its hollow.

Frank rescued him by pulling on his arm. "This is Adrian Lawrence, Libby."

Once on his feet, the monsignor, slightly shorter than Libby, sandwiched both of her hands between his own, massaging them and patting them as he gazed fondly into her eyes and said, "You don't know the half of it, Mrs. Pearsall. You don't have any idea how much good you and your husband are doing out there in your Indian outpost, and I don't mean just the good you're doing the Indians. I mean the good you're doing my young priests."

"Well, we became very fond of Gene DeSmet, Father, and of course Frank and I are friends from way back."

Frank, standing apart from them and regretting that Libby had made him feel suddenly so skittish, so clumsy, watched the old man's warmth melt her pinched look. Color came into her cheeks.

"Lovely, just lovely. Have you had your breakfast? Marcella, what have you got in the kitchen for this young lady?"

"Coffee and grapes," said Mrs. Tatzig, who had backed up to the fire and stood with her arms crossed, her eyes riveted on Libby. The cat, too, was examining Libby, its head hanging over the back of the couch.

"Thanks, I've eaten," said Libby. She smiled warmly at the old priest and seemed in no hurry to take her hands away from him.

"Well, at least coffee," said the monsignor.

"Yes, coffee," said Libby. She turned from the old man and joined Frank at the couch, sat down next to him, sat well forward because the cat, perched behind her, was making a menacing noise in its throat.

Mrs. Tatzig said, "Coffee coming up," and bounced into the kitchen.

"Lovely." The old man backed up to his chair and fell into it. "Wonderful."

Libby looked at the clock on the mantel. "Do you have some free time, Frank?"

"I'm making a school visit, then I'm free for the rest of the morning."

"Verna's in the hospital."

"What happened?" He saw her pinched look come back. He saw the monsignor, sensing a private talk, turn off his hearing aid.

"Something mental," said Libby. "I wonder if you could come and see her with me."

"Sure. Berrington?"

"Yes, her doctor will be there at 10:30."

He looked at his watch. He was scheduled to discuss forgiveness with grades five and six at 9:30. Berrington was an hour away.

"I've done this so often it ought to be easy—gone into strange hospitals and tried to explain Verna to strange doctors—but it's hard every time." Her pinched look softened into sorrow. She turned away. "It's harder than ever today, Frank, for some reason. It ought to get easier, but today it's very, very hard."

Frank went over to the monsignor's chair. "Adrian."

The old man set down his oatmeal and fumbled shakily at his ear, turning up his hearing aid.

"Adrian, are you well enough to take my place in school this morning?"

"I'm fine. You bet. Whose room?"

"Mrs. Pettit's."

"Yes, my boy. Fine. What'll I say?"

"I told them we'd talk about forgiveness, but it's up to you."

"Forgiveness. Lovely."

Mrs. Tatzig came in with a mug of coffee, a pitcher of cream, and a paper napkin. Her sister timidly followed, carrying a silver sugar bowl and a lit cigarette.

"No cream or sugar, thanks." Libby took the mug and the napkin.

"Libby, this is Mrs. Johnson," said Frank.

"My sister," said Mrs. Tatzig proudly.

"Mrs. Johnson, this is Libby Pearsall. She's the nurse at the Indian Health Service in Basswood."

Mrs. Johnson said, "Pleased to meet you," and retraced her

steps to the doorway. She was a pear-shaped woman, round-shouldered and dark-skinned like her sister. She stood at the door waiting for her sister to return with her to the safety of the kitchen, but Mrs. Tatzig, her curiosity not yet satisfied, lingered at the fireplace, her back to the fire, her eyes on Libby. She said, "Hats like that were in style years ago."

"Yes," said Libby. "They're back."

"Not around here."

"No. In Chicago."

"That skirt looks warm, is it wool?"

"Yes." Libby lifted it off her knee. "Just the thing for weather like this."

"You ought to have warmer boots." They were high-topped shoes, black with mauve laces.

The monsignor, who had been following Mrs. Tatzig's commentary from head to toe, said, "I like her jacket, Marcella. You ought to have a jacket like that."

"*Very* warm," said Libby, opening it to display the lining.

Mrs. Tatzig's laugh was disparaging. "That? On me? You're being funny." She drew a Kleenex from the pocket of her shapeless knit sweater and turned around and dusted the mantel and the clock. Her sister, stationed in the doorway, took a deep drag on her cigarette.

The monsignor took up his oatmeal again. "Frank tells me you've been away, Mrs. Pearsall."

"Yes, to Chicago. We used to live there."

"You drove?"

"Yes."

"How were the roads?"

"Fine. No ice, except between here and Basswood, and that was only nineteen miles out of the seven hundred."

"Nineteen? But it's only twelve in winter."

"We don't drive across the lake."

"For heaven's sake, why not? It's a smoother road than most winters."

"My husband can't be talked into it."

Adrian nibbled his toast. "I was in Chicago years ago for the Eucharistic Congress. I took the train."

"Charlotte's husband was in Chicago during the war," said Mrs. Tatzig. "Charlotte went there once to see him." She turned to her sister. "You took the bus if I remember."

Mrs. Johnson, avoiding everyone's eyes, addressed the ash at the end of her cigarette in a thin, unhurried voice. "I took the bus down and the train back. It was bad weather and the buses stopped running. March of '45. Alfred was in the navy at Great Lakes. He had a weekend pass and he met me in Chicago. The things you do when you're young."

"Tell them about the hotel."

"The lobby was all black marble and chandeliers."

"And the show you went to."

"It was onstage. It was singing."

"Negroes, wasn't it, Charlotte?"

"Negroes and whites mixed together."

"Now you see it on television all the time," Mrs. Tatzig explained to Libby, "but it wasn't so common in those days."

"That was the last year of the war," said her sister. "Alfred came home that fall."

Frank's brothers, too, had come home that fall. While Mrs. Tatzig carried on with a few more of her sister's reminiscences, he was astonished to realize how old his brothers must be. Peter in St. Paul had to be at least sixty and Joe in Montana was eight years older than that. For two decades he'd been thinking of his brothers, whom he hadn't seen since his father's funeral eighteen years ago, as men in their middle age, yet they had become as old as Charlotte and Alfred Johnson. Charlotte's hair was white and Alfred was retired from the grocery store.

When Libby and Frank got up to leave, the monsignor rose without assistance and clutched her hands again, praising her work with the Indians. The two sisters retired to the kitchen and Frank followed them to get his coat. He returned to the front door, where the monsignor was calling Libby "my dear" and imploring her to come again soon.

"I will," she said, remaining politely in place while the old man ran his hands up the puffy sleeves of her jacket and fondly squeezed her elbows.

"So that's Loving Kindness."

"Yes."

"I pictured him different."

"I can see why, if all you had to go on was Gene DeSmet's opinion."

"I expected to meet a doddering old fool."

"He dodders, but he's no fool."

"No. He's very sweet. And those red suspenders—I love him."

Frank glanced at the speedometer—seventy—and tensed up. "There's a sharp curve ahead, Libby."

She let up on the gas. The road curved to the left, skirted a frozen pond, then veered to the right and climbed over a railroad grade. Then it straightened and ran flat across miles of farmland. The sun was blinding on the fields of snow.

"I called you last night."

"I saw the note, but not until late. After midnight."

"A sick call?"

"A death call."

She took her right hand off the wheel and gave it to him, gloved. "Is it hard, watching someone die, Frank?"

"For me. I'm new at it."

"I used to be okay with death, but lately I've been getting soft. That Sunday at Roger Upward's, I cried like a baby."

Frank didn't know what to do with her hand. He held it limply, resting his wrist on his knee. When had he last held hands with anyone? Was it in grade two, playing Jack to Sylvia Pofford's Jill in a skit for parents? Last night, as priest to widow, he had held the hand of Mrs. Fredricks beside her husband's deathbed—but holding hands as friend to friend? Not since he was eight.

"Did you cry last night?" she asked him.

"Men don't cry, Libby."

"God, are you behind the times." She took her eyes from the road and smiled at him fondly over her sunglasses. "It's okay now, men can cry."

"Since when?"

"You haven't been seeing the right movies. All the stars are crying these days. I've seen Dustin Hoffman cry twice."

"Ray Milland cried in *Lost Weekend* and they locked him up."

The car was getting warm. She took her hand from him and removed her gloves. She didn't reach out to him again, and he was relieved.

Mrs. Pettit led the monsignor down the corridor of St. Ann's School and into the library, where the fifth and sixth grades were brought together twice a week for their lesson in religion.

"Where's Father Healy?" one of the sixth-graders asked with obvious disappointment. She was a long-haired blonde wearing silver earrings and lipstick.

Another piped, "Father Healy said he was teaching us for the rest of the year." This was a tiny brunette in a Mickey Mouse sweatshirt.

"Father Healy's been called away," Mrs. Pettit announced, helping the old man off with his coat and scarf and earmuffs and mittens.

The girls groaned.

Mrs. Pettit, a youngish woman in black slacks and a red sweater, pleaded for quiet and eventually got it. Then she introduced the pastor, and when she stepped aside to give him center stage, she was horrified to see him leaning sideways, far to his left, with his eyes shut tight as though in pain. She asked, "What's the matter, Monsignor?"

He smiled at her without opening his eyes and began to say something she couldn't understand. She clutched at his black suitcoat, trying to keep him upright, but he tipped over—slowly and carefully—and lay on the floor. She went to her knees and held his head in her hands. "Monsignor, what's the matter?" His eyes remained shut, his face was contorted in pain, but there was a deliberate sort of movement in his lips and a weak sound from his throat as though he were trying to form words. Or was he singing? Up close it sounded like singing. Mrs. Pettit tried to catch the words, and so did the eleven- and twelve-year-olds, who sat engrossed in the spectacle, the girl in the Mickey Mouse sweatshirt peeking through her fingers, the girl with the silver earrings biting her nails.

Up and down went the old man's quavery voice. He was reciting a line over and over that Mrs. Pettit recognized from this morning's liturgy: "The spirit of the Lord God is upon me, the spirit of the Lord God is upon me."

24

"Hope is closed to visitors until evening," said the woman behind the information desk in the lobby, "unless you're family."

"I'm her mother."

The woman, a chubby, middle-aged redhead, pointed her pencil at Frank and an inquiring look at Libby.

"He's my priest," Libby told her.

The redhead looked skeptical but let them pass. "Hope's on four."

In the elevator Libby drew open his coat and tugged playfully at his shirt. "Where did you get this?"

He looked down at his faded rugby shirt of blue and red stripes. "St. Ann's annual rummage sale."

"Don't you ever wear priest clothes?"

"Not very often—they make people stiff. They make *me* stiff."

Wide double doors led to Hope, a vast, brightly lit room of Formica tables and tubular chairs with a nurses' station at the far end. The walls and ceiling were painted three shades of yellow. Two patients, an old woman wearing a gray sweatsuit and a young woman wearing a violet bathrobe, sat at opposite ends of the room. Two spacious hallways, one blue and one green, led to bedrooms and offices.

There were three staff members behind the counter of the nurses' station. One of them, a woman of about fifty with a deeply wrinkled face, told Libby that Dr. Pella would see her in a few minutes.

"I'd like to see my daughter first," Libby replied.

"Your daughter's in Special Care."

"I know."

"We suggest visitors to Special Care wait until late afternoon at the earliest. We don't like to interrupt the program over there." The woman wore a name tag—*Roberta Brink, RN*—over the pocket of her black blouse.

"I'm sorry, but I haven't seen my daughter for over a month. It's urgent, just for a minute."

The woman rearranged her wrinkles into a deeper state of concern. "I'll have to clear it," she said. "Have a seat."

"Please clear it for both of us. This is my priest."

"Please have a seat."

They crossed the tile floor to the nearest table, removed their coats, and sat. At the next table the old woman in the jogging suit sat reading a letter and weeping silently. In the distance the young woman in the bathrobe was scissoring something out of construction paper.

The old woman raised her head and asked through her tears, "Is it nice out?"

"It's cold," said Libby.

"It looks nice out."

"Yes, it's sunny but very cold."

"I've been here since Christmas," she said to Frank, wiping her cheeks with her fingertips. "I had a nervous breakdown at Christmas. Off my rocker, my husband calls it. 'Pauline,' he says, 'you're clean off your rocker.' I didn't think I was having a nervous breakdown. I thought I was just feeling bad. But what I'm learning is that if you feel really, really bad, pretty soon you can feel bad enough to have a nervous breakdown. The Hope Unit is where you learn things like that. I'd been feeling bad for ten winters without realizing I was going off my rocker. I think it's good to learn things, don't you?"

She appeared to be asking Frank, who replied, "It's always good to learn things."

"Even if it's bad news, don't you agree?"

"Yes, probably."

"No news is bad news."

"It can be, I suppose."

"Bad news is good news."

"Mmmmm."

"Well, isn't it?"

"You've lost me, I'm afraid."

"Just take it slow," said the old woman sternly. "I was feeling bad for ten years before I knew I was having a nervous breakdown."

"Yes."

"Then I was told I was having a nervous breakdown."

"I follow you."

"That was news."

"News, yes."

"That was *good* news."

"Because?"

At this, the woman drooped in discouragement, her head hanging, her arms dangling. When next she spoke, it was to Libby: "Are you checking him in?"

Roberta Brink, RN, summoned Libby to her desk and said Special Care wasn't ready for her but the doctor was. She pointed to the green hallway. "Down there on the right." When Frank made a move to follow, the nurse added, "Alone."

"He's my priest," said Libby.

"Alone—the doctor wants to see you alone. You'll find his name on 422. Dr. Pella."

Frank accompanied her to 422. She knocked and a voice called, "Come in." She went in. Frank continued on to the window at the end of the corridor and stood looking out. The hospital stood on a hill and he saw, spread out below him, the heart and arteries of Berrington, an unattractive city of small factories, a great many empty store buildings, and a population that had been shinking for ten years or more. Once a thriving rail hub at the intersection of three lines, Berrington had seen two of those lines swallowed up by the third, which then moved its division point farther west, leaving the abandoned rail yard, unsightly and vast, stretching across the city's midsection like the scar of a mortal wound.

He returned to the table in the dayroom and had been paging through *People* for ten minutes or so when the double doors to Hope swung open and clusters of people entered the room chattering noisily. Most, perhaps two dozen of them, were young, but a few were Frank's age and older. From their talk and their wet hair he gathered that many of them had been swimming. Somewhere in the building was a pool; he could smell the chlorine. A few of the young people drifted down the two hallways, apparently to their rooms, while others entered a smoky TV alcove, but most settled at the tables with cans of soda or cups of coffee. The old woman at the next table got up to leave, pausing to tell Frank, "Activity hour gets them all worked up. You're going hate it here. You're going to have people milling around like this day and night, and you're going to get plenty sick of it." She hobbled off down the green corridor.

Soon a tall man wearing a suit and tie and tennis shoes came hurrying through the room calling, "All right, people, it's time, come along now, it's time," while a young woman with a clipboard stood in the blue hallway shouting out names. From a speaker in the ceiling a croaky female voice said that the second-level class on medications would meet in two minutes. When Libby emerged from the green hallway, the dayroom was empty of everyone but Frank and the young woman in the violet bathrobe cutting things out of construction paper.

"The staff called Dr. Pella in the middle of the night to get him to admit her, which he did by phone," said Libby, sitting down, folding her jacket on her lap, smoothing it nervously. "They put her in Special Care because she was threatening to kill herself."

"Is she still?"

"No, not this morning. Dr. Pella wasn't in yesterday, so he didn't get his first look at her till about an hour ago. I told him

Verna threatens suicide about once a day, so it probably isn't necessary to keep her in Special Care—those are usually such dismal places—but he says he doesn't take chances with patients he's never met before, and he wants her there till he gets her medications straightened out."

She spoke fast. There was a heightened color in her cheeks, a quickening in her eyes. Frank recalled from years ago these sexual signals in Libby whenever she met a boy or a man who aroused her interest. He assumed that Dr. Pella was handsome and engaging.

"What's his diagnosis?"

"You mean what's *my* diagnosis. Depression, at the moment. We went over her chart and I could see her mood's been swinging like mad. She's probably been off her meds, or she's been sniffing something or popping something that neutralizes her meds. She'll get reckless like that whenever something bad happens to her. It's usually a broken love affair that does it."

"Do you suppose she broke up with Judge Bigelow?"

"God, Frank, can you imagine?" Her face clouded. "Judge Bigelow with my daughter?"

"He's not much to look at."

"You know what makes my skin crawl? I keep wondering what their intimate moments must be like."

"You probably shouldn't."

"I know I shouldn't, it makes me sick."

Two men in suits came through the double doors. Their heels were loud on the tile as they crossed to the nurses' station. The older man, whose baldness gleamed in the fluorescent lighting, wore squeaky shoes. This man leaned over the counter and spoke to Nurse Brink—Frank heard him ask for Dr. Pella—while the other man, who was taller and younger and wore his crimson tie hanging loose from his open collar, surveyed the room, his eyes returning again and again to Libby and Frank.

"It's tricky regulating meds for manic depression," said Libby. "You give her something to lift her up when she's low and it's liable to make her zany. Or you give her something to calm her down when she's high and she's liable to hit rock bottom."

Frank watched the two men stroll to the far end of the room, where they bought coffee from a machine and sat at a table. They looked like detectives in movies.

"I'm going to talk to Caesar Pipe and his wife when I get back to Basswood," Libby went on. "I'm going to thank them for bringing her here instead of to jail. Caesar is quoted on the chart as saying she was disturbing the peace at the Homestead. That's a misdemeanor, you know. He could just as well have taken her to jail. She was in jail twice, in Chicago."

"For disturbing the peace?"

Libby nodded. "One time it was that. The other time it was assault. She beat up her boyfriend and he called the cops. She's not very big but she knows how to fight."

Nurse Brink, the phone to her ear, called to the two men, "Dr. Pella will see you in Room 422," and she pointed down the green hallway. As the men left the dayroom, the nurse said to Libby, "You can see your daughter now, you and the father." She pointed down the blue hallway.

The door to Special Care was locked. Beside the door was a sign instructing visitors to press the red button and speak into the grille in the wall. Libby did so, and the lock clicked open. Frank followed her into a rectangular room, not large, crowded with a dozen patients wearing pajamas and robes. The door swung quickly and heavily shut behind them. Some of the patients sat on couches watching TV, and others sat at small, round tables watching each other. Most were young, a few were old. Bedroom doors stood open along three of the walls.

Here the nurses' station was a cage. A young man with a mustache spoke through the wire mesh, asking Libby and Frank to sit down and wait—Verna needed coaxing out of her room.

"Has she talked about suicide?" Libby asked.

He pulled at his mustache. "Not to me. I guess she did when she was admitted, but I haven't heard her talk that way."

"Go easy on the Levilil."

The young man looked insulted. "We give out the medication prescribed."

"I'm her mother and I'm a nurse and Levilil isn't the best way to bring her out of depression."

"You'd have to tell the doctor that, Mrs. Highsmith."

"I did. His orders will come through, but I'd like you to stop the Levilil right away. And my name is Mrs. Pearsall."

"Here she comes," the young man said.

Frank and Libby turned. Led from a bedroom by a young man wearing jeans and a name tag on his sweatshirt, the hem of her oversized robe dragging like a train, approaching with her head turned sideways and looking fearful and deeply self-involved, was Libby's daughter.

Libby gave her a hug, which Verna did not return.

"This is Frank Healy. You've heard me talk about him."

Verna glanced at him without interest, then settled her eyes on the TV across the room.

They made room for themselves at one of the tables, opposite two men sitting side by side. Frank tried not to eavesdrop on the questions and reassurances that Libby, in her softest voice, directed at her daughter. Verna, folding her arms on the table, said nothing, seemed incapable of speech. The eye she turned toward her visitors—the right eye—was concentrating on something deep inside herself and displayed no flicker of comprehension, no acknowledgment of what her mother was telling her. Her other eye was partially hidden under her pale brown hair, which hung tangled and unwashed. She had dark eyes and a delicate chin—features resembling her mother's but not adding up to her mother's beauty. Verna's was a face that might have been pretty if infused with a happy spirit, but now, sunk in gloom, it had a dead look.

"Verna, can you tell me what happened at the Homestead Saturday night?"

No reply.

"Can you tell me how you're feeling?"

Glum silence.

"Can you give me a little smile? Can't you say anything?"

Nothing.

"Verna, last night on the phone you wanted to see me."

Her daughter slowly lowered her head and rested her forehead on her folded arms.

What anguish! thought Frank. Did you, dear God, foresee this when you made the sun, the moon, and the stars and told your creatures to propogate? Did you know that some of the people you claim to love would be confined to this cramped room with a lock on the door, their moods and behavior out of control? And this parent who devoted years of her life to the care and loving of her only daughter—did you foresee her coming here today to find that all her efforts have gone into the formation of this unraveling wreck?

Instead of waiting for an answer—God sometimes took forever—Frank turned his attention to the two men sitting across the table. One, young and bearded, was smoking the tiny stub of a cigarette. The other, old and flaccid, was staring down at a few Cheerios floating in a plastic bowl of milk. The young man kept his eyes fastened on Libby's lips as though reading them as she spoke. The old man was trying to submerge the Cheerios by pressing them down with his spoon. Across the room the TV was tuned to a game show. Behind the nurses' cage the man with the mustache spoke on the phone. In a nearby bedroom Frank saw a middle-aged woman lying across a bed on her back, her head hanging over the side, her long gray hair nearly touching the floor. She was looking at Frank upside down. Someone on TV won a four-man tent. Someone watching TV began to cry. The old man offered Frank his bowl of Cheerios, but Frank said he'd eaten. The young man put out his cigarette, bending low to inhale the fumes from the ashtray. Libby got up to go.

Verna lifted her head, raised her eyes to Frank as he was getting to his feet. "Don't go," she said softly.

They sat down again, exchanging chairs, Frank next to Verna. He laid his hand on her arm. She gave him the vaguest of smiles and lowered her head again, pressing her forehead to the back of his hand.

A minute passed. The flaccid man put his bowl to his mouth and drank. The young man went to the cage and asked for another cigarette, was given one, put it to his lips and pressed his face against the wire mesh as a match was struck for him. He returned to his chair and his study of Libby.

Another minute passed. Frank said, "Verna, we'll come again."

She raised her head and looked him full in the face. Again the vague smile came to her lips, but not to her eyes.

"Get well," he said.

She nodded deliberately.

"We love you," said her mother.

Her daughter turned to face the wall.

Frank followed Libby out. Waiting at the elevator, he saw the sorrow in her haunted eyes, saw the wrinkles of worry around them, saw that unlike her daughter, Libby lost none of her attractiveness when her spirit was clouded, saw that her face, shaded and softened by sadness, was more beautiful than ever.

"Worse than you expected?" he asked.

She nodded. "More withdrawn. More depressed."

"She gave me a smile, at least."

"She has a smile men can't resist." Libby frowned at him. "And she can't resist men who respond to it."

The two men resembling movie detectives joined them in the elevator.

"I suppose one day more or less doesn't matter," said the younger man wearing the loose tie.

"Not much we can do anyhow, if she's out of her mind," said his bald partner.

"Let's check out her father."

"Let's eat lunch."

They dropped swiftly to the lobby, where the clock behind the information desk said noon. Stepping outside into the frigid sunlight, Libby said, "Those men—I had the odd feeling they were talking about Verna."

So had Frank, but he didn't say so.

25

Dr. Tom Pearsall told Judge Bigelow to wait while he put his order together.

"I got all day," said the Judge, smiling slyly at Tom and lowering himself onto the small chair between the scale and the examination table.

Tom closed his visitor in the examination room and crossed the hall to the kitchen. He secured the kitchen door by bracing a chair under the knob, then he went out the back door. The sun on the snow made his eyes ache. He let himself into the garage, a sturdy, windowless structure built last summer by the Upward brothers and still smelling of new pine lumber. He switched on the light and unlocked the built-in tool cabinet. Instead of tools the cabinet contained a small, plaid, soft-sided suitcase. This he carried into the house and laid on the kitchen table. He unlocked it and removed two shirts and some underwear, revealing a dozen plastic bags lying on a bed of bath towels. Under the towels lay a number of small, colorful packets containing capsules and tablets. He selected two green and three red packets and set them on the table. Next to these he placed four plastic bags, each packed tightly with smaller bags of marijuana.

He heard the front door open, and froze. He listened. This

couldn't be Libby already, could it? She'd left for Berrington only an hour and a half ago. He heard two footsteps on the wooden floor of the hallway. Only two. Either the visitor was standing in the hallway or had gone into the carpeted waiting room. Removing the chair from under the knob, he opened the door and peered out. No one in the hallway. He shut the door and returned to the table, where he stood over the suitcase, examining his inventory and wishing the Judge would take some cocaine. He had cocaine this time, worth a fortune, but the Judge's clients were interested only in pot and pills.

"Doctor?" A voice from the waiting room. Not the Judge's voice, but that of a younger man.

Quickly he selected another bag of pot and two more packets of pills from the suitcase, then he replaced the shirts and underwear and locked it. He picked up the chair standing in front of Libby's easel and moved it over in front of the sink. He stood on it and stashed the suitcase into the overhead cupboard.

He realized he was shaking. Not from fear, he told himself. Merely the boozer's morning tremble. He'd had it before. Weak in the knees. A little light-headed. He went to the refrigerator for a beer. Trembling, he opened the can, tipped it up, and drank. He stood in front of Libby's easel, waiting for the shaking to stop, his back to the sunny window, his eyes on her unfinished painting. It wouldn't do to have the Judge see him with the shakes. He might think it was fear.

If you scare easy, this is a good line of work to stay out of, he'd been told last spring before he left Chicago. It was the pharmacist who'd said it, Tom's supplier. They were having a farewell drink in a dark bar on a suburban street after locking the drugs and dope in the trunk of the BMW. "I don't scare easy," Tom assured the pharmacist, who was drinking mineral water with a lemon twist. "All the same, I hate to see a guy like you get into this. You've got a good income without it."

"I'm being paid peanuts for the next twelve months," Tom explained to him. "I'm on salary with the Indian Health Service."

"So what good's money on a reservation? What's to buy? You'll probably come back with a savings account."

"It isn't just the money," Tom explained. "You've got to

realize I'm going out to the edge of the universe and live there for a whole goddamn year. I need to take some of the city with me."

"Take a woman."

"I've got one." Correcting himself, he added, "I've got two."

What Tom didn't explain to the pharmacist was his expectation that reservation Indians weren't likely to accord their new doctor the respect a doctor liked to have, the sort of respect he'd built up in the Silver Park Clinic. He was afraid of feeling insignificant. Tom, a child of impoverished parents, didn't aspire to being surgeon general, but he did require a position higher than the rabble he'd been born into. Drugs would give him status on the reservation, he'd assumed, at least among users.

And that's exactly how it had worked out. With his marijuana and his medicines he'd earned the respect of the man he most respected in Basswood, Judge Bigelow. He'd set Judge Bigelow up in the drug business, was helping him turn his tavern into a thriving little supply depot for all the Ojibway who needed pharmaceutical comfort. That Tom would leave Basswood in the spring was no reason their partnership couldn't continue. The Judge had mentioned the possibility of setting up branches on other reservations, reaching out to other tribes in need.

But he'd lose the Judge's respect if he couldn't quit shaking. He held out his right hand. Soft. Pale. Trembling. Not fear, he told himself again, even though the trembling had begun when the stranger's voice called, "Doctor." Who was it, a cop? Of course not—out here law enforcement was entirely the business of Caesar Pipe. It was probably some Indian kid with a cold, or maybe the younger Upward brother grazed again by a bullet.

So why didn't his shaking stop? He drained his beer and opened a second can. He regarded the half-finished painting on the easel—Libby's distorted view of the world outside the kitchen window. She'd begun it a month ago and abandoned it a couple of days later. It was a flat painting. No depth. Between two narrow bands of rose (the sky above and the snowy foreground below) the tall jackpines were rendered left to right across the canvas as a greenish black curtain that kept the eye from entering the scene. Indeed, it repelled the eye—layer upon layer of thick paint laid in with a knife and forming a barrier as solid and ugly as a cement wall. What sort of mind would produce such a painting?

"Hey, Doc," said the Judge, opening the kitchen door and startling Tom. "What the hell's taking you so long?" The morning sunlight falling across the room illuminated the Judge's jacket of red nylon. His dyed black hair, greased and combed straight back, shone like patent leather. "You got somebody waiting."

"I know it," said Tom, relieved to discover his voice didn't shake. He gripped his beer with both hands, suppressing his outrage that the Judge should enter the kitchen uninvited.

The Judge's eyes fell on the medication and the plastic bags. "Aaah," he said, closing the door and stepping over to the table. He picked up the packets one by one, peered closely at the printed matter, and pressed them into his pockets. He made a pouch of his jacket by fastening the zipper and he stuffed the bags of marijuana around his belly. Closing the zipper to his throat, he said, "How much?"

"Seven hundred," said Tom, avoiding his eyes.

"Seven hundred bullshit."

"Seven hundred." Tom's trembling, overlaid with anger, was diminishing.

"Come on, Doc."

"Put the money on the table."

The Judge caught Tom's angry tone. Patting his middle to make sure his waistband was holding his merchandise in place, he chuckled and moved over to stand beside him. He looked at the painting. "Hey, I didn't know you were an artist."

Tom took a deep breath, restraining himself from telling the Judge to get out. Judge Bigelow, gross in appearance, dissolute in his habits, purveyor of manifold addictions to the Indians and whites of the surrounding forest, had no business standing here looking at his wife's painting. It revealed too much of the artist for the likes of the Judge to lay eyes on.

"I'm a Sunday painter," Tom lied.

The Judge backed up a step or two, eyed the canvas, and said, "I like it."

"You do?"

"Yeah. What is it?"

"My psyche."

"Your what?"

"My true self."

"Here."

Tom looked at the five bills the Judge was spreading like a fan in his right hand.

"Seven," said Tom.

"You said five."

"That was last time."

"Same stuff."

"My cost went up."

Judge Bigelow thrust his hand forward, wrinkling the bills against Tom's chest. "Take it or leave it."

"*You* take it or leave it."

The Judge patted his jacket, grinning. "I'm taking it." He laid the money on the table on his way to the door. "Tell you what, I'll pay you more if my clients pay me more, fair enough?"

Tom said nothing. His rage was making him sick to his stomach.

"You see, Doc, you're buying this stuff at city prices, but I've got to sell it at country prices. No way these folks out here can come up with that kind of money. I'll be lucky to break even at five."

"You owe me two hundred dollars."

"Not if my clients won't bear the increase."

"Then there's no sense in me supplying you anymore."

"Are you threatening me?" Anger flashed in the Judge's eyes. "'Cause if you're threatening me, you're threatening the wrong man." After an ominous silence, the Judge grinned. "Listen, Doc, I see us in business for years to come. Just get yourself a different wholesaler."

Tom stared at the Judge, his wry grin, his blazing red jacket, his icy eyes, and he felt such revulsion that he cried, "Get out!" before he quite knew what he was saying.

"Jesus Christ, there's no need to get pissed off."

Quieter: "Just get out." Tom was fighting the need to throw up.

"Listen, Doc, I'm only telling you the facts of life. Seven hundred in the city is five hundred in the boondocks." There was an interval of silence before the Judge added, "Well, anyhow, I think you folks got yourself a real cozy kitchen here." Another pause. "And I think you've got real promise as an artist, Doc. Keep it up."

Tom crossed the room and opened the door to the hallway. "Could you just leave?"

"I'm ready. Lead the way." When Tom didn't move, the Judge tipped his head toward the waiting room. "I mean, shouldn't we both come out of your office? I'm here for medical reasons, remember."

They went across the hall and through the examination room to the waiting room, where a teenage boy was sitting on the couch with a magazine on his lap. The boy said, "Hi."

"Do you have an appointment?" asked Tom.

"No, my grandma said I probably didn't need one."

"You don't. Come in." Tom retreated to the examination room.

Judge Bigelow stepped over and stood in front of the boy, preventing him from standing. "What's your name?" he asked.

"Billy." The boy wore jeans and tennis shoes. His red and green flannel shirt was fuzzy and new.

"Billy what?"

With athletic agility, the boy slid sideways on the couch and sprang to his feet. He was taller than the Judge. "Annunciation," he told him, smiling. "And you're Judge Bigelow."

Across the Judge's fat face spread a momentary flush of pleasure at being recognized. "Jerry Annunciation's son?"

The boy nodded and joined Tom in the examination room.

"Where you been?" the Judge called after him.

"The Cities," the boy called out to him.

"Drop in at the Homestead, I'll treat you to a few games of pool and some soda pop."

Tom shut the door on the Judge's offer.

"Creep," said the boy.

"What?" Tom was washing his hands at the sink. He no longer had the shakes.

"He's a creep—Bigelow."

Tom nodded, wiping his hands and listening to make sure the Judge was departing. He heard the outer door close, a car door slam, an engine start up. When the sound of the car died away, he said, "Now what do you need a doctor for?"

"Physical for school."

"All right, take off your shirt and shoes and stand on the scale." Tom gathered instruments from drawers. "How do you know Bigelow?"

"I used to live here."

"Yeah?"

"Long time ago. Fifth grade."

Tom wrote down his weight and height (6'1", 168) and told him to sit down. "Your parents move back?"

"Nope, I'm with my grandparents. I'm your neighbor across the road."

"The Pipes?"

The boy nodded, flinching a little at the touch of the cold stethoscope.

"Take a deep breath."

26

Leaving the hospital with Frank, Libby struggled against her grief. It was a familiar old grief, renewed each time her afflicted child was hospitalized. In the past it had been replaced, upon Verna's release, by hope, but now that Verna was twenty-six her complete recovery was becoming unimaginable. As she crossed the parking lot to the BMW, the unbearable prospect of checking her daughter in and out of hospitals for the rest of her life visibly aged her, bent her eyes to the ground.

She unlocked the car and they got in. The sun had warmed it. She started the engine and sat staring ahead, picturing the two men in the elevator.

"Do you think they were talking about Verna, Frank?"

"Chances are they weren't. There are dozens of patients on that unit."

She looked at him. "But I had a bad feeling. Like it was about Roger."

"I heard them say they would check out the woman's father next. Is it likely they'd look up Vernon Jessen?"

She shrugged. "Why not? They'd have to start somewhere. Or maybe they meant Tom."

She put on her sunglasses and drove out of the parking lot.

As they moved downhill toward the center of Berrington, Frank asked, "Were you ever in touch with Vernon after you left him?"

"Not a letter or a phone call from the time of the divorce until I took Verna out to the farm last summer. I'm sure our marriage—if it ever crosses Vernon's mind—seems as incredible to him as it does to me. Were there ever two people less suited to each other, Frank?"

"Surely you knew that when you married him."

"I suppose." She smiled weakly at the street ahead. "But he had that new green pickup." She stopped smiling. "And I had his baby."

"But even so . . ."

"Don't forget, we're talking about ages ago, Frank. If you were pregnant in those days, you implored the father to marry you, and if he did, you were indebted to him for life."

"But you married his farm as well."

She grimaced. "And his mother. The farm was bad enough. Realizing I'd married Mrs. Jessen was worse."

"You didn't know she was part of the package? Did you expect her to move off the farm?"

"I can't say what I thought about her, but I liked Vernon's father, you know."

She drove in silence for a few blocks, picturing the farmhouse kitchen, its blue and red linoleum worn gray at the doorways, tomatoes ripening on the windowsill over the sink, the wood-burning range smoldering and smelling. She moved her memory into the living room, so cold in winter, so gloomy year round, the walls bare except for three or four small photographs hanging high up under the molding, the floor covered with the same blue and red linoleum. It covered the floors in the bedrooms as well, Vernon's mother having found the ugly pattern on sale somewhere and bought a lifetime supply. There was a thick roll of it standing on end in the machine shed, waiting to be cut up and put down when the first layer wore out. Mammoth red roses on a powder blue background.

Libby braked at an icy intersection, skidded to a stop. "Vernon's father was a nice man," she said. "It could be that I was looking for a new father for myself. I think I had my heart set on learning from him how to be a farmer's daughter, while learning from Vernon to be a farmer's wife. Does that make sense?''

"Or was it the other way around, Libby? I mean did you see Vernon as your father and Vernon's father as your husband? I know it sounds crazy, but didn't Vernon resemble your father?''

She pondered this, then nodded. "I'd grown up learning how to live with a man like that. How to be his charming little sweetheart. How to deflect his anger with jokes and smiles. How to be quick on my feet and stay out of his way when he flew off the handle.''

"So it's no wonder, with those skills, that you married Vernon.''

She moved the car cautiously through the intersection and down the curving, sloping street. "And is it any wonder I also wanted to live with his father? I was dying to know what it was like to be with a man day after day who was all-around nice. But he died, you remember, and there I was, sharing the house with his son and his grieving widow.''

"I remember Mrs. Jessen from the egghouse. A mousy woman.''

"Right. Not overbearing like her son, but her mousiness could be overpowering in a way. I mean she followed me around all the time, not criticizing or complaining exactly, but always breathing down my neck.''

"Did she help with the baby?''

"Yes, of course. Her only grandchild. She taught me how to be a mother. But it was eerie how intimidated she was by Vernon. It was demoralizing to watch him boss her around.''

"I went through the eighth grade demoralized by Vernon. He kept beating me up.''

"He never hit me. He used to shout and he used to beat his cows and goats with sticks, but he never laid a hand on me in anger.''

"How did he treat the baby?''

"With a total lack of interest. He wanted a son. Where are we going, Frank? Do you have time for lunch?''

He looked at his watch. "Good idea. There's a place called the Bavarian Wursthaus on Twelfth Street.''

They continued downhill and Frank pointed out a landmark: "That's where I spent last summer and fall. The Cathedral of the Holy Family."

Through the bare trees Libby caught sight of a spire on a hill, a wall of Gothic windows, an adjoining house of enormous size. "From that to Linden Falls?" she said. "Are you in exile?"

"More or less, thank God."

"So that's where Gene DeSmet lives. I thought he was going to bust his buttons when they notified him he'd be moving to Berrington. He brought two bottles of champagne out to Basswood and the three of us drank them down like water."

"Well, he's safely sequestered up there with the champagne crowd now. If he can keep drinking without becoming a drunk, and eat a huge dinner of red meat every night without heart damage, he'll be rector there someday." Frank craned his neck for a final glimpse of the place. "It's a country-club parish."

"Country club? In this town?"

"You don't see it driving through, but most of the money from Berrington's better days has attached itself to the cathedral. There are two other parishes serving the real people."

"Frank, are you a snob, in reverse?"

"There's hardly a meal on that hill that isn't catered."

"The rich need priests, too, don't they?"

"Sure they do, as the bishop kept telling me."

Libby, braking, skidded again, inches from an accident. When the car came to a halt, she dipped her head to look at Frank over her dark glasses. Chagrin. "Would you like to take the wheel?"

"I would."

But the driver behind them honked. She proceeded slowly. "I have trouble picturing Gene living with a bishop," she said. "He's such a boy. So free and easy."

"So is the bishop—for a bishop. He has this idea that his parishioners expect him to act like a Renaissance prince. They flock to his brunches. Caviar and muffins."

"Mmmmm."

"Canadian bacon and three kinds of melon."

"I'm salivating."

"Eggs Benedict and usually somebody playing Scarlatti in the background."

"So civilized."

"It's beyond civilized. It's decadent."

"No, Frank, it's biblical. Feed my lambs, feed my sheep—isn't that what the gospel says?"

"You're right." He chuckled. "Feed my lambs caviar, feed my sheep eggs Benedict."

A stoplight. "Where's Twelfth Street?"

He directed her to the restaurant. She parked, removed her sunglasses, and twisted the mirror in her direction.

"What about your second husband?" Frank asked, opening his door and letting in a swirl of icy wind. "Who was he?"

"An older man, a nice man," she said, looking in the mirror and poking at her hair. "But a pervert."

Seated at a small table in the Bavarian Wursthaus, where the luncheon special was quiche, the music flamenco, and the wine upstate New York, Libby shook off the pall of the Hope Unit. During her three weeks in Chicago she had imagined this lunch alone with Frank, had imagined a series of lunches—they had a quarter century of catching up to do.

"I left Vernon when the baby was three. I moved off the farm and into town and lived with my mother. I felt so absolutely trapped on that farm. Did you ever see it?"

"Once. I went out there with a veterinarian to see a cow."

"Can you imagine me at eighteen and nineteen and twenty living in that gulch, a boor for a husband, chickens on the porch, cow manure on the breeze, getting to town only once a week, no friends, nobody I could pick up the phone and talk to?"

"Not even Sylvia?"

"Especially not Sylvia. She dropped me the minute I got married. I'd go home to my mother on Saturday afternoons and cry, and she'd tell me to bear with it. She said it was hard to adjust to marriage sometimes, but it always worked out if you stuck with it. Think of it! My mother, the wife with bruises on her face, telling me it would work out."

Three young businessmen at the next table, catching a few of these words, turned and looked Libby over. Without quite facing them, she felt their eyes on her face. She was warmed by their attention. She lowered her voice only slightly.

"My father and my brother were out of the picture by the time I left Vernon. My brother was in the army. My father had left town on a freight train. He was loading grain one day, and when the freight car was full, he handed his shovel to his partner and said 'So long' and headed west." Libby sipped her wine and smiled. "My mother had some good years after he left. When I came in from the farm, I got a job at Dagwood's and my mother took care of Verna. Remember Dagwood's, next to the grain elevator?"

"Thick malts."

"Well, I'd heard Dagwood's was the place to work if you wanted to meet men, so when I got that job, I thought my life was taking a definite turn for the better." She rolled her eyes. "There were men all right, but they were mostly farmers, and a farmer was the last thing I was looking for. I went out with a couple of traveling salesmen but found them lacking, so I decided to somehow get me and my baby and my mother back to Minneapolis."

"Lacking in what way?"

"The salesmen? Lacking in availability. They were married."

Their quiche was served, their wine replenished. Libby glanced at the clock behind the bar and wished she had Frank to herself for the rest of the day. She wanted to spread out the entire crazy quilt of her life for him, wanted him to feel it, comment on it, compare it to the life he'd been leading. His, of course, had been orderly, thought out, apart from the mainstream. How could it have been otherwise, given his upbringing? She'd known from the start, from the day she saw him wade into the river with his football, that Frank would proceed through life with his ear cocked for music no one else was hearing. And wasn't that a large part of the fascination—how different they were? He'd been prudent while she'd been careless. He'd been patient and she had not. His thinking transcended the physical, where Libby felt at home.

She'd be lucky to get through the Harris Highsmith phase of her life by the time she dropped him off at the rectory for his two o'clock appointment. The trouble with the Harris Highsmith story was that it needed a preamble. You couldn't just blurt out that your husband was having sex with your little daughter. You had to approach it slowly and dance around it for a while. Coming at it head-on, you ran the risk of breaking down.

"Getting out of Linden Falls was complicated. What would I do in Minneapolis to support all of us? Say I got a job in the city like my job at Dagwood's, I could never rent a place as cheap as the house in Linden Falls. You know what we were paying for that house on Pincherry Street? Forty-five dollars a month."

"How much were you making at Dagwood's?"

"Thirty a week plus tips, which came out to about sixty. Not bad in those days, but rent in the city was two or three times higher. It was clear that we'd need two incomes, so I came up with this scheme. I coaxed my mother out of the house and got her a job at Dagwood's. We alternated shifts, so one of us was home with Verna. My mother had cleaned for people, she'd taken in washing and sewed, but she'd never worked in public. She was a battered wife with talent as a seamstress and cook but with no self-esteem. Her first few days on the job were torture. She was so shy. She'd never handled money before. But she hung on and began to take an interest in Dagwood's kitchen, and before long she was back there doing the cooking, making the best meals in town, and Tippy Olson was pleased as punch."

"Dagwood."

"Right. Tippy Olson was his real name, or at least the Olson part was. With my mother in the kitchen his diner became the *in* place to eat, and he gave her a big raise, and that's when I started working on her to go back to the city with me. She resisted for a while—Dagwood's was her place of triumph—but I knew that deep down inside she missed the city nearly as much as I did, and finally she agreed to go. We found an apartment in one of our old neighborhoods, and we found jobs in separate eating places, and we alternated shifts as before. But the place I worked was no better than Dagwood's for meeting men who met my standards. They were mostly truck drivers."

"Tell me about your standards."

"College degree, good looks, and money."

He pondered this for a moment before asking, "Then why did you come to me in the seminary? I had none of those things."

"That was earlier, when I was leaving Vernon. I was still hung up mostly on good looks, along with that gentle way you had about you—so different from him."

"Good looks?" Frank seemed surprised.

"Oh, Frank, you're so innocent. You had no idea, did you, that you could have had any girl you wanted simply by giving her the time of day. You were the Gregory Peck of Linden Falls. All the girls were waiting for you to notice them, and they were all very disgusted when you went off to the seminary."

"Any girl I wanted? I wanted you."

"No, you didn't. I went to your seminary and asked if you wanted me and you said you didn't."

"But before that, in high school."

"No, not then either. You weren't ready. You wanted a friend, not a girlfriend, and so that's what we became—friends."

"The best of friends," he said.

She touched his hand. "Just the very best ever."

Falling silent, they exchanged a look that made Libby's blood rush. She felt her cheeks redden with pleasure. She read in his earnest, dark eyes the message that time had done nothing to loosen their bond. Moreover, she felt that time had done little to change either of them at the core. Boy and man he was the same good heart. Girl and woman she was the same . . . whatever she was.

Reluctant to break the sweet spell of this silence, she waited for him to speak. She watched him taste his soup, look around at the crowded room, sip his wine. He seemed to be composing a difficult statement. At last he divulged it.

"I couldn't imagine you being my girlfriend in those days, because you were too beautiful."

"I wasn't."

"I swear to God. Beauty I somehow didn't deserve."

She wondered why he said this with sorrow written on his face. He looked pained, like a messenger arriving late with urgent news. Some twenty-five years late. "Beauty like I never saw again," he added.

This she modestly denied with a shake of her head.

"Until I found you in Basswood last month."

She allowed herself to savor this before replying.

"There was that sort of thing about you, too, Frank."

He forced a laugh. "My beauty."

She didn't laugh. "I mean your unapproachability. I couldn't . . . no girl could . . . cross over from being your friend to being your girlfriend. You were too mystical or something."

"Mystical, hell. Stunted was more like it."

"Yes, that too."

He fidgeted with his napkin and spoke slowly to his silverware, telling of his childhood, his teens, his training at the hands of the strict nuns and the kindly pastor and the doting housekeeper of St. Ann's. She watched his eyes. Why is it that some people display themselves in their eyes, she wondered, while others do not? Her own eyes, she well knew, usually displayed only what she wanted them to, while people like Frank seemed unable to dissemble, unable to hide even the most fleeting thought. You couldn't help trusting eyes like that. Verna, though deeply disturbed, had looked into Frank's eyes and smiled.

"Girls made me very nervous in high school. Danny Ash— you remember him—went to sock hops and learned how to dance. I remember how shocked I was the first time I saw him gliding around the gym to the tune of 'Chattanooga Choo Choo' with Sharon Griggs in his arms. Remember Sharon Griggs?"

"Breasty," said Libby. "Not very bright."

"'What's she like?' I asked Danny the next day. I was referring to her personality because I'd heard Sharon Griggs was below par mentally, and Danny said, 'God, Frank, girls are soft.' I thought he was going to swoon. His eyes rolled up in his head. 'So goddamn soft,' he said. 'You've got to feel one, Frank, to know what I mean.'"

Libby laughed. "So did you feel one?"

Frank, eating, chuckled and shook his head. "Not for another year. Not until I danced with you at the Loomis Ballroom."

"Was I soft?"

Closing his eyes and smiling with his mouth full, he nodded.

They were interrupted by their waiter, a young man wearing a soiled green apron and a curly blond perm who splashed water into their glasses and recommended the chocolate cake. Frank sent him off for more wine.

"But we're sidetracked, Libby. You were working at a truck stop in the city."

"No, tell me more of your story. We'll get back to me."

"It's hardly a story, there's no drama to it. I became a teacher and taught at Aquinas Academy and then it closed down. It's a vocational school now. And I'm trying to redesign my vocation, trying to learn the pastor business. I think I'm starting to catch on. Up until a month ago I was lost. I couldn't seem to find my way."

"How did you find it?"

He slowly twirled his wineglass. "Hard work. Prayer. Rum."

She nodded. "I've always imagined it's hard work, doing what you do."

"Teaching was hard enough. Pastoral work is teaching plus living." He looked at his watch. "I'll have to be getting back."

"It's probably like nursing," she said. "It will eat you up if you let it. Except your hours are worse. Nurses usually aren't on call."

"It's like going into a mine. It's dark down there, and you have to bring your own light."

Her response was immediate: "Love is like that."

He looked skeptical. "Love?"

"Love can be deep like that. And very dark."

"Deep I grant you, but dark?"

"Oh, so dark." She paused. She was about to say that her second husband had led her much deeper into darkness than Vernon had, but Frank was calling to the waiter, asking for the check.

Looking into his billfold, he said, "But you know something, Libby? Now for the first time since the Academy closed I'm not wishing I was back in the classroom."

"Good," she replied, hoping he'd say she was at least a part of the reason.

"I'm too busy at St. Ann's to wish anything."

Disappointed, she wondered if it was his newfound sense of mission that had prevented him from taking her hand this morning in the rectory. On the night his stove blew up, he'd taken her hand quite naturally, had not flinched from her taking his. Was a hardworking priest more troubled by a woman's touch than a priest at loose ends? Was she now a threat where a month ago she'd been a consolation?

As they rose to leave, a man called, "Father Healy, what are you doing back in town?" and Frank crossed the room to shake several hands. Libby sat down again, waiting, and felt herself under the scrutiny of the three businessmen on her left. She wondered what conclusions they were drawing about her. Was she attractive to them? Was her tam too chic for Berrington, and did it mark her as an outsider? Could they see that she was growing uneasy under their examination? Had they been able to tell throughout the meal that she was in love with her lunch partner?

27

"I was a waitress by day and an avid reader of the want ads by night, especially those in the health field because my dream of dreams was to marry a doctor."

Frank, glancing in the mirror as he speeded up, saw the midday sun hanging low behind the car, its light dimmed by the gray haze hanging over Berrington's factories.

"And it wasn't long before I was hired as the night switchboard operator at Unity Hospital," Libby continued, unfolding her sunglasses, checking the lenses for dust, touching away a speck here and there, slipping them on. "But the switchboard was located in a cubbyhole behind the admitting area, and I had nobody to talk to all night long except nurses."

"No men," said Frank, glancing at his watch. One-thirty. He'd be late meeting with the Fredricks family to plan the funeral, and his other appointments would have to be pushed back—the engaged couple planning their wedding; the liturgy committee planning for Lent; the plumber bidding to remodel the rest rooms in the church and school. He pushed the BMW over the speed limit. Compared to Adrian's Olds, it hummed along without effort. He hadn't had a ride this smooth since the time he took a group of Academy boys down a placid stretch of the Badbattle in canoes.

"Absolutely a woman's world," said Libby. "But a blessing, as it turned out, because those women made me realize what I wanted to *be* in life. Watching them work and listening to them talk about their jobs, I decided I wanted to go into nursing. I told that to one of them, an old nurse named Ernestine Paulson, who said the best way to be a good nurse was to rise up through the ranks the way she had. Nurse's aide, LPN. Not that I had a choice. I mean where would I get the money for nurse's training? My mother and I were barely making ends meet."

Libby unzipped her jacket; the car was warming up. "If this gets boring, Frank, don't stop me—I've got to tell it."

"When have you ever bored me?"

She acknowledged this with a smile and continued.

"Every day Ernestine Paulson went snooping around the personnel office for me, and the minute they put out a call for a nurse's aide she told me who to apply to and she coached me for my interview and I got the job. Oh, that was wonderful, Frank. Have you ever made a move in life that was better than you dreamed? It seemed like I'd been making the wrong moves all my life, but as soon as I put on that uniform and gave my first patient a bath I swear to God I felt like I was starting out fresh in life, doing what I was born to do."

"The classroom was like that for me. I'd never given teaching a thought until the bishop steered me into it, and suddenly there I was—where I was meant to be."

"Exactly. I seemed to know instinctively how to take blood pressure and give backrubs and make beds with people lying in them. And lying in one of them was a man with heart disease and I fell in love with him."

"He was a doctor?"

"No, I waived that requirement. He was the business manager of the Palladium, which has since gone bankrupt. It was on Hennepin and it was where touring companies put on all the big musicals. His name was Harris Highsmith and I was mad for him. He had the most handsome face and the most gracious manner. He had interesting people visiting him. He looked like he had money."

"And a college education?"

"No, I waived that, too. He was a self-made businessman. He owned some movie theaters, and when I met him he had just gotten into producing plays. Which explains why he had such fascinating visitors in the hospital. They were theater types and he wanted me to meet them all. He'd call out my name—he had this clear, ringing voice—and I'd go to his room and he'd say to his visitors, 'I want you to meet the most beautiful girl in the world.' Well, you can imagine what that did for my ego. His fourth day in the hospital he asked me for a date. I told him yes, and he asked me where I'd like to go. I said anywhere but Sammy's Truckstop in Northeast. He said, 'I was thinking more in terms of Miami,' and he had me call his travel agent and make reservations. Well! After Miami I followed him home. I'd have followed Harris Highsmith to hell."

"You married him."

"Not right away. I lived with him."

"And Verna?"

"My mother kept Verna."

"But your mother was working."

"We hired a baby-sitter. Harris hired her."

"You kept working?"

"Oh, yes, I simply had to. Not that I was above being a kept woman, but I simply loved the hospital. I'd dreamed of being a nurse, you see, and now I saw it was possible. Harris had enough money to send me to nurse's training."

"This guy's out of a fairy tale."

"Yes . . ."

Frank looked across at Libby. She was absently fondling an earring as she stared ahead at the road. Behind the dark glasses he saw that her eyes were unfocused, far off. They rode through a mile of hilly farmland without speaking. At the windblown crest of each hill the impoverished soil of Berrington County showed red through the snow. Farmsteads huddled in the lee of their piney windbreaks. A farmer, spreading a bronze line of manure across a snowy field, waved from his tractor, and Frank waved back. A deer grazed in a stand of aspen, nibbling the bare twigs.

"Harris taught me a lot. First and foremost he taught me there's more to love than what I'd felt for Vernon. Maybe a teenager's heart is too small for big love, I don't know, but what I felt for Harris was very, very big. I was twenty-one. I sometimes wondered if it was his money I loved. His house in the suburbs. The exciting people he knew. But no, it was more than that. It was Harris. I tell you, Frank, I loved him so much. . . ."

"That you married him."

"On stage at the Palladium, one morning in June. One of his actors recited a poem and another recited the Song of Solomon— 'Lovely are thy breasts,' and so forth. Verna was my flower girl. Quite a few of the guests thought I was an actress, or would become an actress, but 'No,' I told whoever asked, 'I'm going into nurse's training.' Well, hardly anybody at the reception believed it. They gave me this curious look, like why with all of Harris's money would I want to go and do a dumb thing like that. But Harris was all for it, and do you know why, Frank?"

"He was sick."

"Exactly. He knew the sort of death he was going to die. Like his father and grandfather before him, his heart was going to get weaker and weaker, and he wanted a nurse in the family. His first wife had been a secretary when he needed a secretary and his second wife had been an actress when he was trying to break into show business, and now he needed a nurse."

She looked at Frank. "I know what you're thinking. You're remembering the girl you knew in high school and wondering how a fun-loving, boy-crazy girl like that ends up in nurse's training when she's got the means to live the life of leisure. Aren't you thinking that?"

"No, I'm assuming your time on the farm made you more serious."

"Serious? I don't know. Maybe a little. But what pushed me through nurse's training was the fact that under the smooth surface of my life with Harris Highsmith I had a scary feeling about him."

Frank gave her a sidewise look, a raised eyebrow.

"It was eerie. I'm not sure I was even aware of feeling scared when I was feeling it. I mean it may have been later, after the truth came out, that I first realized that all the while I was married to this nice well-to-do husband he was filling me with a vague sense of dread, and this dread was what kept me out there pursuing my own career. It's hard to explain, Frank. It was nothing he ever said or did. He was always very good to me."

A long pause.

"It was the way he'd look at me sometimes. I'd catch him looking at me and I'd feel chilled. It was like he was saying, 'You will never entirely understand me, Libby. Or entirely belong to me. Or entirely love me.'"

Another pause.

"And this was very confusing to me because I *did* love him. I was mad for him, as I've said. He was so wise and funny and he took me to opening-night parties all over the city and he bought me things and he was never owly like Vernon or violent like my dad. And I'm convinced he never saw other women. But there was this constant worry at the back of my mind. Of course it was partly worry about his health. He had his sixtieth birthday before I was twenty-five, so I was going to be a widow sooner or later, and the way his heart was behaving it looked like sooner. And partly it was worry about money. He promised I'd be taken care of when he died, but how could I be sure? He never let me in on his business affairs. We lived in this great house on this stately street and we drove two new cars and Verna went to an expensive preschool and then to an exclusive elementary, but what if he died and left me as dead broke as my father and mother always were?"

They were silent for a very long time. Finally, when the Linden Falls water tower came into view above the gray trees, she asked, "Can you skip your appointment, Frank?"

"I don't see how. I have several."

She sighed. "I was a registered nurse by the time Verna was eight. By the time she was eleven, Harris was dying by inches. Blood clots. Little strokes. Angina. My mother moved in with us and took care of him while I was at work. My mother was ten years younger than my husband—isn't that amazing? And because he was dying, he seemed even older than he was, and because he had a fatherly way of acting toward both of us, we felt more like sisters than mother and daughter. Two sisters waiting on Daddy. Or rather three sisters, because Verna was very grown up for her age. My mother liked Harris quite a bit, but when I brought it up one day how I never felt I understood him entirely, she said she knew what I meant. She said there was something a little false about him. I'd never thought of him as false so much as hidden, but false was my mother's word for him. Exactly the right word, as it turned out—false and evil!"

She gripped Frank's arm. He looked at her. High emotion colored her face.

"He died and left me nothing. There wasn't much to leave, and what there was went to his first wife. But that's not the worst of it, Frank. When Verna went into therapy at fourteen, it came out that she'd had sexual relations with Harris beginning when she was seven."

Frank, scowling at the road and shaking his head, felt a burning sensation spread through his chest. It was sorrow and it felt like heartburn.

"You aren't shocked?" she asked, her grip tightening.

"I don't know what to say. It's awful."

Letting her hand slip from his sleeve, she turned to look out her side window. A wide spot in the Badbattle. A man trudging between two boxy fish houses. Three crows picking at something dead on the ice. They drove the remaining mile in silence.

Turning down the street to St. Ann's, Frank said, "Would you like me to see Verna again? I had the feeling she might warm up to me."

Libby removed her sunglasses. "I was right about that, wasn't I? I told Tom—remember?—that Verna might talk to you."

"Tom didn't seem to care for the idea."

"That's because he didn't think of it. We have this arrangement, you see, where Tom gets to have all the good ideas."

"And you get . . . ?"

She uttered a bitter little laugh. "Not much anymore."

He waited for her to expand on this, to shed light on what

struck him as a malfunctioning marriage, but she shifted back to Verna.

"You'll see her?"

"Tomorrow. I'm free in the morning."

"Tomorrow we're conducting sight and hearing tests at the reservation school."

"That's all right, it might be better if I see her alone."

"Oh, Frank!" she cried, and he touched the brake, thinking she saw danger—a child darting into the street?—but the way was clear.

"Oh, Frank," she repeated, bringing her hands to her face and shuddering. He pulled up in front of the rectory, switched off the engine. "Frank, I never used to be like this. I used to be strong no matter what. Don't all those years of being strong . . . ?"

The question hung between them, unfinished, as a new wave of sorrow swept over her. He had never seen anyone so utterly lost in the throes of weeping. Her shoulders heaved and she shook her head from side to side like a swimmer fighting for air. He laid his hand on her arm. At his touch her body went limp. She released her seat belt and leaned into him, melted into him, laying her head on his shoulder, laying her arm across his chest. He felt the small contractions of her dying sobs. He felt the heat of her breath on his neck, and put his hand to her face. Gently rubbing the wetness from her cheeks, he said, "Talk to me, Libby."

It was a long time before she spoke. "Everything's wrong."

He saw the Oldsmobile coming down the street. Mrs. Tatzig, no doubt, returning from the grocery store.

"Everything's wrong," she repeated in a voice not her own, speaking slowly, heavily, as if asleep and dreaming. "Everything's been wrong for a long time." She sighed a long sigh. "How come I'm not strong enough anymore?"

It wasn't Mrs. Tatzig, but her sister Mrs. Johnson who passed in front of the BMW as she swung into the driveway. Advancing toward the garage, she craned her neck and stared back at Frank and Libby with undisguised curiosity, and only at the last moment did she wrench the wheel and narrowly miss the doorframe. Why was Charlotte Johnson driving the pastor's Olds?

"My life, Frank. It's always wrong."

"Always?"

"Ever since I was little." Her voice was little.

"Haven't things ever been right?"

"Never." She sat up, drawing a wet strand of hair away from her face and gazing at him. He had never been looked at like this by anyone. Her eyes were intense and yet unfocused and trance-like. She seemed to be looking through him, or at something so deep inside him he didn't know it was there.

He looked away, looked at Mrs. Johnson, who emerged from the garage carrying grocery bags and made her way gingerly along the icy path to the kitchen door. The BMW cooled. He restarted it to get the heater going, and this stirred Libby out of her trance. She found a hankie in her purse and dabbed at her face. She said, "You can't possibly know how deeply you're affecting me."

For the better? For the worse? Both, he suspected.

A car pulled up behind them. The engaged couple. Libby and Frank watched them walk to the front door and ring the bell. They wore matching jackets. The man was very tall, the woman was short. They were holding hands.

"Well, this is it for us, isn't it, Frank?"

"For today."

She smiled at him. It wasn't her smile of amusement or joy. It was a crimped smile, devoid of humor. There was impatience in it. And sadness. And blame, of all things. What was she blaming him for?

"I'll be going," she said rather sharply, sitting forward, ready to move over behind the wheel, her crimped smile held firmly in place.

He got out, feeling oddly chastened. "I'll talk to Verna and call you," he said.

"Fine," she said flatly.

"Good-bye, Libby."

She pulled the door shut and drove off without glancing back or waving.

Frank followed the engaged couple into the house and there learned from Charlotte Johnson that the monsignor had been carried off to Berrington in an ambulance.

28

Caesar, at the wheel of his pickup, stared out at the two holes in the ice his grandson was holding him responsible for. In the farther hole the red and white bobber made three quick dips underwater, then was still. He hoped the fish would go away. It was too cold to be getting in and out of the truck. He wished he were home lunching with Joy instead of sitting out in the middle of Sovereign Lake eating potato chips and staring at holes in the ice like a fish-starved white man.

"Win a few?" asked Billy.

"Yeah, the first summer we burned up the league. Ten wins and three losses." They were discussing Caesar's recent two-year stint as manager of the softball team for Linden Falls Redi-mix. "The second summer we fell apart. Our best hitter moved away and our best infielder got fired from his job at Redi-mix and the girl who played second got knocked up."

"You had girls playing?"

"It was a mixed league."

"Sounds sissy."

"It *was* sissy. Softball's a sissy game. Ball the size of a grapefruit."

"Then how come you managed?"

"Felt like it." Caesar's small bead-black eyes grew wistful. As a young man he'd spent two seasons in the Class C Northern League as the second-string catcher for the St. Cloud Rox. When it became apparent that Class B was beyond his skills (he was a sucker for anything low and outside; his throw to second was erratic), his manager advised him to quit, which he did. He came home a hero—Basswood's only professional athlete ever. He chose fishing as his vocation, working with Carl Butcher and his gill nets for several years before the tribal council voted him half a living wage as tribal leader and the county sheriff added the other half by making him a part-time deputy. His first summer home he'd organized and coached a reservation baseball team that earned its way into the Badbattle League of town teams— Linden Falls, Staggerford, Owl Brook, Bagley, and Basswood. They played on Sunday afternoons not for pay but for fun and glory. But after a few seasons baseball gave way to softball in these towns, and the Basswood Indians disbanded along with the Badbattle League.

"Johnny Upward was working for Linden Falls Redi-mix," Caesar continued. "They asked him to talk me into managing their softball team, and I said okay. I was missing baseball a lot. We hadn't had a reservation team for I don't know how long. Fifteen years maybe."

"Not that long," said Billy. "I was batboy, remember? When I was about six?"

"Yeah? Ten years then." Caesar shifted in his seat, trying to relieve the pressure of the steering wheel on his belly.

"I remember Stan Fox played first that year, and one of his brothers caught," said Billy. "The brother that caught hit a bunch of home runs."

"Yeah, that was a hell of a team, Billy. We beat Bagley that year."

"We beat Linden Falls, I remember."

"Hell, we always beat Linden Falls." Caesar saw in memory the Basswood ball diamond as it looked in those years—the grass cut in the outfield, the infield raked smooth, no gopher mounds, no holes in the backstop, bleachers full of fans behind the plate. He looked at Billy, his little batboy now nearly a man. "There wasn't a year back then we couldn't have fielded a team of women and girls and beat Linden Falls."

"Hey, a bite!" Billy threw open his door, draining the pickup of warmth, and ran to a hole on his side of the truck.

Caesar leaned over and pulled Billy's door shut. He turned the key in the ignition. The idling engine was loud and so was the heater fan. He watched his grandson play the line out delicately across his fingers. The sight made Caesar sad, for this was the white man's method of fishing. Indians, by treaty, by instinct, went after fish with nets and spears while the white man put down a line and gazed at the water as if he could see past the face looking back at him. Indians took the fish they needed while the white man made stupid rules for himself, like fishing with only two lines per man and not catching more than six fish a day, and then he broke the rules.

Billy had been in the city too long. Caesar had disapproved from the start. He'd warned his daughter when she left the reservation that the city would turn Billy into an Indian bum in a white man's world, but she went anyway. Jerry was down there, she insisted. "But Jerry's a bum," Caesar reminded her. "So what," replied his daughter, her eyes flashing with defiance, "he's my husband." Caesar told her, then, that it was well-known that Jerry Annunciation had gone to the city to get away from his wife and child, but Caesar's daughter wouldn't believe it. She had to go to the city and find out for herself, and there she remained, living hand to mouth in a dumpy apartment and catching colds that lasted months and sometimes turned into pneumonia.

Billy had been a fifth-grader when his mother took him to the city. Yesterday when he stepped off the bus in Linden Falls, Caesar didn't know him. He'd grown so tall. His voice had changed. Maturity had transformed his face—no resemblance to the little batboy. He was handsome. He'd inherited his mother's good sturdy chin and wide, smiley mouth. He had the straight nose and the wide-apart eyes of his no-good father. There wasn't one good-looking nose on the Pipe side of the family. All the Pipe noses were pudgy like Caesar's.

Riding home from the bus depot, Joy kept saying, "I can't

take my eyes off you," and Billy kept smiling. It had been three and a half years since they'd last seen him. Three summers ago he'd come up on the bus for a two-week visit. For fourteen days he'd fished morning, noon and night. Fished in a boat like a white man. Caesar had to take a lot of kidding about that from Carl Butcher and a few others.

Yesterday Caesar, too, kept stealing glances at Billy, trying to get used to his face. What bothered him most were his eyeglasses and haircut. They were hippie eyeglasses, small and round with thin wire frames. Did Caesar imagine it, or were the lenses actually tinted a kind of lavender color? And the ungodly haircut—you couldn't see his ears.

At supper there'd been an argument. Billy said he'd like to transfer into Basswood High School a day late, spend Monday taking it easy, unwind, fish. Joy said why not, he'd need to get a physical exam for school anyhow, so why not Monday morning? Caesar went along with the plan, though he warned Billy not to skip school ever again. Then Billy asked if he could take the pickup fishing, and after a little discussion he was given permission to drive it in the afternoon when Caesar was off duty— he liked to make a swing through the reservation each morning— but then it became clear that Billy had no intention of driving over to the outlet and helping Carl Butcher net fish out of the river; he wanted to take the pickup out in the middle of the lake and fish with a hook and line. Caesar argued against it. The argument, come to think of it, didn't involve Billy. Billy was busy eating while his grandparents argued. Joy said Billy could fish any way he pleased and Caesar said it was a disgrace to fish that way when Indians had the right to take fish by the netful.

Joy was unmoved by his appeal to her Native American pride—you could never budge Joy when she had her mind made up—so Caesar fell back on the contention that while the ice might be two to three feet thick overall, there were certain places over springs and currents where it was too thin to drive on. This wasn't a fabrication; he knew of at least two such spots, though they were close to the far shore and not where Billy was likely to fish.

"Then how come everybody drives across the lake all winter?" asked Joy.

"Because whoever plows the roadway knows where the ice is thin and nobody ever veers off away from it."

"Then let him fish on the roadway."

"He can't fish on the roadway. If it's snowing or windy or dark, some driver's likely to come barreling across the lake and not see him and crash right into him."

"Do you know where the thin ice is?" she asked him.

He tried not to raise his voice. "Joy, is there any boot print, rabbit track, or tipped-over outhouse on this reservation that I don't know about? Why did the sheriff hire me over everybody else if I didn't know every square foot of this land and water better than Adam knew Eden?" He paused for effect. "Of course I know where the thin ice is."

"Then take him fishing yourself."

Billy watched the line play out across his fingers, watched it speed up for a moment, then stop and go slack. He feared the walleye had unhooked itself, but no, after a little while the line slowly began to tighten. Then he felt a couple of tugs. Then a steady tension.

"Yank him out of there," his grandfather called from the pickup.

Billy, bending over the hole, shook his head. His grandfather, he knew, wanted to go home. More than that, his grandfather was embarrassed to be out here angling. If his grandmother hadn't taken up his cause, Billy would have had to come out here on foot and stand in the cold wind all afternoon.

"Yank him out of there, Billy, and let's get the hell home."

Again Billy shook his head, hunching his shoulders to keep the cold wind from blowing down the collar of his lightweight jacket. The trouble with Indians like his grandfather was that they spent so many years netting fish they didn't know any other method. Off the reservation, Billy had had to fish like a white. No spearing walleyes in the creeks. No netting. Not that you could ever hope to catch a walleye in Minneapolis by any method. It was crappies and sunfish mostly. Once in a while a bullhead. Many a Saturday and Sunday when the gloomy apartment he shared with his mother made him sad—and a few other days when he felt like skipping school—Billy would take his spool of line and his tin can of jigs and ride twenty-one blocks on the city bus to Lake Calhoun, where he'd borrow an auger from one of the regulars and drill himself a couple of holes in the ice and jig for crappies.

He learned to like that style of fishing. He liked having to guess when to let the fish run and when to set the hook. With the fish on one end of the line and himself on the other, he felt in tune with nature. Sometimes, in fact, if he concentrated hard enough, he could sense the fish's approach before it touched the bait. The regulars, mostly old retired men from the surrounding neighborhood of expensive houses, called him Billy Fish.

The line began to move again. Slowly at first, then fast. Billy counted to five, then tugged hard on the line. It went taut. The fish felt big, maybe three pounds. Big enough to break the line. Let it run. Let it tire itself out. Billy fed out the line little by little. After a minute or so, the tugs weakened, and he turned the fish around and pulled it back toward the hole, hand over hand. He saw it for an instant, a silvery flash at the bottom of the hole, before it was gone again, making its final desperate run. Billy turned it around again, retrieved it, threaded it up headfirst through the hole, and swung it onto the ice, where it bounced and flip-flopped, scatting silvery drops of water that froze before they came to rest. A sleek, beautiful walleye, three and a half, four pounds.

He unhooked it and tossed it into the back of the pickup with the four other walleyes. This was the biggest so far. He opened the Styrofoam bucket standing on the tailgate and plunged his hand into the icy water, snatching out a minnow. He baited his hook and dropped it into the hole. Blowing on his hands, he ran to the other holes and found all three beginning to freeze shut. He broke the thin crust of ice with the toe of his boot and drew up each line to check the bait. The minnow was gone from one of the lines his grandfather was watching. He rebaited it, dropped it down the hole, and hopped into the pickup. Bending forward to spread his hands in front of the heater, he said, "Quite the fish, eh, Gramps. Seven more and we can go home."

"You actually enjoy this?"

"Nothing like it." He beamed at his grandfather.

"You'll get over it."

"I doubt it," said Billy.

"You'll have to get over it. I can't be bringing you out here like this."

"I'll walk out."

"Freeze your ass."

"I'll build myself a fish house to sit in."

"Jesus, Billy, not a fish house." His grandfather made the face of a man insulted. "Basswood Indians don't sit in fish houses."

"Who says?"

"It's not the Indian way."

Billy rubbed his hands until they were warm; then he picked the empty potato-chip bag off the seat, tore it further open, and licked the salt.

Caesar cleared his throat and raised a finger in the air, instructing his grandson, "There's the white way of doing things and there's the Indian way. Your grandmother and I have nothing against whites, but we've always followed the Indian way." He was pleased with having said this much and wanted to say more, but he couldn't think of the words. He wished Joy were here to take up where he left off. Joy always had the words. He lowered his finger, cleared his throat again, and concluded, "It's always seemed to your grandmother and me that we should do our part to preserve the Indian way."

Billy, his face in the bag, said, "You'll get over it."

29

Within twenty minutes Frank was back on the road to the Berrington Hospital, his meetings with the bereaved and the engaged abbreviated, his other appointments canceled. Charlotte Johnson was left in charge of the rectory with its phone constantly ringing as news of the monsignor's collapse spread around town. Mrs. Tatzig had ridden off with the monsignor in the ambulance.

Coronary Care was on the third floor. He was directed to Room 6, in which he found Adrian lying on a high bed with a transparent oxygen mask over his face and three lines connecting him to an electronic screen jutting out from the wall over his head. His eyes were closed tight. The screen, flashing green digits, monitored his blood pressure and pulse rate. It also displayed the shape of his heartbeat—a green line of jagged peaks and dips moving from right to left. Beyond the bed stood a man playing with his stethoscope as he watched the screen. He introduced himself as Dr. Droubie and said it would be a while before the EKG and blood tests told him what he wanted to know. The doctor was a ruddy man whose prominent teeth gave him a smiley aspect—smilier than he meant, judging by the grave look in his eye.

"It's a heart attack?" Frank asked.

"It certainly is."

"Heart damage?"

"Quite probably."

Standing beside the doctor was a floor-to-ceiling window through which the orange-red light of sunset came flooding into the room.

Frank stepped up to the bed and took Adrian's hand. Adrian groaned softly. His fingers twitched. Frank said, "God help you, Adrian." The old man fluttered his eyes briefly but said nothing.

Frank looked at the monitor. From moment to moment the heartbeat changed. At times the peaks and dips were sharp and uniform; at other times scribbly and flat. "Is that alarming?" he asked.

"I should say," replied Dr. Droubie.

A technician in a white smock steered into the room a large, noisy, self-propelled machine that looked to Frank like a miniature cornpicker. Two nurses followed. The machine was parked at the foot of the bed and Frank was asked to leave. Going out, he glanced back and saw the nurses struggling to raise Adrian to a sitting position and the technician slipping a large photographic plate behind his back.

In the hallway he met Mrs. Tatzig getting off the elevator eating a candy bar. She still wore her all-purpose slippers and her shapeless cardigan. "He fell over in school," she said.

"Charlotte told me."

"Did she tell you he's worse?"

"No."

"I called her a little while ago and told her he's worse. All the way in the ambulance he was awake. He talked to me. In the emergency room he talked to the nurses. But once they got him up here to bed, he started fading out."

"Medication maybe."

"Could be." She peeled the wrapper back from her half-eaten Baby Ruth. "You going to stay for a while?"

"Yes."

"I'll go home then. I met Mary Maguire in the cafeteria. She'll give me a ride. Her husband's in with piles."

"It was good of you to come with Adrian, Marcella."

Chewing, she gave him a narrow, accusing look. "Who else was available?"

Farther along the corridor he found a visitors' alcove with a broad window facing away from the city. Woods and fields and a highway of headlights. The sun was gone. A few small, hard-looking clouds hung in the coral sky. Pressing his forehead against the glass, he closed his eyes and pictured Adrian unconscious in Room 6. So withered. So fragile. Dear God, don't take Adrian away from me. This is the man I've been drawing strength from since I was eleven years old. Never a vigorous man. Not a brilliant man. Not a man whose passing will be noted far and wide. But steady. Trusting. Self-satisfied without being self-absorbed. Devout. Good-natured. Undemanding. Even-tempered. Loving. Holy.

The X-ray crew emerged from Room 6. Frank went in and found Adrian unattended. He switched off the bright overhead light, and the purple dusk spilled in through the floor-length window. He drew a chair over to the bed and sat down, fastening his eyes on the monitor. The numbers, glowing green in the dark room, climbed and fell—48 over 18, 80 over 40. Whenever the heartbeat line stretched out nearly flat, Frank felt his scalp crawl; when it recovered its lively verticals, he relaxed.

He relaxed into fatigue. His head felt leaden. His eyes itched. He slouched down in his chair, laid his head back, and dozed. He dreamed Libby was walking with him on the grounds of the Aquinas College and Academy, which were vastly transformed by a glacier that had moved through overnight. Ravines had been cut, trees uprooted. The buildings were ruins. The sky was black. They walked to a treacherous cliff edge where they stopped and looked down and Libby pressed Frank's hand to her cheek and warned him of some terrible event to come.

He awoke with trepidation. He had slept a long time. The floor-length window framed a black sky. He raised his eyes to the monitor. The blood pressure numbers no longer fluctuated so wildly. Minute after minute they flickered around 90 over 50. Adrian slept peacefully under his mask of oxygen.

Nurses came and went. A nurse said it was dinnertime and

asked Frank if he would like a tray of food. He declined. He was feeling too listless to eat. He stirred himself out of his chair and went for a walk in the hallways. Wandering up to the fourth floor, he stopped and peered through the rectangle of barred glass in the door to Special Care. He saw that a few of the patients had changed from bathrobes into street clothes. Verna was one of them. She was watching TV and conversing with a woman sitting at her side. She was altogether more animated than she had been earlier. There was life in her eyes. She was filing her nails. Had her torpid behavior this morning been an act? Should he go in now and visit with her, catch her off guard? No, he would wait until morning. He was feeling torpid himself.

Returning to the third floor, he met Bishop Baker coming out of Adrian's room. The bishop, a balding little man with a ready smile, was tightly belted into a black trench coat.

"Frank, how are you? Sorry I couldn't get here sooner, I was meeting with seven parishioners from Owl Brook unhappy with their pastor." He shook Frank's hand warmly, smiled broadly, spoke loudly. "How are you taking it, Frank? I know there's probably no one you feel closer to than our dear Adrian. Please tell me what I can do."

"Thanks, Bishop, I can't tell you much. The doctor's waiting for the results of some tests."

"Dick."

"Pardon me?"

"Call me Dick, remember?"

"Oh, sorry. It's hard for me to call the Bishop of Berrington by his first name. Bishop Swayles would never have permitted anyone to call him Walbert."

"No wonder, with a name like Walbert."

Frank, putting his head into Room 6, read the numbers. "He's stabilized, compared to an hour ago."

"So I'm told. I'm sure he'll come through. He strikes me as the type who'll surprise you with his resilience."

"Let's hope."

"But, in any case, it looks like you're St. Ann's new pastor, Frank. Any problem with that?"

Frank, astonished, said, "Well . . ." But of course it made

sense. Adrian had been systematically relieving himself of his pastoral duties since the day Frank joined him.

"Don't kid me, Frank. You've been more or less in charge all along."

"All right, but don't make it official."

"Why?"

"Don't call me pastor as long as Adrian's there."

"It wouldn't upset him, Frank."

"I know."

"Then why?"

"It would upset me."

The bishop gripped his hand again. "Whatever you say, Frank. Sorry I can't stay, I'm having dinner with Gene DeSmet and his mother." He looked momentarily downcast. "I wish you hadn't left me, Frank."

"DeSmet's your man."

Bishop Baker smiled sadly, turned, and strode off down the hall. "So long, Frank."

"Good-bye, Bishop."

The little man halted in his tracks. He didn't turn to look back, but stood stock still.

"Dick," Frank corrected himself.

The bishop set off again.

30

The next morning Frank went directly from the schoolchildren's Mass to the garage, backed out the Olds, and drove again to Berrington. It was one of those rare days when January reverses itself by opening up a channel of warm air from the Gulf of Mexico. The woods and farmsteads along the highway were veiled in a gray-blue haze, and the snowbanks of Berrington were seeping into the wet streets.

Passing through the lobby of the hospital, he glanced at the wall behind the information desk and saw a signboard headed CLERGY IN. Three nameplates—Jordan, DeSmet, Lundquist—were attached to the board. Perhaps he'd find Gene DeSmet in Adrian's room. He rather hoped so. He was curious to know how a mental lightweight like DeSmet might view Bishop Baker, who for all his breezy glad-handing was not a superficial man by any means. Frank had it from several parishioners that Gene DeSmet could go weeks without saying anything spiritual from the pulpit. His homilies were based on newspaper articles. Drive safely, he preached on holiday weekends. Have your well water analyzed for impurities, he advised during a pollution scare. Motherhood was his topic not only on Mother's Day, but for two Sundays beforehand and one Sunday after—his own sainted mother apparently being the spool around which he spun the thin, endless threads of his thinking.

Rising in the elevator, Frank brought to mind the complaints of Danny Ash. Shortly after Frank's arrival at St. Ann's he was told by Danny Ash, his friend from boyhood, that seminaries were turning out idiots these days. "Where are the tough, hard-working, he-man priests of the past, Frank? Where are the priests who feared God and nobody else?" Danny Ash, father of six little Ashes built on the same squat, muscular scale as their father, possessed an unshakable faith in such eternal verities as fasting, penance, and excommunication. He was the only Catholic Frank knew who still avoided meat on Friday. In the same breath Danny was able to argue in favor of prayer in the schools and capital punishment. The business of the Church, according to Danny, was law enforcement, and something had to be done about disorder and faintheartedness in the force. "It's been years since the bishop ordained a priest who knows right from wrong, Frank. They're all idiots and mama's boys like DeSmet."

In Adrian's room, Frank found two nurses busying themselves at the bed and a third nurse—a beautiful, cream-haired young woman—standing near the window holding a tray with a glass cover. Adrian, his eyes closed, was mumbling under his mask and twitching. Dr. Droubie came in, nodded at Frank, and bent over Adrian with his stethoscope. Smiling grimly, he straightened up and told Frank, "Your friend has suffered some heart damage. We're going to insert a catheter into his chest. We need more accurate readings than we're getting." The doctor pointed to the tray held by the cream-haired nurse. "We need core readings."

Frank stepped over and looked at the tray. Sterilized under glass and lying curled like a strand of jewelry was a delicate metallic tube eighteen inches long. The doctor explained, to Frank's astonishment, that the tube would be inserted into Adrian's chest near the collarbone, and follow an artery into the heart.

"It sounds last-ditch," said Frank.

"The time has come for extreme measures. The man's lungs are filling, and look there—he's not eliminating waste." The doctor pointed to an empty urine bag hanging at the side of the bed.

"And listen to his talk—his heart's not pumping enough oxygen to his brain. Core readings will tell us precisely what medications he needs."

A nurse said, "We're ready, Doctor."

"If you'll please step out now," he said to Frank.

Before leaving, Frank lifted one of the monsignor's dry hands. God keep you unaware for a while longer, Adrian. Unaware that your lungs are failing, along with your bladder and brain. Unaware that I'm already grieving over your death and speculating about the details of your funeral.

He left the room feeling stunned. He wandered along the hallway to the visitors' alcove and stood looking down at the snowy countryside sloping away to the west. He felt resentful that the day should be so beautiful. He resented the warmth, the pristine blue of the cloudless sky. The sun mocked him with its glittering, stupid, hyperbolic hope. Dear God, if dear friends must die, why can't they do it on cold, dark days when the world as a whole seems doomed? He turned from the window and gazed down the long, tiled hallway. He felt anxious, flat, empty, useless, used up. Symptoms of the big leak. Don't just stand here like a dolt letting your spirit drain away, he advised himself. Go upstairs and divert yourself in the psych ward.

Roberta Brink, looking up from her paperwork at the nurses' station, gave him a weary but welcoming smile and said yes, the clergy was allowed to see patients at any time. (It was for this purpose that Frank had dressed as a priest this morning.) She lifted the phone and spoke briefly with Special Care. "I'm so sorry, Father, Verna's gone off the unit with a visitor. She's doing much better, they say."

"I thought visitors weren't allowed till evening."

"Family can come in anytime—it's her father. They've gone down to the cafeteria, first floor, west wing."

Surely not Vernon Jessen, thought Frank, descending in the elevator. Most likely the nurse meant to say stepfather. Why was he feeling annoyed at having to face Verna in Tom's presence?

He didn't find them in the cafeteria. A waitress suggested he try the annex down the hall where smoking was permitted. This was a small windowless room containing a Coke machine, a sandwich dispenser, and a large round table surrounded by a scattering of chairs, five of which were occupied. Verna and her visitor sat with their backs to the door. Frank immediately recognized her visitor. There was no mistaking the rounded, slope-shouldered, bearlike back and the thick, short neck supporting a head too small for the torso—Frank's old nemesis, Vernon Jessen.

"Hey, Frank," came a voice from across the table, "what are you doing in uniform?" This from Gene DeSmet, who rose to his feet beaming at Frank, pulling an empty chair up beside his own and indicating that Frank should sit in it. On his left sat an old woman wearing a pink satin robe. A pair of curlers hung in her white hair. On the woman's left sat a frail old man in a dark tweed overcoat. The boy-priest was wearing a new mustache, small and blond, which instead of lending maturity to his face drew attention to its seamless innocence. He, like Frank, was dressed in priestly clothes, but of a much better cut than Frank's. The overcoat draped over the back of his chair, according to the label, was cashmere. DeSmet's mother, according to clerical gossip, drove up from St. Paul twice a month with merchandise from an exclusive clothier and a fresh tube of Clearasil.

"Here, sit down, Frank. What are you doing in uniform? I haven't seen you dressed like that since Bishop Swayles's funeral. Here, let me get you a Coke. How about a sandwich?" He was pulling quarters from his pocket with one hand and patting the old woman's shoulder with the other. "Have you met my favorite parishioners, Frank—Violet and C. W. Habnett? Violet, this is Father Healy from Linden Falls." He raised his voice to a shout: "C.W., this is Father Healy."

The old man, flitting his eyes from one priest to the other, brought a sour look to his thin, sagging face.

"They're mainstays of the cathedral from way back, Frank. It was Violet and C.W. who paid for the new wiring in the rectory, and now they're thinking of having electronic chimes installed in the belfry."

The old lady cast a cold, suspicious eye up at Frank and offered him her fleshless hand. "No need to introduce us," she said. "We're already acquainted. I don't think Father Healy liked us very well."

"I liked you just fine," Frank assured her, careful not to injure her fragile fingers with his handshake. "How are you, Mrs. Habnett?" He had last seen the Habnetts at a United Way reception sponsored by the bishop.

"I'm in here with bronchitis," she said, pulling him down into DeSmet's chair. "Listen to this." As Frank settled at her side, she exhaled forcefully a couple of times, giving him a sample of her wheezing. "If you liked us just fine, how come you ditched us?"

"I wanted a smaller parish, starting out. I found the cathedral overwhelming."

"You're pretty old to be starting out."

"Much too old," he agreed, pointing his thumb at DeSmet. "You're better off with the young one."

She was convinced of this—Frank could see it in the warm, chummy glance she raised to DeSmet.

"Coke or sandwich, Frank? Coffee?"

"No thanks, Gene."

"Violet? More coffee?"

"No more coffee, Gene dear. Sit down."

The young priest obeyed, pulling the other chair up close to Frank's and asking, "How's Loving Kindness?"

"Not good."

"I looked in on him, but he was sleeping. He didn't seem to be in distress. But when has Loving Kindness ever known distress?"

"Who are you talking about?" demanded Mrs. Habnett, drawing a long cigarette from the pocket of her robe and putting it to her lips.

"Monsignor Lawrence," said DeSmet, leaning in front of Frank to light it. "He's up in Coronary Care with a heart attack."

"Oh that man." She sighed with disgust, smoke pouring out her nose. "How many years was he in the chancery, and never learned how to give a proper dinner party."

"Loving Kindness won't die like the rest of us," said DeSmet, chuckling. "He'll be carried off by angels."

C. W. Habnett, sitting forward to see around his wife, scowled at Frank and asked, "Are you in stocks?"

DeSmet answered for him: "He's a priest, C.W."

"What?"

Louder: "He's a priest."

"I know he's a priest. Can't a priest be in stocks? Good God, Bishop Swayles owned half of Gladness Shortening before he died."

"I've never played the market," said Frank.

"What?"

"I have no stocks."

"I own quite a lot of uninteresting paper," said the old man, settling back in his chair, "so what I invest in for fun is cattle and pigs. If you want to have a good time with your money, get into pigs."

A breathy sound from across the table—Verna snickering. Verna did not appear to remember Frank from yesterday's visit. She looked vague and sleepy—probably from medication—but not engulfed in the black mood she'd presented to her mother. Frank watched her eyes move laconically from DeSmet to the Habnetts to himself as though she were mildly interested in their conversation. When C. W. Habnett announced that he stood to make a bundle in the next few days on pork bellies, she giggled again, flicked the ash off her cigarette, and turned to see if her father was amused.

Frank wondered what emergency or change of heart could have prompted Vernon Jessen to visit his daughter after a quarter century of being out of touch with her. Why, after giving her the silent treatment when she visited his farm last summer, had he driven to Berrington this morning to seek her out? Though he'd recognized Vernon Jessen from the back, Frank would never have known him from the front. His face had grown wider, his eyelids droopier. His hair had gone from brown to yellowish white. Even his brown eyes seemed to have faded to a lighter, less distinct hue. The biggest change, however, was not in the lines of his face but in his demeanor. Vernon Jessen, all-state tackle, had lost his aggressiveness. You could tell from the way he slumped in his chair and looked warily out of his puffy, insecure eyes that years had gone by since he'd been a bully. This came as a shock to Frank. Indeed, it was more than a shock; it was a blow to his self-confidence. Was his memory faulty? Had Vernon been menacing only in Frank's imagination? Had he so misjudged him as a boy that he'd never sensed any of Vernon's vulnerability? For that was precisely how he looked now: vulnerable.

It was clear that Vernon didn't recognize him. If I tell him my name, thought Frank, will he remember me as the skinny eighth-grader he loved to terrorize in the school yard, or the timid fifteen-year-old who watched Dr. Gilpatrick examine his cow, or the love-struck seventeen-year-old from whose arms he stole Libby at the Loomis Ballroom? Or was I too minor an irritation for him to hold in his memory all these years?

Nor did Verna recognize him—at first. But then suddenly her roving eyes stopped on him and widened in surprise. "You," she exclaimed.

"Hi, Verna."

She fastened her eyes on his clerical collar. "You're the priest from the rezz. The one that tries to keep up with Tom."

"Tries to keep up? What do you mean?"

"Beer for beer."

At the mention of Tom and beer and the rezz, Gene DeSmet was arrested in his chatter with the Habnetts and turned searching eyes on Verna. As she went on in her drugged, lazy, good-natured drawl, the boy-priest's cheery expression gradually changed to one of horror.

"You don't look like I thought you would. Tom told me the Basswood priest was sort of baby-faced. Sort of still wet behind the ears. Sort of, you know, saintly and dumb. A real boozehound, Tom says." She paused to laugh softly. She raised her eyes to Frank's hairline, then studied her father's. "You must be as old as my dad. I thought you were young."

Vernon Jessen looked impassively at his large hands lying inert on the table. DeSmet looked sick to his stomach.

Frank had to reassess this gathering. He'd assumed Verna

and DeSmet had known each other in Basswood, but obviously they hadn't. Frank's heart went out to DeSmet, whose crushing disillusionment was written on his face. His thoughts were there for Frank to read: *Me, a dumb, saintly boozehound? And all the time I imagined the Pearsalls utterly charmed by my visits on Saturday nights. Wasn't I their ray of hope in Basswood, their lifeline in the boondocks? Wasn't I fun?*

Frank corrected her: "Your mother and I were friends in high school."

Verna's eyes narrowed for a moment, then widened again. "Oh, that one! Of course, the friend she liked so much and he went off to be a priest. She used to talk about you a lot."

Father DeSmet, trying to steer the talk elsewhere and struggling to be cheery despite his damaged ego, asked Frank if he missed the cathedral.

"No, I'm too busy. How do you like it?"

The young man worked up an expression of bliss. "It's wonderful."

"You're getting along with the bishop?"

"We're very close. He's so much more human than Loving Kindness. He plays the trumpet, did you know that?"

"He has many talents," Frank agreed.

"Last year I lost big on yearling steers," said C. W. Habnett, "but I made it up on pigs." This might have been for Verna's benefit because at each mention of pigs she giggled.

"My dad hauls pigs," she told the old man.

"We never could figure you out, Father Healy," said Mrs. Habnett, laying a feathery hand on Frank's sleeve. "That time you took your shirt off playing tennis at the country club! Where's he from, we all wondered, Outer Mongolia?"

Verna turned to her father. "Tell him about hauling pigs."

Obediently Vernon Jessen lifted his eyes and faced the old man's flinty gaze. He cleared his throat. "I haul cattle. I make runs to St. Paul."

"Runs?" The old man shook his head. "I'm more on the constipated side. It's my wife who gets the runs."

His wife ignored this, or didn't hear it. She was boring into

Frank with a reproving frown. "You had no idea, did you, that men do not remove their shirts at the Berrington Country Club."

Frank, who had played a few sets there with Bishop Baker, had no memory of the scandal she referred to, but he apologized nonetheless. "Very thoughtless of me."

"We could only assume you were trying to flaunt your priesthood. You thought you were above our silly little bylaws."

"No, Mrs. Habnett, I never thought that."

"The windows of the dining room look out on the tennis courts. Well! We had *nowhere* else to look."

"There's two schools of thought on constipation," the old man said.

"Oh, shut up," said his wife, snapping her head around and blowing smoke in her husband's face.

"Two schools of thought," he repeated.

"Shut up, I said."

As though to distract Frank from this tiff, Father DeSmet said, "I got in a few games on the Berrington course before it snowed. I'm nine over par."

"Good."

"What were you?"

"One or two."

DeSmet looked grieved all over again.

"Don't forget," Frank consoled him, "I coached golf at the Academy."

C. W. Habnett stood up and proclaimed, "They used to say you had to have a movement every day, but they've changed their mind on that. Now they're saying it's okay to skip a day or two."

"Can't you go ten minutes without talking about your bowels?" scolded his wife.

He buttoned his coat. "Come on, Vi. I'll walk you back to your room."

"I just lit a cigarette. Sit down."

"Come on." He hobbled around the table and out into the hallway.

"That man!" she said, putting out her smoke. As she stood

up, DeSmet sprang to his feet and pulled her chair back. He spoke to Frank.

"It's my woods get me in trouble. How about playing a few rounds with me in the spring? See what I'm doing wrong."

"Okay. On the Linden Falls course."

DeSmet made a face.

"Good-bye, Father Healy," said Mrs. Habnett, crossing the room to catch up to her husband. "I'll never forget the time your Monsignor Lawrence invited us to dinner and his dessert plates didn't match."

"So long, Frank." DeSmet followed her out, his coat over his arm.

Vernon looked at his watch, showed it to his daughter.

"Five minutes," she said.

Frank stretched his hand across the table and said, "Hello, Vernon. Frank Healy. Remember?"

Vernon pumped the hand once, weakly, and replied, "Yeah?"

"Second-string quarterback the year you graduated."

The old all-stater seemed interested enough to try to remember. He gave his head a heavy nod and echoed, "Second string, huh?"

"I also had a crush on Libby."

A momentary smile: "Second string there, too."

Encouraged by this evidence of lively thought, Frank offered more. "I worked for the Schultenovers. Candled a lot of your eggs."

Vernon sat back, cupping one hand in the other on the shelf of his belly. "I've cut down on my chickens. Not enough money in eggs anymore, not since the big egg factories came in." He lifted a thumb to his mouth and chewed on a hangnail for a few moments, then said, "Libby's back."

"I know."

"This here's her daughter."

Frank nodded.

Verna, turning to her father and pointing her cigarette at Frank, said, "He was here yesterday. Came with Mom."

This puzzled Vernon. "Why?" he asked. "I mean are you and Libby . . . ?"

"No," said Frank. "Nothing like that."

"You never know now-days . . . about priests."

"Libby's very concerned about Verna. She brought me along to help keep her spirits up."

"That's what you think," said Verna.

Both men waited for her to continue, but she didn't. She looked coy.

"Don't you?" Frank prompted.

"Don't I what?"

"Think she's concerned about you?"

"Sure, I know that. What I mean is . . ." She put out her cigarette, stabbing it to shreds. "Your old girlfriend's got designs on you."

At this, he felt both father and daughter reading his face with great interest, and he wondered what it displayed. He was often too far removed from his feelings to realize which ones he was giving away—indeed, which ones he was feeling. He said, "She told you that?"

"No, but I know her so well. Did she come with you today?"

"No."

"But she sent you."

"I volunteered."

"And you'll report back to her."

Frank nodded.

"Tell her . . ." She wrinkled her brow, preparing a statement. "Tell her I'm sorry about yesterday. I was so *down* all of a sudden. I couldn't help it."

"She'll be glad to hear that."

At this, she smiled at him, bringing prettiness to her face, a kind of injured beauty that tugged at his heart. Was she entranced by her medication, or was she purposely letting the smile linger on him? Did she realize how warm it was? Did she mean it to say she was fond of him?

Her father jolted the table as he hunched himself forward, leaned across it, his arms bent under his chest, his eyes glaring at Frank. His voice was a low, urgent rumble.

"Healy."

"Yes?"

"Are you part of the investigation?"

"What investigation?"

"The BCA. Two guys came to see me."

Frank recalled the two men in the elevator. "Was one bald and the other one young?"

"Yeah, you know them?"

"Saw them, is all. Yesterday, here in the hospital."

"What do they want?"

"I have no idea."

"They came out to the farm and asked me a bunch of questions. That's all government assholes know how to do, mind other people's business. They got no right to be on my farm." Something of the old bully flashed in Vernon's eyes. "I told them to stay clear of my property or they'd get a hideful of buckshot."

This amused Verna. "He thinks they're after him for taxes." She gathered up her cigarettes and lighter and billfold and got to her feet.

Vernon stood. "What I make is my business, Healy. You can tell them for me that there ain't no government assholes going to look at my records." He snickered triumphantly. "There ain't no records to look at. I don't keep any."

"I told you, they aren't after you for taxes," his daughter said.

"You never know, with government assholes."

"Did they ask to see your records?" asked Frank, following them to the door.

"No, they weren't there long enough." He snickered again. "I told them to clear out or I'd get out my shotgun."

Verna spoke to Frank on their way to the elevator: "They're trying to find out how Roger died. They came and talked to me early this morning. The bald one asked the questions. The young one looks like Elvis—you know, that black hair swept back, that long face. I guess they were here yesterday, but Dr. Pella put them off for a day. 'What's the problem?' I asked them. 'You think I killed Roger?' The bald one said, 'Not necessarily.'"

Her father, half a step behind, asked, "Roger who?"

"Roger Upward, a friend of mine."

"He died?"

"Yep."

"Upwards are Indians." Vernon Jessen added a look of pain to his bully expression. "You friends with Indians?"

She ignored the question. "What jerks. Ask them if you're wanted for murder and they say not necessarily. What kind of an answer is that? Christ, it got me all worked up." Her face was animated now, her voice no longer subdued. She hit the elevator button hard. "I can't stand it when people say 'not necessarily.'" There was a pause, then she turned an ironic smile on Frank, as though suddenly realizing that her peevishness might strike him as silly.

It didn't strike her father as silly. "Those assholes," he muttered, between bites of his hangnail.

Frank accompanied them as far as three. "Good-bye," he said, stepping out into the hallway.

Vernon Jessen grunted.

Verna held the door open. "Frank," she said, appealing to him with her injured smile. "Will you come back and see me?"

"Maybe Thursday. I might be coming back to see a friend downstairs." Actually he imagined Adrian dead by Thursday.

"Good," she said. "Without my mom, how about? I need to talk to you."

Adrian, wired for core readings, was lying still and breathing evenly. His eyes were closed. There was a dribble of urine in the bag. Of the medical crew, only the pretty, cream-haired young woman remained, standing by the window in a shaft of sunlight.

"He seems much better now," she said musically. "Let's hope the worst is over."

Frank nodded, allowing his eyes to linger on her for a few moments, arrested by her beauty. Her hair, aglow in the sun, was a halo.

"I'll leave you with him," she said, moving over to the bed and straightening the sheet across Adrian's chest. "We'll be monitoring his signs from the nurses' station. Push this button if you need us."

She left the room. Frank pulled the vinyl chair over to the bed and sat.

Adrian eventually opened his eyes. "Hello, my boy."

"Adrian!" Frank, startled, gripped his hand. "My God, you gave us a scare."

Smiling weakly, the old man moved his eyes from Frank to the clock on the wall. "Is it morning?"

"Yes."

"What day?"

"Tuesday. You've been here twenty-four hours."

The eyes closed. Minutes passed. The peaks of heartbeat moved evenly across the screen. The numbers held steady. More minutes passed. Adrian snored. Frank went down the hall for reading matter, and when he returned with yesterday's newspaper, he found Adrian awake again.

"Frank, I let you down."

"How?"

"Along with Mrs. Pettit and her students."

"Adrian, you collapsed."

"Tell them . . ."

The eyes closed. Time passed. All was well on the screen. Frank read an article assessing Carter's first year as president, another assessing the career of Barbra Streisand. The January thaw would be short-lived, according to the weather map.

"Frank."

"Adrian. How are you feeling?"

"Fine. A little sleepy."

Frank patted his hand. "You can sleep all you want."

"It's my heart, isn't it?"

"It is. Some damage, the doctor says, but you're doing much better."

There was a long pause—Adrian gathering strength to continue. "Frank, I saw an angel."

"You did?"

He rolled his head toward the window. "Over there."

"Yes?"

"I wasn't delirious, Frank."

"No."

"They were getting me settled in bed and I looked over there and saw her. Just for a second."

"I did, too, Adrian."

The head rolled back, the eyes settled on Frank, then slowly went shut. "I'd like to know her name."

There were more conversations as the morning wore on, not about the angel. The numbers held steady. The doctor seemed encouraged. Bishop Baker phoned. A volunteer brought in the mail—a dozen get-well cards from Linden Falls.

Frank took his leave at noon. On his way past the nurses' station he asked the cream-haired girl what her name was. She said it was Cindy.

"Really, Frank? You saw a difference?"

"Day and night." Shifting the phone to his other hand, he spread out the morning mail on the desk. His desk now.

"She actually talked to you?"

"And smiled, and asked me to come again."

"Will you?"

"Thursday. Adrian's there, with a heart attack."

"Oh, that sweet man. How bad is it?"

"Quite bad. Though he seems to have stabilized."

"Coronary unit?"

"Yes."

"How are you—sad?"

"Pretty sad."

"Oh, Frank, I don't want you to be sad. Let's meet somewhere right now. Let's talk."

"Thanks, but I'm swamped at the moment. The bishop has put me in charge of St. Ann's, and I've got a hundred things piling up."

"I've also got to talk to you about those two men we saw yesterday. They *were* detectives. They were out here to see us, asking about Roger Upward."

"They saw Verna early this morning."

"She talked to them?"

"She asked if they suspected her of murder. They told her not necessarily."

"Who are they, Frank? Just what is the Bureau of Criminal Apprehension?"

"Minnesota's version of the FBI. Oh, another thing, Libby—Verna's father was there."

"Where?"

"Visiting her."

"No! Vernon? Why in the world . . . ?"

"He's afraid the BCA is after his money."

"What money?"

"Taxes. He evidently hasn't been paying any. They'd been out to his farm."

Silence on the line. Frank picked up a notepad and ran down the list of messages in Mrs. Tatzig's hand—the plumber and the liturgy committee asking for appointments, the bank questioning an erroneous deposit slip, the insurance office threatening to raise rates if the deteriorating roof on the rectory wasn't replaced.

"Did you talk to him, Frank?"

"A little. He's a pretty glum guy."

"Makes you wonder if that's where she gets her glumness, doesn't it?"

"It does."

"Frank, what about the BCA? Should we be worried?"

"I'm going to call Caesar Pipe and find out."

"Frank, did she say if she wanted to see me?"

He stalled. "Well, let me think. . . ."

"I called her," Libby continued. "She hung up on me."

"I'd like to see her once more alone. I think she'll come around, but she needs time."

"You know what *I* need, Frank?"

"What?"

"To see you."

"Well . . ."

"I'll leave it to you. Say when."

"I'll say when when I get some of this work behind me."

Her laugh was nervous, strained. "You're avoiding me."

"I'm not avoiding you, Libby." But he was.

She asked, "Will you call me?"

"As soon as I learn something from Caesar."

"We *will* go to Berrington together, won't we . . . eventually?"

"We will."

"Good-bye, Frank."

"Good-bye."

"I'm going out for a walk. It's thawing."

"Caesar, what's the BCA up to?" Frank asked.

"Can't tell you."

"You can't tell me, or you don't know?"

"Don't know."

"But you know they're around, asking questions about Roger Upward."

"Yeah, they came out here and talked to me yesterday, but it was all questions and no answers. I don't know what they know. Or suspect. Or don't know. Or don't suspect."

"Caesar, could you find out from the sheriff exactly what they're up to? It would put a lot of people including myself at ease to know what's going on."

"On pins and needles, are you?" Frank, in his mind's eye, saw Caesar break out in his small, insinuating grin.

"Worried, Caesar. For Verna's sake. I'm convinced she had nothing to do with Roger's death."

"Me too."

"Did you tell that to the BCA?"

"Yeah. I told them I could come up with at least a dozen witnesses who saw Verna at the Homestead far into the night. And at least one witness—a big fat one—who slept with her there in the back room till morning."

"Were they impressed?"

"Who knows? Guys like that never let on."

"Could you find out, Caesar?"

"They teach them that in cop school—never let on."

"Could you ask the sheriff what they know?"

"Well . . ." A long pause. "That's not really my style."

"What *is* your style, Caesar?"

"I'm more one to sit back and wait and see what happens."

"But this time, for Verna's sake, for her mother's sake, maybe you could ask the sheriff."

"Well . . ."

"For my sake."

"Could, I guess."

"Do it, Caesar. Ask him."

31

The next morning, after attending the Fredricks funeral (she hadn't missed a St. Ann's wedding or funeral in twenty years) Mrs. Tatzig picked up her sister and sped to Berrington in the Oldsmobile. She protested when a nurse allowed them only ten minutes apiece at the monsignor's bedside, but was mollified somewhat when her sister (shy of priests anyhow, though less shy of Monsignor Lawrence than others, particularly now that he was barely conscious) gave her her own ten minutes. Returning home in midafternoon, having bought dish towels and twenty-five pounds of birdseed at the Berrington K-Mart, Mrs. Tatzig told Frank the old man was doing poorly.

"He's delirious. He said he met an angel."

Frank, sipping coffee in the breakfast nook while keeping an eye out for the plumber, asked, "Did he get her name?"

Mrs. Tatzig gashed open the birdseed bag with a butcher knife, then directed a puzzled look at Frank. "Whose name?"

"The angel's. He told me yesterday he'd like to know her name."

Her expression turned suspicious. "You believe in angels?"

"I do, Marcella. Don't you?"

She squinted, trying to see the invisible. "What's Rome saying these days?"

"About angels?"

She nodded.

"Same as always."

She shrugged. "Then I suppose I do." She scooped out a saucepanful of birdseed. "But it's one thing to believe in angels and another thing to actually see one. That's what separates Christians from loonies."

The phone rang. Mrs. Tatzig, on her way out the door with the birdseed, picked it up, said, "Yeah, he's here," and stretched the cord to the breakfast nook.

It was Danny Ash. "Just back from Berrington, Frank. Had to go on business, so I stopped in and saw the monsignor. He's doing great. Sitting up. Taking soft food. Doctor says at this rate he'll be out of the coronary unit by the weekend. I'm betting on him. Tough old soldier, the monsignor. Not like the new softies they're ordaining these days. Which brings me to why I called. Ran into the bishop at the hospital, and he told me who's coming to help you out on weekends. Damn it, Frank, can't you do something? Talk to him? Change his mind?"

"Who's coming?"

"You haven't heard?"

"No," Frank said. But he could guess.

"DeSmet."

"It makes sense, Danny. He knows the parish."

"And the parish knows him. Talk to the bishop, would you?"

"Sorry, Danny."

"Why not?"

"Why don't *you* talk to the bishop?"

"Chain of command. Lieutenant talks to the captain. I'm a buck private in your army."

"Look, it's only temporary. While Adrian's recuperating."

"Sheesh. If I have to listen to one more of that idiot's sappy sermons, I'll stand up and throw something."

"Go to late Mass. He'll be taking the early one."

"Promise?"

"Promise."

"You won't ever switch with him?"

"I can't. I'm in Basswood for early Mass."

"Basswood? You mean there's still a Mass in Basswood? I thought they closed down that two-bit operation."

"There's a community of believers out there, Danny."

"Can't be many. Why don't they drive in to St. Ann's?"

"They're Indians."

"I know they're Indians. What's that got to do with it?"

"St. Ann's is pure white."

"So what? We're not prejudiced."

"They feel at home in Basswood. I doubt if they'd come to St. Ann's."

"They'll have to sooner or later—the priest shortage and all."

Frank said, "If it comes to that, why not close St. Ann's?" and got the response he expected.

"Close St. Ann's! Christ, we'd have to go to church in Berrington—sixty miles."

"Basswood is nineteen."

"Sheeesh, Frank, are you serious? Can you see us all getting in our cars and driving out there to go to Mass with Indians?"

"Not all."

"Any?"

"Some."

"Who?"

"You."

"Me?" A pause. "Yeah, maybe you're right. But I wouldn't like it."

"Why?"

"Well, Christ almighty, Frank, this is my home parish."

Frank spent the rest of the afternoon in the pastor's office examining desk drawers and files and finding, not surprisingly, that the parish records were not up-to-date and the parish debt was somewhat greater than parish income. Correspondence had been neglected. Nothing disastrous. Nothing wrong that couldn't be righted with a routine of long days in the office and a new appeal to the parishioners' pocketbooks. Adrian, moderate in all things, was moderately negligent.

Closing the last drawer and looking around at the walls bare of everything but a calendar and a crucifix, Frank was struck by the absolute lack of personality in the room. Not one personal letter. No private notes. No photographs. How like my father, thought Frank. The personal effects I gathered up after my father's death did not quite fill a shoe box.

And, dear God, how like me. I never take pictures, I've never kept a diary or journal, and except for a few short-lived exchanges with graduates of the Academy, I've never been one to write letters. When I was a seminarian, I suppose I would have been glad to foresee myself this aloof from the world. In those days I equated remoteness with holiness and strove to perfect an aversion to this life and a love of the next. When did I change? *Why* did I change? Why, this afternoon, am I sitting at this office window watching the sun go down and wishing I owned a photo album? Wishing I had someone to write to. Wishing I had at least one clerical suit as spiffy as Gene DeSmet's. Is it Adrian's mortality that's making me feel so bereft, so unattached, so frightened? Yes, dear God, frightened. I'm feeling frightened. All day, beginning with the Fredricks funeral, my heart has been rising up and sticking in my throat the way it did one time when I was fourteen and skating over a deep stretch of the Badbattle as the ice began to crack. Or the way it did when I was homesick in Montana. Or the way it did when my mother died.

The sun sank, pulling its afterglow with it, and Frank, staring at his reflection in the dark window, felt himself dangerously close to springing the big leak when Mrs. Tatzig called him to the front door where a visitor stood waiting. It was Kelvin Pfeiffer, Eunice Pfeiffer's elderly brother, ill at ease in his faded blue farm clothes.

"Eunice is out in the car, Father. She'd like to talk to you." Kelvin, having removed his cap, ran his hand over his thin white hair. His large face was unshaven.

"Won't she come in?" Frank asked, knowing better.

"No, she says to come out, if you would. It's hard on her breathing, you know—the cold air."

"Sure, lead the way."

They hurried down the front walk, Frank inwardly clenching himself against the cold. Winter was back—zero or below. The stars were ice crystals in the black sky.

"Cold," said Kelvin Pfeiffer, holding the back door open.

"Too cold," Frank replied, getting in. It was a ten-year-old Chevrolet smelling of earth and pipe smoke. The engine idled; the heater fan whirred at high speed. The dome light was on. Eunice, in front, turned to look at him. A face mask hung from a thin elastic band around her neck.

"You shouldn't be out without your coat, Father."

"It's all right, Eunice, your car is warm." It was suffocatingly hot.

"I'd come in, but my breathing . . ."

He conveyed his understanding with a nod, and it wasn't only her asthma he understood. He knew that she hadn't once set foot in the rectory since Mrs. Tatzig replaced her two decades ago.

Kelvin got in behind the wheel and gunned the engine. The dome light brightened.

"We've been to Berrington to see the monsignor," she said. "He told me you didn't visit him today."

"Mrs. Tatzig went in my place."

At the mention of the woman's name, ice appeared momentarily in Eunice's eyes. "Will you go and see him tonight?" she asked.

"I'm meeting with the liturgy committee tonight."

"Tomorrow then."

"Yes."

"The shut-ins want to pay the monsignor back for all his visits. Will you take them with you?"

"But they're shut-ins."

"Gert Graham's the only one confined to bed. I'll arrange it with Selma Schultenover and the Hallorans and we'll be ready whatever time you say. I'll have Kelvin bring me in to Selma's."

"All right," he said obediently. "Ten o'clock."

"Now, Father, we have to talk about where the monsignor will live when he gets out."

"Why? He'll live here," he said, hoping to forestall what he sensed was coming.

"With that woman?" The icy look again. "He'll need care."

"Marcella is capable."

Eunice Pfeiffer looked insulted, pained. "Capable, yes, maybe. But caring, Father?" A brief, scornful laugh. "No, not by any stretch of the imagination is that a caring woman."

Frank sighed, resenting (as he had years ago) her habit of meddling, her judgmental nature, her pushiness. He said softly, "Where would he go, Eunice? What are you getting at?"

"I was with him all those years—those wonderful years when you were growing up—and now it's time for us to be together again."

Frank picked his words carefully; nothing outraged Eunice more than the suggestion that she was behaving outrageously. "We can't turn her out, Eunice. It's her livelihood. She's sometimes a little harsh, true, but she's adequate for the job."

"Who's talking about turning her out? Do you think at my age I'm going to come in and be your housekeeper? Don't be silly, Father. I'm talking about the Kittleson Arms. There's one room open now, and another death expected any day. I've given it a great deal of thought. We belong in those two rooms, the monsignor and I."

Frank pictured the Kittleson Arms, a two-story cube of green stucco on Main Street. Sixteen bed-sitting rooms, four bathrooms, meals in the basement, bingo and TV in the game room, the smell of disinfectant throughout.

"Let's wait, Eunice. Let's see how he is when he gets home."

"The rooms will have to be spoken for."

Kelvin lifted his foot from the accelerator. The dome light dimmed.

"Frankly, Eunice, I can't see either one of you in the Kittleson Arms. Think of how cramped those rooms are."

"I think how *warm* they are." She shifted her gaze to her brother. "A person could freeze to death in our house."

Kelvin, reading his gauges and cocking his head for engine noises, paid her no attention.

She turned back to Frank. "And what's he going to do about the stairs? He can't be going up and down the rectory stairs after a heart attack. The Kittleson Arms has an elevator."

"We'll have to see what the doctor says, Eunice. I've actually heard of cases where stairs were recommended for exercise."

"And he'll need nursing. There's a nurse stopping in five days a week at the Kittleson Arms."

He continued to reason with her for a time, though he knew it was useless; never in his life had he been able to alter this woman's thinking. So he relaxed and gave up, realizing that her scheming, bold as it was, would be no match for the monsignor's inertia and charm. Once he got home—if he got home—and settled himself into his soft reclining chair, there'd be no moving the old man to the Kittleson Arms. She'd lay out her scheme for him over the phone and he'd say, "Tut tut, Eunice," and she'd fold. Why did she allow Adrian the last word, but never himself?

"Did he talk to you?" Frank asked.

"Oh, yes, he was sitting up taking food. He had apricots he didn't care for. I did my best to see that he ate them. He's never cared for apricots—you know that, surely—but he was always one to clean his plate. Has he fallen into bad habits, Frank? Not cleaning his plate?"

"No, he usually cleans his plate."

"The meals at the Kittleson Arms look tasty. I've been there visiting at mealtime."

Kelvin Pfeiffer pressed the accelerator in a manner indicating impatience.

"He told me an angel came to see him."

"Yes, he said that yesterday."

"Doesn't that convince you?"

"Of . . ."

"Of his needing care. His mind is going."

"Don't you believe in angels, Eunice?"

"Of course I believe in angels, but you can't see them."

"Mary saw Gabriel."

"Not in Berrington, she didn't."

Frank nodded acquiescently.

Her brother raced the engine, and Eunice adjourned the meeting. "We'll talk more tomorrow, Father."

Frank opened his door. "Adrian's the one to talk to."

"Not necessarily. Not if he's non compos mentis."

"We'll wait and see if he bounces back."

"Don't go out again without your coat."

"I won't." He got out.

"Father."

"Yes?"

"Are you eating right?"

"Yes, I am, and too much. Good-bye, Eunice, I'll see you tomorrow."

"Think about it now. He'll need care. He'll be a burden to you."

"I will. It's good of you to be concerned."

Kelvin got out of the car, saying, "I left my cap in the house."

Following Frank into the entryway, the old man said, "I have to tell you she's not easy to live with, Father." He drew his cap out from inside his jacket, where he had concealed it. "Impossible to live with, is more like it. She's on our backs, my brother and mine, day and night, harping on this and harping on that. We'd like to see her in the Kittleson Arms."

Frank, chilled to the marrow, shut the door and said "I see."

"Maybe the old monsignor doesn't belong in the Kittleson arms, but Eunice sure does. If you could, you know, talk to her about it some more. . . ."

"I could, but I don't carry much clout with her, Kelvin."

"Who does!"

"The monsignor does. It's possible he could talk to her."

"I mean more than talk to her. I mean talk her *into* it."

"That's asking a lot."

Kelvin put on his cap, swiveling it down tight. "If you knew what it was like to be harped at all the time . . ."

"Have you and Raymond talked to her?"

"About the Kittleson Arms? No."

"Or about her harping?"

"No."

"Maybe you should."

"We don't talk to her, period."

"That's terrible, Kelvin. Why not?"

"She doesn't like us."

"Maybe if you had conversations with her, she'd like you."

The old farmer, standing with his hand on the doorknob, spent a few moments pondering this. "Conversations about what?"

"Well, I don't know. The farm."

"We don't farm anymore."

"The neighbors."

Kelvin frowned, apparently trying to imagine such exchanges. He shook his head. "We never see the neighbors."

"The news in the paper."

"We only get the Linden Falls *Leader*. Not much news in that."

"Listen, Kelvin, women like to talk. Women *need* to talk. She's probably *starving* for talk, that's why she nags you. Get her mind on other things and she'll forget about nagging."

"We're not talkers, me and Raymond."

"Don't you talk to each other?"

He searched his memory. "I guess we did when we farmed. You have to, you know, sometimes talk about what to plant."

"Well, that's my advice, Kelvin. Maybe you're right about the Kittleson Arms. Maybe she'd like it there. Maybe that's why she's bringing it up—she wants to move there with or without the monsignor—but as long as she's in your house you ought to talk to her."

"I told you, we're just not talkers."

"You're talking to me."

"This here's different. This here's an emergency."

They heard the horn toot twice. Kelvin hung his head and opened the door. Mrs. Tatzig's voice carried in from the kitchen: "Supper in ten minutes!"

Kelvin lifted his head, tipped it toward the kitchen, and asked, "You talk to that one?"

"I do. Not as much as I should, maybe. The monsignor talks

with her, watches television with her. That's another thing, Kelvin. Do you ever watch television together?"

"Me and Raymond sometimes—sports."

"I mean the three of you."

He shook his head. "She won't watch sports."

"You could watch what she likes."

"'Rockford Files'? It's all made-up stories."

"The news."

"Same thing there. They make it all up."

"Well, that's the best I can offer, Kelvin." Winter was flowing in over the doorsill, freezing Frank's ankles. "Just try talking to her."

The old man turned away. "Thanks anyway, Father. If she brings it up to you again, you know how we feel. We'd like to see her in the Kittleson Arms."

"If I get the opportunity, I'll do what I can."

Kelvin stepped out into the night. "Cold," he said.

"Terrible. Good night, Kelvin."

"Good night."

Frank went to the kitchen and mixed himself a drink. Mrs. Tatzig, standing at the stove, was listening to the daily obituary notices on the radio. He carried his glass into the dining room, switched on the small TV standing on the buffet, and stood looking at John Chancellor while picturing the Pfeiffers on a winter evening, Kelvin and Raymond switching channels on the big TV in the living room looking for sports, Eunice bundled up and shivering in her cold sitting room watching James Garner. He forced himself to picture Kelvin leaving the living room and going down the dark hallway and asking Eunice if she'd like to see her program in color for a change ("Come on out and sit on the couch, Eunice, it's warmer out there")—an enormously charitable gesture for this reticent man, a breakthrough, the first step toward harmony in the farmhouse. But no. Without willing it—indeed, while trying to stave it off—Frank saw the invitation rejected, saw Eunice turn in her rocking chair and announce coldly, looking wounded and proud, "I'm used to black-and-white."

Dear God, the barriers between us. The walls. He turned and

looked at the wall between himself and the kitchen. He took a wineglass from the china cabinet and went into the kitchen, where he searched the liquor cupboard for a bottle of the wine Mrs. Tatzig liked. He removed the cork, poured a brimming glass, and crossed to the stove, holding it out to her.

"Yeah?" she said, pushing her hair up off her brow with her wrist. "What's this all about?" She took the glass.

He raised his own. "Cheers, Marcella."

She swallowed deeply and smacked her lips. Then turning back to her burners, she handed him the glass. "Cheers yourself," she said. "I'm busy."

32

The next day was blustery, overcast, and cold. Frank parked in front of the furniture store and spent twenty minutes helping Bert and Tricia Halloran into their coats and down the stairs and out onto the icy sidewalk, where the wind blew Bert's hat off. Frank guided them to the car, then retrieved the hat and set it firmly on the old man's head. "Get in," he said, opening the back door, but they didn't get in. While Frank folded Bert's walker and put it in the trunk, they stood at the open door arguing about where Tricia should sit.

"Here, sit in back with me," ordered Bert. "Let Eunice sit in front."

"Eunice and Selma can sit in back with you," Tricia sang out happily, pulling the front door open. "I want to sit with Father."

"Your place is with your husband."

She gave her husband a pleasant little smile, then a firm little push, which caused him to teeter. "My place is wherever I want it to be."

Frank settled the contest by helping Bert into the back, Trisha into the front.

"A wife's place is with her husband," Bert muttered as the

Olds moved through a squall of snow flurries toward Selma Schultenover's home in the remodeled egghouse.

The front door of the egghouse opened the instant the Olds came to a stop, and the two women stepped out into the wind. Eunice Pfeiffer led the way, her black scarf tied around her head so that only her eyes were exposed. Selma Schultenover, bent small by her infirmities, seemed even smaller outdoors. She was bundled up in a billowy, down-filled coat that swept the ground. She wore earmuffs and a floppy flat hat. Frank helped them across the icy sidewalk and held open the back door. Bert Halloran appeared unwilling to make room for them until Selma Schultenover gave him a vicious poke in the leg with her cane.

Excited to be out, to be traveling, to be in one another's company, the four shut-ins threw themselves into a spirited and sour discussion that lasted all the way to Berrington. They started with the weather.

"Horrible."

"Depressing."

"Worse than last year."

"One night above zero since December twelfth."

"Dreadful."

"Worse coming."

"Are the roads icy, Father?"

"No, they're clear."

"Just wait, they'll be icy if this snow keeps up."

"I don't mind the cold, but I hate the snow."

"I hate the cold."

"I hate the cold and snow both."

"I hate winter. Everybody's so grouchy."

"There isn't the old friendliness anymore, not in any season. In the old days people were friendlier."

"There isn't the friendliness and there isn't the respect for age."

"There isn't the patriotism."

"There isn't the ambition."

"There isn't the quality of food."

"There isn't the respect for the elderly."

"You already said that."

"Potatoes especially. Where can you buy a good potato nowadays?"

"And prices, my lord."

"Horrible prices."

"Dreadful prices."

"Worse coming, they say."

"Do you know what you pay for a good baking potato nowadays? You can pay as much as thirty cents."

"That's criminal."

"That's outrageous. I paid fifty cents for ten pounds of russets in 1955."

"Where will it all end?"

"It's outrageous."

"It's depressing."

"It's the Democrats."

The Linden Falls delegation found Monsignor Lawrence sitting in a chair saying his rosary, free of all tubes and wires except for a line of oxygen attached to his nostrils.

"Ahhh, how lovely, how lovely," he purred as his four old shut-ins took turns lifting his limp hand, patting it, asking how he was, interrupting his answer with news of their own (the wind, the snow squall, the thirty-cent potato), then carefully replacing the hand on the arm of the chair. Eunice pulled up a second chair and sat down beside him while the other three settled themselves side by side on the bed. Though the monsignor smiled and nodded and continued to mumble his pleasure at seeing them all, Frank, standing beyond the bed, caught in his eyes the look of a man whose serenity had been invaded, and he was the only one to notice when Adrian, leaning forward to lay his rosary beads on the bedside table, surreptitiously pressed the call button. This brought immediate help, not from the angelic, cream-haired nurse, but from a stern older woman, who ordered the visitors out of the room. "One at a time," she scolded as she herded them into the hallway. "We're strict about that on CCU, only one at a time. How did the bunch of you ever get past the nurses' station?"

Eunice Pfeiffer, appointing herself first among equals, went back into the room while the other three hobbled after Frank to the visitors' alcove. They were no sooner settled on chairs than they decided they wanted a snack. Frank helped them to their feet, guided them to the elevator, and told them how to reach the cafeteria. They begged him to come along—Tricia Halloran snatched at his sleeve, trying to pull him into the car as the door was closing—but he said he had someone to visit upstairs.

Through the double doors of Hope, he saw Libby and Verna sitting together at a table in the dayroom. Most of the tables were occupied by dozens of chattering patients on mid-morning break. He held back for a moment, trying to size up Verna's state of health. She was dressed. She was wearing white over white over white—open cardigan, buttoned cardigan, and blouse. Her jeans were white as well, and so were her shoes. Her outfit was stylish, worn in the careless ill-fitting mode of the day. She looked sulky. She was smoking. She wore makeup for a change, so much eye makeup that her eyes looked bruised.

He went in. Libby, seeing him, smiled happily. She was wearing black slacks and a black turtleneck under her gray jacket. How should he greet her? Instead of a kiss he shook her hand and felt stupid doing it. Libby chuckled. Verna turned to him and scowled. Sitting down at their table, he sensed that Verna had been fighting off her mother's attempts to converse.

"She's out of Special Care," said Libby. "Isn't that wonderful?"

"Wonderful," he echoed with forced enthusiasm. "She didn't belong there in the first place."

Verna studied her painted fingernails.

"The nurses say she's doing much better."

"Wonderful," he said again, while thinking, Dear God, we'll never get anywhere with this girl if we keep fabricating happiness.

Verna drew an emery board from the pocket of her sweater and did some delicate work on a thumbnail.

"Any news from the BCA?" asked Libby.

"Nothing, except Caesar's convinced the death was accidental."

"Yes, you told me. Nothing more?"

"He hasn't called me back."

They fell silent. Amid the surrounding din of chatter, their silence felt awkward. Frank broke it, finally, by leaning close to Verna and suggesting they take a walk.

Verna looked up from her nails. She nodded.

"I'll stay here," Libby wisely offered.

Frank accompanied Verna to the desk, where she signed out for fifteen minutes, her maximum allowance of freedom. With her pencil poised at "Destination," she said, "Let's go outside."

"Okay. But it's cold."

"I haven't breathed fresh air for days."

She went down the green hallway to her room and returned wearing a green satiny jacket. It was several sizes too big for her. The name ROGER was stitched on the front. On the back were large block letters: LAR'S BAIT AND TACKLE.

The snowfall had stopped, but the wind continued to blow. They walked the hospital grounds, following paths between snowbanks, Verna continually drawing her windblown hair out of her face and Frank recounting his conversation with Caesar Pipe.

"He's checking with the sheriff, but he himself thinks there was no foul play. He's convinced that Roger fell and hit his head, then got into his bed and froze to death."

"*Our* bed!" wailed Verna. She stopped and looked up at Frank with tears in her eyes. "Not *his* bed—*our* bed. Oh, God, what am I going to do without Roger?"

They were standing next to a snow-covered tennis court. Verna turned and pressed her forehead against the wire fence. "Roger," she called at the top of her voice. "Rogerrrrrrrr." She spread her arms wide and knitted her fingers into the wire mesh.

Frank laid his hand on her shoulder, spoke to her back. "You loved him."

"Roger was so good to everybody," she sobbed through the fence. "He was so good to his brothers. He was so good to his sister. He was so good to me. Oh, Rogerrrrrr."

Frank repeated, "You loved him."

"I did—oh, I did." Suddenly her knees buckled and she hung for a moment by her outstretched hands locked in the fence; then, losing her grip, she sagged further and Frank caught her under the arms. Standing close behind her, he laced his fingers into the fence and held her up by the armpits as he spoke close to her ear. "You loved him, Verna. Did he love you?"

The head bobbed. The voice was husky. "He loved me and I treated him like shit. I kept jilting him. I jilted him that night. He walked home because I jilted him. I never thought how cold it was. How drunk he was. All I thought about was treating him like *shit*." Her final "shit" was a shriek.

"You're sorry for it now."

"Oh, God," she cried softly. "I treated him like shit."

"Listen, Verna." The snow-chilled wind was blowing directly into their faces. Frank bent his head first right and then left to wipe his watering eyes on the shoulders of his coat. Verna's hair was whipping in his face. "I'll tell you something, Verna. If you and Roger loved each other, then you had the most precious thing in life."

"We did. We loved each other."

"Not everybody gets that out of life, Verna. Don't forget how good it was."

"We loved each other and I treated him like shit. That's what I do when people are good to me. I treat them like shit."

"Who's them, Verna? Who besides Roger?"

A long pause. A small voice: "My mother."

"Who else?"

The head shook from side to side. "Nobody else is good to me."

"Tom?"

He felt her body stiffen. "No, Tom's not good to me. Tom says he's good to me, and everybody thinks he's been such a great stepfather, but he's not good to me at all. Tom's bad to me."

Frank, holding her up, felt his arms growing weak. His fingers ached, gripping the cold wire. He should have worn gloves. Again, right and left, he wiped his watering eyes on his coat. "Do you know why you treat your mother like shit and why you treated Roger like shit?"

"No. I love my mother. I loved Roger."

"That's why."

"That's why?" At last Verna stood without his help. She turned around and looked up at him.

He took a step back, rubbing his hands, flexing his fingers. "When you love people, you want to take them into your soul. You want them to know what you're like. So you make them feel like shit because then they'll understand how you feel." He reached out and drew a wet strand of hair away from her eyes. "You've got to stop feeling like shit, Verna, otherwise you'll never be decent to people you love."

She stepped up to him, into him, took hold of his lapels, stared at him. Her wind-reddened face, her eyes, reminded Frank of the starving faces he'd seen in the news from East Africa. The eyes in those photos never had the desperately hungry look he expected. They were meek faces. They were fixed on the camera in a kind of passive, fatalistic stare. Do what you will, those faces said. Snap the shutter. Feed me or don't feed me. I'm too weak to care.

"Verna, has your doctor talked to you about these things?"

"He's not much of a talker. He's more of a chemist."

"Doesn't he get into why you feel so bad about yourself?"

"I don't let him."

"Why?"

"There's things I can't tell him."

"What things?"

Emotion returned to her eyes. Anxiety. Defiance. "Why should I tell you?" Then she let go of his lapels, drooped her head, and said softly: "They're too awful. They'd hurt people."

He assumed it was sex with Harris Highsmith. "Who would it hurt, Verna?"

"My mother."

Not sex with Harris Highsmith then. Libby knew about that.

"Verna, you're hurting your mother the way it is."

Verna shrugged. "Let's go back, I'm cold."

They retraced their route, the wind at their backs. They didn't speak until they rounded the corner of the hospital near the entrance; then Verna asked, "Did you know my grandfather?"

"Which one?"

"Mother's dad."

"Not at all well." Frank pictured the man on the platform of the grain elevator. "He was handsome. He reminded me of Clark Gable."

"Who's that?"

"A movie star."

"Manic-depressive behavior can be hereditary. I keep thinking I got it from him. He was a pretty horrible guy, from what my mother says. He treated his family like shit."

"I'm not sure you can blame your low self-esteem on your mood disorder, Verna. I've seen manic depression before. A student of mine had it. He was inclined to the opposite view—an inflated opinion of himself."

They went into the lobby. Frank dabbed at his cheeks with his handkerchief.

"God," Verna said, "are you crying?"

"Wind makes my eyes water." He blew his nose.

"I bet my eyes are a mess."

"No," he said. But they were. Smeared makeup. Matted lashes.

Waiting at the elevator, he said, "Whatever your secret is, please tell your doctor."

She faced away from him, shook her head.

"Or tell me," he said.

She turned and studied him. "I might . . . someday."

The elevator opened.

"Will you tell me now?" He took her arm, holding her back, indicating a pair of armchairs in the corner of the lobby.

She answered by pulling away and stepping into the elevator. He followed.

Upstairs, the afflicted were called back to their classes and therapy sessions. Sitting down next to her mother in the empty dayroom, Verna lapsed into silence again, but she looked less ill-tempered than before, less sullen. By revealing her dark feelings she had talked herself into a somewhat lighter mood. And had evidently worn herself out, for she looked exhausted. She slid her hand over and rested it on her mother's arm.

Libby, smiling, patting the hand, said, "I saw your doctor. He says you're making progress."

Verna raised her eyebrows slightly as if to ask, Progress toward what? Then she lowered her eyes to the table. Frank and Libby exchanged a few pointless remarks in an attempt to draw Verna out, but soon gave up and surrendered to her silence. There was something like repose in Libby's smile, and Frank was struck once again by her strength, her resilience, her facility at appearing serene in the face of trouble. It was a great part of the attraction he felt for her.

Verna moved her hand slowly up and down her mother's arm as though to assure her that this was not the silence of animosity. It was preoccupation. Fatigue.

The nurse Roberta Brink came over and reminded Verna that she was expected in med class. The three of them rose from their chairs and walked slowly to the double doors, where Verna allowed herself to be kissed on the cheek first by her mother and then by Frank.

"Will you come back?" she asked, looking at Frank as though his answer mattered a great deal.

"Sure. Early next week."

She looked relieved. She stood in the doorway, watching them walk away, and when they reached the elevator, she called to Frank.

He returned to her and bent his head to hear her whisper: "There's something you maybe should tell her."

"What?"

Verna peered around Frank at her mother, who stood in the

elevator doorway, holding it open, smiling a fixed, tired smile. Verna's eyes lingered on her—the meek, East Africa stare—as she whispered, "You could tell her . . . I love her."

When he conveyed Verna's message in the elevator, Libby's smile weakened and she covered her eyes.

Getting out on three, he left her in the elevator, weeping.

He waited for the last of the shut-ins, Selma Schultenover, to emerge from Adrian's room, then he took his turn. He found Adrian sunk low in his chair, worn out by his visitors, groping for his rosary.

"Frank my boy, would you help me into bed?"

He did so. The old man seemed to have shrunk, seemed to weigh no more than a sack of dry leaves. He covered him, brushed his hair flat, handed him his rosary.

"I may not get back until the first of the week, Adrian. You seem fine here on your own."

"Much better, much better." He smiled wearily.

"Sorry to bring such a crowd with me, but Eunice insisted."

"Lovely souls, every one of them."

"Marcella sends her best. She'll be coming to see you again."

"Lovely." The old man closed his eyes.

Frank, looking across the bed and out the window, saw the wind bending the bare treetops. He said, half to himself, "It's a hard winter, Adrian."

The old man uttered an agreeable sigh, already entering sleep.

Dear God, I should not have left Libby weeping in the elevator. She, in her way, is no less troubled than her daughter. She's on thin ice. Who will she cling to when the ice gives way? Me, I'm afraid. I feel her grip tighten each time we meet.

Adrian opened his eyes. "I forgot to tell you, Frank, the angel's name is Cindy."

Eunice Pfeiffer took the front seat. The other three, grunting and straining, packed themselves into the back, and the

Olds stirred the powdery snow into clouds as it sped home under the low, gray sky.

"He's so weak."

"He's so shaky."

"You wonder if he eats right."

"Yesterday he didn't clean his plate."

"The meals are good there. I was in there with my hip, and they fed me good."

"When I was in for gallbladder, they fed me hog slop."

"Maybe because he's a priest, they let him get away without cleaning his plate."

"I thought he looked pale."

"He's always been pale."

"Not this pale."

"Oh, yes, even as a young man he never had much color."

"I never used to be able to eat ham, but ever since my gall-bladder operation I can eat as much ham as I want."

"Did you see all the cards he got?"

"Cards? What cards?"

"Tacked to his bulletin board. Thirty-one, I counted them."

"My husband missed his ham, but I couldn't stand the smell of it cooking."

"Be careful, Father, it might be icy."

"Such a winter."

"Dreadful."

"I don't mind the cold, but I hate the snow."

"I hate the cold."

"I hate the cold and snow both."

33

Saturday was warmer—three below and climbing—
when Mrs. Tatzig and her sister drove to Berrington and found
that Adrian had been moved across the hall to a unit called Te-
lemetry. There he shared a room with a car salesman from Be-
midji and a schoolteacher from Staggerford. Each man wore, on
a cord around his neck, a small electronic box by which the nurses
at their station kept surveillance on his pulse.

"The car salesman said he flew planes in World War II," Mrs.
Tatzig reported to Frank when she returned home in the late
afternoon, "but you can tell by his eyes he's got Indian blood in
him. I asked Charlotte if they let Indians fly planes in wars, and
she said maybe they did if the manpower shortage was bad
enough. Somebody hit a horse. We saw it in a ditch. They had
a sale on paper towels at K-Mart." She emptied eight rolls out
of a large plastic bag onto the kitchen counter.

Frank, sitting in the breakfast nook, stirring a cup of instant
coffee, asked, "Was it dead?"

"Was what dead?"

"The horse."

"Dead as a doornail. And we saw a fender bender in Berrington. Saw it happen right in front of us. Some moron ran a

327

light." She turned to Frank. "Adrian says Gene DeSmet's coming for the weekend."

"Yes, he ought to be here any minute."

"You didn't tell me."

"I forgot, Marcella. Sorry."

A car door slammed under the kitchen window, causing her to brighten and exclaim, "Speak of the little devil."

Father DeSmet burst through the kitchen door carrying a Gucci overnight bag and a paper funnel of cut flowers for Mrs. Tatzig, who stepped into his embrace and nearly smiled. Frank was amazed. He hadn't realized that Mrs. Tatzig was a hugger or that DeSmet was such a favorite. Even the cat sidled up to him for attention.

"'Love Boat's' on at nine," said Mrs. Tatzig, ripping open the paper and burying her nose in the red mums and white daisies.

"We'll watch it together, Marcella." DeSmet dropped his cap and gloves and coat onto the seat of the breakfast nook opposite Frank. "Unless the pastor's going to make me go out to Basswood."

"The pastor's in the hospital."

"No, he's not. He's sitting right here in your kitchen."

She turned slowly to Frank, her eyes narrowed. "Since when."

"Just the other day," said Frank. "And just while Adrian's laid up."

She looked resentful. "You might have told me."

"I'm sorry, Marcella. I forgot."

"I swear, sometimes you act like I'm invisible."

"I mean I forgot I was pastor."

She nodded as if to say she wouldn't put it past him to forget his name. She turned back to the counter, drew a vase from the cupboard, lifted an enormous shears from a drawer, and snipped away at the stems.

"What about it, Frank? You aren't sending me out to Basswood, are you?" The boy-priest tried to deliver this in a nonchalant tone, but Frank caught the apprehension in his eyes and recalled Verna's loose talk in the smoking annex of the hospital cafeteria. With a few rash words—"a saintly, dumb boozehound"—she had destroyed forever DeSmet's pleasure with the Pearsalls.

"No, I'm keeping Basswood for myself. You'll take the eight o'clock tomorrow, and confession before and after my five o'clock this afternoon."

"That's it?"

"That's it."

"Super." He picked up his leather bag. "Which room, Marcella?"

"Front." By which she meant the larger of the two guest rooms upstairs, the one expensively furnished and decorated in case a bishop ever found himself in need of a bed in these parts. "There's extra blankets in the closet."

"Super."

Mrs. Tatzig turned from the counter, holding the vase of flowers for DeSmet to admire.

"Like them?" he asked.

She smiled. "Just beautiful."

Frank, regretting that in his sixty days as her housemate he had not once earned from her a smile like that, put on his coat and went out to unlock the church. He opened the switch box in the sacristy and turned on a few lights. He turned up the thermostat. He walked down the middle aisle and unlocked the street door and switched on the light over the steps. He sat in a pew near the back, loosened his coat, and gazed around at the silent interior. The church smelled vaguely of old incense, old prayerbooks, and the glue holding down the new carpet. The stained-glass windows facing south were lead gray; those facing north were black. Up front, the crucifix was barely visible in the dim light. The flame in the sanctuary lamp was a pinpoint of red suspended over the altar.

Dear God, I feel no more like a pastor than I did as a teenager when I would sometimes steal into church on dark winter afternoons and sit in this pew and wonder what place you would find for me in the world. I'm still wondering. Does this pew turn out to be my place? Wondering my endless role?

The door behind him opened, and the first of the afternoon's penitents filed in. He watched them move down the side aisle—

three adults and two children—genuflect, and settle on kneelers near the confessional.

Dear God, I was beginning to feel at home in the rectory, but with Adrian gone it's clearly Mrs. Tatzig's house and I feel like an intruder. The flowers DeSmet brought her lit up the kitchen. Warmed it. Drew the two of them together like a fire in the hearth. What pals they are. How kind of him to bring her flowers. How obtuse of me never to have thought to do so. Forgive my self-pity, Lord, but am I destined to go through life feeling like an outsider in my own house?

Two hours later he turned up the heat in Our Lady's Church in Basswood, rebaited the mousetraps, and carried the dead mice outside by their tails and dropped them in the snow for cats to find. He returned to the Olds for the bag containing his pajamas, electric razor, tin of Communion wafers, and a bottle of altar wine. He deposited the bag on his cot, then went next door to the Pipes' and found them in the middle of supper. They introduced him to their grandson Billy Annunciation and insisted he join them for dessert. They were eating late, they said, because Billy had just come in from fishing.

"He's the grandson we told you about," said Joy Pipe, moving a chair up to the table for Frank. "He's here to finish high school." Joy was wearing a black sweater and silver earrings and devoting part of her attention to a small TV on the counter separating the kitchen from the living room. This was Frank's first visit beyond the front door of their trailer house. It was roomier than it looked from outside. A plate of cake was put in front of him.

"The kid fishes like a white man, but otherwise he's okay," said Caesar, who was eating with his deputy jacket on—a bulky tan jacket with a silver badge pinned to the front and a colorful insignia sewn on the sleeve.

"Grandma says you might have a job for me, Father."

"Yes, possibly."

Billy's small, round glasses, in Frank's opinion, were unsuited to his long face, and his hair needed cutting, but he was a handsome boy, lean and athletic looking.

"I'm pretty good with my hands. I used to help a guy in the city assemble little electronic gadgets once in a while when he fell behind, and he said I had the small-chore dexterity of a woman. I thought it was an insult but he meant it as a compliment. And last summer I worked Sundays in a gas station and learned a few things about cars, but I learned more about what a drag it is to take the wife and kids to the beach. The station was near a beach, and by the end of the day the kids were crabby and the wife was hollering at them for getting sand all over the seats and the husband was complaining about how much they'd spent on candy and tanning lotion and how much I was charging him for gas, and it was all just a drag. Like, it was Sunday and why couldn't they all just shut up and be happy? I think that's what I had against the city more than anything. Nobody seems very happy down there."

Billy Annunciation had a forceful voice and an expressive way of using his eyes. There was an intensity untypical of Indians in his manner of conversing. Frank asked him, "How are you at shoveling snow?"

"Have you got a snowblower?"

"No," said Frank. "A shovel."

"I'm better with a snowblower, but I can handle a shovel."

"How are you at painting?"

"You got a sprayer?"

"No, a brush."

"Yeah, I can handle a brush."

"Do you drive?"

"I'm a good driver. Ask Gramps. I've been driving his pickup."

"How about coming to town next Saturday? I can give you some odd jobs around St. Ann's and some errands to run."

"What time?"

"Midmorning."

"Sure. I'll fish till nine, then come in. Gramps will lend me his pickup."

"Like hell," said Caesar. "What am I supposed to drive?"

"You can take him in," Joy told her husband.

Caesar shook his head. "Let him catch a ride with somebody going in. Everybody goes to town on Saturday."

"Yeah, I'll catch a ride," said Billy. "You want to come out and fish with me, Father? I found the hot spot."

"*Who* found the hot spot?" asked his grandfather.

"Gramps found it. The sandbar out in the middle. Twelve feet of water. Set your bobber so your bait's a foot and a half off the bottom and you've got yourself a mess of walleyes."

"It's warming up tonight," warned Caesar. "They'll move."

"No, they won't," said Joy. "TV says cold again tomorrow."

Ten minutes passed before Frank was able to transfer the conversation from fishing to the investigation. "What about the BCA, Caesar?"

"They're gone," said Joy.

"Yeah, they're gone," said Caesar.

"You mean the fuzz?" asked Billy.

"The Bureau of Criminal Apprehension," his grandfather explained.

Billy nodded slowly, knowledgeably, respectfully. "Man, that's a bad-ass outfit. I knew a guy they put away for life. He deserved it, he was big-time into drugs, but I never thought he'd get caught."

"Tell him what the sheriff said," Joy instructed her husband.

"Sheriff says those two guys from the BCA lost interest in Roger Upward."

"Good," said Frank.

"Says neither Verna nor nobody else is suspected of murder."

"Good."

"Says the more they looked around up here, the more they got interested in dope. They went home to St. Paul but . . ." There was a long silence as Caesar looked askance at Frank and Billy. Then he turned to his wife, who spoke for him.

"This isn't public knowledge, you understand."

Frank, eating cake, said he understood.

Both Pipes looked at their grandson.

"Swear," said Billy, raising his hand oathwise.

"They went home to St. Paul," Caesar continued, "but they plan to send up an agent posing as a druggie."

This made everyone thoughtful for a moment, except the announcer on TV: ". . . the lashes every woman dreams of and every man falls in love with."

"What's the point?" asked Billy. "Why don't they just close down the Homestead and be done with it?"

This surprised his grandfather. "Why, what have you heard?"

"Everybody in school says you can buy pot and pills, as much as you want, from the midget that works for Judge Bigelow. The Judge brings in the supplies and the midget does the dealing." His grandparents' questioning look gave him pause. "Well, isn't *that* public knowledge?"

"Look," Caesar said to Frank, "do you mind if we change the subject before my brilliant grandson puts the BCA out of business?"

"Well, isn't it?" Billy asked his grandmother. "Doesn't everybody know about the midget and the Judge? Can the entire student body of Basswood High School be wrong about where to buy pot?"

"Okay," said Caesar. "That's well known. What isn't well known, and what the BCA wants to find out, is where the Judge is getting it."

"Why don't they ask me?"

"You know?"

"Not yet. Give me a day or two."

Frank looked at his watch, stood, and said it was time for confessions.

"Confessions!" said Billy. "Who goes to confession anymore?"

"I've got a few regulars."

Caesar accompanied Frank to the door, stepped outside with him, and stood in the peach light of the street lamp.

"'Preciate it if you can find some work for the kid."

"A few hours on Saturdays, Caesar. Send him in around ten."

"What do you make of him, Padre?"

Frank turned up his collar against the wind. "First mouthy Indian I ever met."

"Yeah, he's a real pain in the ass. When I was his age, I never passed up a chance to keep my mouth shut."

"Caesar, what about the Pearsalls? Do they know Verna's off the hook?"

"Hard to say."

"You haven't told them?"

"Figured you'd tell them."

"I wish you'd tell them, Caesar. They're worried."

"Why don't you tell them?"

"I've got confessions."

Caesar narrowed his eyes, peering across the road. "Tell you the truth, Padre, that geek doctor makes my skin crawl."

"Just knock on their door and tell them the BCA's satisfied there was no foul play. Take you half a minute."

"Could, I guess."

"Do it, Caesar. Tell them."

Looking out from the sacristy, he saw two of his half-dozen regulars waiting for him, Bernadine Butcher lighting a candle at the Virgin's altar, her mother kneeling in a pew near the back.

With his stole draped over his overcoat, he strode down the aisle with his eyes lowered to the squeaky wooden floor—a habit from the days not so long ago when no penitent was willing to be identified. The confessional stood at the back of the church near the oil burner. He sat down in his stall and waited. Dear God, if it's numbers you're after, we might as well board this place up, but, please, let's carry on here for a while longer. I don't understand why—maybe it's because I'm such an outsider everywhere else—but I feel more at home in this clapboard church in this desolate outpost of humanity than in any place I've been since the Academy shut down.

His stall was partially curtained off, so that he could see neither the pews nor the altar. He had a view only of the oil burner, and above it, on the wall, a small ceramic portrayal of the Eighth

Station, *Jesus Speaks to the Daughters of Jerusalem*—Jesus and three women with their heads together, he wearing a crown of thorns and encumbered by his cross, the women weeping into their cloaks.

Mrs. Butcher, preferring the pretense of anonymity, entered the dark, curtained side of the confessional and spoke invisibly from behind the grille. Her voice was an expressionless little whine. As usual, the transgressions she spoke of were mostly her husband's—he was lazy, irritable, tight with money, and worst of all, he was an occasion of sin for her, forcing her again and again to lose her temper and swear at him.

Frank's advice was minimal: forbearance. Some weeks ago when he'd recommended that she and her husband try to talk over their problems, Mrs. Butcher had cut him off with "Hah! How do you talk to a stump?" So he settled on forbearance as the best possible advice for her—it was easier for her to ignore. He absolved her and said, "Go in peace."

Next, her daughter Bernadine came lumbering over from the Virgin's altar and settled her great weight on the chair at Frank's right hand. She wore a new green coat ballooning with down. Its shell was noisy nylon.

"Hello, Bernadine."

"Hello, Father." She shook her head to indicate there'd been no improvement. She whispered the same complaints as last time, and the time before that. Nobody ever asked her out anymore. She was too fat to be asked out, so she stayed home and ate. Was she to spend the rest of her life at home with her bickering mother? Was she destined never to find a man as generous and good-natured and ambitious as her father? Her sin, she said, was blaming God for her problems.

Frank said, "Look for the good in yourself, Bernadine."

"What good?"

"Try to make inroads into your despair by doing one small thing each day in which you can take satisfaction. As for blaming God, it isn't all that great a sin, Bernadine. God's big enough to absorb the blame. But he can't plant hope in you until you prepare the soil."

"Yeah? How?"

"With prayer and giving up sweets," he advised, not meaning to be flip but fearing that he sounded so.

She sighed. "So what's my penance?"

"Doing that one small thing each day you can be proud of. Please come back next week and tell me about it." He blessed her. She smiled sadly as she heaved herself up from the chair.

Watching her move heavily away, he thought of the days when a priest was expected merely to admonish people and dole out penances ("Ten Our Fathers and ten Hail Marys and make a good Act of Contrition") like a judge consulting a sheet of sentencing guidelines. Well, that oversimple time was dead and gone, and good riddance. But, dear God, how do I respond to these latter-day penitents who ask—as well they should—for more than absolution? I can't give Mrs. Butcher a tranquil spirit. I can't restore hope to Bernadine. You can do those things, but I cannot.

He heard several others entering church. There were heavy footsteps and the scuffing sound of children in boots. There were light footsteps approaching the confessional and slipping into the curtained side. He was about to raise his hand in preliminary blessing when a voice said, "Hi."

"Libby?"

"Thanks for sending Caesar," she said through the grille. "What a load off my mind."

"Is this a social call, Libby? If so, why don't you move around where I can see you?"

"No, I thought I'd just pop in and see what this rigmarole is all about. Is this all you get for confessions—half a dozen people?"

"Up from one or two a few weeks ago."

"A priest must feel very neglected in this post-Christian age."

"Who says it's the post-Christian age?"

"My husband the doctor."

"Tell him for me he's got his prefix wrong. Until the Second Coming everything's pre-Christian."

"God, Frank, you actually still believe in all that, don't you?"

"More or less. I do some picking and choosing among the details, but the big picture will always make sense to me."

There was a long pause before she said, "I guess I love that. I mean what you believe leaves me cold, but for some reason I love you for believing it."

"Quaint, what?"

She laughed.

"Keep it down, Libby. Nobody laughs in confession."

"Sorry." She was silent for a moment, then asked, "Frank, will you come across the road for dinner?"

"I have to decline, Libby. I need to be available."

"Please, Frank, just tonight, just for dinner. To celebrate Verna's exoneration. You don't have to stay the night."

Heavy footsteps approached the confessional and halted near the curtain. Carl Butcher was waiting his turn—Frank recognized his wheezy breathing. Someone else came and stood behind Carl.

"Now you're trapped," Frank whispered. "When you're seen leaving, you'll be thought a Catholic."

She lowered her voice and continued (presumably without realizing it) in the hushed monotone of the experienced confession goer, a mumble loud enough to be heard beyond the curtain but not understood. Carl Butcher and whoever else waited in line would assume Frank was hearing a list of vices when in fact he was hearing this:

"Cranberries. Walleyed pike, broiled. Wild rice. Baked potato. Homemade buns. Blackberry jelly. And lots of rum."

"Bless you," said Frank. "I'll be there."

With a suppressed giggle she slipped away.

Carl Butcher's sins, of a minor nature, were related to alcohol. The woman who followed had sexual stories to tell. She was followed by a thief. Next, someone young had lied and disobeyed her parents. Then sex again, lying again, sex again, and the inflicting of bodily harm. There were eight confessions in all (not counting Libby's popping in), which was better by two than his previous high. The numbers were sent to the chancery.

His final penitent gone, Frank came out from behind the curtain and found Millie LaBonte waiting for him in a pew near the front. She said, "Father, can we talk?"

"Sure, Millie, what is it?" She looked agitated. One of the six-year-old twins was stretched out sleeping in the pew beside her. The other twin stood against her mother's knee, dreamily weaving her fingers in and out of the holes worn in her snowsuit. The boy, Lanny, was lighting a few dozen candles in front of Our Lady's statue.

"It's about my brothers." She gathered up her purse and the children's stocking caps. "Where do we talk?"

"Right here." Frank sat down in the pew in front of her.

"Here?" She looked furtively at the tabernacle, as if afraid of disturbing the Presence.

"There's no place to sit in the sacristy."

Lanny, wearing moon boots and an oversized jacket hanging to his knees, left Our Lady and came over to introduce himself to Frank. "I'm the Incredible Hulk," he said.

"Lanny!" his mother scolded. "Don't start that Hulk business."

"I'm the Incredible Hulk."

Frank shook his little hand. "Happy to know you, Hulk."

The boy smiled a satisfied smile and went back to the candles.

Frank turned to Millie. In her eyes he saw nothing of the furies that used to drive her to fits of temper in school. The eyes were slow moving now, the face heavy. She had put on a lot of weight. There was a tremor in her hand as she smoothed the hair of the twin standing at her knee. And her other hand, fiddling with her coat buttons, trembled as well. The furies had apparently left her eyes and gone to her hands.

"What is it, Millie?"

"It's about Roger. The BCA's decided to drop it, as maybe you know."

Frank nodded. "Caesar told me."

"Well, my brothers don't think it should be dropped. Pock and Johnny. You remember them from the funeral? They were two of the pallbearers."

"I remember." He pictured Pock, the older of the two by several years, a broad-shouldered man in his thirties with a nickname obviously related to his deeply pitted face. His forehead and right cheek were particularly disfigured. He pictured

Johnny—lanky, fidgety, taller than his brother, darker of skin. Johnny was perhaps twenty-five. He had a spotty little mustache. Encrusted on his deformed right earlobe was a thick black scab.

"Do they suspect somebody, Millie? Are they saying it was murder?"

"They're not saying it was murder. Maybe it was murder, maybe it wasn't. Roger could have hit his head, like they claim. But the thing my brothers keep saying . . ." She paused to look around and make sure the church was empty. "Roger was high on booze and drugs." She wrung her hands and raised her voice. "It's been going on around here too long, drugs and drunks. It's getting worse. Roger never would have hit his head if he was sober." The sleeping girl stirred; her twin sister put her thumb in her mouth and fell forward, swoonlike, to lie across her mother's lap. "And who let him walk home without his jacket when it was below zero?"

"Are you blaming Verna for that?"

Millie dismissed this with a wave of her hand. "Verna? Verna's in the same boat Roger was in. No, I'm talking about somebody who gets people drunk and keeps pouring booze in them till they can't hardly stand up and lets people go out when it's below zero without their jackets on, and sells drugs besides."

"Judge Bigelow."

She nodded. "My brothers are out to clean up the Homestead."

"How?"

"Who knows how? That's what's got me worried. They think they're Starsky and Hutch."

"Tell them to go to the authorities, Millie."

"You can't tell those two goofballs nothing." She studied Frank. "What authorities?"

"Caesar Pipe."

"They been to Caesar. Caesar says wait."

"And they won't wait?"

"No, they say why wait? They say—which is true—the Cashman boy who committed suicide was on drugs. Were you here when that happened?"

"No."

"Terrible. Sixteen years old, my daughter Elaine's age. And Arnold Countryboy drank antifreeze because Judge Bigelow had been getting him sloshed every night for months and then all of a sudden cut him off because he was broke. You weren't here when Arnold died of drinking antifreeze."

"No."

"Every so often somebody kicks off around here from booze or drugs, and that's why my brothers can't wait. They're going after the Judge and whoever the Judge gets his drugs from."

"And you're afraid they'll—"

"Shoot themselves in the foot."

"And you've come to me because . . . ?"

"Because I'm so worked up about it."

"Ouch!" cried Lanny, dropping the stub of a match and stamping on it. The sleeping girls stirred a little.

"Millie, how can I help?"

"Well, I wondered if you'd talk to Caesar. Or maybe the sheriff. They're the ones should be looking into all the crap going on out here."

"They're going to, Millie."

She looked surprised. "They are?"

"That's why Caesar told your brothers to wait. Something's going to be done."

"When?"

"I don't know. Soon."

"You positive?"

"Yes."

She nodded. "If it isn't soon, there's no stopping my brothers." With trembling hands she worked a tight stocking cap onto the head of the girl bent across her lap. She called to Lanny, who came over and shook Frank's hand again.

"I'm the Incredible Hulk."

"I know it."

"Stop that crazy talk, Lanny."

Frank carried one of the girls out to the bronze Chrysler and laid her on the front seat. The other two children scrambled into the front as well, shivering and whining. Their grandmother got in and started the engine. "Well, thanks, Father." She put the car in gear.

Frank held the door open. She looked at him curiously.

"Millie, where does Judge Bigelow get his drugs? Do you have any idea?"

"Ma, let's go, it's cold."

"We've got a real good idea."

"Where?"

"Maaaaa, it's cooooold."

Millie dug into her purse and came up with a pill bottle. "My brothers brought home some pills the other night they got from a guy they were playing cards with." She shook the bottle and held it up to the streetlight. "They were the very same as these pills I got from Dr. Pearsall for my nerves."

The little girl whimpered. Lanny chanted nonsense. The girl lying on the seat woke up and howled.

"I'll talk to Caesar, Millie. I'll try to get them to hurry up."

"Good."

He closed the door. The car turned in a circle under the streetlight and rumbled away, followed by its swirling cloud of exhaust.

He stood under the streetlight for a minute, his back to the wind, his eyes on the Pearsalls' house. Tom Pearsall dealing in drugs? It wasn't hard to believe. Did Libby know? Surely not. Libby the victim. Again.

He returned to the sacristy chilled to the bone. He removed his stole. After a moment of indecision, he lowered the flame in the oil burner, certain of being offered the Pearsalls' guest room and of lacking the resolution to come back here and climb into this cold sleeping bag on this flimsy cot. He dug his electric razor out of his bag.

Dinner was delicious, Libby was high-spirited, and Tom had drunk enough to be fairly cordial, but Frank, preoccupied with his drug suspicions, found it hard work to be their cheerful guest. Over dessert they heard the wind come up and howl outside the window, which set Tom off on a tedious diatribe against Minnesota weather, and although he couched his complaints in terms meant to be humorous, Frank's mood darkened as he listened, and soon after they left the table he pleaded exhaustion and went up to bed.

More than exhaustion, he felt trepidation. His intuition told him there was a great deal more trouble under this roof than he could put his finger on. He feared for Libby. He feared for Verna and Tom. Further, he couldn't shake his conviction that he was unwise to accept their hospitality week after week. Why did he feel so uncomfortable—imperiled even—entering this house, lying in this bed? Dear God, protect us all, he murmured, allowing the wind to lull him to sleep.

Soon he woke up and heard the Pearsalls preparing for bed in the next room. He heard Tom's voice, then Libby's. He heard water running in the bathroom. He heard a dog bark. He dozed. He woke again, this time to the throaty sounds of lovemaking. These noises set off a turbulence in his heart which he found alarming, a sexual feeling more powerful than anything he'd experienced since his youth, a tidal wave that had been gathering itself far out of sight for a very long time and was sweeping in now to engulf him. He buried his head under his pillow, but still the sounds were faintly audible, a rising and falling sigh together with an undertone of pain. When the sound did not diminish after several minutes, he sat up, listened more carefully, and realized he'd been mistaken. His agitation had been caused by the rising and falling of the wind under the eaves.

PART FOUR

34

February. The first Saturday of the month. Snow at dawn, followed by a clear sunrise. Clouds again at noon, and a biting northwest wind.

Lunch was walleye, supplied by Billy Annunciation, who sat shoulder to shoulder with Frank in the breakfast nook. In the opposite seat Mrs. Tatzig, using her fork and her forefinger, picked her portion to shreds in search of bones. When she found none, she leaned to her right and picked apart the monsignor's portion.

The old man, pressed into the corner of the breakfast nook with his housekeeper's shoulder in his chest, asked, "What are you doing, Marcella?"

"Looking for bones." She refrained from adding that since Adrian had come home from the hospital with his brain impaired, she couldn't trust him to remember what he was eating. He'd had two spells, his second occurring three days ago when he got up in the morning and made a beeline for the basement to fill the stoker. There hadn't been a stoker in this house since the neighborhood converted to natural gas in the early sixties. The day before that he'd come down from his nap dressed in his clericals and sat by the front window expecting a visit from Bishop Swayles, a dead man.

Billy Annunciation assured her, "Don't worry about bones, Marcella. I get out the bones when I clean them."

"You can't get them all," said Mrs. Tatzig, continuing to pick and to probe. "When I was a girl, I knew a kid got a fishbone in his throat and it made him talk funny for the rest of his life."

"There *aren't* any bones," Billy insisted. "I've been cleaning fish since I was eight."

"You can't get out all the bones," Mrs. Tatzig repeated, her voice edged with irritation. She didn't mind serving Indians at her table as long as they were charity cases—a few had come begging at the back door like hobos over the years—but this young buck dragged home by Father Healy and given spending money out of petty cash seemed to think he was as good as the company he was eating with. He had opinions, he contradicted his elders, and his clothes looked practically new. Worst of all, he'd accomplished in three weeks what Mrs. Tatzig had been trying and failing to do for nearly two months: he'd gotten next to Father Healy.

"Marcella, I'm hungry," said the old monsignor softly, his fork clenched in his fist, his fist resting on the windowsill. On the other side of the glass, sparrows were squabbling over seed in the feeder.

"Look," she said triumphantly, holding up a tiny bone.

"Oh oh," said Billy. "I missed one."

"Marcella," said the monsignor a little more insistently, "let me eat."

"Go ahead, eat," she said, transferring her attention to Frank's plate, leaning across the table but stopping short of putting her fork in his food. "Be careful," she warned him.

He assured her he would.

It was a matter of secret shame to Mrs. Tatzig that after psyching out every last clergyman assigned to her at St. Ann's, she'd finally been served up a priest she couldn't read, couldn't get next to. "What's cooking in that Father Healy?" she'd asked her sister more than once, not that her sister would know, and her sister's reply was, "Maybe nothing." Not the right answer by any means. Mrs. Tatzig had known a couple of priests with nothing cooking in them. They were lazy men, living for their next meal and their next drink. They stood at the altar like sticks and delivered sermons that put you to sleep. No, there was something definitely cooking in Father Healy. He had a seeking, unsatisfied look in his eye. He liked his food and he liked his rum, but food and rum weren't enough for this man. His mind was on something more.

A woman?

If so, she knew which woman. The reservation nurse. There was that time a month ago when she called at the rectory and hauled Father Healy off to Berrington in her foreign car. To visit her daughter in the hospital, he claimed. Maybe. Maybe not. Did he think nobody knew the two of them used to be an item? Mrs. Tatzig's sister had heard it from Trisha the ditsy Halloran, who'd heard it from Mrs. Graham, that the mother of the young woman who'd been shacking up with the Indian who froze to death before Christmas had been the high-school sweetheart of Father Frank Healy. Pretty hot news, considering how old it was.

And then there were the midnight phone calls. Ordinarily Mrs. Tatzig, whose bedroom was behind the kitchen, wouldn't have been aware of these calls because at bedtime all the phones in the house were disconnected except the one upstairs in Father Healy's room, but one night about three weeks ago, she'd forgotten to unplug the kitchen phone and she heard it ring once at midnight and didn't hear Father Healy go out on a sick call. So she kept it plugged in after that and sure enough that single ring came at the stroke of twelve about three nights a week. She imagined him lying in bed talking sweet talk.

Monsignor Lawrence, chewing carefully, said, "This walleye is delicious, Billy."

"Best-eating fish in the world," Billy agreed. "They been in eight feet of water for a week now. They been real hungry. They'll bite on anything—dead minnow, live minnow, fake minnow—just put it down the hole and you've got your limit of walleyes inside of an hour. Why don't you come out and fish in my house, Monsignor? I'll have a stove in it by next weekend."

"Next weekend the fishing season will be over," said Mrs.

Tatzig, whose husband had done quite a little fishing in his day, in and out of season, and had never gotten out all the bones.

Billy said, "No, Marcella, not on the rezz it isn't."

"Oh?" She scowled at the boy, irked that he should be using her first name, irked that Indians were exempt from fishing regulations.

The monsignor said, "My doctor tells me I shouldn't be out in the cold, Billy. I'm supposed to get my exercise walking indoors. I walk in church."

"I can take you out in my gramp's pickup. Drive you right up to the door. Frank's coming out with me one of these days, aren't you, Frank?"

Frank nodded. "Let me know when the stove's in."

The foursome ate silently then, and Billy, holding his fish house in mind, examined it with pleasure. With Frank's help, he'd hammered it together from old sheets of plywood and two-by-twos they'd found in the basement of the church. Last Saturday they'd hauled it out onto Sovereign Lake in his grandfather's pickup and christened it Graceland. It tilted slightly to the north. It was a two-man house with a door on spring hinges and two small windows and a shelf for tackle and candles. It contained a box for firewood but as yet no stove, and that's why—to Billy's dismay—Elaine LaBonte refused to go fishing with him. He'd taken her out there last Sunday and she'd gotten so cold she said never again unless he installed heat. He needed his grandfather's help with the stove; Frank didn't know anything about metalwork. He hoped they could install it tomorrow, because Sunday was Elaine's only chance to go fishing, what with her job at the Health Center on Saturdays and every day after school.

The job was a joke. Eight or ten patients in an average week, and maybe a dozen phone calls. Billy had phoned her today before lunch and she said there'd been no drop-ins or phone calls since the Pearsalls left for Chicago on Thursday. The government let the Health Center go too long without a doctor, according to Elaine, and everybody in Basswood got into the habit of seeing Dr. Clayton in Linden Falls. "Dr. Clayton at least looks like a doctor," said Elaine. "Dr. Pearsall, so pale and bent over for his age, looks like he *needs* a doctor." Then she'd cut the conversation short, saying she saw her uncles pulling up in front of the Health Center in their van.

The monsignor, finishing his fish, turned to Mrs. Tatzig and said, "Marcella, do you pray for the dead?"

Accustomed to this sort of spiritual eruption in the old man's thinking, she said, "Yup," without looking up from her plate.

"Frank, you pray for the dead of course."

"I do."

"Billy?"

"Yeah, for my grandma Annunciation, when I remember. Usually I forget."

"Well . . ." The old man picked up his spoon and his plastic cup of yogurt. "I'm wondering if there's been something missing all these years in the theology of prayer. Frank, have you ever wondered about that?"

"No, Adrian, I haven't."

"Billy?"

"Not me."

"I hate to say it, but I think Rome's teaching on prayer is flawed." He smacked his lips over his tart yogurt. He turned to his left. "Marcella, have you ever wondered—"

"Nope."

He shifted his eyes to Frank. "I am currently praying for seven hundred and five departed souls."

Frank was astonished. "Every day?"

"I try."

"That's too many, Adrian."

"That's what I'm thinking. The list begins with my grandfather Lawrence, who died when I was seven, and it extends down through the years to Hubert Humphrey. A man my age can't support that many faithful departed. I can't get through the list anymore. Ever since my heart attack I get up into the four hundreds and I fall asleep. Now what I want to know is, Frank, why doesn't the Church impose a sunset law on prayers for the dead?"

Frank broke out in a smile.

"Don't laugh at me, Frank. Do you know what I mean by a sunset law?"

"Yes, I see what's coming, Adrian. It's a superb idea."

"Marcella, do you know what I mean by a sunset law?"

"Who wants dessert?" Having left the breakfast nook, Mrs. Tatzig was removing a packaged cake from the freezer.

"Billy, do you know what I mean by a sunset law?"

"Yeah, a law stops being a law at the end of a year or something, unless it's voted into law again."

"That's it exactly. And wouldn't it make sense to limit the length of time you pray for a soul who's passed into the next life?"

"I s'pose."

"Why should I still be praying for my grandfather Lawrence? He was a shoo-in for heaven, everybody knew that. I haven't once skipped my daily prayer for him since his funeral, and that was sixty-four years ago. Somewhere along the line the Church ought to let us off the hook. Say ten or twenty years of praying for somebody and then clean the slate." He shook his head sadly. "I simply can't make it up to seven hundred and five anymore. Frank, is this heresy?"

"It's perfect sense, Adrian."

"Not a sin of omission?"

"Not by any means. I suggest you go through your list backward, Adrian, starting with the most recently dead. And then stop after a dozen or two."

"Is that what you do?"

"More or less."

"But there's no precedent for it."

"I do it—there's your precedent."

"But I mean officially. I don't think Rome would approve."

"I'll bet the pope does it that way."

The monsignor looked skeptical. "I doubt you there, Frank. The pope's very holy."

"And very busy."

"Yes, isn't he! My! And such a traveler. I'm sure he prays in the air. Think of the prayers you could say between Rome and New York."

Mrs. Tatzig brought three wedges of frozen chocolate cake to the table, her own the largest, and sat down to dig in.

"Marcella," said the monsignor, "I believe I'll have a little of that cake."

"Nope."

"I mean just a taste."

She shook her head. "Your diet. Your heart."

"The damage is done, Marcella. There'd be no harm in a taste."

Her lips turned up in a little smile as she handed him a forkful of cake covered with thick frosting. He put it in his mouth and closed his eyes in ecstasy.

She took back her fork and ate a small bite.

He said, "One more, Marcella."

She dipped her head, still smiling. "Don't be a tease. You've got your yogurt."

"You're the tease, Marcella. Just one more."

Her smile—sweet, self-satisfied, almost girlish—swept over Billy and Frank before she fastened it on the ceiling, and there it remained as she handed the monsignor her fork, moved her plate between them, and produced a fork for herself from the pocket of her apron.

Frank was touched. Adrian's heart attack had softened Mrs. Tatzig, had somehow made her happier than before, almost lighthearted, had worn through her grouchy façade and exposed a bright sort of playfulness. But not where Frank and Billy were concerned. With Frank she was never anything but serious, guarded, suspicious. With Billy she was crabby.

"Are you going to want a meal tonight before you go out to Basswood?" she asked Frank, her smile gone now, her scowl seeming to indicate that either answer—yes or no—would present problems.

"I'll take a sack lunch, Marcella. A sandwich or two."

"Not eating with the doctor and his wife?"

"They've gone to Chicago."

"Again?"

"Once a month. They visit her mother in a nursing home."

The monsignor, his mouth full of cake, asked, "How is that poor girl of theirs, Frank? Did they straighten her out?"

"Pretty well. She's being discharged on Monday."

"After how long?"

"Nearly a month."

"My, that's a long time. My three weeks seemed like forever."

"Where's she going to live?" asked Mrs. Tatzig.

"There's a halfway house in Berrington that'll take her in as soon as they have a vacancy. Till then, she plans to be in Basswood."

The doorbell sounded.

"The reservation!" sputtered Mrs. Tatzig, getting up and crossing the kitchen. "Worst place in the world for a nutcase."

"Basswood's heaven on earth," Billy said proudly, defiantly.

"Not for whites," she replied. "Put her back on the reservation and she'll be off-the-wall in a week."

The monsignor reproved her quietly—"Now Marcella"—but she was gone.

The phone rang. Frank answered it: "St. Ann's."

A female voice, small and high-pitched: "Father Healy?"

"Yes."

"Frank, it's me—Verna."

"Hi, Verna."

"I'm getting out Monday."

"Yes, I haven't forgotten. Are you feeling ready?"

"Jeez, it's been a month. I'm going stir crazy."

"Then you're ready."

"Frank, can you come right away?"

"Why, what's going on?"

"Could you just come? I mean right now? It's an emergency."

He looked at his watch. "I can come for a little while. Please tell me what's wrong?"

"I can't say it on the phone. You have to come. Please!"

"All right."

"If you don't come now, it might be too late."

"I'll be there at two."

"Oh, Frank, you're so wonderful." She hung up.

Mrs. Tatzig returned to the kitchen and told Frank there was an Indian at the front door. He found Millie LaBonte standing in the entryway trying to restrain Lanny from advancing into the living room.

"Hi, Millie, come in and sit down."

"No, the twins are out in the car." Step-by-step, Lanny was tugging her into the room. "I'm in town for groceries and I wanted to tell you my brothers are real antsy."

"As usual, right?"

"More than usual. There's no holding them back anymore. Right now they're at the Health Center giving Elaine a hard time." She brought Lanny to a halt in front of the cold fireplace and gave him a hard slap on the seat. "They're out to prove Dr. Pearsall's dealing. I don't know what to do—if I should tell Caesar Pipe or what."

"How are they going to prove it?"

"By searching the Health Center. They aren't bad men, Father, but they're so goofy sometimes. They go off half-cocked."

"I think you should tell Caesar."

"I called him up yesterday. I asked him when the law's coming in to clean up the Homestead, like you said. Caesar told me it probably won't happen."

"Why?"

Millie shrugged.

Lanny continued to struggle, trying to break his mother's grip. He stopped when Frank gave him a quarter. He studied it, heads and tails, before putting it in his mouth.

"Lanny, get that out of your mouth."

He looked up at his mother, cross-eyed.

"Lanny!"

Frank held his hand under the boy's chin and said, "No fair, Hulk. Either put it in your pocket or give it back."

The boy turned and spat the quarter into his own hand and held it behind his back.

Millie said, "The trouble with going to Caesar, it's like going behind my brothers' back."

"Would it help if I told him?"

"Yeah. But then I think what can Caesar do about it anyway? I mean he can't go following my brothers around day and night."

"No, but he can warn them. Of course if he does, they'll figure out that you squealed on them."

"That's okay, as long as they know I squealed to you. They figure all women are weak and unreliable and have to talk things out and it might as well be with a priest."

"So they'll blame me for telling Caesar."

She gave him a fleeting little smile. "Do you mind?"

"No, of course not."

"They won't think any less of you." She smiled again, more broadly, as if to say, They couldn't.

"Not very fond of priests, are they?"

"No. But there's priests they can't stand even the sight of, which isn't the case with you. They liked what you did with Roger's funeral."

"Good."

"It was Father DeSmet that turned them off. They think he's a jerk."

"So do a lot of priests."

Millie laughed silently.

"I'll talk to Caesar."

"Thanks." She opened the door and they watched Lanny dash out to the car displaying the quarter for his sisters to see.

Frank drew two more coins from his pocket. "Here, for the girls."

"You don't need to do that."

"That's what you think." He pointed at the twins, who were rolling down a window and crying out for quarters of their own.

"Thanks." Millie took the coins and left.

Frank stepped into the office and phoned Basswood. "Caesar, what did you tell Millie LaBonte about the Homestead? She's worried."

"She's always worried."

"What did you tell her?"

"Told her nobody's doing nothing about drugs on the rezz."

"But the BCA, Caesar. The druggie in disguise."

"That's out the window."

"How come?"

"They couldn't figure out how to plant an agent in a place where everybody knows everybody."

"Well, you've got a couple guys in your tribe who've decided to take the law into their own hands."

"Upwards, huh?"

"Right."

A long silence.

"Caesar, are you there?"

"I just went to the window. The Upwards' van's been parked in front of the Health Center for the last hour."

"Go and see what they're up to, Caesar, the Pearsalls aren't home. They could be tearing the place apart, looking for drugs."

"Naw, it's probably family business—Elaine's over there minding the place."

"They're angry, Caesar. The Pearsalls are gone, and they're trusting me and you to keep an eye on their house."

"Live and let live, Padre."

Frank said heatedly, "Caesar, Millie told me and I'm telling you. Her brothers are playing private investigator. Just go across the road and see what they're up to."

"Could, I guess."

"Do it, Caesar, go over there."

35

The older Upward, Pock, having gone through the drawers of the dressing table and the two nightstands, was now standing at the large oak bureau folding Libby's silky underthings and trying to remember how they had been placed in the drawer.

"Jesus, they own a lot of clothes," said his brother Johnny in the closet, where he had checked the pockets of all the shirts and pants and dresses hanging on hangers and was now on his knees examining a basket of dirty laundry.

"Lots of underwear," Pock agreed, folding a slip into a small square.

"Bunch of nice sportcoats in here. How come he always dresses like a bum?"

"Because that's what he is."

"You think he'd miss one if I took it home?"

"What for?"

"For dress-up."

"You got no need to dress up."

"Never know. Elaine and Billy might put on a wedding. Eh, Elaine?" Johnny, kneeling, stuck his head out of the closet and laughed. "Where is she? Elaine," he shouted, "when are you and Billy Annunciation getting married?"

Elaine came into the bedroom, fuming. Room by room, she had followed her uncles through the house, scolding them as she put things back where they belonged. Now, seeing her uncle Pock with Libby's slip in his hands, she blew up. "Not her underwear!" she cried. "Leave her underwear alone! You guys are going to lose me my job. Get away from there." She snatched the slip from him and refolded it.

"I ain't looked in the bottom drawer yet."

"I'll look, just get away!"

Johnny emerged from the closet wearing a tan sportcoat over his black and green flannel shirt. "Check it out."

"Put that back!" cried Elaine.

"How do I look?" he asked his brother.

"Like a doctor."

"Put that back!" she repeated, flying at him and clutching the collar of the coat, trying to strip it off.

"Just let me see how I look." Shaking her off, Johnny went to the dressing table and turned left and right, admiring himself in the mirror. The coat was drawn tight across his shoulders and his muscular arms bulged in the sleeves, which left an inch or two of thick wrist exposed. "Jesus, he's a dinky little shit."

"He's *real* dinky—look." Pock pulled a T-shirt from the bottom drawer of the bureau and held it up daintily, his little fingers sticking out. "Looks like it would fit Lanny."

"That's his wife's," said Elaine, grabbing it from him.

"You ought to see his shoes," said Johnny. He stepped back into the closet and emerged with a pair of wingtips fitted over his hands. "Dinky feet," he said, clapping the soles together.

"You guys stop it now."

"Dinky feet." Clap, clap.

Pock found a frilly garter in the bottom drawer. He stretched it over his head, bringing it down to his eyebrows, and said, "Dinky head."

"Dinky feet." Clap, clap.

"Dinky head."

"Stop it!"

"Dinky feet." Clap, clap.

"Hey!" A voice from downstairs.

All three fell silent.

"What's going on up there?" It was Caesar Pipe.

Elaine ran to the head of the stairs. "They're making a mess of everything. You've got to stop them or I'll lose my job."

Caesar climbed the steps, muttering.

"They took everything out of the cupboards in the kitchen," said Elaine, "and they messed up the examination room and now they're going through Mrs. Pearsall's underwear, and I'm the one's going to catch hell for it."

Caesar, puffing from the climb, unzipped his deputy jacket as he crossed from the head of the stairs to the bedroom Elaine pointed to. He stood in the doorway, glaring. "What the hell you guys doing in here?"

Johnny, dropping the shoes, looked to his older brother for the answer. Pock scowled at Caesar and said, "We're doing what the law ought to be doing but isn't." His words and his glare, owing to the lacy garter circling his brow, were not as commanding as he intended.

"Get the hell out of here." Caesar advanced into the room.

Elaine, at his heels, said, "There's no way I can get all this stuff back the way it belongs. If I lose my job, you creeps are to blame."

Pock stood his ground, raising his hand to hold off Caesar. "You know as well as I do where the pot and pills are coming from and we're sick of waiting for the law to do something. Roger died seven weeks ago tonight and nobody's doing a goddamn thing about it."

Caesar looked from Pock to Johnny. "So you dress up in other people's clothes? What's that supposed to accomplish?"

Elaine pleaded, "Caesar, make him take off that coat."

"Take off that coat, Johnny."

Doing so, Johnny ripped open a shoulder seam.

"Oh, God, now look what you've done." She took the coat from Johnny and held the ripped seam under Pock's nose. "You creeps! You jerks! You assholes."

"Found anything?" asked Caesar, crossing to the bureau and lifting the lid of a jewel box.

"Nothing so far," said Johnny.

Caesar next opened a drawer containing socks.

"I looked in there already," said Pock.

Elaine cried, "Caesar, not you, too!"

"Don't hurt to look as long as I'm here." He closed the sock drawer and opened another.

She reached around him and slammed the drawer shut. "Don't you dare, not while I'm responsible for this house."

Caesar opened a drawer containing sweaters.

She went to the nightstand and picked up the phone. "I'm calling the sheriff."

Caesar, undaunted, carefully ran his hand between and beneath the sweaters.

She changed her strategy: "I'm telling Joy."

Caesar instantly shut the drawer and turned to her. "Don't," he said.

"Then get out."

"Come on, you guys." Caesar went out into the hallway and over to the stairs. "If you guys ain't found nothing by this time, there probably ain't nothing to find."

"Out!" she repeated, pushing Johnny after him.

Pock followed, telling Caesar, "There's still the garage."

"Take that garter off your head!" ordered Elaine. Her voice was shrill and tremulous.

Pock handed her the garter and followed the others down the stairs. Elaine descended halfway, to make sure they left the house. "Go on," she urged when they stalled in the front hallway. They ignored her.

"There's still the garage," Pock repeated, "but it's locked and we can't find no key."

"Yeah, it's the one place we *gotta* look," said Johnny.

"When we put up the garage, he had us build him a big tool cabinet with a padlock on it."

Caesar stood staring out the window of the front door. He looked thoughtful.

"It's gotta be the place," said Pock. "What's a dude like him want with a tool cabinet? He ain't got no tools."

"Get us in there, Caesar. We'll show you."

"How am I supposed to get you in there?"

"Get a search warrant and bust the door down."

"Where's your warrant for searching the house?"

"We never had to bust no door down."

Caesar squinted out at the sun on the snow-packed road.

Johnny said, "What's the matter, Caesar, don't you believe us?"

Pock's tone was needling: "Can't you get no warrant? Ain't you got no clout with the sheriff?"

Caesar spoke softly, as though to himself, his nose nearly touching the glass. "Let's say you guys are right, the doctor's dealing. He's bringing it onto the reservation from someplace, right? And where would that place be? It would be Chicago, because he comes from Chicago and he's been back to Chicago every month since he got here." He turned and faced the brothers. "And where is he this weekend? Chicago, right? And if he's in Chicago and he's hauling a load of drugs, there's no sense looking for anything before he gets back."

"There might be something left from last time," said Pock.

"It's a lot easier looking when he's not here," urged his brother.

"And another thing, how come it's only the doctor you're accusing? What about his wife?"

At this, for some reason, the three men turned and looked at Elaine on the stairs.

"You're out of your minds," she said with venom in her voice. "The three of you are out of your tiny little minds."

36

Verna had been waiting in the hospital lobby downstairs, and the instant Frank stepped through the door she sprang up from her chair, held him by the lapels, and kissed him. She wore a black dress with a long-stemmed daisy up the left thigh, and black, low-heeled pumps. "Let's get out of here before they find me," she said, slipping into her green oversized jacket, throwing her hair back over the collar, and grabbing her purse off the magazine table. She was smiling. The color in her face was not entirely makeup. Was it excitement he read in her eyes, or edginess? He'd never seen her healthy before. "I didn't sign out," she said. "When they discover I'm gone, they're going to just shit."

"Let's go back and sign out," urged Frank, following her out the door.

"No." Her step was light and lively. She was leading him toward the parking lot, her satiny bait-shop jacket gleaming in the sun. "Don't worry, I'm coming back." She looked delighted with herself.

He unlocked the car and she slipped in. He got in behind the wheel and said, "Well?"

She gripped his arm tightly, shook it roughly. "You're my

best friend in the world, Frank, and I have something very ugly to tell you. Can we find a Mr. Donut? I haven't had anything gooey to eat since I checked into this place."

They ate two gooey concoctions apiece, sitting on stools.

She said, "I'm getting out Monday."

"Then why are you running away this afternoon?"

"Because I've had it up to here with that place, and because I need a test run as a normal person." She transferred her bearclaw from hand to hand, licking her fingers. "And because I talk better in doughnut shops. Aren't these super?"

"Delicious."

"Couldn't you just live on them?"

"Three meals a day."

She ate, giggling.

Farther along the counter sat a woman about Verna's age. Judging by her dress, her makeup, her low-heeled pumps, Frank guessed she was on coffee break from the office building next door. Meeting as strangers, you'd never guess the same about Verna, and Frank wondered why not. What made Verna so obviously a misfit, the other woman so obviously involved in serious work—as a legal secretary, say, or a lawyer? They weren't dressed so differently. Their makeup was applied in the same slightly overstated style. Their shoes might have come from the same shop.

"I'm going to live with my mother till a place here in Berrington has room for me."

"Yes, she's told me."

"Two weeks at the most, they say. It'll be good being with her again. Getting reacquainted."

"Then how long in the halfway house?"

She shrugged. "Till I'm ready to leave."

"Then what?"

"Then the real world."

"What will you do? Be?" She had dropped out of college

twice, out of countless jobs. Her most successful employment, according to her mother, had been five weeks in a pizza parlor.

"I'm going to be a travel agent. It's offered at the Berrington Vocational School." She stirred her coffee at high speed, setting up a little whirlpool that spilled over the rim. "I used to wish I was a flight attendant, but I got to know some flight attendants and it isn't the glamorous job it seems to be. Nothing is, I guess, but I'd really like to spend my life on the move. I think part of my trouble is living so long in one place."

"You've only been in Basswood since May."

"I know." She turned to him and her hair flew. "But time slows down in Basswood."

It dawned on him then. Verna would never be mistaken for an office worker on coffee break until she curbed her gestures and developed a settled look in her eyes. There was an unrefined quality in the careless way she drank her coffee and wiped her mouth and tossed her head when she talked. Her eyes were continually darting, searching. Between this hyped-up Verna and the silent, depressed Verna, was there a Verna normal enough to complete a travel-agent course?

Customers came and went. Frank and Verna lingered over their coffee and crumbs.

"Verna, why did you call me?"

"I need to rehearse something with you."

A long silence. She fidgeted. Her eyes were jumpy, shifty.

"Go ahead," he prompted.

"Well, see, I'm finally going to tell Dr. Pella my secret." She swiveled on her stool, facing away.

"What is it?" he asked.

"Will you go with me when I tell him?"

"If you want me to."

She swiveled back to face him, to murmur, "Sex with my stepfather." When Frank showed no surprise, she added, "You're not shocked?"

Frank, too, lowered his voice, though there was no need; they had the counter to themselves and the waitress was in the back room. "Your mother told me."

Now Verna looked shocked, then skeptical. "She never did."

"Yes, some time ago."

"No, what she told you was about Harris Highsmith."

It took a moment to register, then he slumped on his stool, stunned. He actually felt groggy, as if clubbed on the head. Though his tone was incredulous—"Tom? Not Tom!"—he believed it.

"Tom." She sighed, nodding, smiling ruefully. Her eyes were settled now, aimed at her empty coffee mug. "I used to think I could get better without telling anybody—I mean imagine what this is going to do to my mother—but I don't think so anymore. I've been carrying it in and out of treatment for years and years, and today it finally hit me—I've got to unload it. I'm getting out on Monday, and if I don't unload it, it's going to make me crazy again."

Frank, nodding in agreement, felt hate for Verna as well as Tom building up in his bloodstream, felt his pulse pounding in his head. Libby betrayed—doubly betrayed by her husband and daughter. Verna at once the betrayer and the betrayed. Dear God, please soften my anger at Verna. And forgive me for hating Tom Pearsall, but don't make me quit hating the son of a bitch. If I try to suppress my hatred for him, sooner or later I'll explode. Just allow me to sit here in Mr. Donut and seethe.

"So I'm telling Dr. Pella this afternoon. What's the matter, your ears are all red."

"I'm hot." His voice was high and tight. Dear God, I haven't felt emotion like this in years. My fingertips tingle. Libby the victim all over again. "Coffee!" he shouted, and the waitress came out and refilled their cups.

When the waitress retired again to the back room, Frank spoke in a tremulous voice: "Tell me this, Verna, are you aware of the evil you and Tom have done to your mother?"

"Oh, God." Her lip curled in a sneer. "I knew I shouldn't tell a priest."

"Just answer yes or no."

She looked angry. "I thought you were different. I didn't think you'd preach."

He held her with his eyes until hers brimmed with tears and she turned away, saying, "Yes," making a long hiss of it.

"Okay, that's good. That's the last I'll say about that. Now, are you aware of what a bastard your stepfather is?"

"Is he? I was the one who started it." She wiped her eyes with a paper napkin. "I came on to him."

"When you were how old?"

"When I was fifteen."

"Then I don't care who started it. Tom Pearsall was, and is, an outlaw."

"Even if I started it?"

"Of course. Courts put men like that in prison."

"I always had this feeling that he was rotten, but he said he wasn't."

"He's rotten," Frank assured her.

"He always said *I* was rotten. He always kept reminding me who started it and I got all confused."

"If you were fifteen, he was responsible, so stop being confused."

Frank's tone being harsh, Verna leaned away from him. A new surge of tears came into her eyes. "Do you hate me?"

"I'll get over it. Now let's get moving on this. We'll go back to the hospital and tell your doctor. Is he there on Saturdays?"

"No, not usually, but watch this." She opened her purse, dug out a coin, and moved to the end of the counter where a pay phone hung on the wall. Frank watched her dial, watched her examine her fingernails as she waited for an answer. She said, "Hope Unit, please." A moment's pause. "Who is this? . . . Val, this is Verna. . . . Val, just calm down, I'm fine, nothing's wrong. . . . Why, what are they doing?" She laughed, dabbing at her eyes. "Tell them to call off the search. I'm coming back, but under one condition—I want Dr. Pella to be there. . . . Because I need to talk to him. . . . I know he's not, but tell him it's an emergency and I'm not coming back unless he's there. . . . Val, it's none of your fucking business where I am. Just tell me, can you get him to come in or can't you?"

There was another pause, a very long one, during which Verna pointed to her coffee mug. Frank delivered it to her and sat at her side. He offered to take the phone, to talk to the Hope staff, but she shook her head, smiling, obviously enjoying the power she exerted over them.

"Val, just call him up and tell him. Is it too much to ask a doctor to see a patient when she needs him? Just call him up and tell him."

There were a few more brief exchanges at long intervals, after which Verna hung up in triumph. "He'll be there in half an hour."

They sat in Dr. Pella's office, waiting. The dark brown walls were unadorned, the furniture was steel, and the single bookshelf held no books. They waited so long that Frank feared Verna might change her mind.

But she didn't. The moment Dr. Pella showed up, she spilled out her secret. She did it with chilly detachment. Dr. Pella, a short, stocky young man with a blond, carefully trimmed beard, was the brusque sort of practitioner who gave off no warmth and who, by his reticence and the noncommital set of his face, encouraged his patients to keep their emotional thermostats turned down. Frank didn't like him much. How could a man so distant and ungiving be successful in this line of work? Was he resentful at being called away from his weekend? He looked the part of a doctor all right, but not—you saw it in his eyes—a doctor of the human soul. He made his work look like pure science. A chemist, Verna had called him.

But never mind the brittle atmosphere, she did what she had to do—she lanced the boil. Sex with Tom shortly before her sixteenth birthday, she said. She herself the initiator. Sex with Tom at irregular intervals thereafter, usually when she was between boyfriends but sometimes not, sometimes while going steady. She was almost always the initiator, and Tom was always willing, but not always able. Less and less able the last couple of years, now that he was drinking so much.

"Where?" asked Dr. Pella.

"Where? Well, lots of places. Motels. Tom's office in the clinic in Chicago. Once on a boat. Sometimes at home. More often at home than you'd think. A couple times, for fun, right there in my mother's marriage bed."

"And it's still going on?"

"The last time was before Christmas. The Sunday Roger Upward died."

"And how was it?"

She looked askance at her doctor. "What do you mean?"

"Enjoyable?"

She shuddered. She looked to Frank as if for the answer. She lowered her eyes. "I loved it." She shuddered again. "I hated it."

"And how do you feel about it now?"

She raised her eyes. "Like shit."

The three of them sat for a few moments in silence; then Frank, who had been growing steadily more agitated, got to his feet and paced. "Tom and her mother are coming back from Chicago tomorrow night," he said. "She's got to be told right away."

The doctor shot back, "You're getting ahead of yourself."

"She can't go on in ignorance. She has to be told."

The doctor's eyes flamed. "She'll be told here, in my presence. By Verna."

"All right," said Frank, continuing to pace. "Monday morning. I'll come in."

"Tuesday afternoon."

"Tuesday?" he shouted. He wanted Libby to know the worst immediately. He felt dishonest, knowing the truth while she did not. "Why Tuesday?" he pleaded. "It's cruel to let this ride."

The doctor shrugged one shoulder, raised one eyebrow. "What's twenty-four hours after nine years?"

"Ten years," said Verna, correcting him.

"Give me one good reason for waiting."

"There are several," said the doctor, and added coldly, "Please sit down."

Frank sat and heard him out.

You didn't call the wronged party into a showdown meeting without having thought through the consequences, without being ready with suggestions. Libby would need advice about how to handle her shock and her grief, about how to relate from now on to her daughter, about how to avoid poor choices on the rebound if she decided to leave her husband, which, surprisingly, not all that many women did in cases like this. Moreover, said Dr. Pella, you didn't confront the perpetrator without being prepared to place him under arrest if his sexual relationship with his stepdaughter constituted a felony, which it probably did—Dr. Pella would need more details from Verna and then he'd check with the county attorney.

"And don't forget," scolded the doctor, his disdain for Frank manifest in his hectoring tone, "it's the patient whose welfare we're primarily responsible for. Verna's primary counselor, Mrs. Brink, and the staff from social services will need time to revise their paperwork so that Verna's hospitalization can be extended—"

"What?" said Verna. "I'm checking out Monday!"

The doctor ignored her. "Extended a week or a month or whatever time it takes her to get through the emotional fallout. And besides all that," he concluded, getting to his feet and opening the door for Frank's departure, "I have no free time till Tuesday at three."

Frank turned to Verna. "Do you want me to be here for the meeting?" He intended to be present; indeed, he didn't see how he could stay away. He felt like the only man in Libby's life who had been faithful to her.

Verna didn't hear his question—she was repeating to the doctor her determination to check out on Monday—but the doctor heard him and responded, "I'd rather you didn't take part in the actual meeting, Father Healy, though you may want to be waiting in the wings."

This was followed by a five-minute argument between Verna and her doctor, at the end of which she grudgingly agreed to remain in the hospital at least until Tuesday.

Frank left the office feeling chastened, having promised not to speak of the matter and not to intrude on the principals until the meeting was over.

Verna, a nervous smile playing across her face, accompanied

JON HASSLER • 369

him down the green hallway and across the dayroom. "Not a fun guy, is he?"

"Hard as nails."

"Knows his meds though."

"And I suppose he's right about Tuesday. You can't go into a meeting like that unprepared." Dear God, he thought, how could anyone possibly prepare?

"But he's wrong about my staying on. I'm leaving here the minute the meeting is over. I checked myself in and I can check myself out."

"Don't be too sure. You don't want to cut yourself off from help."

"Listen, my follow-up program reads like a full-time job. Besides a halfway house, I'm supposed to be outpatient here for six months."

They came to the double doors and halted.

"Well, just don't close your mind to it. You might feel different on Tuesday."

She gripped him roughly by the arm, turned him to face her. "Please, Frank, don't try steering me ways I can't go." Her smile remained but he saw a steely resolve in her eyes.

He said, "Right."

Her eyes softened a little. "You know what I like about you, Frank?"

"What?"

"You've been here to see me, what, four times?"

"Five."

"Five times, and up until this minute you haven't given me a single piece of advice."

"Fair enough," he said, lifting his hands in surrender.

"Can you imagine how much advice I'm given, Frank?"

"Lots, I'm sure."

"Tons. All my life, tons and tons. My mother and my stepfathers, tons and tons of advice. My teachers, my doctors, my lovers, tons and tons and tons. After a while it gets so you're living a life totally mapped out by other people. I can't stand that, Frank. That's why I get wild sometimes. At least when I'm wild, I'm on my own."

He reversed this on her, just so she understood: "So you're advising me. . . ."

Gripping his lapels, she gave him a shake. "I have to, Frank. I don't want to stop liking you."

He nodded submissively. "No more advice then."

"We need you for other things, my mother and I. Please be here on Tuesday."

"I'll be down in the lobby. Pick up the phone."

"Promise."

"At three."

She let go of his lapels, stepped back, and looked at him with her eyes steel-hard again. "Why don't I believe you?"

"Because you've never known a man you could trust."

37

Leaving Berrington, Frank stopped for a red light on Great Northern Avenue and was honked at and grinned at by two men in an old maroon van with most of its glass covered with frost. It wasn't until the van sped past him that he noticed UPWARD CONST painted on the door and realized he was waving at Johnny and Pock Upward from Basswood. He saw them slow down some distance beyond the stoplight and turn in at Continental Overhead Door.

He drove home enshrouded by his sorrow for Libby. It felt like a thick and smothering pall. It obscured his vision. He couldn't see beyond Tuesday at three. He couldn't foresee how she would react. At times he thought of her as strong and resourceful; she'd survived more than her share of adversity. At other times she seemed on the point of collapse. Dear God, keep her strong.

In Linden Falls, he stopped at the rectory only long enough to pick up his overnight bag, his lunch bag, and Billy Annunciation.

"I took a call for you while Marcella was at the grocery store," Billy told him as they sped out of town. "Long distance from Chicago."

"Yes?"

"Mrs. Pearsall."

"Yes?"

"Said she'd call you tonight at her house."

They rode a mile or two in silence, Billy searching for music on the radio and Frank preoccupied with Verna's revelation. His anger at Verna had dissipated. It was replaced with apprehension. Verna, emerging from the hospital, could go either way. Would she call up the strength of will to set herself a new course, or would she continue down the long slide to self-destruction? Dear God, make her strong.

"I finished painting the downstairs bathroom," Billy said. "The molding was a bitch."

"Cleaned the brush, did you?"

"Yeah."

What he felt for Tom was very intense, but harder to define. It wasn't entirely contempt. It was something even darker, like horror. However, it didn't seem to be abhorrence at what Tom had done so much as a mysterious, deep-seated dread of what he was yet to do. Dear God—

"We'll need another can of paint for the upstairs bathroom."

"I'll get it. You can paint next Saturday?"

"Yeah."

"How did Adrian seem?"

"He's fine. I watched part of a game with him. The Gophers and Michigan."

"No hallucinations?"

"No, but he keeps trying to get those seven hundred dead people prayed for. He's got this little notebook with their names in, did you know that?"

"He's carried it with him all his life."

"He kept opening it during time outs. At halftime he asked me if I planned on praying for his soul when he died. I told him he wouldn't need prayers because he was going to shoot straight to heaven."

"You're right."

"But he doesn't think so. He said nobody can read the mind of God and know who's going to be saved instantly and who's going to need a little developing in purgatory. You'd think death was a fish hatchery, to hear him tell it."

"A fish hatchery?"

"I mean purgatory sounds like these holding tanks they have in hatcheries where we'll have to hang around and develop to the point where we're ready to be set free in the big lake, which is eternity."

Frank was amused by the analogy. Indeed, ever since taking him on as his Saturday sidekick, Frank had been continually charmed by Billy's brightness, was a little envious, in fact, of his headlong manner of blurting whatever crossed his mind. Billy was the loquacious extrovert Frank would never be.

"Who won the game?"

"Michigan. We lost it on a missed free throw."

Another mile of silence, broken by Billy.

"Frank, what's with the Pearsalls? Are they as screwed up as they look?"

Frank gave him an inquiring look.

"I mean he's such a wimp and she could be in movies. Elaine says their medical practice is a joke. My grandma says if Dr. Pearsall stays here long enough, he'll have a decent practice, but my grandpa says he knows a loser when he sees one and Dr. Pearsall is one of the super losers of all time and he'll be a failure at whatever he does and wherever he does it. He says not all the failures in the world grow up on reservations."

"The Pearsalls have been dislocated, Billy. Dislocation can knock you off balance—I speak from experience."

"Yeah, I know, I felt dislocated in the city for seven years." Billy crossed his arms and gazed at the road ahead. "Seems like everybody's meant to be in a certain place, doesn't it?"

"It does."

"And if you're in the wrong place, you can't live your life right."

"I believe that."

"My place is here, Frank."

"Likewise."

"It's like I'm a compass and I have to keep pointing north."

"Me too."

After a pause, Billy said, "It seems like Adrian's in touch with God more than most people."

"True."

"He's weird."

"Adrian? Weird?"

"No, I mean God. What's he like, do you suppose?"

Frank called to mind his four years of graduate theology and reduced them to a word: "Merciful." To which he added, "I hope."

"I don't mean that. I mean does he have a personality?"

"It's probably up to each of us to imagine his personality."

"What do you imagine?"

"I imagine someone a lot like myself. Lots of appointments. Guardedly optimistic. Tired of winter."

"Could God be a woman, Frank? Elaine says God could be a woman."

"To Elaine, God could be a woman."

"But she says men, too—they can think of God as a woman."

"Some men, I suppose."

"Not you?"

"No, not me."

"Why?"

"Force of habit," said Frank, advising himself not to reveal the other, more forceful reason, namely that whenever he tried thinking of God as a woman, the image of Eunice Pfeiffer came to mind. Eunice Pfeiffer, from whose array of important virtues mercy was missing.

"Frank, what if we get to heaven and God turns out to be like Mrs. Tatzig and hates Indians?"

"Depressing thought."

"Or maybe God's like the monsignor."

"I'd like that."

"Sort of vague in the head, I mean. That wouldn't be so great, would it?"

"But so full of concern for everyone's soul. That would be ideal."

Billy laughed. "And in love with women on TV." He shifted

in his seat, rearranging his long legs. "What do you think of Elaine LaBonte, Frank? You've never said."

"I like her."

"What do you like about her?"

"She seems to know her own mind."

"Do you think she's good-looking?"

"Very."

"Do you think we're good together?"

"I've never seen you together."

"In church you have."

"Oh. So I have."

"Are we good together?"

"What do you think?"

"I think we are."

"Then I think so, too."

They came to Sovereign Lake. Frank turned off the road and drove carefully down to the ice. Crossing the lake, he gave more thought to God's personality. Most of God's attributes were a mystery to Frank, but not God's ambivalence concerning his people. God was a loner, no doubt about it—thousands of years of scrutiny by prophets and theologians and he was still as evasive as ever. Yet, like Frank, he was apparently a loner who wanted it both ways. He was always urging you to follow him, always out there ahead of you, calling to you from over the next hill or from deep in the trees, promising to fulfill your hopes. And so you toiled on and on, searching him out.

Halfway across, they passed the lopsided fish house they had hammered together.

"Ain't she a beaut?" said Billy.

"An architect's dream."

"Frank, do you realize my grandpa's got a snowmobile in the toolshed he's never used?"

"I've seen it there."

"It was issued to him by the sheriff's department and it's been just sitting there for about five winters."

"For emergencies, I suppose."

"For fishing, from now on. I talked my grandma into talking him into letting me use it. Could you help me get it started? It needs oil and stuff. My grandpa doesn't know the first thing about engines."

"I don't either, Billy."

The boy gave Frank a dark look. "You know why I'd never be a priest, Frank? Priests never know anything outside their field. They're all so spacey."

"Sorry."

"I'll ask Elaine's uncles. They bring her mother's Chrysler back to life whenever it dies."

Driving up off the ice, Frank pointed to the old pickup that had been standing near the Homestead for nearly two months, the driver's door ajar, one of its tires flat. "Can't they get Roger's truck going?"

"It needs a part they can't get. A coil or something."

"And a tire patched."

"Yeah, Johnny shot a hole in it so nobody'd drive it off."

"How could anyone drive it off if it doesn't start?"

"Don't ask me. Johnny's insane."

Frank heard twelve confessions. After absolving each of the twelve, he asked them to pray for a secret intention of his own, and later, before leaving the empty church, he sat in the front pew with his eyes on the crucifix and added his prayer to the twelve. Dear God, watch out for Libby and Verna and Tom. There's danger ahead and only Verna knows it. If there's no way for the three of them to avoid heartbreak, please see to it that they heal up in good time.

Sensing that God wasn't giving him his full attention, Frank repeated the prayer. Again he felt ignored, uneasy, frustrated. This worried him as he crossed the road to the Pearsalls' house. Frank was not given to psychic experiences on a grand scale, but he was visited occasionally by small premonitions. A lifetime of cultivating his spiritual life had taught him, for example, that when a prayer led to anxiety instead of peace, something ominous was looming ahead.

Something in the Indian Health Center, his prickling scalp told him. Was it his sixth sense that alerted him in the front hallway, or was it merely the faint smell of cigarette ash? He sensed intruders. He sensed a struggle. Looking through the downstairs rooms, he found two cigarettes stubbed out in the waiting-room ashtray and another in the kitchen. Nothing unusual about that: Elaine LaBonte had been on duty, receiving patients and sending them away; Elaine probably smoked. He climbed the stairs and found another cigarette in a dish beside Tom and Libby's bed. Neither Tom nor Libby smoked. If Elaine smoked, why in the master bedroom? He considered calling Elaine, then remembered that Billy had taken her to town in Caesar's pickup to see *Taxi Driver*. He looked out the bedroom window. The pickup wasn't home yet.

Because the guest room had no phone for him to take Libby's call, he carried a comforter downstairs and lay on the couch watching a TV retrospective on Hubert Humphrey, who'd been dead two weeks. After that, gazing at the news, he fell asleep and dreamed he was walking beside a large body of water. In a cove he came upon a middle-aged woman sitting on a rock and looking sad. She might have been his mother. She might have been Libby. She was being comforted by a little boy who was murmuring something in her ear. He was her son, obviously, for the two of them had the same eyes and cheekbones. Soon they were joined by an older child, a daughter of twelve or thirteen, who had her mother's mouth and complexion. This girl put her arm tenderly around the woman's shoulders and sat silently beside her, listening to the little boy continue with his message of solace.

The phone rang at midnight. The sound of Libby's voice renewed Frank's anxiety. Not that she sounded anxious herself; on the contrary it was her buoyant tone that increased his dread of the Tuesday meeting. The higher her spirit, the farther the drop.

"We just got in from a play, Frank. Neil Simon. A so-so play, but it's such fun to rub shoulders with play goers. The city is my tonic, you know. I'm lighter on my feet in Chicago."

"You must dread coming back."

"Well, I do and I don't. I miss you."

There was the sound of the Pipes' pickup slowing to a stop

across the road, followed by the sound of its door slamming shut.

"Tom's the one dreading it. All the way down here on Thursday he kept insisting he wasn't going back to Basswood."

"Did he mean it?"

"Yes, that's the trouble. He's said it before, but always as sort of a joke, but this time he wasn't joking, he was dead serious, and I think if I wasn't here to reason with him, he'd risk his probation and not go back."

"With four months to go."

"That's what I keep telling him—four months and we're free. I know I'll have to drill it into him again in the morning to get him going. Frank—I have to ask you—after I move back here, will you come and see me?"

He told her he would, but when he tried to picture such a visit, he couldn't do it. And why did she say "I" and not "we"?

"Often?"

"Not often, Libby. It's seven hundred miles."

"But only an hour by air from the Twin Cities."

"Libby." Did she need to be told the obvious? "Libby, I work for an outfit that doesn't like their men getting involved with women."

"I'm not saying we have to get serious." There was petulance in her voice. "Anyhow your outfit is so medieval. Aren't you ever, once in your life, going to step out of that role and see what real life is like?"

He bristled. "What I'm doing seems pretty real, Libby."

"You know what I mean—break out of that sterile existence. You keep avoiding me."

"If it becomes sterile, I will, but I'm still finding my way in this line of work. If I ever leave the priesthood, I'll want to be sure—"

"God, Frank, I'm not asking you to leave the priesthood. I'm asking you to take a three-day vacation in Chicago sometime."

"Which I've said I'll do."

"But you're so evasive. You keep avoiding me."

"When have I avoided you?"

"The last two times I've asked you to ride along to Berrington."

"I had appointments, I told you. I had a wedding and I had the dentist."

"But you never suggested another time."

He sighed. More and more often lately Frank found himself involved in something like a lovers' skirmish. "I have never avoided you," he said. Which was not precisely true. Feeling increasingly besieged, he no longer initiated meetings with her, and although he enjoyed talking with her on the phone, he depended on her to place the calls. "Look how often we talk," he said. "Have I ever once cut a phone call short?"

Plaintively: "The phone is your way of avoiding me, don't you see that, Frank? To you, life is all words."

He allowed a few silent moments to pass, then changed the subject: "Libby, are you splitting up with Tom?"

A long pause. "I don't know. Why do you ask?"

"Because you didn't say 'after *we* move to Chicago,' you said 'after *I*.'"

"Oh, what I meant was, I'm not coming back here right away when our year is up." Another pause. When she continued, it was in a businesslike tone. The skirmish was over. "It's because of Verna. She'll be in that halfway house for at least six months, and I want to be there when she needs me."

"You'll stay in Basswood?"

"No, God no. Berrington. I'll get an apartment in Berrington and work at the hospital. They need nurses. I've already applied, and they'll hire me anytime. I'm hopeful about Verna, Frank. She's come a long way in the last week or two. Have you seen her lately?"

"I saw her today."

"Oh?"

A lie: "I had to go to Berrington on church business, so I stopped by to see her."

"And?"

"You're right, she's a new woman."

"It's Dr. Pella and Mrs. Brink. They're wonderful. Isn't it ironic that we move to the boondocks thinking she'll be helped by seeing her father, who doesn't give a damn for her, and instead of that we hit on just the right hospital? I think she's been able to say things to Dr. Pella she hasn't told anybody else."

He suppressed his need to explain how correct she was. "Her discharge has been moved back a day, Libby. Tuesday instead of Monday."

"Why?"

"Dr. Pella's schedule."

"But he doesn't have to be there for discharge."

"He wants to be. Tuesday at three. Can you be there?"

"Sure."

"Can Tom?"

"Tom never goes to these things. Verna's never wanted him to."

"She wants him this time. So does the doctor."

"You saw Dr. Pella?"

Another lie: "For a minute."

"On Saturday? He's never there on Saturday. What's wrong, Frank? Something's wrong. Tell me."

A third: "Nothing's wrong. He just likes to see the whole family at discharge time."

"Why don't you tell Tom, Frank. He's right here. I'll call you tomorrow night when we get back. Okay?"

"Okay."

"Good-bye."

"Good-bye, Libby."

Tom's voice on the line: "Frank, what's the weather like?"

"The same."

"Shit."

"Tom, Verna's doctor wants you to come to her discharge conference."

"Tell him I never do that."

"Verna wants you there, Tom. *Needs* you there."

"Why?"

"Needs, Tom. You know how needs are. You can't always define them."

"Needs money, is what she needs."

"That may be. Will you be there?"

"I might, when is it?"

"Tuesday afternoon. She won't be released unless you're there."

"That's bullshit, she can leave anytime."

"I'm only telling you what they said, she and her doctor."

"Playing hardball, are they?"

"So it would seem."

"Tuesday?"

"At three."

Tom spoke to Libby. Their voices were faint on the line for nearly a minute, then Tom said, "Frank, would you put a note on the front door for us? We're staying here an extra day. We'll start back late Monday and stay overnight in Minneapolis and show up at the discharge meeting on Tuesday. Write 'The doctor is out,' and tape it to the front door, would you?"

"I will."

"Frank, how's the weather?"

"The same."

"Shit."

After Mass the next morning, Frank stood on the front step chatting with his parishioners on their way out the door. When Elaine LaBonte came out, coughing and holding her little twin sisters by the hand, he told her about his sense of unpleasantness in the Pearsalls' house. He asked if she had put a cigarette out in the master bedroom.

"That must have been my uncle Johnny, he smokes," she said.

"They got upstairs, did they?" As Frank asked this, they were joined by Caesar and Joy Pipe and Billy Annunciation.

"Looking for drugs," explained Elaine. "He and my uncle Pock, yesterday. I had to call Caesar to kick them out."

"Couple of amateur detectives," said Caesar.

"Couple of idiots," said Joy.

"Hey, there they are," said Billy. He dashed across the road to speak to the Upward brothers, who were climbing into their van.

"Wants them to look at our snowmobile," Caesar explained to his wife.

"What are they doing here?" asked Joy. "They weren't in church, were they?"

Frank said they weren't.

"Probably snooping around the Health Center again," said Elaine. "If they lose me my job, I'll kill them."

Joy turned to her husband. "You keep them away from there."

"Don't worry," said Caesar, taking his wife's arm. "Come on, I'm hungry."

Joy didn't budge. She stood there waiting for Billy, who was standing at the driver's window of the van talking to Pock and Johnny. Pock called out, "Hey, Caesar," and Caesar responded with a timid little wave. Pock raised his hand in the air, giving him the V-for-victory sign.

"What's that all about?" asked Joy.

"Damned if I know," said Caesar. "Let's eat."

The church emptied. Frank, securing the door and returning to the sacristy, speculated that Caesar probably *did* know. He speculated further that the V-sign might have meant that the Upwards had found the doctor's stash. Having built the Pearsalls' garage last summer and having visited Continental Overhead Door yesterday afternoon, weren't the brothers likely to be in possession of a duplicate garage-door opener? And wasn't Sunday morning the best time to use it, the ever-watchful Joy Pipe being in church?

38

Tom approached the double doors of Hope expecting the worst, while Libby, at his side, expected the best.

Halfway between Minneapolis and Berrington, the possibility had dawned on Tom that he'd been invited to this conference because Verna had revealed their secret; and so, stopping along the way for lunch, he'd knocked back several brandies, and then, approaching Berrington with Libby at the wheel, he'd rolled a joint and smoked it in the car. Brandy and pot endowed him with a powerful faith in his ability to defend himself. Who was going to believe the accusations of a mental cripple like Verna against the word of Dr. Tom Pearsall, the Albert Schweitzer of the Basswood Indians? Besides, didn't everybody have a dirty little sex-and-drug secret these days? Verna's psychiatrist, doubtless concealing secrets of his own, would be sympathetic. The fraternity of physicians and all that.

Libby expected this to be the first in a series of happy days. Always in the past when Verna moved home after an extended absence, harmony had descended on the house and remained for quite a long time. A week, anyway. Two or three weeks sometimes. If it wasn't love Libby got from her daughter during these cease-fires, it was at least respect. Or, if not respect, at least restraint. No brooding. No tongue-lashings. No coffee cups or hair dryers hurled across the room. And this time Verna, having been promised admittance to a long-term halfway house, was likely to be relocated before the harmony came to an end.

They found the dayroom empty of patients. Libby noticed a man sitting near the coffee machine drinking from a Styrofoam cup—a very large man wearing a tan jacket with a badge pinned to the front and an insignia sewn on the sleeve. A deputy sheriff.

"Mrs. Pearsall, over here," Dr. Pella called from the doorway of a small conference room.

"Doctor, this is my husband, Tom."

Dr. Pella, not much taller than Tom, shot out his hand, smiled a mechanical smile, and said, "Hi, happy to know you." He was wearing loafers, jeans, and a sweater vest over his button-down shirt. Libby, regarding the two men, was struck by her husband's languorous manner and unhealthy pallor in contrast to the other man's vigor and ruddy complexion. That she much preferred color to pallor, vigor to languor, was something she tried to expel from her mind at this moment.

"Hi," said Tom. His reactions retarded by alcohol and marijuana, he caught hold of Dr. Pella's hand just as he was about to withdraw it. "How's it going?"

"We'll meet in here," said Dr. Pella, dropping Tom's handshake. The room was too small for the long table and the eight upholstered chairs it contained. Seated on one of the chairs was Roberta Brink, RN. She nodded to Libby and then looked Tom up and down as she told him, "I'm Verna's primary counselor."

"Hi," said Tom. He took her hand while straightening his hair. "How's it going?"

Like Dr. Pella, she seemed to need only a moment to size up Verna's stepfather. Cutting short the handshake, she turned her attention to a well-worn manila folder on the table before her. Tom, sitting down next to her, saw that the file was labeled "Highsmith."

"That's my stepdaughter," he told her, breathing alcoholic fumes.

"Yes," she said.

"So how's it going?" he asked again.

"Fine," she said sternly.

Libby squeezed her way around the table and took a seat with her back to the window. The table was blond Formica grained like oak and the chairs were newly upholstered in plum. Seated, she felt suddenly in peril, felt herself stiffen, felt her happy expectations drain away. What sort of dark energy was at work in this room? Why were the doctor and nurse so abrupt and formal today? She noticed the nurse's jaw muscle tightening and untightening like a pulse. Dr. Pella, waiting for Verna in the doorway, nervously tapped his thighs with his thumbs. Looking past the doctor, she saw that the eyes of the deputy sheriff were directed alertly, expectantly, toward this room.

Tom leaned close to Roberta Brink again and said, "This is a bad-smelling room."

"Verna requested a room she could smoke in," the nurse replied. The upholstery and drapes, new as they were, reeked of cigarettes.

"Where is she?" Dr. Pella asked.

"She's on her way," said the nurse, busily shuffling papers and avoiding everyone's eyes.

"It smells like a tavern. Libby, doesn't it smell just like the Homestead in here?"

"Not quite," said Libby, smiling at her husband, hoping he would do them all the favor of extending his present mood to the end of the meeting. Tom at this stage of inebriation—relaxed, chatty—was good at dispelling tension.

"This is my wife," he explained to the nurse. "Have you had the pleasure?"

"Oh, yes," said Roberta Brink, her attention still directed at her papers. "We've met many times."

"Yeah, she's been here a lot."

Silence.

"But not me. This is my first visit."

"I know." There was a hint of reproach in the nurse's reply.

"The reason is, see, I've got this medical practice on the reservation and it's hard to get away."

No response. Tom, shrugging, made eyes at Libby as if to ask, What's eating this dame?

"Hi, Mom." Verna came in smoking, carrying a plastic saucer as her ashtray.

"Hello, dear." Squeezing the wrist of her daughter's cigarette hand, Libby read her eyes and judged her to be slightly tipped in the manic direction—six or seven on a scale of zero to ten. Zero was Verna as she had been during Libby's first visit to Special Care, Verna the zombie in deep depression. Ten was all-out manic, Verna wildly distraught. Five was the peaceful middle ground, the ideal, the true Verna, her behavior at its best, her thinking unimpaired by drink, drugs, or mental aberration.

Verna sat down opposite her stepfather and studied him for a time with great intensity, blinking now and then as smoke rose into her eyes but not taking her gaze from him. She said, at length, "Hello, Tom."

"Hi." Grinning, he lifted his hand and wiggled his fingers. "How's it going?"

Six or seven wasn't bad, Libby told herself, though volatility lay in that direction. It was better than three or four, the down side. At three and four the eyes were clouded, sleepy, sad. At six and seven the eyes were lively and responsive. For the past month Libby had watched her swing from one end of the scale to the other as Dr. Pella worked at regulating her medication. Last week Verna had been at her best.

Dr. Pella motioned to the law officer, and when this large, uniformed man came in and sat down next to Tom, the room shrank and Libby's alarm was turned up a notch. Tom seemed not to be uneasy or even curious.

The doctor said, "This is Larry Malmquist from the sheriff's office. I've asked him to sit in for reasons that will become clear."

Tom shook the man's hand and said, "How's it going?"

"Not bad," replied Larry Malmquist, a round-faced, young-ish man with striking blue eyes and blond hair cut very short and standing on end. "Wish it would warm up."

"Me too," said Tom.

Dr. Pella sat down at the head of the table, opposite Libby, his back to the door, which he had left standing ajar. He aimed his mechanical smile at Tom and said crisply, "Verna would like to begin the meeting with a statement."

Long moments passed as Verna lowered her eyes, fiddled with her cigarette, and moved her lips as though rehearsing. Libby recognized the necklace her daughter wore—Roger Upward's necklace of talons and teeth. She remembered Roger wearing it on that day last fall when she went to his house searching for Verna. Libby had no idea that day, nor had Roger, that Verna was in Chicago with Tom. When Tom phoned that evening and told her, she'd hit the ceiling, shouted, said things she could never say to his face. How dare they go off without telling her! How dare he leave her stranded in Basswood without a car! Hanging up, she'd trembled with astonishment at how easily she had released this torrent of anger on the long-distance line. She'd felt strangely exhilarated.

"The thing is," said Verna. She put her diminished cigarette to her lips for a final drag.

"Come on, Verna," said Dr. Pella impatiently. "We'll help you along, but you've got to get it started."

"The thing is."

She put out her cigarette and looked around the table. Her eyes came to rest on Libby as she spoke.

"Tom's been screwing me."

This was followed by nearly half a minute during which Libby—shocked as she was—felt becalmed, distant, amazingly at ease, as though unconsciously she had been expecting her daughter to utter these very words, as though they were somehow liberating. And during this long, numb half minute, her emotions held at bay by her long habit of repression, she regarded the other five people coolly, analytically. They might have been mechanized sculptures in a gallery, pieces in which she had only a casual interest. She saw the eyes of Roberta Brink darting swiftly between mother and daughter, with a quick side glance every so often at Dr. Pella. She saw Dr. Pella tapping his lower lip with his forefinger, his eyes boring into Tom. She saw Tom sniff and bring his lips tightly together and look as though he were absorbed in a slightly irritating thought. She knew the look well. This was how he confronted anything distasteful or threatening—conveying by his facial expression that he was above it all. There was nothing at all to read in the smooth, round face of Deputy Malmquist, who sat with his arms folded and his head lowered, his eyes on his wristwatch. Verna, her lively eyes fastened on her mother, lit another cigarette. She inhaled deeply. Smoke came pouring out with her words.

"Father Healy says I have to tell you this, and I know he's right. Dr. Pella says I have to say it in front of both of you, and I know *he's* right. Do you hear me, Mother?"

Her mother nodded, dazed now. Dizzy.

"Tom Pearsall, my stepfather, your husband, has been screwing me since I was fifteen years old."

Tom leaned over and confided to Roberta Brink: "I never did it. She wanted me to, but I never did it."

"Frank?" murmured Libby. "Frank knows?"

"He's the one I told first."

As the nurse shifted away from Tom, he leaned farther over and nearly fell off his chair. "Damn it," he said sharply, righting himself and placing a hand on his lower spine. "I threw my back out."

"How long has Frank known?"

"Since Saturday. He wanted you to know right away, but Dr. Pella said we should wait."

Libby turned to Tom, then turned suddenly away, feeling nauseated, clutching her stomach.

"It's taken me a long time to say this, Mom. It takes time to work up to it. There's a lot of shit I had to think through first." A deep drag on her cigarette. A long stream of exhaled smoke. "And now there's a lot of shit *you* have to think through."

Tom, both hands pressed to his spine, turned to Dr. Pella and explained, "She's a highly sexual person, Verna is. She came on to me like gangbusters, but I never did it. I might have to leave this meeting early—I just threw my back out."

Verna spoke to her mother: "I want to live with you for a while. I'm ready to come out, see. I mean I'm starting to deal with things now and I don't want to be in here anymore. But there isn't room at Hanson Manor right now and I have to live somewhere and I sure as hell don't want to go back to Judge Bigelow, so what I'd like to do is live with you in the meantime."

"Yes," said Libby dully. "That's what we planned."

"But I can't be in the same house with Tom."

Dr. Pella raised a cautionary hand. "Verna, haven't our plans changed? Didn't we decide . . . ?"

Rapid-fire: "You decided—I didn't."

"But we agreed, didn't we, that how your mother worked this out would be separate from how *you* worked it out?"

Testily: "So what's the problem?"

"So you shouldn't be implying that your mother leave your stepfather. That's for her to work out."

"Well, I can't stay in the same house with him, can I? And where else am I going to stay?"

"Here," said Dr. Pella. He, too, was beginning to sound irritated. "We decided you'd wait here till Hanson Manor has room."

"I never decided that. I can't stay here another fucking minute."

He took it slow: "Verna, your social worker arranged for an extra two weeks' hospital funding, remember? And didn't we set up counseling sessions? And think about it, Verna—aren't you behaving impulsively this afternoon? Haven't we talked about your impulsive behavior and where it has led you in the past? Haven't we—"

"Don't take that condescending tone with me."

Tom spoke up: "Listen, everybody, I hate to run, but I threw my back out." He rose carefully to his feet and leaned on the table as he addressed Dr. Pella, physician to physician. "It's apparent to me that Verna's heading into another episode. It's always a sign when she hallucinates like this."

"Sit down," said Dr. Pella.

"I can't sit down. I threw my back out." Tom made for the door.

"Stay where you are, or I'll have you arrested," ordered the doctor. Deputy Malmquist, rolling his chair, blocked the way.

"Arrested!" said Tom, scowling in turn at the doctor, at Verna, at Libby. He returned to his chair and carefully lowered himself onto it. He looked at his hands and saw that they were trembling. He dropped them to his lap. He scowled at Verna.

"For Chrissake, she's been coming on to me like gangbusters since she was in junior high. I never did a thing."

Libby made a sound that startled everyone. She was gasping for air. Her shoulders were shaking. The cramping in her stomach intensified. She got shakily to her feet and moved around the table, stopping for a moment behind Verna's chair and pressing her daughter's head against her abdomen; then she flew out the door and across the dayroom to the lavatory.

"She's not a strong person," Tom explained, getting to his feet once again. "She needs me."

"Sit down!" ordered the doctor, and the deputy again blocked the way.

Kneeling over a toilet vomiting, Libby tried to think what to say. What to do. "I can't be your wife anymore." She repeated this aloud between fits of quaking and throwing up. When her retching came to an end, she said, "I can't be your wife anymore and I don't ever want to see you again." Her voice was small and husky. She forced herself to say it louder, speaking to the tiled wall over the toilet. "I can't be your wife anymore. I can't stand the sight of you anymore." She sobbed, "God, Verna, what you've been through!" She got to her feet and said it all over again. "I can't be your wife anymore. I can't stand the sight of you anymore. God, Verna, what you've been through."

Stepping out of the toilet stall, she found Roberta Brink running cold water, moistening a handful of paper towels. She took the towels from her and stepped up to a mirror. "I have to make a phone call."

"The priest?"

Libby nodded.

"He's downstairs in the lobby. I'll call him for you."

Libby pressed the cold towels to her eyes, then dried them and stood gripping the sink, leaning toward her image in the mirror.

"Are they actually arresting him?" she asked.

Nurse Brink said, "It's a felony, what he did to Verna before she was eighteen."

"They'll put him in jail?"

"I don't know. I suppose a judge will decide. There's a drug charge pending as well."

Libby, who seemed not to be listening, backed slowly away from the sink and cried, "I *hate* that woman!" She was pointing at herself in the mirror.

Dr. Pella stood with Verna in the dayroom, trying once again to convince her to remain in the Hope Unit until the halfway house had space for her. "That way you and your mother will have the time and the distance from one another to work out your problems separately. No interference from either side, at least for now. Later on, when the healing process is further along, you and she can start to repair your relationship. Everything is too chaotic at the moment, feelings too raw, for proper communication."

Verna, smoking, tapping her ashes into the plastic bowl, nodded as her doctor made these points, then, when he finished, she shook her head vigorously. "No."

He said sternly: "Verna."

"No! I want to be *with* her. Now!"

"Eventually you can be with her all you want, but wait awhile."

"Now!" she cried.

"Under arrest?" Tom's voice rose in the conference room. "What do you mean I'm under arrest? Under arrest for what?"

"Sexually molesting a minor, for one thing," explained Deputy Malmquist, who remained seated beside him, attached to him now by handcuffs.

"You've got the wrong man. That was the husband before me. Harris Highsmith."

"Come on, Dr. Pearsall, let's get a move on."

"My wife was married twice before. Her second husband

had sex with her daughter when she was just a little girl. Whew, talk about perversion."

"Come on, Dr. Pearsall," the deputy repeated patiently as he rose to his feet. "Let's go downtown."

Tom remained in his chair. "There's such a thing as a statute of limitations, you know. Even if what you allege was true—are you out there, Dr. Pella? I want you to hear this."

The doctor put his head in.

"Even if it was true, it would be beyond the reach of the law. Verna is twenty-six. She hasn't been a minor for eight years."

"The statute of limitations can be waived in child-abuse cases," said the doctor.

Tom shot a burning look at him—hatred mixed with fear. "I don't believe you."

"Ask your lawyer."

"Verna will tell you anything to avoid blaming herself for her troubles. She'll tell you the whole world is screwing her. When she gets out of here, she'll probably tell people *you've* been screwing her." Tom covered his eyes for a moment. His inebriation, to his profound regret, was evaporating. When he looked up again, he found the doctor gone from the doorway. He raised his voice. "Hear that, Dr. Pella? We're all in the same boat." He sighed and said to the deputy, "Verna's got a horny imagination."

"We've got a drug charge against you, too," said Malmquist.

Astonishment and fear: "What the hell are you talking about?"

"Possession of controlled substances."

"Who, me?"

"In your garage."

"That's medicine. I'm a doctor, for Chrissake."

"Drugs and pot. Come on." The deputy tugged Tom to his feet.

"The pot belongs to my wife."

The deputy led his prisoner out into the dayroom, where a group of teenagers was coming through the double doors wearing their coats and caps. They were carrying food and drink from the Dairy Queen. They removed their wraps and settled quietly at tables to eat.

Tom said to Malmquist, "I've got to take a leak."

"Then so do I, I guess."

Crossing the dayroom with Deputy Malmquist at his side, his back pain momentarily forgotten in his extreme need to relieve himself, Tom noticed Libby and Verna sitting at one of the tables. He was struck by the beaten-down slouch of Libby's shoulders in contrast to Verna's upright posture. He'd never seen the two of them positioned quite this way before, the daughter looking like the stronger of the two, the more determined, the more alert and resilient, while her mother seemed to be drooping, shrinking, aging moment by moment. He'd never seen Verna's arm around her mother before. The sight made him feel empty. He was cut off from both of them now. He felt a sudden and urgent desire to go over and sit with them. He needed them.

Entering the lavatory, he turned and snapped at the deputy, "Chrissake, can't a man even piss in private?"

39

Frank, sitting in the waiting area off the lobby, had been groping for bits of wisdom to offer Libby and coming up empty. She would need direction across terrain Frank had never explored, had scarcely known existed. Dear God, does one continue to live with one's husband after a horror like this comes to light? Surely not. But where does one go? And does one take one's daughter along (if one's daughter is willing to go), or does one kick the daughter out of one's life? Or maybe one *does* stay with the husband. Maybe, if one is as man-dependent as Libby, one somehow retrenches and carries on.

Frank had chosen a chair near the information desk, having alerted the woman in charge that he was expecting a call from upstairs. He'd been sitting there for twenty minutes when a voice called to him, "Well, if it isn't my weekend pastor. What's up, Frank?" Gene DeSmet, smiling his toothy smile and removing his overcoat, was advancing upon him. "What brings you to town, Frank, another parishioner laid low? Don't tell me Loving Kindness had a relapse."

Getting to his feet, Frank, said, "I'm seeing Libby's daughter in Hope."

"Why not come back to the clergy lounge? There's coffee and rolls."

"No thanks, I'll be called upstairs any minute."

The boy-priest's smile turned soft and sappy—pastoral concern. "What's the kid's trouble, Frank? Is it drugs?"

Frank shook his head. "A mood disorder."

The smile was replaced by an analytical squint. "Inherited from Tom, do you suppose?"

"Tom's not her father."

"Oh?"

"Libby was married before, didn't you know?"

"No."

"Twice."

A pained and pensive look came over DeSmet, which allowed Frank to read his mind: My closest friends in Basswood and I knew next to nothing about them. "You mean Tom's her third?"

"Yes."

"Who was the girl's father?"

"His name is Jessen. You saw him with her that day in the cafeteria."

Disbelief: "That man was married to Libby?"

"Her first husband."

"But he looked like a farmer."

"That's what he is."

"You're kidding."

"They weren't married long."

"What about the second one? What was he?"

"A businessman."

They stood looking across the lobby at a group of slick-haired teenagers who had come from swimming and were waiting for an elevator.

"Farmer, businessman, doctor," mused DeSmet. "At least she worked her way up."

At that moment an elevator opened and Dr. Tom Pearsall, moving stiffly and listing to his left, emerged side by side with the sheriff's deputy.

"What in God's name . . . ?" DeSmet exclaimed when he saw that they were linked by handcuffs.

Frank was summoned to the phone.

Watching through the double doors, Libby saw Frank step off the elevator along with a crowd of wet-haired teenagers. Swimming had made the youngsters energetic. Prancing into the room, they shouted and squealed. Their high spirits infected the group that had returned from the Dairy Queen, some of whom got to their feet and shimmied and sang. In the midst of this noisy nonsense, Libby embraced Frank. She clung to him desperately, feeling love pouring out of her heart and into his. All of her love. Every last bit of it, including the portion that until this afternoon had belonged to Tom. Frank would know what to do. Frank would help her get settled somewhere apart from Tom. Frank would look after her always. Frank would love her till the day she died. This was inevitable, she knew, because the day Frank didn't love her she would die.

Verna came over and embraced them both.

Frank would help her look after Verna. He would help Verna recover and get started on a career. It would be the three of them then—Frank, Libby, Verna—the way it should have been to start with. She'd known it decades ago. She'd been on the right track when she drove to the seminary and tried to convince Frank that the religious life was not the only avenue to happiness.

They broke apart, stepped back from one another. She studied Frank. She said, "You knew."

He nodded. "On Saturday."

"I'm finished with Tom," said Libby, wiping the corner of her eye with the heel of her hand.

"I'm sorry." Frank said. "I'm not surprised."

Libby felt sublimely content for a few seconds, and then suddenly she was angry. It was anger at Tom, she assumed, but when she linked arms with Frank and faced Verna, she realized that she was mad as hell at her daughter.

"Verna," she barked with fire in her eye.

"Mmmm?" Verna was lighting a cigarette.

"Are *you* finished with Tom?"

Verna seemed unperturbed by the question. She lifted her chin and blew smoke at the ceiling. She said quietly, "Jesus, yes."

Libby clutched her daughter's wrist, raised her voice. "Say it!"

Irritably: "I said yes."

"Tell me you're finished with Tom. Say it in those words: 'I'm finished with Tom.'"

"I am. I'm finished with that rat."

Libby wailed hysterically, "Say it! Say his name. Say, 'I'm finished with Tom.'"

"I am," screamed Verna, wrenching her arm from her mother's grasp. "I'm finished with Tom!"

Most of the youngsters in the dayroom were silenced by this exchange. They turned and watched, not with avid interest, it seemed, but lazily, their eyes oddly passive as if shouting matches were commonplace in Hope and a bit boring.

Nor was there any urgency in Roberta Brink's manner when she came over and gently lifted one of Libby's hands to lead her away.

Libby withdrew the hand and embraced Frank. She laid her face against his chest.

"We'll finish the interview in Dr. Pella's office," said the nurse, and added, looking at Frank, "You may join us."

Sitting in his brown, bookless office, the three of them listened as Dr. Pella, with support from Nurse Brink, ran through their plan for detaining Verna.

Verna once again voiced her refusal. Libby, when asked her opinion, shook her head and wept. Frank, not asked for an opinion, kept his mouth shut and speculated that the doctor's plan, while sensible and perhaps the healthiest alternative, was doomed to fail. Verna wanted out immediately, wanted to be her mother's daughter once again, wanted to atone somehow for being Tom's sex partner. Let Dr. Pella advise till he was blue in the face, there was no keeping these two women apart right now. They might very well fly apart within days, thought Frank, but the strongest force in this room at the moment was Verna's willfulness, and she would get what she wanted.

"I can't live with Tom anymore," said Libby. Her voice was toneless, despairing.

"We'll find a place," Verna told her.

"Well, you won't find it tonight," said the doctor. "That's another reason Verna should sit tight. Give yourselves time to relocate."

"We can check into a motel," said Verna.

The doctor sneered. "Don't be silly."

Verna flared at him: "What's silly about it? Is she supposed to go home with that rat and pretend nothing's wrong?"

"I've got to go home," droned Libby. "All my things."

"We'll go get your things," said Verna.

"There's truckloads."

"I mean just the things you need."

Energy and heat returned to Libby's voice: "I can't go around living in motels." Then softly: "Verna, just stay here long enough for me to find us a place."

"Not another minute. You can't live in a madhouse without going mad yourself."

"Just a day or two. So I can go home and pack up my things and look for a place."

"Go home with Tom?"

"Just for a day or two."

"Go home with that rat?"

"He may or he may not be home," said Dr. Pella, "and this brings us to the legalities." He lifted a page of handwritten notes off his desk. "Your husband is on his way to the sheriff's office to be charged with criminal sexual conduct with a minor and possession with intent to sell controlled substances. The county attorney says the seven-year statute of limitations might very well not apply to the sex charges because the crime didn't come to light until now. It's assumed in cases like this that coercion was exerted on the victim to keep her from reporting the crime. Now, of course, charges imply a trial, depending how your husband pleads and whether it can be settled out of court, and a trial means your daughter must testify—not a happy prospect, going

public with your sex life—but Verna and I have talked it over
and—"

"Oh, God," moaned Libby. Her moan went straight to
Frank's heart. He longed for the meeting to be over.

The doctor addressed Libby. "We've talked it over and she's
willing to do it, Mrs. Pearsall. She understands—you as a nurse
understand—that her testimony, her public acknowledgment,
will be an important step in her recovery." He folded the page
of handwritten notes and put it into a drawer. "Now, taking the
next few days into account, Mrs. Pearsall, would you feel safer
if your husband was held in custody until you left home?"

"No, Tom's not dangerous. Not in that way."

"He wouldn't hurt you?"

"No more than he already has."

"You see, he's likely to be released on bail or possibly on his
own recognizance, but if he poses a danger to you, I'm sure a
court order can be arranged to keep him at a distance from you,
at least for a few days."

"You mustn't put him in jail."

"You're sure."

"You mustn't." Libby's father had been in jail more than
once. As a girl she had grown accustomed to his brutality but
not to his being in jail. She'd been horrified, watching the police
take him away.

"I'm not staying here and I'm not going to Basswood," said
Verna. "I'm checking into a motel."

"No," said her mother.

"No," said Frank—his first spoken word since entering the
office. They all turned to look at him.

"Come home with me," he said. "Both of you come home
with me."

40

Mrs. Tatzig glanced out the kitchen window, saw a second pair of headlights follow the Oldsmobile into the driveway, and scurried into the living room to ask the monsignor if Father Healy was bringing somebody home for supper. "I'm low on coffee and there's only pudding for dessert."

Adrian Lawrence, his attention on the evening news, said, "Relax, Marcella."

"I like to be told when I've got company coming."

"I've never known you to prepare an inadequate meal, Marcella."

"There's always a first time."

The back door opened—she felt the draft on her ankles—and Frank came in lugging a large suitcase and calling, "Marcella, we have visitors." He was followed through the kitchen and into the living room by the reservation nurse and a young woman Mrs. Tatzig assumed was the daughter she'd heard so much about—the mental case. She saw the resemblance in their dark eyes and the way they carried themselves. Mrs. Pearsall looked washed out, whipped. The young one, pale and wide-eyed, was smoking a cigarette. Two suitcases and a cardboard box were deposited at the base of the stairway and Frank introduced the young one as Verna. Her hair was light, the color of hay, and needed trimming—a pageboy cut grown shaggy. The monsignor, whose unfailing chivalry struck Mrs. Tatzig as ridiculous, stood up and held the hands of both women simultaneously, assuring them that nothing in the world made him happier than receiving guests.

"And Marcella Tatzig, our housekeeper," said Frank.

Mrs. Tatzig came forward, hoping the young one understood that in a Catholic rectory the term "housekeeper" stood for a great deal more than dusting. "Pleasure, I'm sure," she said without pleasure, nodding curtly at Verna. And then, turning to Libby, she softened, for she saw the distress in the poor woman's red-rimmed eyes, saw the knotted brow, saw the exertion smiling required of her. She sensed lines of tension running between the two women. Even Father Healy was looking a little strained. Something peculiar was going on.

Frank said, "These two friends of mine have suddenly found themselves homeless."

The monsignor was visibly affected by this announcement. He renewed his grip on the women's forearms and shook his head in commiseration, declaring, "You both have a home here at St. Ann's as long as you need it."

Mrs. Tatzig made the room assignments and helped carry the luggage upstairs. She gave Libby the larger guest room with the sunny exposure and the view of the street (DeSmet wouldn't be needing it until Saturday) and she showed the daughter into the smaller room at the back of the house. The daughter was the gushy type, breathy and high-strung—running (Mrs. Tatzig assumed) on some high-octane medicine. She enthused over the brass bed, the patchwork quilt, and the small green and yellow flowers in the wallpaper. Genuine or chemically induced, this praise went straight to Mrs. Tatzig's heart. A decade ago she'd furnished and chosen the wallpaper in both guest rooms and had never once been told how nice they looked, which was one of the problems in running a house for men. Men, she'd complained to her sister again and again, didn't know an oak wardrobe from a two-hole privy.

The luggage, as it turned out, belonged entirely to the daughter, and Mrs. Tatzig went down to her own room behind the kitchen to collect things for Mrs. Pearsall, who hadn't brought so much as a toothbrush. What was up? Had her house burned down? Was she fleeing a deranged husband?

She served supper (spaghetti and meat sauce) in the dining room on her second-best china (not on the Haviland kept in reserve for bishops) and was rewarded with the deliciously shocking truth: Dr. Pearsall was in jail. Mrs. Pearsall stopped eating after two mouthfuls. The daughter ate like a horse.

Lordy, how frustrating to wait for a chance to phone her sister. She couldn't very well interrupt supper to do it, and afterward Frank and the two women lingered so long at the table within earshot of the kitchen phone that she finally went upstairs and used the phone in the monsignor's bedroom. (The monsignor had left the table to catch the final episode of Billy Graham's Crusade in London.)

Her sister said she wasn't surprised. You heard things, she said. The doctor, you heard, had several times been seen plastered in the Linden Falls Municipal Bar and Lounge, and last summer he'd insulted a cashier at the grocer's who'd told him he couldn't shop barefoot. Well, put that together with the fact that he came from Chicago, and you wondered why he wasn't in the hoosegow long before this. What was the charge?

Mrs. Tatzig sadly had to admit she didn't know, but she'd try to find out.

"Drunk driving's my guess," said her sister.

Mrs. Tatzig returned to the dining room and found Father Healy and the two women still at the table. Clearing away the dishes, she learned that they were planning Mrs. Pearsall's future. She started the dishwasher and hurried back upstairs to the phone.

"It's something worse than drunk driving," she said to her sister. "They're talking like their marriage is on the rocks. They're talking about moving the missus to Berrington so she can be near her daughter. She'll work at the Berrington Hospital."

"Maybe malpractice, do you suppose?"

"Malpractice? What practice? He hasn't got hardly any practice. I was thinking more along the lines of a crime of passion."

"Passion!" exclaimed Charlotte Johnson. "I've seen him. He's a shrimp."

"So?"

"You can't get passion out of a shrimp."

"It'll be in the Berrington paper tomorrow. Who do we know that gets it?"

"The Sparkmans get it."

"Call the Sparkmans."

Later, in the front bedroom, Libby slipped Mrs. Tatzig's voluminous nightgown over her head and stood at the window, feeling sick. She watched a man pass briskly along the sidewalk, led by a small dog on a leash. A soft shower of snow was falling into the circles of light under the lampposts. She felt shaky. She felt her heart pounding in her ears. She had come upstairs feeling exhausted, leaving Verna with the monsignor in front of the TV, but now she was wide awake. She felt an aimless sort of urgency, a compulsion to accomplish certain things before she lay down to rest, but she didn't know what those things might be. Talk with Frank? With Verna? Commit suicide? Scream and weep? Phone Tom?

Phone Tom, that was it. She must talk to Tom immediately and tell him their marriage was ended. She hadn't told him at the hospital. He'd been led away by the deputy before she'd composed herself. She'd tell him now. He'd argue, but she'd be adamant. She was only dissolving a union he had already destroyed.

She put on the brown terrycloth robe Mrs. Tatzig had laid out for her. This, like the nightgown, was much too large, a garment perhaps left behind by some visiting clergyman, judging by the laundered shreds of pipe tobacco in the pockets. She put on Frank's large slippers and went down the hall to his room. She rapped lightly.

"Yes?"

"Frank, where can I use a phone?"

"Just a second."

When he opened the door, she had to smile, seeing him in a robe identical to her own. She tugged at the lapel. "The bishop issues these?"

"The housekeeper. They were on sale at K-Mart."

"Did I wake you?"

"No, I was reading."

"Frank, I have to call Tom."

"Help yourself." Edging out of the room, he pointed to the phone on his bedside table.

"You don't have to leave."

But he did.

Sitting on the narrow bed with the phone on her lap, she studied the austere room. Two mismatched rugs. A bookcase and a chest of drawers. The walls white and unadorned, except for a small crucifix over the head of the bed. On the bedside table were periodicals she'd never heard of. *The Tablet. Commonweal. National Catholic Reporter. The Sporting News.* So this was where he took her midnight phone calls. Here's where he lay, saying reassuring things to her in the dark. The room had a calming effect on her. It seemed to speak to her in Frank's voice. It said *Simplify.* It said *Relax.* It said *Rest.* She ought to live in a room as plain as this. She would, she resolved, in Berrington.

She dialed information and asked for the number of the Berrington County Jail. She found a pen in the drawer of the bedside table and jotted it down on the cover of *The Tablet.* She took a few moments to collect herself. Then she placed the call. She was put through to her husband without delay.

"Tom, I'm calling to see if you need anything."

"Libby, for Chrissake, why would a wife have to ask what I need? I need underwear, socks, shirts, my electric razor, and I might need money for bail. I also need a drink very badly, but I suppose there's no way you can smuggle it in. I know you don't believe Verna—she's a mental case, for Chrissake—but do you realize the trouble I'm in if the doctor and the nurses and the cops and the judge believe her? And besides that, they've got me mixed up with somebody else. They're saying I'm a drug peddler. I've got a lawyer named O'Brien. He's calling some guy in Minneapolis to arrange for the bond, if there is one. We don't know what the deal is because the judge is out ice fishing. Can you believe it, Libby? There's not a single bail bondsman in this county and the only judge within two hundred miles is out ice fishing while I sit here in this dirty slammer reading dirty magazines. Libby, listen to me, when this is over, you and I are getting the hell out of Minnesota and never coming back. We're kissing the sticks good-bye."

She took a deep breath and said, "I'm finished with you, Tom."

"O'Brien says I'll be out of here within forty-eight hours, and then in a few days there'll be a hearing, and if there's a trial, it'll be later in the spring. O'Brien's worried it might come to trial. He says the circuit judge scheduled to hear cases this spring is prejudiced against the kind of thing Verna's accusing me of. He says a lot depends on who handles the hearing. He says if we get the local judge for that, we're probably in the clear."

"Tom, did you hear me?"

"What I'm saying is this could be serious, Libby. You've got to talk to Verna. She's framing me, for Chrissake, and she doesn't realize how serious it is."

She took another deep breath and said again, "I'm finished with you, Tom."

There was a long silence before he replied, softly, "Libby, don't be stupid."

"It's over, Tom."

"You need me, Libby."

She said nothing.

"Libby, don't be stupid."

She said nothing.

"For Chrissake!" he shouted. "Don't do anything childish till we talk it over."

She said nothing.

"You hear me, Libby? You need me."

She hung up. She didn't get up to leave. She remained on the bed, waiting for Frank to return. Though she'd been in his company for the past six hours, they'd had no private moments. It wasn't talk she needed. It was his presence at her side. His touch. She sat with her eyes on the door, willing it to open, willing him to come in and sit down and hold her.

But he didn't come in. She went into the hallway and called his name softly and got no response. At the end of the hallway the door to her room was closed. Had she closed it? Was he in there? Yes, of course, he'd gone there to wait. She'd find him in the rocking chair by the window. He'd stand and hold her in his arms for a few minutes. Words wouldn't be necessary. Just to be held. Just to feel the old, everlasting bond renewed.

She hurried into her room and found it empty. Her agitation returned. Her nausea. Her pounding heart. She stood at the window, waiting for Frank's footsteps in the hallway. The falling snow formed an amber nimbus around the streetlights. The man with the small dog hurried past in the opposite direction, the dog's back and the hood and shoulders of the man's parka white with snow.

Minutes passed. Her nausea went away, but not her agitation. She regretted coming here for the night. She felt trapped. If she were at home, she could busy herself. She could begin packing. She could go to her kitchen and make herself a cup of something hot. She could phone Frank at midnight. She shouldn't have allowed herself to be confined to this room in this house of strangers. There were moments here when even Frank seemed a stranger. Why had he left her alone in his room and not returned to comfort her? She knew why. By coming here—never mind his invitation—she'd advanced too far into his life. She must be careful with Frank. He was skittish and she must not frighten him. If he forsook her, she would die.

And it was no less a house of strangers for Verna's being here. Who was Verna but a stranger? For years now, it hadn't been clear to Libby how she should feel about her daughter. Should she pity her as the victim she was, the lifelong victim she'd been? Should she be tough with her, demanding that she reform? Should she be indifferent and wait for her to straighten out on her own?

Did she love her? Libby, watching the snowfall thicken for a time and then diminish again, sorted through her feelings. At the moment she wasn't feeling pity and she wasn't feeling love.

She wasn't inclined to be tough and demanding, nor could she call up the patience or strength or whatever it took to be indifferent. Far from indifferent, in fact, was the emotion building up in her breast and causing her heart to beat in her ears. What she was feeling was fury.

Having left Libby in his room, Frank had gone downstairs and stood for a minute watching a TV show that Marcella, Adrian, and Verna seemed to be enjoying. Then he'd gone into his office, where he opened a ledger and became absorbed in the year-end statistics he'd been preparing to send to the chancery office. The columns of figures refreshed him. They formed a colonnade that seemed to support his spirit, holding it high above the unrelenting misery of the afternoon and evening. Throughout his teaching career, mathematical problems had been Frank's diversion, indeed his distraction, his refuge from the less manageable problems that sometimes cropped up in the lives of the adolescents in his care; and figures diverted him now from the haunting sight of Libby, haggard and bereft, at his bedroom door. He'd wanted to take her in his arms and kiss her sad eyes.

St. Ann's: new parishioners down from the year before; baptisms down slightly; confessions and counseling sessions up; weddings, deaths, and income virtually the same. At Our Lady's in Basswood almost everything was down. Only death was on the rise. Frank resolved to visit the bishop soon and try to forestall his plan to lock up Our Lady's. He'd point out to the bishop that confessions, counseling sessions, and income had been rising gradually since Christmas. The bishop, in turn, would point out that Frank was spreading himself too thin now that the monsignor was out of commission. He'd probably claim that Father DeSmet could no longer be spared for weekend duty. Frank would plead for time. He'd present a plan. He'd enumerate certain goals for Basswood, certain numbers to be achieved by the end of the year. He drew a tablet from a drawer and began to make a list of these goals.

The late show ended and the party in the living room broke up. Adrian put his head in the office and said good night. So did

Verna. She looked tired, but happy. She thanked Frank. Stepping over to his chair, she gave his head a tight little hug and caught sight of his bare feet. She laughed and said they were the longest, thinnest feet she'd ever seen. She called the monsignor back to have a look.

Adrian agreed. "They look like skis."

"Stork feet," said Verna. "Storks have feet like that."

"You two go to bed," said Frank.

"So do cranes," said Adrian, brimming with chuckles and smiles. "You see feet like that in zoos."

"Stork feet," Verna repeated, laughing.

Covering his right foot with his left, Frank said, "You've never seen a stork, now go to bed."

"Stork feet," she repeated, leading Adrian out of the room.

Frank laughed silently, listening to their chatter up the stairs:

"Blue herons too," said Adrian. "Long, ugly talons."

"Storks and cranes and herons," Verna said.

"All aquatic birds," said Adrian, "but herons especially. Feet like that are good for clutching fish."

Verna's laughter died away and the house fell silent. The mantel clock marked midnight with its blunt, deliberate tone.

Then a shriek sounded from upstairs. Frank rushed into the living room and heard another scream, followed by a despairing moan. He raced up the stairs. Voices came from Verna's room. He advanced down the hallway, listening. Then, catching the words, he stopped.

Libby's voice, raised in anger: "But my *husband*!"

Verna's, hysterical: "My *stepfather*, don't forget! My fucking rotten stepfather!"

"But your mother's husband! You're a whore! You've got the instincts of a whore!"

A scream: "Get out, get out of my room!"

"Never thinking of *me*. How I'd feel. Never in your life paying any attention to me. Always hurting me. Over and over, hurting me."

"Get out!"

"Never on my side. As far back as I can remember, always against me."

"As far back as Harris Highsmith, right? I was seven and he taught me how to screw, right?"

"I'm talking about Tom. My husband Tom. What we had together. You've destroyed it."

"What you had together? You had nothing together. Your marriage was shit and you know it."

"You made it shit."

"All your marriages have been shit."

Libby's voice rose to its highest, shrillest note: "Shut up!"

"How do you find men like that? How do you manage to find shitheads like that, one after another, and bring them into my life?"

Libby's voice fell: "Oh, Verna." A hoarse whisper: "Oh, Verna . . ."

Her daughter, too, lowered her voice: "It's my life, too, you know, not just yours."

The quiet sounds of sobbing. The blowing of noses.

Frank pushed the monsignor's door open, imagining that anyone leading a life as unnaturally serene as Adrian's must be terrified, or at least mystified, by the shouts and screams. But the room was dark and Adrian appeared to be sleeping. How could he possibly have slept through the uproar? Frank stepped closer to make sure the old man wasn't dead. No, he was peacefully asleep, his breath softly whistling in his nose.

He left the room and found Mrs. Tatzig standing at the head of the stairs in her brown terrycloth robe. "What's going on?"

"A family spat," Frank told her, gesturing for her to go back downstairs.

"Woke me up."

"It's over," he said, following her down. "They're going through a hard time."

"It sounded like bloody murder."

"They got it out of their systems. It'll be quiet now."

"You think they'd like some Ovaltine?"

"No, let's wait and see."

"I never heard such a racket."

"It's over, Marcella."

"I think I'll have some Ovaltine. Cup of Ovaltine and I'm out like a light. Aren't you going to bed?"

"I want to finish up some office work."

"Want a cup of Ovaltine?"

"Sure."

She brought it to him in the office.

"Thanks, Marcella."

She raised her eyes to the ceiling. "I didn't catch the words up there."

"Well . . ." Sitting back in his chair and blowing into his hot cup, Frank weighed his options. He knew the Ovaltine was a bribe and that by satisfying Mrs. Tatzig's curiosity he would take a very large step toward winning her friendship. And didn't she deserve to know? After all, weren't the two women her guests as well as his, eating her meals, residing in her rooms, disturbing her sleep? And within twenty-four hours wouldn't the Berrington paper be out with the facts? And yet to tell her seemed a betrayal of Libby and Verna.

"Such a racket, screeching and shouting," she said, lowering herself into the chair facing the desk. "Would you like something with that? A cookie?"

"No," he said, "but bring your cup in, Marcella. Let's have a little talk."

She sprang out of her chair, bustled into the kitchen, and returned with her cup and a plate of Oreos.

"They've both been through a terrible day," he told her. "They've watched Dr. Pearsall be led off to jail. They were attending Verna's discharge conference at the hospital when a deputy sheriff arrested him and actually led him away in handcuffs."

Mrs. Tatzig sat forward in her chair. "No."

"The Indian Health Center was searched and drugs were found. He's suspected of dealing."

"Aaah," she sighed with satisfaction, like someone slaking a thirst.

"It may be a mistake. He claims it was medicine for his practice."

She sat farther forward and said confidentially, "It wasn't medicine."

"How do you know, Marcella?"

"You hear things."

"What things?"

"Things."

"You've heard he's a drug dealer?"

"No, but he's a drunk and he insulted a checker at Sammy's Food. It all goes together."

Frank watched her sit back in her chair and sip from her cup, looking relaxed, gratified, absorbed by the information. Good, he thought—I don't intend to get into Tom's sexual misconduct.

But after a few moments her inquiring expression returned and she sat forward again. She scrutinized him closely and said, "What else?"

What did she know? How did she know it? Some of the shouting upstairs—the exchange about sex—must have been intelligible in her room below.

"You're right, Marcella, there is more, but I can't tell you."

She nodded and put up her hand to silence him. It was a condoning, sympathetic gesture. It said, You've been more than generous, I don't want to press you.

They heard footsteps upstairs—Libby returning to her room.

Mrs. Tatzig pointed to the page of scribbled numbers on the desk. "Is that the household budget?"

"No, some figures on the Basswood church."

She brought a look of distaste to her face. "Lost cause, no?"

"I hope not, Marcella. I want to keep it open."

"Why?"

"There are about fifty people who seem nourished by it."

"Indians." If she'd said this with the sour expression still on her face, Frank might have reproved her, but she'd had the good sense to remove it and replace it with an impassive, far-off, long-suffering look that reminded him of the typical Ojibway expression he faced each Sunday in Our Lady's Church. And then— all of a sudden—he understood that her wearing the facial expression of an Indian was more than a coincidence. She *was* an Indian—or at least one of her ancestors had been. Those small black eyes of hers with their vaguely Asian aspect, eyes that he'd always assumed came down to her from some Lapp or Mongol far back in her family tree, were Indian eyes. They were actually her most striking feature, a distinctive gift from the Ojibway nation, but a gift she despised and worked incessantly, with cosmetics and bombast, to conceal.

"I was going to say—the household budget needs hiking up. You bought groceries lately?" she asked.

"No."

"Prices out of sight."

"I'll see what I can do."

"I'm a careful shopper. I don't want you to think I splurge."

"I know you don't, Marcella. Let me know how much more you need and I'll find it somehow."

She sipped from her cup and ate a cookie. Frank was struck by how relieved she looked, as though she had dreaded asking him for money. Was he that hard to talk to? Had he unwittingly appeared unapproachable all these weeks? Boy and man, had he lived too long alone to learn common household civility, and had Mrs. Tatzig's coolness been simply a reflection of his own? It was high time he treated her like the ally she was.

"We have our hands full upstairs, Marcella, and I don't mean just the two women."

Her nod told him she understood.

"His two spells," he said. "I worry about him."

"Another one today," she told him. "He talked about going to a family reunion."

"His doctor says it's the arteries to his brain."

"He talked about seeing his cousins at the reunion. They promised him a ride on their toboggan."

They finished their Ovaltine in silence. Then Mrs. Tatzig asked in a tone Frank hadn't heard her use before—it was soft and chummy—"Why do you worry about him, Father?"

"Why? It's obvious, isn't it? He's losing his mind."

"No, he's not. He's just going into different *parts* of his mind."

"Well, I suppose that's one way to look at it."

"And he always comes out of it."

"But maybe someday he won't."

"So what?" This sounded callous, but he saw no callousness

in her eyes. She sat there looking serene and sleepy. He also saw that without face powder her skin was coppery. She continued: "There's worse ways to get old than rummaging around in your memories."

"But they aren't memories, Marcella, they're hallucinations."

"Call them memories, you'll feel better."

She stood, tightened the belt of her robe, and gathered up the plate and the cups.

"Thanks, Marcella. That hit the spot."

"My husband was high-strung, too. Ovaltine settled him down."

"You think of me as high-strung, do you?"

She ignored his question. She went to the door and turned to look at him. "Our problem isn't upstairs, you know."

"Oh?" He was curious—her tone was ominous.

"Our problem is Eunice Pfeiffer. She was on the phone with him again today."

"She'll never budge him, Marcella. She'll give up eventually."

"Maybe." She didn't look convinced. She looked tired. She yawned. "Well, I just wanted you to know we might have a problem there."

"Good night, Marcella." He was pleased by her phrasing— *we* might have a problem. They were allies.

"If I hear another ruckus upstairs, I'll take up some Ovaltine."

In the dim light of dawn Verna woke to find her mother sitting on her bed. She was dressed. She had her coat on. She was smoothing Verna's hair and asking, "Can we start over? Can we forget last night and start over?"

Verna struggled to sit up, struggled to speak. The process of waking up, due to her new medicine, was like climbing out of a well. It was hard to hold her eyes open, to lift her head. She took her mother's ice-cold hand and pressed it against her forehead. "Have you been outside?"

"To start the car. I'm going to Basswood and start packing. Will you be all right?"

"What time is it?"

"Seven-thirty."

Verna sank to her pillow.

"Can we put last night behind us, Verna?"

"Last night . . .?"

"Our fight. I'm sorry."

"Oh, that."

"We can start over?"

"Sure, if I can just sleep a little longer." She rolled over and buried her face.

"I'll talk to you later."

"Sure." She felt her mother rise from the bed, heard her cross the room, and was asleep before the door closed.

Frank, emerging from his room in his robe, saw Libby's door open, saw her sitting in the rocking chair with her coat on. She beckoned. He stood in the doorway.

"Where are you going?"

"I'm leaving, Frank. I'm going to start packing and house hunting."

"Now? Stay for breakfast at least."

"I can't. I'm so embarrassed about last night, I can't face your housemates."

"Forget it."

"Our screaming must have sounded horrible."

"Bloodcurdling, actually."

She lowered her eyes in chagrin.

"Forget it, Libby. Adrian slept through it, and Marcella was ready to bring you Ovaltine." He looked at his watch. "Wait an hour. I'll be back from Mass and we'll talk."

"No, my car is running. I can't sit still another minute."

He crossed the room to the window. Narrow streaks of cloud spanned the rosy sky.

"Will you come back?" he asked.

Her swift answer—"No"—made him turn and look at her.

"I don't belong here," she explained. "I don't like throwing my-self on your mercy."

He made a deprecating gesture, which she ignored.

"God knows you're my one and only support, but I don't feel right living in your house. I have to get busy or I'll fold."

Below him he saw the heavily bundled Mr. and Mrs. Heul-skamp trudging through the snow to church. They were a vig-orous couple, retired from the hardware business, for whom daily Mass was the midpoint break in their four-mile walk at dawn.

"Which are you doing first," Frank asked, "packing or look-ing for an apartment?"

"I'll decide when I get in the car."

"Tell you what. After Mass I'm free till evening. I'll go to Berrington while you go to Basswood. I'll find some places for you to look at."

"Thank you," she said, rising and buttoning her coat.

"You're welcome," he said, shaking her hand.

Downstairs she thanked Mrs. Tatzig, who sent her off with a cup of coffee and a muffin.

41

After two nights in jail, Tom was released without posting bond so that he could return to his "noble and humanitarian work among the Native Americans." The phrasing was that of the circuit judge, who set the date for pretrial hearing. J. T. O'Brien, Tom's lawyer, speculated that the drug charges might not stick because the Upward brothers had found the stash without any authority to be snooping in the Health Center. Further, he advised Tom to maintain that the marijuana belonged to his wife; surely the county attorney couldn't prove otherwise. But the sex charges, said J. T. O'Brien vaguely, the sex charges were something else again.

Tom, hopeful and fearful by turns, returned to Basswood and became so lonely after Libby left that he called up Elaine LaBonte and asked why she wasn't coming in after school. Elaine, who had helped Libby pack her bags and move out, told him she'd had to quit her job because of play practice. But the truth was (as she said to Billy) she wouldn't go near that pervert for a million dollars.

Billy took Elaine out to his fish house after Mass on a Sunday morning in late February. They sped over the ice on his snowmobile, their faces covered with ski masks and helmet visors.

They built a roaring fire in the little stove, opened two holes in the ice, and they sat there—he on the wood box, she on a stool—gazing at their bobbers and comparing their impressions of the Pearsalls. Elaine said she missed Mrs. Pearsall, who was now working in the emergency room of the Berrington Hospital, and more than that she missed her job. "Just when my life was going right for a change," said Elaine.

Billy described for her the place where Verna was living, a halfway house called Hanson Manor. He'd been there with Father Healy. It was full of recoving people, he said.

"Recovering from what?" asked Elaine.

"Everything from narcotics to idiocy, from the looks of it. Retarded and addicted people all mixed up together. Verna hates it."

Meanwhile Libby, on the way home from her night shift in the emergency room, was leaning into the wind sweeping along Great Northern Avenue. Because of Sunday's limited bus schedule, she hadn't been deposited at her bus stop until 9:30 A.M., an hour and a half after her shift ended. Hurrying along with her nose buried in her red scarf, she promised herself that next Sunday, having received her first paycheck, she'd take a taxi. Or maybe by next Sunday the weather would improve and she could walk. She guessed the hospital wasn't much more than two miles away.

Or maybe she'd get Tom to buy her a car. Twice on the phone she'd asked him, but he changed the subject. She hadn't thought she'd need a car, at least not until she could afford one, but Berrington's one and only bus route, a modified figure eight lying east and west across the city, came nowhere near Hanson Manor on the north side. She'd been there only twice since Verna moved in, once with Frank and Billy Annunciation, the other time in a taxi. She wanted to see more of Hanson Manor in order to prove her first impressions wrong.

On both visits she'd had the feeling that Verna was misplaced in that huge remodeled wreck of a house. On the ground floor— the women's floor—she'd been introduced to a pair of severely retarded old ladies and a pregnant teenager in whose darting eyes you saw some raw and desperate form of psychosis. Among the men who drifted down from upstairs was one who gave off such clear signs of ill will that Libby cringed. He was a muscular, black-bearded young man wearing a lumberjack shirt with the sleeves torn off at the shoulder and black, high-heeled boots studded with silver swastikas. An evil coldness flowed from his eyes as he paused on his way to the TV lounge to regard Verna with undisguised lust, and when he turned the same look on Libby, she saw a fresh cut on his lip.

This cut he had acquired (Verna told her) in a fistfight that had broken out in group therapy. Group therapy was held three times a week in the basement, conducted by the house counselor, Mr. Trygseth. Mr. Trygseth was a meek-looking chain-smoker whom Verna claimed was ineffectual and ignored by all the residents except the retarded old ladies, in whom he inspired adoration. Throughout his shift the two old ladies followed Mr. Trygseth around the house at a little distance, smiling sublimely, and when he was off duty, they sulked.

A block from the bus stop, Libby followed a narrow driveway between a pair of small story-and-a-half houses, one yellow, the other blue. Her apartment was the upper portion of the blue house, a remodeled attic with four slope-ceilinged rooms. The traffic on Great Northern was noisy, her bedroom was never dark, and the outdoor steps leading up to her kitchen door were snow-packed and treacherous, but these had been the only decent quarters available on the bus line at the time Libby and Frank went looking. And the rooms were warm, thank God, warmer than the Health Center in Basswood. Suffering through this endless, incredibly cold winter, you came to a new understanding of warmth. You went hunting for warmth in drafty rooms. You went shopping for it like any staple, bringing home with your groceries a hot-water bottle and an electric space heater. Libby had made sure the heat was adequate before she signed the lease. She had asked the landlord to please open up the pipes and she had stood with Frank in the empty living room waiting for the radiators to heat up.

The next day she moved in. The move was orchestrated by

Frank, with the assistance of Caesar Pipe and his pickup and his grandson and Elaine LaBonte. They brought from Basswood the bare essentials—the bedroom set from the guest room, the table and three of the chairs from the kitchen, and enough furniture to make the small living room comfortable—leaving Tom with nearly everything else they had acquired in their twelve years of marriage. She would delay any fair and equal division of property until they divorced, which she was determined to do despite Tom's pleading. But not yet. She needed to feel stronger, less weepy, before she could face it. She needed to catch up on her sleep. Working nights, she was falling further behind every day.

Her insomnia had begun the first night she lived here. Pining for Frank, she lay awake until the orange neon light flooding her bedroom from across the street (NOONAN'S CAR WASH) was replaced by the gray light of dawn.

Having spent a night at St. Ann's rectory and three more nights at the Health Center, one of them with Tom fresh out of jail and drunk, she relished the privacy of her own place, yet she missed Frank acutely and was deeply disturbed that he'd come to visit her here only once, and then with Billy Annunciation tagging along. This afternoon, forsaking his shut-ins, he was coming again.

Unlocking the door at the top of the icy steps, she glanced at the thermometer beside the kitchen window—twenty or more below zero. Her forehead and temples ached with cold. She put her shoulder to the door, bumped it open, and stepped into the healing warmth of the kitchen and the sound of the ringing phone. She knew who it was before she answered.

"Libby."

"Yes?"

"I'm cold."

"Put on your long johns."

"I'm cold and lonesome."

"Put on your long johns, Tom, and go to the Homestead."

She heard her husband sigh. She slipped out of her coat, laid it across a kitchen chair, and backed up against the radiator. Looking down at her white uniform, she was relieved to see that she could work tonight's shift without washing it.

"You don't get what I mean, Libby. What I mean is, I'm in Basswood and you're in Berrington and it's all very absurd."

"I know. You told me yesterday."

"Absurd, Libby."

"And the day before yesterday."

"Absurd."

"Tom, are you drinking?"

"Not a drop, swear to God."

"You sound like you're bombed."

"I'm sad."

She felt a pang of sorrow, the urge to cry. She stuggled to suppress her tears, to be as tough with him as Dr. Pella recommended. She and Verna had been meeting with the doctor. *Be brief and blunt with your husband. Stop letting him manipulate you.* She took two or three quick, shallow breaths before saying, "Well, I'm sad, too, Tom, and there's nothing we can do for each other."

"You're wrong there, Libby. We need each other. All our years together—are we supposed to just forget them?"

All our years together—this wounded her every time. As Tom well knew. The one time he'd come to see her and she hadn't let him in, he'd stood at the top of the icy steps and said, "All our years together," and she'd burst into tears on the other side of the door.

He continued: "I don't want to be living alone in this house in the middle of nowhere and you don't want to be living alone in that house on the ugliest street in the Midwest. We're both cold and lonesome and sad and we want to be together."

She didn't reply. She was afraid she might weep out loud. Her tears were becoming a major worry. She cried several times a day.

"We do, Libby, we want to be together, we need each other. I've always known you needed me." He paused, then lowered his voice as though revealing a secret. "And now I'm realizing I need you as much as you need me." His voice cracked. Was he crying? "I didn't know that before, Libby. I didn't know how much I needed you."

She kept silent.

"You hear me Libby? We need each other."

"Tom." She swallowed the urge to sob. "I asked you not to call in the mornings."

"I know, were you sleeping?"

"No."

"Well, good. No harm done then."

But the harm *is* done, she thought, wiping her cheeks with a paper napkin. Never mind his message, the very sound of his voice harmed her whenever he called, and she was at her most vulnerable between work and sleep.

"Tom," she said resolutely.

"What."

"I don't need you."

"Yes, you do. You've never been one to know what you need."

"You're wrong, Tom. I know what I need."

"You do?"

"Yes."

"All right, what do you need?"

"A car."

42

Verna, encouraged by her doctor and her counselors to make amends, particularly to her mother, for what they called her "inappropriate behavior," phoned her father and asked him for a car. She used the pay phone in the front hallway of Hanson Manor.

"It's for my mother," she told him. "She's living in Berrington now—she's left Tom—and she needs a car."

"Who?" asked Vernon Jessen. "Who needs a car?"

"My mother. Libby. Your former wife."

"Who is this calling?"

"Your daughter."

She heard her father turn from the phone and say, "Here." After a few moments her grandmother came on the line and made a noise that sounded like "How?"

"I want to talk to him."

"He don't like the phone. Who's calling?"

"This is Verna."

"How?"

"Your granddaughter Verna."

The old lady's voice, fading, said, "It's Verna." Her father's voice was fainter yet: "Better hang up."

"Don't hang up, please. My mother needs a car for a while, till she can buy her own. You've got two cars and a pickup, I saw them last summer. Please let her use one."

The old lady's voice was suddenly loud and vigorous, too close to the mouthpiece: "We got no cars."

"You've got two cars. I saw them."

"Them you saw is on the blink."

"Maybe one of them can be fixed."

"Hang up now," ordered her father. "It's about taxes I never paid."

"It's about cars," said his mother.

Her father's voice advanced closer to the phone: "It's a trick to get to the taxes."

The dial tone sounded.

"Shit," said Verna, hanging up and sitting down on the steps of the wide oak staircase. Except for the hum of a hair dryer upstairs and the faint voice of a TV evangelist down the hall, the house was quiet. Sunday mornings in Hanson Manor were incredibly boring. Several of the residents had been taken to church and the rest were mostly still in bed. She opened her pocketbook and picked through the coin pouch. She sighed, finding too little change to call Basswood. She looked across the hallway at the open door of the staff office. Mr. Trygseth was on duty this morning. She saw him in there, standing in front of a cabinet examining medicine and other valuables. He was smoking. She disliked Mr. Trygseth, he was such a mousy little tease. She detested Hanson Manor, it was boring, it smelled funny, and it had rules like a prison.

Getting to her feet, she checked her green wool skirt for lint, straightened her dressy tweed jacket, and made sure her hair was in place before she crossed the hall and stood in the office doorway.

The small, myopic Mr. Trygseth squinted at her across the room. "Good morning, Verna," he said cheerily.

"Can I have a smoke?" she asked. The staff, to reduce Verna's intake of nicotine, had locked up her cigarettes.

He glanced at the clock on the mantel. "On the hour," he said. It was 10:40.

"Give me a break, Mr. Trygseth."

"Mel."

"Give me a break, Mel."

He gave her a dumb smile. "Why should I?"

"It's Sunday."

"So it's Sunday, so what?"

She gave him a dumb smile in return. "So give me a break." He was the only staff member you could talk into bending the rules—if you could put up with his stupid teasing.

He drew her carton of Marlboros from the top shelf of the cabinet and fished out a half-empty pack. "You're getting low."

"Let me see." Stepping into the office and around behind the desk where residents were not permitted, she took the carton from him. "Goddamn it, somebody's smoking my cigarettes."

"Not me," said Mr. Trygseth, losing his smile and looking a little frightened.

She put a cigarette to her lips and returned the others to him. She lit up, inhaled deeply, exhaled slowly. She said, "I need to use your phone."

Placing the carton back on the shelf, he said, "You look nice this morning, Verna."

"Thanks."

"Your mother taking you out?"

"Probably. Mel, I need to use your phone."

"Local?"

"More or less. Basswood."

"That's not local, you'll have to use the pay phone."

"I'm out of quarters."

"I can change a dollar."

"I haven't got a dollar."

"Sorry then." He closed and locked the cabinet.

She laid her hand gently on his neck. "Mel," she said sweetly, "be a sport."

He colored and smiled shyly. He said, "Rules." Besides telephone rules he might have been referring to the restriction against touching, but Verna knew he liked to be touched. She touched his ear and said, "Give me a break, Mel."

"Why should I?"

"I'll pay you back this afternoon." She gave his ear a rough little shake. "My mother's bringing me some money."

"Don't tell me you've spent your whole assistance check already."

"I'm not on assistance yet. It doesn't start till the first of the month." She let go of his ear and took another drag. "I'm living off my mother's charity."

Mr. Trygseth relented, stepping over to the desk. "I'll have to dial."

"Thanks, Mel." She rewarded him with a one-armed squeeze around the waist.

While all the rooms in the house were haunted by Libby, it was in the kitchen especially that Tom Pearsall was shot through with pangs of loneliness. She had taken the kitchen table and the clock off the wall and left him only one chair to sit on. Gone, too, was the easel with her intriguing and unfinished rendition in oil of the jackpines out the window. His table was now the typewriter stand from the reception room, and there he sat, eating toast, when the phone rang. He answered it hastily, expecting to hear his wife say she'd changed her mind and was coming home.

"Tom, it's Verna."

Her voice loosed in him a sudden and confusing mix of feelings—fear and anger as well as something soft that might have been remorse. "Yeah?" he said with trepidation, fear quickly becoming primary. Here was a woman capable of putting him away for one to seven years.

"Tom, my mother needs a car."

"Yeah, she told me."

"Well?"

"Well what? Does she think I'm made of money? Do you know what they pay me for running this clinic? Peanuts. They're paying me peanuts."

"You've got other income."

"I have not."

"You've got a car worth thirty thousand in the garage."

"Seventeen thousand. I had it appraised in Chicago."

"You used to say over thirty."

"Depreciation." Actually the appraisal came in at twenty-seven thousand and he had bundles of cash squirreled away in various rooms of the Health Center, but if there was ever a time for keeping secrets, it was now. If Libby divorced him and if his case came to trial, he stood to lose a bundle.

"Tom, that's still a lot of car."

"What are you saying—give it to Libby? How am I supposed to get around? It's a hell of a long wait between buses in Basswood."

"I'm saying sell it and buy two cheaper cars."

"Sell it? Who'd buy it? Nobody's got that kind of money up here."

"Go to a city. Minneapolis."

"Verna." He searched his mind for something tender to tell her. She had a harder shell than her mother, but it wasn't totally inpenetrable. He said, "All our years together, Verna." Maybe this would soften her. It always worked with her mother.

"What?"

"You might think I'm mad because you got me in trouble, but I'm not. I understand how it was with you."

"Jesus, I don't believe this. I'm the one supposed to be mad."

"Being medicated, I mean, and being under pressure from your counselors and your doctor. I guess I have to respect you for all the times you *didn't* say anything."

"Lay off me, Tom. I'm talking cars."

"And I'm talking relationships. I'm saying don't let everything go to hell before we're sure it's the right thing."

"Tom, are you going to get my mother a car or aren't you?"

"I will, if we can all make up and put this behind us."

"Tom, you're a rat."

The dial tone sounded.

He hung up and sat looking at the phone, sick to his stomach with fear. The hearing was scheduled for Wednesday. Tom's lawyer had said that if he didn't soften Libby and Verna, he was a dead duck. "We're up against the worst possible odds," Lawyer O'Brien had told him yesterday. "The county prosecutor's a fire-breathing crusader. We might still wiggle out of the drug charges, but sex is always a can of worms. The judge they've assigned to the hearing has a reputation for sending sex offenders to the slammer with instructions to throw away the key."

Sitting there staring at the phone, Tom decided to run.

Toad Majerus was behind the bar sorting through last night's beer bottles, culling the refundables from the throwaways, and Judge Bigelow was emptying a bag of money into the till when the phone rang. "Answer it," ordered the Judge, and the midget, stretching to his full height, tipped the receiver off its hook and caught it as it fell. He said, "Homestead," and paused. When he said, "Hi, Verna," the Judge snatched the receiver away from him and laughed into it. "Long time no see, baby. Where are you?"

Verna, in her softest voice: "I'm in Berrington, Puppy."

"Your dad says you're out of the hospital."

"He's not my dad."

"Your stepdad. He sure as hell got his tit in the wringer, didn't he?"

"Puppy, I need a car for a week or two."

"No, you don't. Just come back to Basswood and move in with your big sugar daddy, you won't have to go nowhere."

"It's for my mom, till she can make a down payment on a car of her own."

He laughed. "You asking me for my car?"

"It just sits there. You always drive the Bronco."

The Judge smiled sublimely. "Do you miss me, baby?"

"And how. I'm living in a houseful of weirdos."

"You better come home where you're appreciated. What do you say I come pick you up this afternoon? Just for a few days. When you leave, you can take the Datsun."

"Okay, Puppy. But just for one night."

"Two nights at least. I been missing you bad."

"What time can you come?"

"You name it, baby, I'll be there."

"Not here. Do you know Berrington?"

"Sure."

"There's a 7-Eleven on the north side, on Randolph near the freeway. You know where that is?"

"I can find it."

"Two-thirty. Just pull up outside."

"Two nights, baby, and you get the car."

"One night, Puppy."

"Two."

"We'll talk about it."

"It's nothing to do with taxes," Mrs. Jessen said, picking up a piece of her jigsaw puzzle and scanning the half-completed Grand Canyon on the kitchen table. "Her mother needs a car and I don't see why you can't get one of them cars out back running for her."

Vernon, slumped in his easy chair next to the refrigerator and watching a ten-year-old episode of "Dragnet," ignored her.

"It's little enough to do. We never did nothing for her all her life and now the time comes she needs something I say go ahead and do it." The piece didn't fit where she thought it should, even though the colors matched. Again and again she tried pressing it into the picture. She cleared her throat and added, "The Ford—there's still four tires on the Ford." Her voice was the raspy mumble of someone who seldom speaks.

"Verna's on government welfare," her son replied. "There's no way I'm getting mixed up with anybody connected with the government."

"No way to avoid it. The government's got everybody's number."

"Not mine, they ain't."

"They have, too. The minute you sign up for social security they got your number."

"Not if I burned my card."

"Burn your card—*you* haven't got your number, but they still got it."

"Like hell."

"In their files in Washington."

Vernon stood up. He was wearing faded overalls over the Nehru shirt his mother had bought him ten Christmases ago. He opened the wood-burning range and jabbed at the fire with a poker. He threw in a stick of wood and replaced the lid. He moved to the sink and looked out at the thermometer. Seventeen below. He looked beyond the thermometer at the old Ford and the old DeSoto resting up to their bumpers in snow. He went to the table and stood beside his mother's chair, looking down at the Grand Canyon with holes in it. This puzzle, his latest Christmas gift to her, was taking her forever because the muted browns and oranges and tans all ran together and her eyes were going bad. Last year's gift, the five-hundred-piece Duesenburg with its distinct lines and brighter colors, had been easier to put together. Her favorite was the puzzle of Holsteins in a pasture, which he'd given her eight or ten years ago. She got that one out nearly every spring and worked on it through the summer.

"If they got my number, how come they never come after me for taxes?"

"Because you never once paid in any," replied his mother. "Mrs. Essig says her husband paid in a little one year, and after that they never let him alone. She says the way to do is never once pay in any."

"Which I ain't."

Standing over her, he noticed that the tremor in his mother's head and hands was more pronounced than ever. There was a light and steady rapping on the table, produced by the knuckles of the hand holding the puzzle piece.

"She says it gets worse every year, what they take. And now she says the state of Minnesota's after him over and above what he pays in to Washington."

"It's all a big rip-off," said Vernon, picking up a dark piece and fitting it into the shadowy depths of the Canyon. His mother pressed it down smooth. The burning wood shifted noisily in the range. Wind rattled the outdoor thermometer. A cat ambled across the room and stood over its empty dish looking thoughtful.

"How come the Ford don't run?" asked his mother.

"Fuel pump."

"That all?"

"Far as I know." He found another piece that fit.

"Ought to get a fuel pump and turn it over to Verna."

"Can't afford it." He scanned the table, determined to find only one more piece and then go back and sit down. He limited himself to three at a time so the puzzle would last. She got restless without a puzzle-in-progress.

"What've we done for Verna all her life?"

"About what she deserved," muttered Vernon. "She left us, remember."

"Her mother left us. Verna was three."

"Well."

His third piece—blue—fit into the sky. He returned to the range and lifted the lid. He threw in two more sticks of wood and poked at them. He checked the thermometer again. Seventeen below. He returned to his chair and Joe Friday.

"It's time we did our part," droned his mother. "She's your daughter."

"My daughter ain't the one needing the car."

"Your daughter's the one asking."

43

Judge Bigelow wasn't surprised that Tom Pearsall should be his first customer when he opened at noon. Since his night in jail the doctor had spent more of his waking hours at the Homestead than he had at home.

"Judge, we gotta talk."

"We're talking, Doc." He drew the doctor a beer.

"Judge, you and I have come to a fork in the road. Let's go sit in a booth."

Tom carried his beer across the dance floor and chose a booth next to a window facing the lake. The Judge mixed himself a dark drink and followed, calling out, "Toad, mind the store."

The midget emerged from the shadows at the back of the dance floor, climbed up, and sat cross-legged on the bar.

"I got to leave in about ten minutes," said the Judge, sucking in his belly and squeezing himself into the booth. "Now what's this about a fork in the road?"

"Judge, I'm in trouble."

The Judge laughed. "You really went and got your tit in the wringer."

Tom looked out the window. Far out on the lake he saw

movement around Billy Annunciation's fish house—someone mounting a snowmobile. "It could be serious," he said.

The Judge continued to laugh silently, his head thrown back.

Tom faced him, trying to look stern. "You got to realize, when I'm in trouble, you're in trouble."

The fat man's laugh came to an abrupt halt. He eyed Tom with undisguised hate. "What in the hell are you talking about?"

"A plea bargain. They'll probably offer me a plea bargain."

"What in hell's a sex pervert like you got to bargain with?"

Tom seethed. "I can tell them who's been buying from me."

Emotion made the Judge's jowls quiver, made his voice come out dry and tight: "Is that a threat?"

Tom averted his face again. "It's a fact we've got to face. Cops take an interest in drugs." The snowmobile was moving swiftly toward the Homestead, carrying two people wearing black helmets.

The Judge said, "Listen, Doc," and then was silent for a time, cooling down. The snowmobile, trailing dirty little puffs of exhaust, came bouncing up the bumpy slope from the lake. The engine noise grew deafening and rattled the panes as it came to a stop under the window. When the driver turned off the ignition, the Judge continued. "You're going at this backward, Doc. It's never your customer the cops care about, it's your supplier."

Both figures stood up from the snowmobile. They wore black woolly face masks under their helmets; the tiny mouth holes were bordered with whiskers of frost. "You hear what I'm saying, Doc? I'm saying the cops couldn't care less about my little two-bit operation."

Tom faced him. The Judge's angry expression had been replaced by his benevolent look, and Tom, though he knew the Judge to be ruthless, grew a little less nervous, gained a little confidence. It was time to remind the Judge of their profitable past, of their rosy future together. "Don't forget who set you up in business, Judge. I mean a year ago you were nothing but a bartender."

The Judge's expression softened further as he nodded and said, "I can't deny it, Doc. You showed me the light."

"And I've kept you supplied. Filled all your orders."

The Judge nodded agreeably.

"And in years to come I'm your pipeline. Expand to other reservations, I'm your man. We're talking big business, Judge."

"Music to my ears," he said softly. But a spark of anger glinted in his eyes. "So what's this about a plea bargain? We're not talking no big business if you're squealing to the law. We're talking out of business and down the drain."

Tom came up with a pretty good imitation of a chuckle. "I'm not squealing on anybody. I just said that to get your attention." He leaned across the table. "What I'm asking is for you to do me a favor."

"A friend in need."

"I'd like to believe that."

"Believe it."

The door opened and a shaft of bright, cold sunlight fell across the dusty dance floor. The Judge turned to watch the pair of snowmobilers enter. They stamped the snow off their boots and removed their helmets and their woolly masks. They were Billy Annunciation and Elaine LaBonte.

"Hey, you two," called the Judge, "where'd you get that fancy sled?"

"My grandpa's," said Billy.

"Go on! Caesar bought a sled?"

"Got it from the sheriff. It belongs to the county."

Unzipping their jackets, they went over to the pool table. Elaine selected a cue from the rack while Billy fed money into the coin slot and the balls rumbled down their chute. The Judge turned his attention back to Tom.

"Quite the boy, Billy."

Tom nodded and lifted his glass to his lips.

"More up-and-coming than most. More like a white."

Tom tipped his head back, draining his beer.

"Got himself quite the little girlfriend there. You know her— Millie LaBonte's daughter?"

Tom lowered the glass and nodded again.

"Nice little piece, wouldn't you say?"

Tom looked away and steeled himself for what he guessed was coming.

"You're a good judge of young stuff, Doc. Ain't she a nice little piece?"

Tom's fury blurred his vision. He laid his right hand over his eyes, took a deep breath, and said, "I need another beer."

"Hey, Toad, two more," called the Judge.

Billy racked the balls. Elaine took aim and scattered them with a mighty stroke, dropping two.

"Okay, Doc, what's the favor? I got to be on the road in two minutes."

"I've heard about people who drowned in this lake and were never found. Tell me about them."

"Why?"

"I've heard there were at least two."

"Two in my time. Could be more."

"How did they drown?"

"You writing a book?"

"I just need to know."

"The last one fell out of a boat. Some stupid broad from St. Paul. It was a year ago last September. Her and her husband were up for the weekend, staying in a campground on the north end. She went out in the boat alone and that was the last they saw of her. Out over there"—the Judge pointed out the window—"is where they first saw the empty boat. It was going around in a hell of a big circle, running half throttle. I mean a *big* circle, a mile or more across, so how do you look for a body in a case like that? She could have been anywhere when she fell in—nobody saw her. Nobody's out on the lake in late September. The wild rice harvest is over and it isn't cold enough yet to stir up the autumn walleyes."

The midget came waddling across the dance floor carrying a beer and whatever the Judge was drinking. He set down the glasses, took the five-dollar bill Tom gave him, and handed it to the Judge, who reached across the table and stuffed it into Tom's vest.

"The sheriff sent up a plane and the pilot reported a cushion floating about three-quarters of a mile north of Pigeon Point. You can't see Pigeon Point from here, it's way the hell north."

"And a hat," said the midget, lingering at the booth to listen.

"Yeah, a hat and a cushion," said the Judge. "So that's where the sheriff's water patrol started their search, north of Pigeon Point, but that's all they ever found, that hat and that cushion."

"They sent a diver down," said Toad Majerus.

In a sudden movement, the fat man swept out his hand, aiming for the midget's head and missing his ear by an inch. "Get the hell back to work," he ordered, and the midget, laughing nervously, retreated to the bar.

"The diver dived for three days and never found her," said the Judge. "So after that the sheriff sent the plane out over the lake once a day till freeze-up, just in case the body came to the surface, but it never did."

The midget hopped up on the bar and sat watching the pool players. Billy Annunciation pocketed the eight ball by mistake and cried out in horror. Elaine LaBonte, smiling demurely, lit a cigarette.

Tom turned his eyes to the window and gazed pensively at the lake. "Did it ever occur to anybody that she might have made it look like she drowned but she really didn't?"

"Why would she do that?"

"To run away."

The Judge shook his head. "No, that was never brought up."

"But maybe that's what happened. Everybody thinks she's dead and she's living a new life somewhere."

The Judge studied his watch. "Doc, get to the point, would you? I got to make a trip to Berrington."

"What about the other one?"

"The other what?"

"The other body they never found."

"That was winter. Hell of a long time ago. Indian by the name of Jones. His car went through the ice."

"Where?"

"Over there across, where the river comes in." He pointed. "You know, where the ice road runs close to the open water."

"I never take the ice road."

"You never take the ice road?" The Judge looked incredulous. "You been going the long way all winter?"

"I'm not crazy about driving across water."

"Jesus, the ice is three feet thick."

"But I hear there's thin ice."

"Sure there's thin ice, but that ain't where you drive." He pointed again. "See across there? It's thin ice where the river comes in, but there's oil drums set up to show you where it's dangerous."

Tom peered at the thin line of gray woods that marked the far shore.

"This Jones guy worked for Carl Butcher on the nets. He was taking a shortcut home from work and drove on the thin ice. Carl Butcher saw him go under."

"Drunk, I suppose."

The fat man shrugged. "Maybe, maybe not. A diver went down and found the car, but he wasn't in it. Jones managed to roll down his window and get out, and they figured the river current pushed him way out in the deep water. That spring when the ice melted, everybody in Basswood went around with one eye on the water looking for his body and the other eye up in the sky to see if the buzzards and eagles and crows would be any help, but Jones never turned up. It's real deep out there, and the bottom's covered with old waterlogged deadheads from the logging days."

"Deadheads?"

"Tree trunks. Branches. A body gets snarled up in that stuff and never comes up."

Tom shivered. The Judge drained his glass. "I gotta go." He began to heave himself out of the booth, but fell back when Tom clutched his forearm with both hands and spoke in a hushed voice.

"I want to do that."

The fat man raised his flaccid eyelids. "Do what?"

"What that woman did." Tom tightened his grip. The Judge's forearm was hairless and hard and enormous. "Only I want to do it the way the man did it."

"What the Christ are you talking about?"

"I want everybody but you to think I went through the ice and drowned like Jones did."

"Jesus."

"And then I want to go away and start a new life, like that woman did."

"I don't believe she did that."

"Well, I'm doing it."

The Judge uttered a scoffing noise from deep in his throat. Tom loosened his grip on the massive arm and held the Judge with his eyes, pleased to see the Judge's expression gradually transform itself from scorn to something like fascination.

The pool balls rumbled down their chute as Elaine and Billy began a new game. The door opened and two men entered. One of them went around behind the bar and switched on the television, then joined his companion on a stool. The midget dropped down off the bar to serve them. A golf tournament materialized on the screen.

"I can't do it alone," said Tom, "and I can trust you not to tell anybody, because in my new life I'll continue to be your pipeline."

The fat man looked thoughtful. "It could be done, Doc, it could be done."

"It's got to be done soon. My hearing is Wednesday."

The Judge frowned. "There's a couple problems."

Tom inquired with his eyebrows.

"I can't see you dumping your BMW under the ice."

"I wouldn't do that. My wife's after me to sell the BMW and buy ourselves two cheaper cars. What I'll do is get her something cheap and myself something cheaper and I'll stash the BMW somewhere so everybody thinks it's sold and I'll put my cheapie through the ice and drive away in the BMW."

"Stash it where?"

"That's where you come in. Details like that."

The Judge read his watch. "I'm late." He gripped the table with one hand and the back of the booth with the other, preparing to rise.

"Wait a minute. We've got to work this out."

"I gotta go to Berrington."

"I'll come back tonight."

"You might not like it here tonight."

"Why not?"

"Verna's taking a little vacation from treatment. I don't want you coming in here and spoiling it for her."

"We're on good terms. I was on the phone with her this morning."

"You were?"

"Listen, Judge, I've got to be dead by Wednesday."

Judge Bigelow got to his feet. "Okay, we'll talk tonight, if you promise not to spoil Verna's little vacation."

"Figure out the details," said Tom, standing, following the fat man across the room. "Like where I buy the two cars and where I hide the BMW and how I get to it after I drown."

"Plus there's another problem you ain't thought of."

"Solve it."

"It's going to look strange, you driving through a hole in the ice when you never drove on the ice all winter."

Tom pulled on his gloves. "There's always a first time."

"Start driving the ice road today, Doc. This afternoon. So people see you out there."

Tom nodded, trying not to look apprehensive. "Okay."

Judge Bigelow laid a heavy hand on his shoulder. "I'll miss you, Doc."

"Like hell."

Returning to the bar for another beer, Tom watched the Judge lumber over to the pool table and exchange a few words with Billy; something funny, evidently, for Billy laughed. The Judge then moved toward Elaine, who edged away from him and did not respond to his playful remarks but averted her face and peered at him warily from the corner of her eye. When the Judge put out his hand to touch her, she hitched her pool cue up under her arm, lancelike, training the point on his breastbone.

Tom sat on a stool. The golf game blurred and faded from the screen. The man on Tom's left sneezed and said, "Sure in hell been cold, ain't it?"

"Inhuman," said Tom.

The midget came along with a beer and Tom leaned over the bar to take it from him.

The man sneezed again, explosively, blowing a little stack of napkins off the bar. He said, "Twenty below again tonight."

"Inhuman," Tom repeated.

The Judge, after conferring with the midget, left by a back door. There was the sound of a reluctant engine grinding and finally starting. Tom, swiveling on his stool and looking out the window facing the lake, saw the Judge move across the snowy ground in his Bronco and down the slope and out onto the ice. The Bronco was red and black, with a snowplow attached to the front. An extra pair of headlights stood up on stems to shine over the top of the plow. Tom sat watching it cross the lake. Another sneeze. The click of pool balls between songs on the jukebox. By the time it climbed to the road along the far shore, the Bronco was diminished to a dark speck.

Tom turned back to the bar. The golf game returned to the screen. Somewhere there was green grass and blue water and people wearing short sleeves and sandals.

44

Libby served dinner at her kitchen table, on which she had laid a lace cloth and placed a squat green candle in a saucer. The salad was magnificent, the roast highly seasoned, and the potatoes underbaked. Frank, eating hungrily, asked about her work and she, eating very little, struggled to be scintillating on two hours' sleep.

The hospital, she said, seemed well managed, a good place to work. Hospital nursing was more demanding than she remembered it; she'd allowed herself to become lazy at the Indian Health Center. After tonight's shift, she'd have two nights off, thank God. She liked most of the people she worked with, and her patients, of course, she liked without exception—they needed her. She wished Dr. Pella met his outpatients elsewhere, however. She and Verna approached their weekly therapy session with increasing reluctance, and Libby thought this was due in part to their being overexposed to the place.

"She's doing okay?"

"She's trying very hard to fit in and straighten herself out, but I worry. You know what Hanson Manor is like."

He nodded. Having helped Verna move in, he'd sensed that the place was unsuitable for her. It harbored all manner of the

mentally afflicted—some cases obviously severe—and his intro-
duction to the director, a fragile-looking man named Trygseth,
had done nothing to allay his misgivings.

Libby said, "I mean I'm not sure if being a good resident of
Hanson Manor has much to do with straightening herself out."

"And there's no better place?"

"Not within a hundred and fifty miles. Not with the kind
of supervision she needs. Didn't it give you the willies, Frank?"

"Not very stimulating, I'm afraid."

"I told her we'd come and see her this afternoon."

"Of course." He sensed Libby's edginess. She was making
nervous little movements with her hands. Her voice was strained.
She was hard to look in the eye.

"I should have a car. I told Tom I need a car."

"You're in touch?"

"He calls every day. Wakes me every morning just as I'm
falling asleep. He times it like torture. He wants me to come back
to him."

"Will you . . . ever?"

She shrugged. A train hooted in the distance.

"Do you miss him?"

She ate a small bite of salad and smiled again, sadly. "Not
as long as I have you."

Hearing these words as he reached for the salt, he burned his
wrist on the candle flame. She didn't see him flinch.

"I have to say it, Frank. I know it's the last thing you want
to hear, and it presents all kinds of problems, and you know it
anyway without my telling you, but I have to say it. I have to
say how much I love you."

He responded by putting down his silver and studying her.
She seemed no longer agitated. She was sitting back in her chair,
her eyes wide and weary. Having made this declaration, she had
apparently achieved some sort of repose.

"Think of it, Frank, our love goes back twenty-five years.
Before Vernon and before your seminary, there was our love for
each other."

"Yes, we go back a long way." He, too, felt curiously composed, unruffled. There was a kind of relief in facing this subject

at last, and an even greater relief in knowing that he was *ready* to face it. He couldn't have spoken of it a month ago. Perhaps not even a week ago. Until now he'd been confused.

"Before Tom," she said.

"Yes, before Tom." He no longer felt confused. He was becoming absorbed in his work. He suspected that he was actually doing some of his parishioners some good. Both at St. Ann's and at Our Lady's, he could sense a vague kind of spiritual unity taking shape around him. More and more people were coming to him and opening up their souls and either asking for advice or—more often—asking for confirmation of the advice they'd been giving themselves. More and more of his people were receiving the Sacraments; he sensed a heightened regard for the Eucharist and he might be the only priest in the diocese—indeed, in America—to report an upswing in the number of confessions. He was becoming increasingly aware of himself as surrounded by two small communities of faith, one Indian, one white, and being nourished by them as he strove to nourish them. They did not follow him so much as cluster around him. He was not so much their leader as their center. They were not his followers; they were his family.

"Before Verna," she said. In finding repose she had apparently found sorrow as well, for her wide, weary eyes were glistening with tears. The train hooted again. It was closer now, louder. "Before Chicago and before Basswood," she added.

"Yes, before all that," he agreed. He loved Libby. He would never *not* love her. She knew more about him, understood him better, than anyone since his mother, and to someone as private and inward as Frank, this amounted to a kind of sacred intimacy. Like his mother, she absorbed him.

"Before life turned bad," she whispered.

He carefully folded his napkin. "Just how bad is it for you, Libby?"

"Very bad."

The train, its whistle blaring, rattled through the neighborhood, causing the kitchen floor to tremble.

He leaned forward, took her hand across the table. He said, "Libby, there's a limit to what I can give you."

A fleeting shadow of fear passed across her face and was followed by her urgent question: "You do love me?"

"Yes, I do love you."

"Then why don't we just leave it there." She rose to serve coffee.

"Because you need to know there's a limit."

"No, I don't," she said sharply. "That's Tom's line. He's always telling me what I need." She poured coffee. "If there's a limit to your love, I don't need to know it right now."

"But I need to say it."

"All right, say it." She returned to her chair and steeled herself.

He began by asking bluntly, "What kind of love are you talking about, Libby? Love with sex?"

"There's another kind?"

"There's brother-sister love."

"Oh, God, that!"

"It's the best I can offer right now." He went on with precisely the words she'd been dreading. His priesthood. His parishes. She didn't listen carefully. Something about his being the center of a spiritual community. It was all so abstract and unintelligible. She tried to conceal her disgust. She tried to bring him back down to earth.

"There's been sex in this from the beginning, you know. From the first night you walked into the Health Center, I've been conscious of how I look for you, what clothes you'd like to see me in. How do you like this shirt?" It was white with pink stripes, half-unbuttoned. She fingered the collar. "I thought I'd wear something plain and unprovocative."

"I like it. It provokes me."

She smiled with satisfaction.

"This is not an affair, Libby. It stops short of bed."

"So far."

"And for some time to come."

"Then why have you been courting me?"

He looked offended. "I haven't."

"You've been *seducing* me!"

It was the stridency of this remark—it was painfully shrill—

that alerted Frank to her precarious state of mind. He looked past her, through the living room and out the front window. It was a long train. With his eyes on the roofs of the moving boxcars, he spoke softly.

"Maybe you're right, Libby. Maybe I've been courting you without knowing it. If I have, I'm sorry."

She was silent for a long time before asking, "Do you ever think of leaving the priesthood?"

"All priests do from time to time, I suppose."

"I mean for my sake."

He looked her in the eye and said, "No."

This was followed by a few awkward half sentences, which finally led Libby to say in a voice drained of emotion, "Let's not talk about it. If we talk about it, we might lose what we have."

Frank nodded, relieved.

"What we have isn't much," she said, "but it's—"

"That's where we differ, Libby. I think what we have is very important."

"I'll try to see it that way."

"Please."

"I'll try to be your sister."

They rose from the table and put on their coats.

Hanson Manor smelled of sweat and meat loaf. Mr. Trygseth, dabbing at his lips with a paper napkin, ushered Frank and Libby into the staff office and asked them please to wait— he would be back in a jiffy to speak with them.

"We're here to see Verna," Frank told him, but he ignored this and hurried from the room.

Frank removed his coat and sank deeply into an overstuffed chair with a sprung seat. Libby chose a straight chair next to a bookshelf containing a hardbound set of Zane Grey, a tattered joke book, and small box of Band-Aids. She kept her coat buttoned and her gloves on. The house was drafty.

"Reminds me of your rectory," she said.

Frank nodded, casting his eyes around. "Same era."

"The oak. The beveled glass."

"The brick fireplace," he added. On the mantel over the boarded-up fireplace was a vase, a tennis shoe, and an alarm clock with a loud tick. It was 4:15.

"Did he seem upset, Frank?"

"Jittery, I thought."

"A problem with Verna."

"Or we interrupted his dinner."

"I should have called ahead."

"It's an odd time to be eating."

They fell silent for a while, then Libby repeated, absently, "I'm sure it's a problem with Verna." Saying this, she felt an unusual sense of equanimity. She felt strangely aloof, secure, out of harm's way. Had she achieved a kind of immunity? Was she truly and finally beyond Verna's reach? Or was it merely a numbing lack of sleep?

Mr. Trygseth returned, carrying his paper napkin, followed by a young woman whose baggy sweatshirt was tucked into her tight jeans. He introduced her as Marilyn, a counselor. She said "Hiya" to Libby and "Hiya" to Frank. She wore her golden hair in a long braid. A pair of small round glasses rested on her nose.

Mr. Trygseth sat down behind his broad walnut desk and said, "Verna's not here. We haven't seen her all afternoon. I sent Marilyn up to her room when dinner was ready and she wasn't there. I thought she was there—she's been napping a lot—but she wasn't there. Her overnight bag is gone, and she didn't sign out." For corroboration he looked to Marilyn, who had backed up to the cold fireplace as though for warmth and was playing with her braid, which she had brought forward over her shoulder. Her voice was husky.

"She took her makeup, her hair dryer, things like that."

Mr. Trygseth, having spread his paper napkin flat on the desk, now folded it neatly in half. "She was on the phone long distance this morning." He folded it in fourths. "Is there someone she might have called, Mrs. Pearsall, to come and pick her up?"

"I don't know," said Libby, smiling serenely, feeling scarcely a trace of motherly alarm. "It doesn't surprise me."

Another fold of the napkin. "I know she placed at least one call to Basswood."

Frank asked, "Have you looked for her?"

"We don't actively search in cases like this, but we do notify the police."

"And they search?"

"If we suspect foul play."

"Do you suspect foul play?" With each question, Frank turned up the urgency in his voice.

"Not in Verna's case."

"So nobody's looking for her?"

"Not at the moment." Mr. Trygseth assumed a pained expression and directed it at both of his visitors in turn. "You have to understand our people are not confined here. They take up residence by their own free will, and if they choose to leave—well, it happens."

Frank shot back, "It's below zero, and she's on medication."

Libby turned to him, startled by his tone, amazed that he should be so agitated while she felt impassive and limp. Her lost empathy for Verna seemed to have found, like a parasite, a new host in Frank. What a pleasure, what a vast relief, to sit back and hear him protest.

"I can't believe you aren't out looking. She doesn't have clothes for weather like this."

"Father Healy, where do you look in a city of twenty thousand people?"

"The police should be looking. She can't be far if she hasn't any money."

Mr. Trygseth spoke patiently. "She's a grown woman, Father Healy, capable of planning her departure. Indeed, she's a schemer." He turned to the girl at the fireplace. "Ask Marilyn."

Marilyn, picking something very small out of the brushy end of her braid, said faintly, "She can take care of herself."

"And as much as we'd like to think we're indispensable," Mr. Trygseth continued, "a woman of twenty-six is entitled to her independence. Instead of sending out a search party, I'm sure we'd be further ahead if we could think who she might have been summoning on the phone. Mrs. Pearsall, any ideas?"

"Yes."

"Well, there you are." He turned to Frank. "There's your

first clue." He stood. "Come on, Marilyn, before Rupert and Dick eat all the meat loaf."

Frank got to his feet. "We're on our own, then?"

"Yes—we have a policy. We wash our hands of residents when they reject our help." Mr. Trygseth wore the unassailable expression of a man who treasures policies.

"Your help doesn't extend very far, does it?"

"You're right, Father Healy," he said with distaste. "It stops at the front door." He came around the desk unfolding his napkin and tucking it into his belt. "We can't be all things to all people."

A tiny, misshapen old woman edged into the room. Her soiled pink dress hung to her shoe tops. She wore a hearing aid and her glasses contained a frosted left lens. Behind her came a second old woman wearing two hearing aids. Mr. Trygseth addressed them tenderly. "Go back, girls, go back. Rupert and Dick will eat all your meat loaf." He gently turned the old women around.

Marilyn said "So long" to Frank, "So long" to Libby, tossed her braid over her shoulder, and left the room.

"Go back, girls," Mr. Trygseth repeated, and the two old ladies sidled stiffly away, their three rheumy eyes cast back at him in worship.

Mr. Trygseth, letting Libby and Frank out of the front door, alerted them to another policy. "I'm afraid she'll have to have a second intake conference if she wants to return. We can't have her running away and then coming back and pretending it didn't happen. She'll have to show us she wants our help, otherwise what possible good can we do her? A certain predisposition is required of our residents if Hanson Manor is to be a viable half-way house."

"Halfway to what?" asked Frank, stalking out onto the wide front porch.

Mr. Trygseth said, "Good-bye, Mrs. Pearsall," and closed the door.

Libby took Frank's arm down the steps. "I never saw you steamed up before."

Frank smiled grimly. "Smug little creep."

She laughed to herself, momentarily elated. As long as Verna had a hold on him, so did she.

They got into the car. He started the engine, adjusted the heater controls.

"Are you thinking it's Judge Bigelow?" he asked.

"It has to be Judge Bigelow."

"I'll go get her."

She laughed softly.

"What's so funny?" he asked.

"You." Her laugh continued. "You're beside yourself."

"The Homestead's no place for her." He looked puzzled and a little hurt. "Aren't you concerned?"

"I'm so tired I'm giddy," she said, turning to cast her eyes back at Hanson Manor, her breath fogging the window. "There isn't much point in going after her. She won't leave the Judge till she's good and ready."

"I have to try. I have to tell her she's throwing away everything she's gained over the past month."

"She knows that."

"Well, I have to tell her anyway. I think she'll listen."

They drove slowly along the street. This was the cathedral neighborhood, where the houses, built by railroad and lumber barons during Berrington's golden years before World War I, were large and substantial and showing their age. Some were in need of paint. Several were empty. Each time they passed a house in superb repair, Libby craned her neck to gaze at it and imagine the lives of comfort within.

"Can't say I blame her for running off," said Frank.

They drove a block or so before she responded, laconically, "I don't blame anybody for anything anymore."

"Libby." There was reproach in his voice.

"I'm sorry." She continued to keep her face averted, her eyes on the houses. "It's almost five. I get the blues around five." This wasn't precisely true. Of late her blues came and went without regard to time of day. What depressed her at the moment was Frank's imminent departure for the Homestead.

"If she doesn't want to come back here, she doesn't have to. She can come back to the rectory."

No response.

"Okay, Libby?"

Silence.

"She was happy at the rectory, wasn't she?"

"Of course she was—a fatherless girl in a house with two fathers." She smiled at him briefly, and then faced straight ahead, holding her tears in check.

"Then if she's serious about the travel-agent course, she can move back to Berrington when spring term starts."

Libby nodded. "But not to Hanson Manor," she said.

"No."

They came to Great Northern Avenue and crossed the city swiftly and in silence.

"Please come up," said Libby as they drew up in front of the blue house.

He looked at his watch. "I should get to the Homestead before she settles in."

"What's twenty minutes? I'll make coffee."

"Do you have some rum to put in it?"

They took their cups into the front room and sat shoulder to shoulder on the couch, their eyes on the window, on its fringe of icicles, on its rectangle of colorfully dying daylight. They didn't speak. Neither was willing to take up the subject of love again, she being too sleepy and he not wishing to delay his leave-taking. It was enough, Libby told herself, simply to be sitting here with him. Or no, not quite enough.

"Would you put your arm around me?"

They set down their cups and she nestled into the hollow of his shoulder. Closing her eyes, she gave her attention to the whistle of a train. She guessed it was approaching the Twenty-fourth Street crossing.

Frank's eyes moved from the window to the easel in the corner of the room and the unfinished painting begun in Basswood.

"Canadian National," she said softly.

"Pardon me?"

"Canadian National. Chicago Northwestern. Port of Galveston. The days here can get pretty long. I've been memorizing boxcars." During her first two or three nights in the apartment, the trains had interrupted her sleep, but lately she had somehow managed to reroute them through her unconscious, where they did not wake her up but quite often bore down upon her in dreams. "Conrail," she added. "Frisco."

The painting disturbed him. The shades of violet and pink made a pleasing harmony, but the tree line made his scalp tingle. There had obviously been a violent sort of abandon in her technique, the greens and blacks having been laid thickly and recklessly over one another with a palette knife and allowed to dry in wartlike bumps and razor-sharp edges.

"Montana Rail Link and Illinois Central," she droned. "Rock Island, Soo Line, and Burlington Northern." Night before last, waiting for the bus to work, she had heard a train announce itself at the Twenty-fourth Street crossing and she impulsively ran across Great Northern Avenue and hurried through the dark passage between Noonan's Car Wash and the Buena Vista Apartments and stood at the base of the railroad embankment with her eyes on her moonlit watch. She was timing the train's approach. All that day she had been feeling listless and depressed. She and Verna had quarreled again on the phone. Tom had called twice, drunk. She had tried calling Frank, but he wasn't home. Suddenly, led by its shimmering headlight, the train shot out of a curve and sent a thrilling shiver up her spine as it roared and clattered past. Such stupendous authority. Such weight and speed. Such a deafening noise. She wanted the train to be endless, she wanted its mechanical racket to blot out her grief, and when it disappeared, she felt profoundly let down.

"I've got to go, Libby."

When he rose from the couch, she lay full length, her eyelids drooping with sleepiness. Through the bedroom doorway he saw a quilt folded at the foot of her bed. He went in to get it and covered her.

"Union Pacific," she mumbled.

He chuckled and kissed her on the cheek.

She slept for a moment and woke when the kitchen door

closed. She listened to his descent down the steps and recalled how curiously elated she'd felt on the bus the night before last after watching the train go by. Staring out the bus window, she'd felt her spirits rise and it took her a few moments to figure out the reason. She was consoled to realize how fast the train had drawn abreast of her house after first calling to her from the Twenty-fourth Street crossing. If she ever needed to destroy herself, all she had to do was listen for the distant whistle, and when it blew she'd have only fifty-five seconds to live.

45

Frank parked in the rosy glow of the Homestead neon and went inside to find Toad Majerus sitting cross-legged on the bar watching "Sixty Minutes."

"Hi, Father Healy, what'll it be?" In a swift, apelike movement, the midget dropped off the bar and disappeared behind it.

Frank settled himself on a stool and opened his overcoat. Johnny Cash sang cheerlessly from the jukebox. On television Mike Wallace spoke to a woman who bit her lip between statements. Toad Majerus kicked a tattered vinyl hassock along the floor to a point opposite Frank, hopped up on it, folded his arms on the bar, and grinned. "What'll it be, Father, a beer?"

"Rum and Coke."

"Coming right up." The midget dropped down, kicked his hassock along the back bar, and rose up near the rum bottle.

"Go easy on the Coke."

"You bet, Father."

Surveying the room, Frank saw only four other patrons. In a booth near the pool table sat three Indians, a man and two women. In another, far back in the shadows, a man slept.

"Slow night," said Frank.

"Sunday," the midget explained.

"Is Judge Bigelow here?"

"In back. Should be out pretty soon. He'll be glad to see you."

"He's had a change of heart then."

The midget chuckled. "Naw, he likes you just fine, always has. He'll get crusty with people now and again, but that's a sign he likes them." He carried the brimming drink carelessly and spilled quite a lot of it as he reached up to set it before Frank. "Me, he talks rough to me all the time, but he don't mean nothing by it. He says when I get too old to earn my keep, he's going to put me in a cage with a rug over it and charge a quarter for people to look." The midget laughed again, retrieving his hassock. "No, the crustier he is with somebody, the more he likes them."

Frank's drink was straight rum. He handed it back. "Could you cut this a little?"

The midget added a squirt of cola from a hose and returned it to him. "Judge Bigelow used to be justice of the peace, did you know that?"

"So I've heard. Incredible."

"Yessir, held court right here where I'm standing. Trooper'd bring in speeders and the Judge'd hear the case and fine them thirty-five dollars plus cost and send them on their way. This might have been the only place in the world where people brought before the bar were actually before a real bar."

When the midget's convulsive laugh subsided, Frank asked, "Is Verna here?"

Instantly Toad Majerus's meaty face clouded. A fretful look came into his protuberant eyes. He stroked his underslung jaw for a moment before answering. "I ain't seen her." He took Frank's money and kicked the hassock over in front of the cash register. "The Judge is real good to Verna." He rang up the sale, scooped out change.

"Please tell her I'm here, would you?"

"I ain't allowed in the Judge's rooms."

"You could knock on the door and tell her."

"That ain't allowed neither."

"Then I'll wait."

"That'll be swell." He took up his position opposite Frank, spreading the change on the bar. "It don't seem like the same old Homestead since the state did away with justice of the peaces. It was more of a respected place then, and the Judge had more gumption. I don't know what it is, it's like he's lost some of his pride." The midget's eyes brightened. "Like the night he threw me in the lake along with the outhouse I was sitting in. Things were more fun back then. You had live music Saturday nights, you had a stripper now and again, you had Johnny Upward going around betting people he could open beer bottles with his teeth, you had just a plain old good time."

"You were in the outhouse and he threw you in the lake?"

Toad Majerus uttered a shrill laugh. "He was mad at me for something and I ran out back and locked myself in the outhouse—that was before we had indoor toilets—and he tipped it over and rolled it down the bank into the water."

"You could have drowned."

"Almost did"—more laughter—"but the Judge waded in and pulled me out."

"Has it occurred to you that your boss is a dangerous man?"

Toad Majerus shook his head, smiling. "Swell guy to work for. 'Just remember, Toad,' he tells me, 'the Judge is your shepherd, you shall not want,' and he's right on the money about that. I'd be a freak in a carnival if it wasn't for the Judge, and a second-rate freak at that. Ain't no future in being a midget when you're up against a two-headed boy and a lady with scales for skin."

A door opened at the far end of the dance floor. Frank and Toad Majerus, peering into the shadows, saw the dark mass of the proprietor fill the doorway. The door closed. The hulk shambled forward into the light.

Toad Majerus laughed merrily. "Hey, Judge, look who's here."

The Judge's movements were heavy, his eyes puffy with sleep. He shoved the midget off his hassock and stood looking at Frank. His growl was deeper than normal. "You lost?"

"Verna's lost."

"So?"

"Let me talk to her."

"Who said she's here?"

"My bones."

"I told him about the time you threw me in the lake. God, was that a night!" The midget spoke laughingly yet warily, as if afraid of offending his boss while trying to divert him. "Remember how stupid I looked wringing wet? God, I tell you, that was a night."

The Judge turned and threatened Toad Majerus with a backhand stroke. The midget fell silent.

"I have a message from her mother," said Frank.

"Her mother sent you?"

Frank nodded.

The Judge said, "Toad, give me your undershirt."

The midget removed his green flannel shirt, then his T-shirt, which he handed to his boss.

"Now go back and tell Verna her mother's eunuch wants to see her."

"Her mother's what?"

"*Eu-nuch!*"

The midget put on his flannel shirt and scurried off, buttoning it. The Judge soaked the midget's undershirt in the sink and wrung it out. He moved off down the bar, cleaning it with the undershirt. One of the Indian women left the booth and fed coins to the jukebox. Harry Reasoner, standing in a park, spoke to the camera. The midget returned and was about to climb back onto his hassock when the Judge ordered him away to clean toilets. Debby Boone sweetly wailed, "You light up my life."

Verna came out of the shadows. White jeans, black sweatshirt, triangular spangles hanging from her ears. She looked happy, composed, glad to see Frank. She approached him eagerly. "Let's sit in a booth."

He followed her to the booth with the view of the dark lake.

"What's going on, Verna? We went to Hanson Manor, your mother and I."

"That dump." This was said lightly, with amusement in her eyes.

"You knew we were coming to see you."

"Haven't you got a drink? Let me get you one. Rum and Coke, right?"

She went behind the bar. Frank noticed something deferential in the Judge's manner of moving aside for her while she mixed the drink, sensed something good-natured (though he couldn't hear it above Debby Boone's singing) in his conversation with her. She returned with a tray—his drink, her Coke, two bags of peanuts.

"Too bad you came clear out here. I thought of calling and telling my mother, but she probably wouldn't believe it."

"Believe what?"

"Why I'm here. I mean I wouldn't blame her, I've been lying to her since I was seven." Sitting, she opened a bag and spilled peanuts into Frank's hand. "I'm getting the Judge's car for my mother, she can have it as long as she needs it, the Judge never uses it. I'm going to take it to her in the morning." Her smile was soft, agreeable, relaxed. Frank assumed that on the scale of zero to ten this was the five Libby had spoken of and he had never seen—the golden mean of normalcy. Dear God, is it too much to hope that Verna has at last outrun her furies?

"Forget the Judge, Verna. Let's get out of here."

Verna settled herself against the window, her feet up on the seat. "My mother's instructions?"

"Nobody's instructions. Your mother, as you may have figured out by now, has given up on you."

"I'm changing. That's why I'm getting her a car—to show her."

"Not from the Judge, Verna."

"Who else? I asked my dad. I asked Tom."

Headlights approached off the lake, bounced up the incline to the Homestead.

"Get your things and let's go. We'll buy her a car."

"We?" She laughed. "I'm broke."

"So am I, we'll get a loan. I've got a friend in the bank."

"I'm a bad risk."

"So am I, but St. Ann's isn't."

She looked amused. "Are you serious?"

"Come on."

She looked defiant. "I'm not going back to that dump. It's full of jerks."

"I know it. Come home with me."

"You mean . . . ?" Her eyes widened in wonder. "To stay?"

"Why not? Your room's empty."

"Hey," she said, distracted by the headlights pulling up and stopping under the window. "That's the BMW."

Returning from his evening meal in Linden Falls, Tom rolled to a stop under the window. Having called up courage he didn't know he possessed, he'd taken the ice road over and back and he was still somewhat astonished that water, chilled, could hold up a car. On the way over, in daylight, the two or three pressure ridges had been easier to see and slow down for; on the way back he'd hit a couple of bumps that rattled his teeth; but otherwise there was nothing to it and he chastised himself for not driving that route all winter like everybody else. It cut off ten minutes to town. Getting out of his car, he was surprised to see the two-tone Oldsmobile from St. Ann's.

The Homestead was quiet, except for one of the lighted beer signs humming and clicking like an injured insect. No music. No audible talk. No one at the bar. He saw three booths occupied, one by Frank and Verna.

"Hi, Doc," grunted the Judge, drawing him a beer.

Tom planted himself on a stool, took the glass, and nearly drained it in one pull. Wiping his mouth, he indicated the booth with a flick of his eyes. "What the hell's going on over there?"

"Verna's had enough of the big city." The Judge leaned forward, grinning. "She come home to Daddy."

"And brought him along?"

"He come sniffing after her. Come to save her, don't you know."

Both men considered this funny. Snickering, they regarded the booth. Neither Verna nor Frank acknowledged Tom, and he assumed they hadn't seen him come in. He thought it strange that they should be wearing expressions of lightheartedness. Verna, in fact, broke out in a laugh as Frank, speaking with animation, made a sudden expansive gesture, his hands flying up over his head.

"Chummy," said Tom.

The fat man chuckled. "Watch her, she'll charm that bastard right out the door."

They saw Verna stop laughing and grow serious. She was intent on something Frank was explaining. If he was pleading for her to return to the straight and narrow, why was she acting so agreeable instead of responding with her customary fit of temper?

The Judge said, "I got it all fixed if you still want to die. I been on the phone with a guy named Ron, he's got a body shop in Berrington and a bunch of used cars. . . . Hey, Doc, are you listening?"

Tom, swiveling around to face him, said, "Looks to me like the priest's horning in on your woman."

This struck the Judge as enormously funny. He laughed out loud, his fat front jiggling, his head thrown back, his hand over his mouth. When he finally subsided, he wiped his eyes with the bar rag and said, "You crack me up, Doc."

"Okay, tell me about the car."

"Horned in on by that eunuch." The Judge began to quake all over again.

"You were saying . . . ?"

The Judge gathered himself, wiped his eyes again, wiped the bar, picked up Tom's beer, and wiped the bottom of the glass. "It's real simple, you drive to Ron's place in Berrington tomorrow morning. I told him you're coming. He's on Concord Boulevard, out near Highway 2, you got to look for it. It's behind a Union 76 station. Ron's Body Shop—you got that?"

Tom nodded.

"Ron's a guy I knew when I was justice of the peace, always took an interest in my traffic cases, always on the lookout for banged-up cars. You still see him in here once in a while, trying to sell some wreck to some Indian. Tall guy with glasses."

"What did you tell him about me?"

"Told him you needed two old cars, one for yourself and one for your missus, and you needed to keep your BMW out of sight for a couple of days. Says he's got a peach of a car for thirty-eight hundred dollars your missus'll be crazy about. It's old, he says, but it runs like a little sewing machine and the upholstery's like new. Belonged to a minister."

"Sure."

"Presbyterian, I think he said." The Judge shook with silent glee for a moment, then went on. "I told him you needed a cheapie, too, the heavier the better, and he says he's got a beater he can let you have for under a thousand. A real heavy old hog, I guess, from the days when Detroit was making cars like army tanks. What you do is, you pull up in front of Ron's around ten in the morning, you honk your horn, and he throws open the door and you drive right in and he throws a tarp over your car. Ron works alone, so you don't need to worry about anybody getting curious. You give him forty-eight-hundred dollars and he gives you the keys and off you go."

"In two cars?"

Judge Bigelow shrugged.

"How do I drive two cars, Judge?"

"You need me to blow your nose and comb your hair?"

"Details, Judge—you said you'd take care of the details."

"Okay, so what's the problem? You drive the Ford to your wife's and have her take you back to Ron's."

Tom shook his head. "I don't want her seeing the BMW at a body shop. I want her to think I'm rid of it."

"She doesn't see it. It's inside."

"So what if he opens the door while she's there?"

"It's under a tarp."

"So what if she wonders where it is?"

"Jesus! Forget delivering her car. Pay Ron to deliver it."

"But I want to see her."

The Judge sighed noisily, angrily. "Listen, I got you the cars and I got you the hiding place, I ain't into marriage counseling."

Tom drained his beer and handed over the glass. The Judge refilled it and picked up a pen and a napkin from the back bar. "Okay, now we come to the good part. We put the beater through the ice tomorrow around midnight."

"No, Tuesday."

"Tomorrow." The Judge spread the napkin on the bar.

"I need time to gather up my belongings. I got to mail some stuff to Chicago."

"No, you don't. Dead men travel light."

"Tuesday."

"No, it's got to be Monday because that's when we're closed and that's why you're out in your car coming home from Linden Falls after midnight."

Tom pondered this.

"And since we're closed, I can be gone and nobody'll wonder why. I can be out there in my Bronco to pick you off the ice and deliver you to your BMW."

Judge Bigelow scribbled on the napkin, getting the ink to run. The napkin tore. He dropped it on the floor and went to get another. The midget emerged from a rest room, dragging a mop. He called, "Hi, Doc, great to see you." The Indian man stood up from the booth where he had been sitting with the two women and joined Toad Majerus at the jukebox. They made a selection and drew pool cues down from the rack.

The Judge spread out the new napkin and drew a long wavery line. "This here's the far shore," he explained. Then lightly, delicately, he blackened an area extending out from the shore in the shape of a banana. "This here's the thin ice where your car goes in." Raising his head, he smiled at Tom and added, "Usually it's open water because of the current, but being it's this cold, it's got an inch of ice over it." The smile faded and was replaced by an expression Tom had never before seen on the fat man's face. It was a deeply inquiring look. And then it deepened further, becoming so grave and unsettling and prolonged that Tom finally had to avert his eyes.

The Indian racked the balls, and the midget, raising his cue shoulder-high, broke. Crystal Gale cried out from the jukebox, asking, "Don't it make your brown eyes blue?" Frank Healy got to his feet, buttoned his black overcoat, pulled on his gloves. Verna, remaining in the booth, spoke to him earnestly with raised eyebrows. The look on her face was intense. Tom wondered if she was off her meds and going wacko again. No, he decided, this expression was different. The wild abandon was missing.

This was a controlled look. It was focused. It was eager. What were the two of them cooking up?

Then Verna sprang out of the booth, flew into the shadows, and entered a back room. Frank stepped over to the bar.

"Hi, Tom."

"What's going on?"

"Verna's leaving." Frank was addressing Judge Bigelow.

The Judge said nothing, made no objection, but his expression suggested he was holding back anger.

"Seen Libby lately?" asked Tom.

"I saw her this afternoon."

"How's she doing?"

"All right."

"Verna hallucinates about sex, you know."

Frank ignored this. He said, "You'd be doing Libby a favor if you didn't call her before evening. She sleeps mornings."

Tom flared. "It's your business when a man calls his wife?"

Frank turned away, his eyes on the pool game. Verna came out wearing her green satiny jacket and carrying a shoulder bag.

The Judge said softly, "Verna."

She sang, "Good-bye, Puppy, see you some other time."

"You're throwing away a car."

"Changed my mind, Puppy."

Tom watched her walk to the door with Frank. He called, "Verna—" his voice breaking unexpectedly and preventing him from saying good-bye.

"See you at the hearing," she said.

The midget sang out, "So long, Verna, so long, Father Healy, it's always great to see you."

When the door closed behind them, Tom fought off a surge of sadness, then turned to the Judge and grinned. "Charmed him right out the door, didn't she?"

The Judge, too, brought a smile to his face and shook his head. "Quite the woman. She could get the pope into bed."

The man in the back booth shifted in his sleep. The midget climbed onto the pool table and lay on his stomach to shoot. Crystal Gale's voice broke with sorrow.

"The bars in town close at half-past midnight, so you'll be

coming home about a quarter to one in the morning. Make it quarter to one on the dot, so I'm not waiting out there freezing my ass." The Judge made a row of dots with his pen. "Okay, you come down off the land and you get out on the ice and you see a line of oil drums. They're orange."

"I saw them," Tom said proudly. "I drove over and back on the ice."

"Atta boy. Do it a couple more times tomorrow so people get used to seeing you out there in the beater. What you do, when you come to the third oil drum, you veer off to the right and head for the thin ice."

"Jesus Christ."

"No sweat, Doc. Them oil drums are a hundred yards from the thin ice. As soon as you make the turn you'll see me sitting in my Bronco with my lights out, facing you. I'll be backed up fairly close to the thin ice, so you know where to stop. You take it slow and easy. You pull up beside me and get out of your car, but you leave it in gear with the motor running. It creeps ahead and goes under. Simple as pie."

"God, Judge, I don't know." Tom was feeling tremors of fear in his hands and face.

"That's all there is to it. You hop in with me, I drive you to Ron's Body Shop in Berrington, and by the time the sun comes up you're halfway to Chicago in your BMW."

"Who said I was going to Chicago?"

"You did."

"I never did."

"You said you had to mail stuff to Chicago."

"Oh."

"On our way to Berrington we'll plan how we stay in business, how you keep me supplied from Chicago. I'm holding you to that."

"Don't worry. There's ways."

"Now another thing. You gotta make sure you roll down the driver's window before you get out of the car. That way they'll figure you climbed out the window after you went under and got carried off by the current. You can't open a door under water because of the pressure, but you can open a window. See, there's no way they can search the whole lake for your body. It's different in the summer when they can send a diver down from a boat, but now they gotta chop a hole in the goddamn ice every place the diver goes down. It won't take long before they'll give up looking and hope you come floating up in the spring, what's left of you, and then—"

Tom shuddered and interrupted: "How does anybody know the car went under in the first place?"

"One of two ways. Carl Butcher knows when he comes to check his nets in the morning. He sees the opening in the ice."

"It'll freeze over by morning."

"Only if it's down around twenty, thirty below. That water's always moving."

"But say it's twenty, thirty below."

The Judge frowned. "I suppose after a day or two when you turn up missing, somebody ought to come forward and say they saw headlights drive out on the lake and disappear. I guess I'd have the midget do that."

"The midget?" Tom squealed. "This is between you and me."

"The midget's my man—no worry there. He'd go to hell for me."

"What have you told him?"

"Ain't told him nothing yet."

"Forget the midget."

The Judge seemed undecided.

"What about tire tracks? They'll see you were out there with your Bronco."

"No tire tracks. The wind's packed the snow hard as cement."

Tom, his heart pounding, placed his shaky fingers on the napkin, crumpled it into a tight little ball and slipped it into the pocket of his vest. He peered into the small inscrutable eyes of the fat man and wondered if he was trustworthy. Yes, he assured himself, Bigelow was an astute businessman; he'd do nothing to jeopardize their future profits as partners. Next, he wondered if he himself had the courage to carry out the scheme. Of this he wasn't so sure. He zipped up his vest and said, "I got to think it over. I'll let you know in the morning."

"Suit yourself," said the Judge, reaching across the bar and thrusting his hand into Tom's vest pocket. He drew out the napkin, smoothed it out on the bar, then struck a match and burned it.

46

Tom woke the next morning with resolve, indeed with a kind of light-headed joy. Shaving, he spoke to his image in the mirror. "The doctor's not in, the doctor's retiring after a long career of toil and sacrifice, no banquets, please." He paused in his shaving to laugh aloud. "The doctor's well loved, he knows that, but please, no gifts or speeches or plaques for the wall. The doctor has his memories."

The doorbell sounded. He stopped laughing. He went to the front bedroom, pulled the drapes aside, and looked down on an old car parked in the road. A young Indian man was helping an old Indian woman up to the front door. He didn't know them. The doorbell sounded again. "The doctor's not in," he said softly, backing away from the window and catching a glimpse, the instant before the drapes fell shut, of Joy Pipe's face in her window across the road.

"The doctor's in, but he's busy," he explained to the mirror as he finished shaving. "He's busy arranging his retirement."

When he went back to the bedroom, the car was gone. He paced between the closet and the bureau in his underwear, looking over his clothes. It was hard to know what to take. He couldn't take much without arousing suspicion. He decided, finally, to take only two suits, two shirts, and a couple of changes of underwear. No suitcase. No more than one overcoat. Dead men traveled light.

After dressing, he went around the house withdrawing his savings. He extracted a thick wad of currency from the armband of his extra blood pressure gauge, and he gathered more from a high shelf in the closet of the guest room. His biggest stash—sixteen thousand in hundred-dollar bills, most of it realized from his pre-Basswood transactions in Chicago—was hidden in the layer of insulation surrounding the water heater in the basement. Most of the money he tucked into the various pockets of his two suits and the rest he buttoned into the inside pocket of his down vest. There remained in the house a couple of small caches of money Libby knew about, and these he did not disturb. Dead men weren't big spenders.

After a pick-me-up of orange juice and brandy, he carried his two suits out to the garage and laid them in the trunk of the BMW. Backing out into the road, he noted that Joy Pipe's face was no longer framed in the window of the trailer.

Driving south on 13, he felt euphoric and agitated and a little sick to his stomach. When he reached the Homestead, he considered stopping in for a fortifying beer and to say he was going through with it, but he decided against it. He would see if the day brought misgivings.

The day was cloudless, windless, and very cold. The sky was blue above but hazy near the horizon. The yellow sun hung pale and fuzzy in the southern sky. Looking in the mirror, he saw that the snow on the ice was packed so hard—as Judge Bigelow had observed—that his tires left no trail. What if, by nightfall, fresh snow began to fall—had the Judge thought of that?

A half mile from shore he slowed down and looked left and right at the vast emptiness of Sovereign Lake, the north end hidden by the earth's curve. Billy Annunciation's plywood fish house, ahead on the left, was the only break in the whiteness. What if Billy Annunciation happened to be fishing tonight and saw the car go through the ice and the Judge's Bronco hightail it for town—had the Judge thought of that?

Nearing the far shore, he accelerated past the nine oil drums on his left, building up speed to climb the bank. At the crest of the bank, he met the Linden Falls road where it came off the bridge over the Badbattle. Here ·he turned the car south and stopped to survey the area of tonight's action. Clouds of steam rose up from the open water beneath the bridge and a hundred yards or so out into the lake. Beyond the steam he could see the wide streak of thin ice extending another two or three hundred yards toward the middle of the lake. The thin ice, darker than the rest of the lake, was shaped like a banana, just as the Judge had portrayed it. The Judge had claimed that a hundred yards of safe ice lay between the oil drums and danger, and now from above Tom saw that this was true, or nearly so. Maybe not a hundred yards, but a good long way.

Sitting there on the promontory over the lake, the engine idling, the heater warming him, he watched himself in his mind's eye drive down the embankment at a quarter to one, travel across the ice to the third oil drum, make a sharp right, and pick up the Bronco in his headlights. He saw himself pull up beside the Bronco, roll down his window, and get out, leaving the car to idle forward onto the thin ice and crash through and sink, saw himself hop into the Bronco and be delivered to his BMW in Berrington and the new unfettered life awaiting him. He had friends in Chicago, professional men not especially keen to follow every last letter of the law. Raymond Ganz, who owned practically every parking ramp within sight of the Sears Tower, had more than once asked Tom to be his medical expert, to live high on a retainer year round and testify in the odd lawsuit once in a blue moon. And there was Stanley Ambler the pharmacist, who despite his tiresome admonitions ("This is no business for somebody who scares easy") had enough connections to see Tom through a long career in the drug business.

He pulled away from the lake, feeling bold and frightened by turns. He drove to Linden Falls at high speed and stopped at the Municipal Bar and Lounge for two brandies and a beer to keep his hands from trembling. He drove the fifty miles to Berrington at an even higher speed and had two more brandies at a dingy bar called the Roundhouse. Leaving the Roundhouse, he felt his bowels go suddenly loose and he rushed back inside to the grimy rest room. He came out trembling. He drove down Concord Boulevard, looking for Ron's Body Shop and lifting his hands off the wheel at intervals to observe their shaking.

On a dead-end street beside a railroad embankment, he found the place. It was a large gray metal building surrounded by cars and parts of cars. He honked his horn and the enormous overhead door went up. A tall, bearded man wearing a furry hat and a dirty gray jacket stood inside smiling and beckoning. Tom drove in and stopped. Ahead were two repair bays. One bay was empty. In the other bay a car was being worked on, a young man with a mask over his nose and mouth buffing its rear fender with a rotary sander that caused sparks to fly. Tom froze. Only Ron was supposed to be here. Ron's was a one-man operation. The Judge had given his word.

Ron (the bearded man's name was stitched in red on his dirty gray jacket) pointed to the empty bay, indicating that Tom should park there. Tom hesitated. He wanted to back out—the scheme was already going awry in its first stage—but the overhead door was closing behind him. He eased the BMW ahead and parked. He got out and Ron threw a tarpaulin over the car and asked for the keys.

"Keys?" Tom said through his teeth.

"The keys to your car," said Ron, smiling agreeably behind his beard. His glasses, like everything else in the shop, were covered with a fine film of emery dust.

"Listen, what is this?" said Tom in his grumpiest voice. "Nobody gets these keys, for Chrissake! Are you nuts?" He felt the brandy moving warmly through his arteries. He felt powerful, belligerent, and dizzy. "Nobody touches that car, see?"

Ron shrugged. "Whatever. Most people leave their keys."

They went outside and looked at the cars Tom was to buy. Libby's car wasn't worth $3,800, Tom could see that. Though its engine purred smoothly, it was a model Tom had not seen on the road for years and it was covered with hail dents. The car for himself, an old green Plymouth Satellite, was riddled with rust holes and sounded, when he started it, like a tractor. He protested angrily about the prices, but the imperturbable Ron shrugged and smiled and said, "Take 'em or leave 'em."

Tom took them, drawing money out of his vest. "I'll be back for the other one in a little while," he said, getting into the hail-dented car.

Libby, home from work, had been asleep only a short time when Tom came pounding on her door. He looked at her through the glass, smiling coyly and holding up a key ring. "I got you a car," he said. She unlocked the door and he stepped in smelling of brandy. Taking her hand, he led her into the front room and pointed out the window. "It's got a manual shift. Can you handle a manual shift?"

She looked down at the bullet-shaped car in the street. It was blue. The roof and hood were pitted. A crack in the back window was sealed with a wide strip of tape. She said yes, she could drive it. Years ago she had driven Vernon's pickup with a manual shift.

"It's had some wear, but it runs good. You want to try it out?" He handed her the keys.

She smiled sleepily. "Thanks, Tom."

"Try her out, see how she runs."

"Not now, I'll take your word for it." She dropped the keys into the pocket of her robe. "Thanks," she said again, intrigued by the mix of emotion in his eyes. Underneath the anxiety and inebriation, there was a rare sort of energy fueling him today, something like excitement or hope.

"I'm selling the BMW, like you said I should."

She was surprised, then skeptical. Yesterday, having suggested he sell it, she'd realized she was asking the impossible.

"You don't believe me? Swear to God."

"How much are you getting?"

"Plenty." He moved close to her and laid his hand on her hip. "Libby . . ."

She smiled and did not move away from him.

"Libby, are you still divorcing me?"

She nodded, quickly sorting through the reasons, preparing to explain the obvious. But he surprised her by not protesting. Instead he put his nose in her hair, his lips to her ear.

"Libby, could we go to bed?"

She pulled back a little, her smile growing sad. She shook her head.

"One last time. There's no telling how we're going to feel about each other after the hearing, and then after the divorce. I mean by the time the lawyers are through with us we might *hate* each other." On "hate" he stamped his foot—a petulant little gesture she had never seen him make before—and then, of all things, tears sprang to his eyes. His tears she *had* seen before, whenever he'd drunk himself tearfully maudlin.

She touched his shoulder. "Tom, how much have you had to drink this morning?"

"Not much. Couple of belts."

"Have you been smoking?"

"No." Wiping his eyes, he turned and faced the window. He lifted his flat cap and ran his wet fingers through his hair. He replaced his cap and said, falteringly, "It just feels like the end of something, Libby."

She wasn't much moved. She faced away so he wouldn't see how little he was affecting her.

"Jesus," he said, "look who's here."

The St. Ann's Oldsmobile was pulling up behind the blue car. Verna emerged from one side, Frank from the other.

"Let them in, would you?" said Libby, leaving the room to tend to her hair.

Frank, rehearsing an apology, climbed the steps behind Verna. He had argued against interrupting Libby's sleep, but there was no dissuading Verna. With the two-thousand-dollar loan approved by Danny Ash, she would take her mother shopping for a car. It was to be her peace offering, her token of atonement. She wouldn't hear of putting it off.

Tom opened the door. Frank, amazed, blurted inanely, "So we keep running into each other."

Verna said coldly, "What are you doing here?"

"Come in," said Tom, grinning. "I'm delivering a car to your mother."

"You are?" Verna stepped into the kitchen. "God, so are we."

Frank followed, shaking the hand Tom held out to him, a hand he'd never been offered before. It was stiff and clammy, with a current running through it. The man was obviously tense. His grin was fastened tightly to his face.

"Thirteen below," Frank told him, for lack of anything sensible to say. He'd decided against "How are you" for fear Tom might tell him. Despite the grin, Tom looked distraught. His eyes were red, his lashes wet.

Verna swept into the front room. "You bought her *that*?" she cried, pointing down at the street.

Both men joined her. "It runs like new," Tom bragged.

Verna rushed to the bedroom, calling, "Mom, we came to buy you a car."

Tom and Frank, sharing an awkward silence, stood watching the traffic on Great Northern. At length, Tom sighed and said, "Healy, I never really got to know you."

"No."

"You're tall."

Was Tom drunk? Frank responded with a nod.

"But you're not as tall as the man I just bought that car from."

"No?"

"No." Tom closed his eyes tight. "That man was taller."

Yes, Frank decided, he was plastered.

Libby, followed by her daughter, came into the room wearing a dressier robe than before. "Frank, what's this about a car?"

He pecked the cheek she offered and said, "I see you already have one. That'll save the parish some money."

Tom addressed Frank: "Why not buy one for Verna?"

Libby answered, "She's on meds and can't drive."

"She won't be on meds forever."

"She can't drive?" asked Frank.

Verna, laughing, said, "I just drove from Linden Falls."

"Your title will come in the mail, I've got to go," said Tom, turning abruptly and leaving the room. Libby followed him through the kitchen, thanking him, reaching out to him, but he evaded her touch and slipped out the door and slammed it shut.

"What's bugging him?" asked Verna.

"The hearing," said her mother.

"Well, it ought to."

Libby turned to Frank. "I almost feel sorry for him."

Tom knocked on the door. Libby opened it. He stood on the threshold weeping.

"What is it, Tom?"

"I forgot." He sobbed for a moment, emitting a little puffing sound through his lips; then he got hold of himself and said, "I need a ride back to my car."

Getting into the Olds with Frank, Tom told him how to reach Ron's Body Shop and they set off along Great Northern. After a few blocks, Tom said, "This might sound funny coming from her husband, but I'd like to see Libby team up with you."

"Team up?"

"Be your woman. I mean, you think I'm blind? You think I haven't noticed every time you're together your little hearts go bumpety-bump? Go for it, Healy, you only live once. She's messed up emotionally, but so are you, so you'd probably get along just fine."

Frank turned off Great Northern onto Concord.

"What you two gotta do first is get your sex life going. I'm talking as a doctor now, Healy. Devote a few months to nothing but screwing, and if that goes good, then you can move on to other things. If it doesn't go good, you'll have to go looking for another woman. I mean there's no telling what kind of sexual hang-ups a priest has to overcome."

"Look, Tom, your instruction is wasted on me. If I team up with a woman, it's not going to be anytime soon."

"Why not? You're not getting any younger."

"Because I'm too busy."

"Too repressed, you mean."

"I said too busy. I'm busy trying to find out what sort of life I'm fit for. If there's a woman in my future—and I'm not saying there isn't—it'll be after I've decided I'm not meant for the priesthood. I don't know that yet."

"Time's running out. Wait any longer, she won't want you."

"So be it."

"Listen, Healy, you know why love comes and goes? Because love is based on needs and needs come and go. If you want a certain woman, you got to get her when she needs you. If she doesn't need you, you can stand on your head and she won't give you the time of day."

They drove the remaining blocks in silence. Frank pulled up in front of Ron's. Tom turned to Frank with acrimony in his eyes. "Healy, get one thing straight, would you?"

"What?"

"I'm not an alcoholic."

Frank took a deep breath. "I didn't say you were."

"I've never missed a day of work because of drinking."

"Good for you."

"I've never been arrested in Minnesota for driving under the influence."

"Good for you."

Tom opened his door, but didn't get out. He peered closely at Frank. "You've never cared for me because I had Libby. Well, now you'll have to think up another reason."

"That won't be hard," Frank said.

At this, Tom smiled. It was his broadest grin, fixed and false. He took Frank's hand off the steering wheel and shook it. He got out and slammed the door.

Frank, driving away, saw him climb into a rust-eaten junker.

The rusty Plymouth, burning oil, laid a trail of smoke from Berrington to Linden Falls, where Tom stopped at the Municipal Bar and passed three enjoyable hours exchanging cancer stories with an unemployed housepainter and discussing politics with a retired CPA. The housepainter, like Tom, had lost his mother to stomach cancer. The CPA, like Tom, had disapproved of Johnson, regretted voting for Nixon, and had helped set the country back on course by voting for Carter. Leaving the bar in midafternoon, Tom shook hands warmly with these two men, regretting that it had taken him so long to find close friends in the north country.

It was midafternoon when he reached the Homestead and pounded on the door until the midget unlocked it.

"Hi, Doc, the Judge says to remind you we're closed Mondays."

"I know you're closed Mondays." Tom pushed the little man aside and entered. "Hey, Judge," he called.

"What do you want?" Judge Bigelow was on his knees behind the bar, repairing a carbonation hose.

"A beer." Tom settled himself on a stool.

The Judge scowled up at him. "Are you out of your mind? What are you doing here?"

"I want a beer."

"Get out of here."

"Why?"

"Why! Because of tonight, for God's sake. People find you dead and remember seeing you come in here and first thing you know I'm getting the third degree."

"Find me dead?" Tom shuddered and raised his voice: "Find me dead? Who finds me dead?"

"Finds your car, finds you missing."

Tom rubbed his nose—it was numb from alcohol—and asked softly, "Can I have a beer?"

"One." The Judge struggled to his feet and drew a glass. "You got the beater?"

"A piece of junk."

"You been back and forth over the ice a few times?"

"I just came over. I'll make another trip."

"Anybody see you?"

"Met two cars."

"Good."

Bigelow lowered himself to his knees and began winding black tape around a hose. Tom drained his beer and said, "Judge, what if it snows?"

"So what?"

"Your Bronco leaves tire tracks out there."

"Snow covers them up."

This answer made Tom extremely happy. After being swept all day by alternating waves of confidence and doubt, he was thrilled by the Judge's wisdom. He felt brave again.

"Give me another beer."

"No."

"Judge, what if Billy Annunciation's in his fish house and sees us?"

"One o'clock in the morning?"

"He fishes all hours."

"Not on school nights, he don't."

This answer made Tom glow. His courage redoubled itself.

"Judge, give me another beer."

"Go away, Doc, you're making me nervous. You ought to be in your office seeing patients."

"What patients?" Tom swiveled around on his stool and surveyed the somber interior of the Homestead. In the absence of heat, light, drinkers on stools, and music from the jukebox, the place might have been an abandoned warehouse. Pale daylight fell through the small windows and glimmered in the water Toad Majerus was slopping on the floor with a mop. The beer-cooler motor came to life, stuttering and coughing and setting up a vibration along the bar. The prevailing smells were of fuel oil and stale cigarette smoke.

"All right," said Tom, stepping down off his stool. "Give me a twelve-pack and I'll go home and see my patients." He unzipped his vest and drew out a hundred-dollar bill.

Judge Bigelow climbed to his feet again, opened the cooler, and lifted out the beer. "It's on the house."

"Thanks."

Judge Bigelow smiled his slack, insinuating smile. "It's nothing, my friend."

Tom lowered his voice: "Did you tell the midget?"

"Yup, any objections?"

"No, I *want* him to know. The more he knows, the harder it'll be for you to go back on your word."

The smile turned hard. "Don't worry, I'll be out there at quarter to one."

Toad Majerus let him out. "So long, Doc, sorry you can't

stay, but Monday's the day we catch up on our work. Good luck now, we'll miss you around here."

On his way to the car, Tom noticed half a dozen snowflakes melting on his sleeve. He opened a beer and drove down the bank and out onto the ice. Driving slowly, he noticed how the snowfall, though not heavy, softened things in the distance. The far shore was hazy. Moving slowly across the lake, he met a car driven by an Indian he didn't know. He waved, calling attention to himself in the Plymouth, and the man waved back. Nearing Billy's fish house, he saw a snowmobile parked beside it. Wispy smoke rose from the pipe in the roof. He honked his horn, hoping to draw Billy to the tiny window. He saw a face at the glass but it wasn't Billy's. It was Elaine LaBonte's. He waved and her face disappeared. In his mirror he saw the LaBontes' old bronze Chrysler trailing him across the ice. He saw it stop beside the fish house. He saw Millie LaBonte get out.

At the far shore he turned around and drove back. Millie LaBonte was standing at the open door of the fish house looking in. Tom honked and she turned. She had a tight, angry look on her face. Tom waved. She didn't wave. She turned back to the open door and leaned inside. Tom opened another beer and drove home.

47

Elaine LaBonte was mortified by her mother's fit of rage. Having skidded to a stop on the ice, her mother had thrown open the door of the fish house and railed at Elaine in front of Billy. "You're supposed to be home watching the kids!" she shouted. "I came home and found them alone. You're supposed to be home every day after school watching the kids."

"Watch them do what?" Elaine shot back. "Watch them watch television?" Elaine never gave in when her mother became temperamental. As long as her mother was civil, she was an obedient daughter, but at times like this she stiffened and fought back. "It doesn't hurt the kids to be alone once in a while. What about when I worked at the Health Center? You never expected me home then."

"That was different. There was a good reason for it."

"Well, there's a good reason for it now."

"What's the reason?"

"I'm fishing."

"Carl Butcher will give us a mess of fish any time we want." Elaine raised her voice. "I'm fishing with *Billy*."

"What's Billy got to do with it?"

"Billy's my *boyfriend*."

At this her mother clenched her fists and made a gargling sound in her throat.

Billy was sitting on the wood box with his head hanging over the hole in the ice, staring at his bobber. He was getting a bite, and just when Elaine's mother reached the high point of her fit—shaking her fists and growling—he pulled a gleaming walleye out of the hole, leaped to his feet, and dangled it in front of her. Hoping to appease her, he said, "Here, Mrs. LaBonte, this is for you."

"I don't want your stinking fish!" she screeched, and just then a noisy car rumbled past the fish house, and the three of them looked out and saw Dr. Pearsall driving an old tin can with a muffler problem. The sight of the doctor in a rusty jalopy was diverting enough to take the edge off Millie LaBonte's anger. In a lowered voice she exchanged a few more unhappy words with her daughter, then she climbed into the Chrysler and drove away.

Her anger had rubbed off on her daughter. Pulling the door shut, Elaine pointed to the wood box and asked, "Is there enough wood to keep the fire going all night, because if there is, I'm not going home."

Billy lifted the lid of the box and said there was. Then he shot her a skeptical look. "You're not serious."

"I'm plenty serious," she said through tight lips. "Let her stew and fret and lie awake wondering where I am all night, and maybe next time she'll think twice before she blows her cork."

She saw Billy's eyes light up and she thought for a moment he was going to offer to stay with her, but his interest was primarily in fish.

"Great," he said. "You'll be here for the three o'clock run." He told her he'd read in a magazine that walleyes were active and feeding around three or four in the morning, but his grandparents never let him fish at that hour. "You'll probably catch your limit," he said.

"I'm not fishing all night, Billy. I'm sleeping."

"Sleeping on what?"

Both of them looked at the damp plywood floor with its scattering of wood chips, ice lumps, and dead minnows. Elaine lay down on the wood box, trying it for size. She fit on it from her head to just below her knees. "Move my stool over," she said. Billy did so, and she rested her feet on it.

"You can't just sleep on a box," said Billy. "You need blankets and stuff."

"Bring me out a blanket when you go home for supper."

"Aren't you going home for supper?"

"I'm staying here till school in the morning." She glanced at her bookbag hanging on a nail over the stove. "I've got my homework. I've got heat. Bring me a couple pillows, would you?"

"Sure, but I'll have to tell my grandma what's going on."

"That's okay, just make her promise to play dumb if my mother calls her up."

Billy nodded. Both of them were confident that his grandmother would play along. She and Millie LaBonte had never been on the best of terms.

"And could you bring me some supper?"

Billy sped home on the snowmobile and came back in the truck with blankets and pillows and hot soup in a bottle and coffee and sandwiches and a sack of cookies. His grandparents, he said, were willing to go along with this scheme as long as he came right back home, because Caesar needed the pickup.

Elaine understood this to be a cover-up for the real reason: Caesar and Joy worried that their grandson and Elaine might have sex in the fish house. They'd said as much to the Butchers and the Butchers told Elaine's mother. Well, they didn't need to worry. Elaine had had sex with Tim Cashman once and it was such a disaster she decided not to do it again until she was good and ready. Billy had been saying he was ready, but Elaine had assured him he wasn't. She said she'd tell him when he was ready.

They kissed and Billy went home. It grew dark. She read her history and did her algebra by the light of three candles. It was eerie on the lake all alone. It was so quiet she could hear the tiny sizzle of snowflakes falling against the stovepipe. Whenever a car drove onto the lake, she saw the water bounce up a few inches in the fish hole. She caught two fish, but after the second one she didn't bait the hook. She read another history chapter and paged through her algebra text to see what mysteries lay ahead. At nine o'clock she blew out the candles so that when her mother began to wonder where she was, she could see from shore that the fish house was dark and she wouldn't drive out looking for her.

48

Tom locked the doors and left the Health Center for the final time at nine o'clock. No moon. The streetlight out. An inch of new snow blanketing 13. The old Plymouth stiff with cold, the engine knocking, one of the headlights winking off and on.

Out on the lake a few snowflakes zigzagged in the headlights. Little drifts were building up on the ice, obscuring the trail in places. Billy's fish house was dark. Nearing the far shore, Tom crept along cautiously, fearful of veering left toward the strip of thin ice. At last the orange oil drums came into view and guided him safely to land.

He timed the drive from the lake to Linden Falls (eleven minutes), ate a steak and french fries at the Deluxe Diner, and then walked along Main Street to the Municipal Bar and Lounge, where he was reunited with the housepainter whose mother had died of cancer and was introduced to a butcher with a college degree in biology and a man whose father had Alzheimer's. A short time later the Upward brothers came in and sat directly across the horseshoe bar from Tom and his friends. Because the Upwards stood for everything Tom despised about the northern wilderness—guns, poverty, inconsequential lives led in squalid

481

little shacks—he was filled with repugnance at the sight of them and moved with his friends to a booth.

As the evening wore on, he grew a little tired of holding forth on the miracles of modern medicine, and he wished the retired CPA would show up so he could talk politics or sports. The housepainter and the butcher didn't have a single interesting opinion between them about the Carter administration and the other man, though he apparently had a theory about the increasing mayhem in professional hockey, was too drunk to express it coherently.

Tom remained sober. He drank a great deal but he couldn't seem to get a buzz on. At closing time he held open the door of the lounge as the painter and the butcher helped the other man outside, and he held open the door of the painter's car as they folded him into the backseat. He stood in the street waving good-bye to the painter, the butcher, and the dozen or so others who drove off into the frigid night. He walked to his car and checked his watch. He was a little early. He considered going into the Deluxe Diner for coffee, but he saw the Upward brothers sitting at the counter. He got into his car and left town. It wasn't snowing now, but the snow that had fallen kept getting up off the ground and swirling around in the wind. He drove very slowly and it was nearly one o'clock when he arrived at Sovereign Lake.

He turned off the road and bounced down the bank, following the tracks of someone who had recently cut through the small drifts. At the third oil drum he turned right and picked up the Judge's Bronco in his headlights. It stood facing him but farther off than he expected. Much farther off. Was it the swirling snow that made it look so far? He rolled down his window and drove slowly and fearfully ahead and was stopped by a drift. He backed up and came at it faster, broke through it, broke through a second drift, kept his speed up and broke through others, drove much farther than he thought safe, but still the Bronco was out there ahead of him—he saw the hulking form of the Judge behind the wheel—and it was only when he felt the ice give way that he realized the Judge was parked on the far side of the strip of thin ice and his cry of horror was engulfed by the freezing water washing in through the window.

Elaine LaBonte saw it happen.

She had slept very little because of the hardness of her make-shift bed and because every twenty minutes or so the fire consumed all the wood she could cram into the tiny stove. At around 12:30, feeding the fire, she had heard the ice groan as it always did when a car approached and she looked out and saw the Judge's Bronco coming from the Homestead. She recognized it by its raised headlights, and she recognized the Judge in the cab as he drove by, his face lit softly by the green glow of the dash lights. She watched the taillights proceed over the ice to a point where she imagined the outermost oil drum to be, and then, curiously, she saw the Bronco make an abrupt turn to the left. The taillights were lost for a moment in a swirl of windblown snow, and when they reappeared, they were moving along the north side of the thin ice, where she had never seen anyone drive before. Then the Bronco turned again, right this time, and stopped. Its headlights shone south for a moment, across the thin ice, then went out.

Elaine stirred the fire. The wood caught and the fish house grew warm again, but she did not lie down. She sat in the dark peering out the small square of glass facing east. Now and then the Bronco's taillights flashed as Judge Bigelow, apparently shifting positions, touched the brake. After a while she saw a car approach the lake from Linden Falls. It was Dr. Pearsall's tin can—she had seen the blinking headlight earlier on his way into town. She watched the car bounce down the bank and out onto the lake, saw it turn north, saw it move toward the Bronco, saw it sink through the ice. She held her breath in horror until water gushed up and flooded the floor of the fish house and then she screamed.

The Bronco's headlights came on and she stopped screaming. The water sank down the holes. Her feet were wet and freezing. The Bronco came toward her. She considered stepping outside and hitching a ride to shore but her instincts warned her not to—not with the Judge, of all people. She crouched down as he drove by. Then she put more wood on the fire—luckily the waterline had not been quite as high as the stove—and prayed that one more car would come along.

One did, a half hour later. Johnny and Pock. She told them what she had seen, and they drove directly to the Pipes' house to tell Caesar.

At two o'clock Judge Bigelow was lying in bed congratulating himself on a job well done and planning his phone call to Ron's Body Shop in the morning ("Paint it black and sell it," he would say to Ron) when he heard the squeaky brakes of a vehicle easing itself down the incline to the ice. Raising himself on his elbow and looking out his window—it was Caesar Pipe in his pickup—he was astonished to see the flashing lights of a patrol car across the lake. Two patrol cars. They were parked near the thin ice. He saw a third patrol car arrive. Next came the flashing blue light of a county maintenance truck or a wrecker. Then another car, not a patrol car. And then another. Spotlights played over the ice.

The Judge heaved himself up out of bed, slipped his red jacket on over his underwear, and went out to the bar to mix himself a drink in the dark. Toad Majerus, wearing a football jersey as a nightshirt, emerged from the room he shared with brooms and shovels and tools and went to the cooler for a can of 7-Up. Neither man spoke. The Judge crossed the room to the booth by the window. The midget followed and sat opposite him. Sipping their drinks, they stared at the lights.

After a while Toad Majerus asked, "What went wrong?"

"Nothing."

"I saw the car go under and you never went to Berrington."

"So what?"

"I thought you were supposed to take him to Berrington."

They gazed out the window in silence until they saw two patrol cars break away from the cluster of lights. When it became apparent that the cars were heading for Basswood, Judge Bigelow shot his fist across the booth and struck the midget full in the face. "You little bastard!" he screamed. "You called the cops!"

"I never did," cried Toad Majerus, toppling flat on the seat, holding his nose. "I never did."

The Judge rose from the booth and gripped the midget by one of his ankles. "You worthless little bastard!" he roared, yanking the little man off the seat and onto the floor. He kicked him once and then kicked air, for the midget was on his feet and running in the dark.

The Judge heard him scramble under the pool table, heard him panting and whimpering under there. He took down a pool cue and went to his knees and probed. When he hit flesh, he jabbed with all his might and the midget uttered a shriek of pain. Bigelow gave the cue another thrust and was suddenly empty-handed. He felt around under the table and was jabbed himself with the blunt end of the cue. A harder jab followed. He reached as far under the table as his bulk would allow and caught the midget by the jersey. He tugged, gained a grip on the midget's arm, and just as he got him out from under the table and was about to put his hands to his throat he heard the cue whipping through the air an instant before it struck him flat against his ear and cheek. Roaring and raging with pain, the Judge fell on the midget, fell across him with his hand over the little man's face, and they lay like that, the midget struggling to breathe and the Judge panting noisily, as the headlights of the patrol cars moved across the ceiling and along the walls.

The cars pulled up at the door, and the tavern was filled with the red strobe of their flashing lights. There was a pounding on the door and then a voice at one of the windows. "Judge, we got to talk to you." It was Caesar Pipe.

Silence. Flashlights at the windows.

More pounding, then more silence.

"Hey, Judge," Caesar called again.

The midget kept twisting his head under the Judge's hand, creating little spaces to get air. He managed to bite the Judge at the base of the thumb, and the instant the hand was lifted away he cried for help.

The door was forced and four law officers, guns drawn, entered with Caesar Pipe. Their flashlights picked out Judge Bigelow getting to his feet and the midget rushing toward them from behind the pool table. One of the officers found a light switch. Light revealed the Judge leaning on the pool table, breathless, sweating, his hair hanging in his eyes, and the midget clinging to the leg of Caesar Pipe and babbling hysterically.

The babble, when they eventually comprehended it, was incriminating.

49

Caesar Pipe phoned Frank at 3:00 A.M. The car had been found in eighteen feet of water with Dr. Pearsall inside. His body had been brought up. His wife needed to be notified.

Frank was out the door and on his way to Berrington at 3:10. Dear God, another life given up to Sovereign Lake. Father Zell was mourned by hordes of pioneers and Indians. Will anyone mourn this reluctant missionary? Will Libby?

Yes. Standing in her bright yellow kitchen in her dark blue bathrobe, Libby broke out in a piercing cry: "Tom! Not Tom!"

"It's Tom. Caesar Pipe identified him."

"Drowned?"

"A diver went down and brought up his body."

She threw her arms around him. "Oh Frank, oh Frank."

He eased her onto a kitchen chair. She sat stiffly and very still. She was not weeping. With that initial cry she seemed to have expelled all emotion. Folding her hands on her lap, she closed her eyes and lowered her head. Was she praying? Dozing? When she finally looked up, it was to ask dispassionately, "Will I get over this?" She might have been inquiring about a sprain or a cold. He told her she would.

"I'm groggy, Frank. I take sleeping pills on my nights off."
Again she closed her eyes.

Frank pulled up a chair close beside her and they sat in silence.
The bright overhead light reflected harshly off the glossy yellow
walls. The faucet dripped. A train announced itself in the distance. He put his arms around her. "He was coming from town,
Caesar said."

"Yes, Monday night," she replied, nodding. "The Homestead's closed Mondays."

"But why on the ice, I wonder. He never drove the ice road."

Libby shrugged. "Drinking made him brave sometimes."

She gave him her hand. It was very cold. His eyes roamed
the kitchen—the flowered potholder on a hook over the stove,
the matching flowered toaster cover, the pots and pans hanging
by their handles, the grocery list magnetized to the refrigerator.

She said, "He wanted to be cremated."

"He did?"

"To get warm."

A joke. Frank chuckled politely. Libby uttered a little moan
and he glanced at her and saw no sign of humor in her face. Not
a joke after all. He fell silent.

"Where's his body?"

"The funeral home in Linden Falls."

"Can you arrange it, Frank? Cremation and burial?"

"Yes."

Staring at the wall, she nodded and said, "Good."

"Do you want a service?"

She pondered this a long time, then shook her head. "No
service."

"Burial where?"

This, too, she pondered. "Anywhere but Basswood."

"What about his family?"

He saw in her eyes that the question didn't register. Several
moments passed before she asked, "What did you say?"

"His brother and sisters."

"Ah. Would you call them?"

"Yes."

"I have their names and addresses in my purse."

The train whistle sounded again, closer now. The hand he held seemed to be growing colder. He enclosed it in both of his own.

"Frank, would you go to bed with me?"

His turn to ponder—not his decision but his phrasing. He settled on "No."

"Please." She was still gazing at the yellow wall.

"I can't."

She shifted in her chair, turning away from him, and sighed. The locomotive drew abreast of the house and hurtled past, its whistle wailing.

"Cotton Belt," she said.

"What?"

"Cotton Belt. Southern Pacific."

"Oh."

"I outlived him, Frank."

"Yes."

"I shouldn't have outlived him."

He squeezed her hand. "Libby."

"I outlived Harris, too, but Harris was old. Tom wasn't old. I should be the one dead."

"Libby."

"Me, not Tom."

"You should not be the one dead, Libby. Look at me."

She slowly turned to him. Her eyes were wide, unblinking, unseeing. She said, "Seattle and North Coast. Conrail."

He shook her gently by the arm. "Libby."

She broke into a slight, distracted smile and rose from her chair. "I'll get the names and addresses."

She was in the bedroom a minute or more before she called to him and he went to the door and saw her standing naked beside the bed. She put her arms out to him. "Lie down with me, Frank."

His animal response was instantaneous and drew him into the room, but it was quickly followed by an even stronger impulse to be be cautious, to quell once more the desire he'd felt for her since boyhood, to lower his eyes to the floor and say, "Libby, you don't understand."

"Look at me, Frank."

He raised his eyes. Libby, beautiful Libby—her head tilted slightly to the left, her dark hair brushing her white shoulder, her dark eyes puzzled and pleading, her arms down at her sides now, her hands open to him, her elbows turned in at her narrow waist, her breasts created to fit perfectly into the hands he was unconsciously cupping.

He picked her robe off the bed and draped it around her shoulders, guiding her hands into the sleeves. She was trembling. As he drew the lapels together over her breasts he reflected not with regret so much as wonder on the superhuman perversity expected of the priest, the contrariness of covering the sublime nakedness of a woman other men—normal men—would naturally disrobe. And yet this did not feel like perversity to Frank. Not tonight. Not with Libby so distracted, so desperate, so vulnerable. It felt like common sense.

"You're absolutely right, Frank. I'll never, *never* understand." She sank to the bed and lay curled on her side, facing him. "Conrail—did I say Conrail?" She drew him down to sit in the hollow of her curl. "Did I say Green Bay and Western?" Her voice was drowsy.

He was still wearing his coat. He sat there for several minutes, leaning forward, his elbows on his knees, her hand lying flat against his lower back. He was thinking about the night years ago when they'd gone walking through the town after the Berrington game, Vernon two-timing her and her father terrorizing her mother, and he'd refused her the refuge of his big silent house on Pincherry Street. *That* was perversity. And then, later, her marriage to Vernon washed up, his refusal to admit that she'd come to visit him in the seminary. That, too, was perversity. Tonight's denial was not. Dear God, help me make her see the difference. He twisted around to explain the difference to her and saw that she was asleep.

"Libby."

Her sleep was apparently deep. Twice more he spoke her name and she didn't stir. He remained sitting on the bed for a while longer, listening to her breathe and staring at his watch. At 4:30 he shook her by the shoulder and her eyes opened.

"Libby, I'm going home. I have a Mass at eight and then I'll make the arrangements for Tom and come right back. Will you be all right?"

The eyes closed.

"Libby, I'm leaving now, but I'm coming back. Will you be all right?"

"I'm dead," she whispered. A faint smile appeared on her lips as she added, "As long as I'm dead I'm fine."

He drew the covers up to her shoulders, kissed her lightly on the temple, and left.

Starting the Olds and pulling away from the curb, he felt a strong force of some kind pulling his attention back up the stairs to her bedroom. The force of lust, he supposed, dismissing it. But the force followed him beyond the outskirts of Berrington and it didn't feel like lust. It felt like fear. Fear of what? Fear that she might despair and harm herself? Again he dismissed it. She had survived worse things than this. The dead man was not her beloved, after all, but the despoiler of her daughter, the husband she was about to divorce. And she hadn't shed a tear. In fact she'd seemed altogether more composed than on her visits to Verna in the hospital. And hadn't he left her falling asleep with something like a smile on her lips?

But thirty miles of highway did nothing to dispel his anxiety. What had she said, "As long as I'm dead, I'm fine"? She'd meant dead tired, hadn't she? And before that—"I should be the one dead, not Tom." And she had sleeping pills. He was well over halfway to Linden Falls when he turned the car around.

At that moment, Libby, dressed in gray slacks and a red sweater, stood at her bathroom mirror brushing her hair. She made a quick job of it, brushing roughly and glancing nervously at her watch every few seconds, and when she finished, she returned to the bedroom and made the bed. She was full of energy and purpose and her heart was beating fast. Frank had no more than closed the kitchen door and descended the steps when she'd been visited by a flash of insight. It was a long-range vision affording her a clear view of the hopeless mess her life had always been and would continue to be if she didn't take control of herself and end it. Rising from the bed, she had gone into the front room and looked out at Noonan's Car Wash and the Buena Vista Apartments and was struck by the absurdity of living alone at the age of forty-four on a grimy street in a frigid city of strangers. She was unable to afford a used car. She was unable to get along with her daughter. She'd had a dolt and two perverts for husbands. She was so unbearably lonely that she'd frightened off the only good man she'd ever known by stripping like a whore in front of him. It was a relief to recognize after forty-four years of mistakes that they could all be gathered together and thought of as one overriding mistake. The mistake of having been born.

She made the bed, and then she straightened the bedroom, the bathroom and kitchen, all the while keeping an eye on her watch, and when she judged that enough time had passed for Frank to reach home, she went into the front room and sat with the phone in her lap, poised to dial his number. Giving him a few extra minutes to get into bed, she studied her painting on the easel. She hated it for its cramped, mean quality. Everything about it was small and hard and inhibited. She had no talent for painting. For loving. For living. Well, there would be nothing small and inhibited about her death. She'd always imagined suicide with sleeping pills, but now she knew that a drugged death would not leave the mark she wanted to make on the world. Her death would be smashing and instantly obliterating. But first Frank must be told he wasn't responsible. True, his refusal to get into bed and comfort her was enough to tip the balance between life and death, but he must not go through life suspecting that.

Adrian Lawrence had to go to the bathroom. He rose groggily from his bed and went out into the hallway, still half-asleep but alert enough to notice Frank's door standing open, his bedside lamp burning, his bed empty. Adrian, what if we had married? asked the voice of Jo Stafford, resuming the dialogue he had been carrying on with her in a dream. What if you had had children, sons and daughters of your own flesh, do you ever wonder about that, Adrian dear? He weaved down the hallway thinking he really should try to come fully awake, but he made no effort to do so because hers was the most beautiful voice he'd ever heard, strong yet soft, low yet distinctly feminine. Not this again, he imagined himself telling her gently, for it was his policy to handle Jo Stafford with a kind of soft resistance. Please, Miss Stafford, we've been through all this.

But do you, Adrian? Do you ever think about what your life would have been like if you had shared it with a woman? Entering the bathroom, he chuckled as he replied, Can't you see I am sharing my life with Marcella Tatzig?

Don't make me laugh, said Jo Stafford.

Adrian chuckled again—he enjoyed teasing her. Standing at the toilet relieving himself, he added, And there's always Eunice Pfeiffer.

Stop it, Adrian. You're not being serious. . . .

The phone rang in Frank's room, silencing Jo Stafford. He left the bathroom and went to answer it, fumbling for a moment with the receiver before he put it to his ear. He had no more than cleared his throat when a woman began speaking to him.

"No matter what happens, please know I love you. Don't blame yourself for anything—just remember that. You have to understand that what I'm doing is inevitable. In fact, if it weren't for you, it would probably have happened before this."

It wasn't Jo Stafford, but the voice was no less appealing. Pressing the phone tightly to his better ear, the monsignor lowered himself to the edge of Frank's bed and sat there smiling sublimely. His fantasy life, so gratifying of late, was becoming downright exciting. The voice continued, breathy and urgent and charged with love.

"What I mean is, having you near is the main thing that got me through the winter."

There was a long pause. He heard her breathing. If he spoke, would he break the spell? Would she vanish? He took the chance, whispering tentatively, "Yes?"

"That's all I can say, Frank. I love you and you're not to blame."

Frank? The monsignor covered his eyes, straining to inscribe in his memory the lovely sensation of imagining for those few moments that she'd been addressing him.

The dial tone sounded.

She put her gray tam on her head and carried her gray jacket into the kitchen, where she laid it across the back of a chair. With a damp rag she wiped off the counter and stove top and then she swept the floor, all the while listening for the sound of the next freight at the Twenty-fourth Street crossing. She opened the refrigerator and threw everything perishable into the garbage. She raised the shade, switched on the outdoor light, and checked the thermometer. Six below. She looked at her watch. It was nearly five. It would be nearly two hours until dawn began to light up the eastern sky. She sat down at the table with a tablet and pen and was writing a brief message to Verna in a scrawl she herself didn't recognize, saying she loved her and she wasn't to blame, when a train called to her. She looked again at her watch. How incredible that in one minute she'd be gone from the world.

She signed the note "L" and put on her jacket. She turned down the thermostat, switched off the kitchen light, and went out, leaving the door unlocked. She paused at the top of the step, under the light, to look again at her watch. She and the train must arrive together, for if she had to stand at the tracks waiting, she might lose her nerve. Unhurried, she descended the steps. She walked along the driveway. She looked both ways and started across Great Northern, but had to step back to let a speeding truck go by. Then she crossed the street at a run, aware of a car pulling over to the curb behind her, aware of its door swinging open and slamming shut, aware of footsteps following her— could the driver have read suicide in her face? She ran faster, she ran between the car wash and the apartment house, conscious of a wonderful buoyancy in her stride, conscious of the train's thunderous weight bearing down on the point where she would meet it, conscious of a syllable or two—perhaps her name—shouted close behind her but drowned out by the screaming whistle. Then she felt a hand brushing her shoulder, her hip, her leg, felt the hand clutch her ankle and trip her, and she fell flat on her face at the foot of the embankment as the locomotive, hooting and roaring, passed overhead.

She fought to free herself, struggled to crawl up the incline to the clattering steel wheels, but the grip remained locked on her ankle, and then the train was gone. In the dark silence, she lay inert in the snow. She knew it was Frank. She refused to stand. He pulled her forcibly to her feet and she refused to walk. He half carried, half dragged her between the apartment house and the car wash. At the edge of the street she recovered enough vitality to stand on her own, and he coaxed her across. He helped her up the steps and into the kitchen. She stood under the glare of the ceiling light with her shoulders slumped and a fixed, empty look in her eyes. Her expression said, All right, if I'm supposed to go on living, you'll have to tell me why. He removed her jacket and led her into the bedroom and slipped off his coat and shoes and lay with her in his arms. He said nothing, and neither did she. Several minutes passed before his breathing slowed to normal. More time passed before she spoke.

"Why is my life so ugly, Frank?"

"Talk about it, Libby."

She was silent.

He prompted, "What's the ugliest part of your life, Libby?"

"Verna with Tom, in that way."

"That's over."

"Not the effect. Not on Verna. That isn't over." Her voice sounded thin and far-off. It was the dull voice of the deaf, devoid of inflection.

"We don't know the effect yet."

"We do. It drove her crazy."

"She's not crazy anymore."

"She's not normal."

"She's getting there. You should see her with Adrian. She's very kind to him. They jolly each other along. It's beautiful."

"Beautiful?" She strung the word out in a kind of moan.

Frank said, "Everything she does around the house, every little act of kindness, is beautiful because you know she's capable of great ugliness."

"She'll go back to it."

"Will she?"

"She might."

"Yes," Frank admitted, "she might."

He fell asleep. When he woke up, it was still dark and Libby was asking in a sleepy voice, "How did you get here so fast? I talked to you on the phone."

"When?"

"A few minutes before I went out."

"You talked to me?"

"I called to say you weren't to blame."

"I wasn't home. I turned around before I got home."

"Somebody answered."

"Adrian."

"I told him I loved him."

"Good."

"I love you."

"That's good, too."

Again he slept and woke.

"Frank, you saved my life."

"I know."

"What are you going to do with it?"

"What do you mean?"

"It's your life. You saved it."

"It's yours, Libby, not mine."

"I don't want it."

"You have to want it."

"Why?"

"It's precious."

"It's worthless."

"It's a gift."

"A gift? I want to give it away."

"There's no one to give it to, Libby. It's yours forever. It will get better. It seems worthless now, but it will get better."

"When?"

"In a few hours, when I take you to the hospital."

"I don't work tonight."

"To Hope. I'm taking you to the Hope Unit."

"No."

"A few days there, Libby. I can't leave you alone."

"No."

Now Libby slept. Frank lay awake. When at length he changed positions, she woke and turned her head to the window. The orange light of Noonan's Car Wash was growing pale. She said, "It's getting light out."

"Finally."

"What time is your Mass?"

"Forget Mass. I'm skipping it today."

"Do you do that often?"

"No."

"Ever?"

"Today."

"Never before in your life?"

"No."

A minute of silence.

"Frank, I'm not going into the Hope Unit."

"Why not?"

"I've seen too much of it."

"What's wrong with it?"

"Nothing's wrong with it. I've just seen too much of it. The walls. The drapes. The chairs. The charts on the bulletin boards. It's all part of Verna's troubles. I can't bear the thought of sleeping and eating there."

"But somewhere."

"There's not another mental-health facility within a hundred and fifty miles."

"So? Why not Minneapolis? Chicago? What's holding you here?"

"You."

"Libby, I can't—"

"Shhh, I understand. I'm not asking for all of you. Just to

be able to see you. Talk to you. I promise I won't harm myself if you never leave me."

He sighed.

She raised herself up on her elbow and looked down at him. "I don't mean full-time, Frank. I mean just to see you every so often, and talk things over. Is that all right?"

"Of course."

"Promise?"

"Yes."

She lay back on the pillow and after a minute asked, "Frank, have you ever been hopeless?"

"Sort of."

"Have you ever felt like killing yourself?"

"No."

"Neither had I, until this winter. It's like hope doesn't reach this far north."

"But it does, Libby. Hope goes wherever you want it to."

"For you it does, but not for me. Not this winter. That's why I need you."

PART FIVE

50

April. Bright morning sunlight. Bird song on the breeze. "God bless Elvis Presley," murmured Monsignor Adrian Lawrence as he let himself out the kitchen door, "and God bless Sir Anthony Eden." He carried a mug of coffee and a copy of *Life* across the backyard to the lawn chair standing between two enormous, leafless maple trees, and he sat down to wait for Frank to emerge from church. Because the sun had not yet burned through the chill of the morning, he wore a green wool scarf tucked into the collar of his black suitcoat and a blue watch cap pulled down over his ears.

"God bless Maria Callas," he murmured, surveying the yard for wind damage. "God bless Peter Finch." According to Mrs. Tatzig, who was now upstairs helping Verna pack her bags, a windstorm had blown through town in the night and brought down several trees and lifted shingles off several houses. Fortunately, except for a scattering of twigs and small branches and a bird's nest lying upside down in the grass, the rectory and its surroundings seemed to have been spared. The nest, it appeared, was that of a robin.

His copy of *Life* was a tattered, year-end issue that he had found at the barber's yesterday and asked permission to borrow, because it contained photos of the many celebrities who had died during the previous year and he couldn't be sure they'd left behind soulmates to pray for them. He leafed through it now, searching for the obituary section. "James M. Cain, may you rest in peace," he said when he located it. He sipped his lukewarm coffee and added, "Joan Crawford and Wernher von Braun, may you rest in peace."

Mr. and Mrs. Robin came swooping down onto the grass, startling Adrian out of his prayers. They hopped around their fallen nest, inspecting it, and then they quickly went to work gathering twigs from the lawn. Adrian watched them fly over the hedge and choose a tree in a neighbor's yard for their new home. He heard them chirping happily on their return flight and imagined their saying, Let's look on the good side of it and consider ourselves lucky that the storm that brought down our finished home has provided us with all these twigs for our new one.

Ah, to be so reconciled, thought Adrian. If only we human beings could learn to accommodate what nature does to us. If only Eunice Pfeiffer in particular would call off her assault on my old age. What distorted sense of nostalgia or wishful thinking compels Eunice to think that I'd care to live out my last years in that tiny room next to hers in the dismal Kittleson Arms? She began her campaign with a rather timid suggestion by letter in January, but since her brother Kelvin's funeral it has become a barrage of phone calls. Poor soul, she's all up in the air. Had it been Raymond who died, she might have stayed on the farm, for Raymond never lifted a finger around the place and would not have been missed as a handyman. It was Kelvin, on the other hand, who saw to the furnace and snowplowing in winter and cut the grass in summer and kept the old Chevrolet in running order, and it isn't the easiest thing to see God's reasons for calling him home. He died of a coronary in the machine shed.

Each day Adrian prayed that Eunice wouldn't call him up. He despised having to feign insanity in order to get her off the phone. The line that worked best with Eunice was the one where he told her he was pressed for time because Bishop Swayles was coming to call. Forgive my shameless deceit, O Lord, and may

Bishop Swayles, along with James Jones and Vladimir Nabokov and all the faithful departed, rest in peace.

Adrian was turning to the next page of dead people when he saw Frank coming across the yard from his schoolchildren's Mass. Frank was pastor now, Frank with all the right gifts for the job—compassion, energy, and a good head for business. A month ago Adrian had suggested to Bishop Baker that Frank take over the reins, and the bishop had readily made the appointment. Too bad Frank had been buried in the Academy for so many years. If he'd been out and around, making his mark in parishes, he might be well on his way to being a bishop himself by this time. The Church, God knew, was in need of his type.

"Good morning, Adrian."

"Ah, Frank my boy, look here. Did you know that Bing Crosby, Ethel Waters, and Guy Lombardo all got away from us in the same year?"

Frank took the magazine and scanned the pictures. "And Groucho Marx."

Adrian chuckled.

"And Gary Gilmore," Frank added.

Adrian frowned. "Yes, executed. Let's hope our Lord is healing him with his loving-kindness."

Frank gave back the magazine. "Is Verna ready?"

"Marcella's up there hurrying her along."

"I'll be gone till four or five. Her mother and I are taking her to the vocational school."

"Yes, so she told me. The travel-agent course of study. How is her mother, Frank?"

"Doing pretty well. Busy at the hospital. There's a lot of old people with flu this spring."

"Such a pity, losing her husband like that. I don't care what comes out against him at Bigelow's trial, he must have been a caring, generous man, doctoring the Indians the way he did."

A large flock of robins glided into the yard on a gust of wind and hopped crazily about, pecking in the grass and uttering a chorus of unmusical sounds suggesting joy. "Ready!" called Verna from her upstairs window, her voice suggesting a similar sort of joy or expectation. Frank hurried to the house.

"Frank," the monsignor called from his chair, but Frank was already indoors. He wanted to ask Frank about two of the recently dead in *Life*. Roberto Rossellini—wasn't he that cardinal from Venice who nearly became pope? And who was Anaïs Nin?

Ten minutes later Verna came flying out the back door and across the yard to plant a kiss on the monsignor's cheek. She held his head in her arms for a moment before releasing him and stepping back to ask how he liked her new outfit—black skirt, cream blouse, leaf green sweater.

"Beautiful," he said, "just lovely." But her makeup was overdone, in his opinion. The bright red lipstick and pink rouge and dark eye shadow made her look clownish in the bright sun. From an inner pocket of his coat, he drew out a fifty-dollar bill, which he folded small and placed in her palm. "For incidentals," he said.

"Oh, Adrian." She kissed him again and was about to fly off to the garage, where Frank was loading her bags into the Olds, when the monsignor detained her by clutching her wrist. "You'll come back and see us."

"Oh, yes, Adrian—all the time. I love it here."

"Lovely." He kissed the hand and released her.

Mrs. Tatzig came out to watch them back out of the driveway. She stood on the step waving a spatula as they sped away. When they were out of sight, she called to Adrian, "Eunice Pfeiffer's on the phone."

He made his way slowly across the yard, stirring up the robins and rehearsing his response. He decided not to play false with Eunice anymore. It was high time he faced up to her pleading. No, Eunice, I'm planted very firmly in the rectory and can't be budged. I will continue to visit you on Sundays as my health permits, but I simply can't join you in the Kittleson Arms. Think of what I'd have to give up? My bird feeder and my Barcalounger. My visits, at whim, to church. My Marcella. My clock, my cat, and my car. In the kitchen Marcella handed him the phone and he said, "Hello."

"Monsignor, if I take the shuttle van to church, will you hear my confession?"

Was this a new tactic? He pictured himself trapped in the confessional, forced to hear her entire argument all over again. Thank God for the silencing dial on his hearing aid. "Of course, Eunice. What time?"

"The van leaves here at 10:25. It's a five-minute ride."

"Fine. Will you come in for coffee?"

"Didn't you hear me? I said, Will you hear my confession?"

"We're hearing more and more confessions in the rectory these days, Eunice. It's more comfortable."

"Confession isn't supposed to be comfortable."

"As you wish, Eunice."

St. Ann's was chilly and damp, its brick interior slow to recover from winter. At precisely 10:30, shivering in the box, he heard her footsteps along the aisle, heard her settle on her knees beyond the opaque curtain, and when her breathing slowed and the rasping of her nylon coat ceased, he said, "Bless you, Eunice, and welcome."

Having rehearsed his reasons for rejecting the Kittleson Arms, he was amazed not to need them. This was indeed a confession. She said, "Ever since Kelvin's funeral, I've been losing sleep over a certain matter, Monsignor, and you'll have to tell me if the matter is a sin or not, and if it's a sin, you'll have to help me make it right. I had thought for many years it was a simply a little white lie that brought about wonderful consequences, but ever since Kelvin passed away, I've been thinking of death and judgment and having this awful notion that maybe it was a terrible sin after all."

A gentle whisper: "What is it, Eunice?"

A long silence. "I can hardly bring myself to tell you."

"It involves Kelvin?"

"No, it's nothing about Kelvin. It's about Father Frank."

Quiet descended upon the confessional. She seemed not to be breathing.

"What about him, Eunice?"

"And about his mother. Her dying words. Remember?"

"Of course. She told you she wanted Frank to be a priest."

"Not exactly. She wanted *Frank* to want to be a priest."

Adrian, not immediately understanding the distinction, put his ear closer to the curtain. "Come again?"

"She said to me, 'Eunice, I hope Frank will want to be a priest.'"

There was another long silence, broken by a little cough or a sob, Adrian couldn't tell which. Then she continued.

"But I didn't quote her that way. What I told everyone was, 'I want Frank to be a priest.'"

"Mmmm," said Adrian. "Yes, I see the difference."

"I thought if I said it that way, it would seem more like his mother's decision than his own. A decision he'd surely abide by, he loved his mother so dearly."

"Oh my," said Adrian, covering his eyes and squeezing his temples—his habit when confronted with moral puzzles. "Let me hear her exact words again, Eunice."

"'I hope Frank will want to be a priest.'"

"And again—what you told him?"

"'I want Frank to be a priest.'"

"You're right," he said. "What you seem to have eliminated is the element of Frank's volition."

"Is that a sin, Monsignor?"

"It's a form of falsehood, all right."

"A mortal sin?"

"Did you give it sufficient reflection before you said it?"

"I did. And I said it over and over, for years."

"With the full consent of your will."

"Yes, with all my heart and will, I said it. Think of the result, Monsignor. I gave God a *priest*."

He didn't respond to this attempt to throw him off course. Surely Eunice Pfeiffer didn't need to be told that ends never justified means. "So it comes down to whether it was a grievous matter," he said.

At this, they were both mute, each waiting for the other to judge. Finally Eunice broke the silence.

"Was it a grievous matter, Father?"

"God knows."

"If God knows, he's not saying. I've asked him, over and over, but he's not answering."

"Frank would know."

To this she didn't respond.

"You see, Eunice, God's silence is directing you to the answer. His silence has sent you to me, and I'm advising you to see to Frank."

"Must I?" There was an uncharacteristic hint of shyness in her voice.

"It's the only way to resolve it, Eunice."

"You talk to him for me, Father."

"I can't. The seal of confession won't permit me."

"Oh, dear, I've got half a mind to forget the whole thing."

"As you wish, Eunice, but of course the other half won't let you."

She sighed and said, "All right, I'll see him."

"Lovely."

Frank left the Olds in Berrington and drove the BMW the rest of the way, Libby riding beside him and Verna sitting in the back. Turning off the highway, he followed the straightened, widened, resurfaced road into Aquinas valley and found that except for the garish billboard announcing BERRINGTON VOCATIONAL INSTITUTE—CAREERS IN THE MAKING, the campus had changed very little in appearance. The Badbattle still bubbled briskly along its western perimeter and the sandstone buildings with their cornices, turrets, and porticos still put Frank in mind of storybook illustrations. It was odd seeing women on campus.

He parked on the vast sheet of tar where the gardens used to be, and he and Libby accompanied Verna along the broad new sidewalk to Christopher Hall, which was now labeled BUILDING ONE. According to a directory in the entryway, it housed Administration on the first floor, the Department of Accounting and Office Procedures on the second, and Mortuary Science on the third. "This used to be the dean's reception room," Frank said, gesturing toward a closed door marked STORAGE.

Going deeper into the building, he noticed that all the interior brick had been covered with pale violet paint and the polished oak floor lay hidden under a brown carpet with violet flecks. Passing the bulletin board where the schedule of Masses had always been posted, he glanced at appeals to join a dating service, a dieting service, and a field trip to the mortuaries of Berrington. "This used to be the chaplain's office," he said when they came to a room labeled REGISTRAR. Verna went in.

Waiting with Libby in the corridor, he asked, "How does she seem to you?"

"Good and balanced." Libby's reply was bright and brittle. Frank had learned to detect this false note of cheer on days when Libby was feeling less than happy. In the ten weeks since Tom's death he had watched Libby struggle against the tides of her sorrow, at times rising above the undercurrent of despair and at other times sinking back into it. Her spirit, like spring in the North, was clouded and clear by turns. Her sunny days outnumbered her dark, but today he sensed her distress.

He laid a hand on her shoulder. "Are you all right?"

Ignoring the question and ducking away from his touch, she asked, "Has she been depressed at all since last week?"

"No, she's been fine." On each of the last ten Wednesdays Frank had delivered Verna to her mother in Berrington for their joint meeting with Dr. Pella, who had agreed, finally, that mother and daughter might try living together. So this was to be his last delivery.

"Does she ever act like she might go over the top?"

He shook his head. "Nothing manic since she moved in with us."

Libby smiled sadly. "We owe you so much, you and the monsignor and Mrs. Tatzig."

"You owe us nothing. She earned her keep."

The smile turned skeptical. "I have a hard time believing that."

"She helped in the kitchen."

Libby laughed. "She's never done anything in the kitchen but heat pizza in the oven."

"Adrian's very fond of pizza."

"Well, he shouldn't be, you know. It's the very worst thing for him to be eating."

Libby was right, of course—about Verna's habits as well as the monsignor's diet. Verna had done only the minimum of household chores, and those rather clumsily, but her presence in the rectory had been a blessing. To Mrs. Tatzig, Verna was not only the live-in confidante she'd been longing for, she was a celebrity besides. Each time the *Leader* carried some item of news surrounding the upcoming murder trial of Judge Bigelow—the midget's plea bargain, the BCA's continued interest in the drug trade, the recovery of the BMW from a body shop in Berrington—Mrs. Tatzig swelled with pride at having Verna in her care. Mrs. Tatzig's sister Charlotte joined the two of them every morning for long talks in the breakfast nook. As for Adrian, Verna had been his tonic and his joy. Nearly every night they'd sat up late together, watching talk shows and old movies and nibbling pizza and feeding crumbs to the cat. Adrian, in the past, had turned down pizza whenever it was offered. Surely, thought Frank, it was out of love for Verna that he pretended to have acquired the taste.

"I'm supposed to go to Travel Services and talk to the chairman," said Verna, emerging from the registrar's office with a packet of admission materials. "Building Eight."

At Frank's suggestion they left Christopher Hall by way of the colonnade leading to the side door of the church. Before going in, he paused and said, "Let's guess what they've made of this."

"Auto Repair." Verna laughed shrilly. The enrollment process was making her high-spirited, drawing her up (Frank guessed) to six or seven on the manic scale.

"A cooking school," said Libby. "I smell fried onions."

He pulled open the heavy, Gothic door that in years past had led him to prayer, and they stepped into the noise of country music and the chatter of four or five dozen students sitting at square little tables. The Church of St. Thomas Aquinas was now the Student Center. They lingered only long enough for Frank to point out that the sanctuary had become a snack bar, the stained-glass windows had been replaced by clear panes, and the choir loft had been remodeled to accommodate pinball machines and video games. "I said a thousand Masses where the fry cook is working," he said. "I preached a hundred sermons on the spot where the Coke machine stands."

Leading them out into the sunshine, he was surprised by his lack of feeling. He wasn't as deeply wounded by the changes as he'd expected to be; nor, considering the quarter century he'd spent here, as nostalgic as he had a right to be. He felt strangely reconciled to the demise of the entire Aquinas operation. Doubtless other academies and seminaries were taking up the slack. Doubtless it had been time for him to explore other avenues of the priesthood. Six months at St. Ann's and Our Lady's and he was feeling like an authentic pastor—challenged, perplexed, useful. He sensed that he would never again be traumatized by a change of assignment. He was out of the valley now, out in the changing world.

On the way to Building Eight, Verna read to her mother from her registration booklet, and as he followed behind them on the crowded sidewalk, Frank was struck by a mother-daughter resemblance he'd never noticed before, a similarity in their stride, in the set of their shoulders, in their manner of tipping their heads to speak to one another. It was warm now, and they both carried their sweaters over their left arms. Both had changed their hairstyles in recent weeks. Verna's blond hair was wavy now and longer than before, silkier. Her mother's hair, very short and resembling a tight-fitting cowl, would have looked severe on anyone else, he thought, but it was becoming on Libby. Did his love for her make him a poor judge, or was Libby truly incapable of being anything other than beautiful? Her flowered dress of pastel colors put him in mind of Easter.

In Building Eight, formerly the clergy residence, Verna asked for Travel Services and was directed upstairs.

"We'll wait outside," Libby told her.

"You're not coming up?" There was a momentary weakening of resolve in Verna's eyes.

"Remember what Dr. Pella said about being independent."

"Then why did you come at all?" asked Verna, looking as if she might pout.

Libby's answer was an encouraging pat on her daughter's shoulder, starting her up the stairs.

Stepping outside, Frank said to Libby, "I'm surprised she insisted that I come along. She could have enrolled alone."

"Moral support," Libby explained, shading her eyes and watching a flock of honking geese pass overhead. She didn't tell him that it was at her insistence that Verna had asked Frank to accompany them. Libby needed to pretend again this week—as she had been pretending for the past ten Wednesdays—that they were a family of three.

They strolled slowly across the campus, gravitating to the spot near the river where their lives had diverged so many years before. All that remained of the apple orchard were a few ancient, gnarled trees putting forth tight little buds and dozens of blackened stumps where the others had stood. She tried keeping her spirits up by speaking of Verna, whose spirits were mostly buoyant these days, but when Frank interrupted her to say, "Libby, tell me what's the matter," she gave in to her distress.

"Nothing's the matter," she said mournfully, turning away from him and facing the swirling river. "I'm feeling better."

"But you look so sad."

She laughed a little. "Feeling better makes me sad." She broke off an apple twig and turned it in her hand, studying its tiny green buds. "Whenever I feel better, I want to go back to the city. Any city. I want to leave the North and never come back."

"And you can't because of Verna?"

She shook her head. "Because of you." One after another, she pressed her thumbnail into the buds. "After her course here, if she's still functioning, Verna can come to the city with me, or not, as she pleases. Dr. Pella says I have to get over my unnatural need to control her." She turned to face him. "He also says I have to get over my unnatural dependence on you." She saw him react to this with a flash of something like disgust in his eyes—disgust at the doctor, as it turned out.

"Let him call it what he likes, Libby. It's natural and it's healthy and it's love."

"But it's doomed never to be . . . complete."

"It's love on a higher plane."

"Higher?" She laughed without humor. "Let's say a different plane."

"All right, different. It's just as real on that plane. Just as lasting. More lasting, maybe."

She couldn't deny it. "And that's why I can't stand to think of leaving you."

"There's always the telephone. The mail."

"And visits? We won't let years go by again?"

He nodded. "Visits, sure."

Or maybe she *would* let years go by. If Dr. Pella was correct in calling her attachment to Frank a dead-end addiction, then maybe they should part without plans to meet again—the way they had parted here in the orchard years ago. Dr. Pella was offering her new ways of thinking about Frank, not that she agreed with them all, but once ideas were planted in your head, how did you obliterate them? One such idea—that Frank was emotionally retarded and incapable of intimacy and thus he employed his priesthood as his defense—she'd vociferously rejected when the doctor put it forth, but she continued to be intrigued by it.

Frank leaned close to her, gripping her shoulder. "You're strong, Libby. I've watched you hit bottom and I've watched you bounce back. You're resilient."

It was true, she thought. Life had been bruising her for longer than she cared to remember, but except for that black night in February when the train invited her to destroy herself, she'd never given up. She'd held her job. Indeed, she'd taken steps to improve her life. With the money found in Tom's pockets and in the trunk of the car he died in, she'd rented a more comfortable two-bedroom apartment in the cathedral neighborhood, which she and Verna would share. Four times a day a bus stopped at their corner on its way out here to the vocational school. Soon, she guessed, Verna would be wanting a car of her own, but for now her medication kept her from driving.

"And I can see why you want to leave, Libby. You've never liked it here."

"The North." She sighed, momentarily fearful that Frank might be urging her out of his life. It was both a lucky and an unlucky thing the way their lives had intersected this second time. It was lucky—Frank would no doubt call it a blessing—that they had come together when Libby needed him so desperately, but terribly unlucky that Frank didn't need her. He'd already come through the worst of his crisis by the time they met in December. What he called his big leak wasn't leaking very much. Their timing was off. "I was able to rent the apartment by the month," she said. "When the North gets unbearable, I can leave on thirty days' notice. Verna can find herself something cheaper."

"You're strong," he repeated, "and you've outlasted your problems, and don't forget, my feeling for you never changes. Since 1949 you've been the woman in my life."

As Frank went on in this vein, she turned to the river, dropped the twig into the water, and watched it float away. She didn't hear everything he said. She was listening to the music of his voice rather than its message. She was comparing him to the boy she came to visit in the seminary a lifetime ago, the boy she frightened back into his bolt hole by announcing that she was available if he wanted her. She had not expected that boy to mature into a man who sounded this self-assured. "You're strong," he was telling her, but he was the strong one. He had a dimension she lacked, a mysterious dimension from which he drew strength, a spiritual dimension she'd never believed existed until she saw it in him. And because she lacked that dimension but needed it nearby, she couldn't imagine being out of touch with him. At least not until she found herself a new partner. All her life she'd been the type who required a partner, yet her choice of partners had been disastrous. Frank himself, when you thought about it, was maybe the worst choice of all, because he seemed not to need a partner. At least not day-to-day. At least not at close range. At least not a woman.

"When would you go, if you go?" he asked.

She looked downstream and said, "Soon." She looked upstream and said, "Not soon." She lifted her eyes from the water to the woods across the river. The trees were alive with birds; she saw flashes of color—finches, jays, redwings—darting among the budding branches. She shrugged and said, "God knows."

Taking her hand and climbing the slope, he realized that her vagueness was a relief to him. For all his brave talk, he disliked the prospect of her leaving, particularly if it brought an end to her nightly phone call. He'd come to look forward each midnight to reviewing his day with her. Her call had become as habitual as the psalm he said before sleep.

Heading back to Building Eight, she told him, as though reading his mind, "I'm going to stop calling you at midnight, Frank. Dr. Pella says I need to loosen the bond and I think the phone calls are the place to start."

Though he nodded and said "Okay," she was almost certain she detected a cloud of disappointment cross his face.

They accompanied Verna from Building Eight back to Building One, where she had more paperwork to see to, and when she was finished, they left the valley. In Berrington they lunched at the Bavarian Wursthaus. It was a very long, convivial meal, featuring Verna's amusing tales from the rectory and Frank's account of his latest visit to the bishop and the bishop's grudging agreement to extend the life of Our Lady's. Libby, while adding very little to it herself, deftly kept the conversation going far into the afternoon, pretending all the while that they were a family of three.

It was evening when Frank returned home and was urged by the monsignor to pay a call on Eunice Pfeiffer. "She has something urgent to ask you, Frank. A moral question." Adrian and the cat were sitting in the living room, both of them with their eyes on the Channel 9 weatherwoman.

"You're the moral theologian in this house, Adrian. She should have asked you."

"She did, and I couldn't help her, poor woman. You'll be doing her a great favor if you can put her at ease."

Because the temperature was mild, the sky a stunning shade

of rose, and the air infused with the smell of freshly turned earth, Frank left the car in the garage and walked across town to the Kittleson Arms, trying and failing to imagine a moral problem too complex for Eunice Pfeiffer to solve.

Her room on the second floor overlooked the street. It was very small and contained as many of her belongings as could be packed into it. The walls were gray and the floor was green tile. She insisted that he take the rocking chair. She sat on the bed, and instead of complaining about her cramped quarters and the noisy resident next door, as she had on his previous visits, she began on a grudgingly positive note. "It's not much, but it's home, Father. What I gave up in elbow room I made up for in heat. When you're old, you like to be warm."

"So you're learning to be happy here."

"When you're old, happy doesn't enter into it."

"You miss Kelvin, I'm sure."

"I miss having someone to drive me places."

"Is Raymond a comfort?"

"None."

So much for small talk, thought Frank, turning away from her and scanning the room. He saw the ribbon-wrapped packet of his letters on the table next to the TV, his ordination picture on the wall, his parents' pictures in stand-up frames on the radiator.

"Adrian said you wanted to see me?"

"Did he say why?"

"No."

"Well, don't worry, it's not about his moving here. I've given up on that."

Frank nodded gravely, concealing his relief. Adrian could relax.

"The Kittleson Arms won't take in people who are out of their minds."

Frank corrected her. "Small lapses of memory, Eunice. He's not out of his mind."

"Of course he isn't, but he pretends to be, because he knows about the restriction. I prayed he'd join me here, but I've had to stop. I can't be responsible for his deception. I can't allow myself to be the cause of his sin."

This was followed by a long silence, during which Frank gazed out at the long twilight. Robins were chirping in the little park across the street.

At length Eunice took two or three deep breaths and then explained about his mother's last words and her own fabrication of them. He listened with his eyes out the window, watching the cars pass below him, watching a dog sniff its way through the park, watching the rose light fade in the western sky. When she finished, there was a long silence, which was broken finally by the squeak of bedsprings. He turned and was startled to see her slumped and shuddering with her face in her hands. He had never in his life seen Eunice Pfeiffer cry. She looked helpless and small, diminished by sorrow. She asked through her tears whether it was a mortal sin.

He said it wasn't a sin. He said there had been nothing reprehensible in her motive. Anyhow, he said, she hadn't misquoted his mother by much. The change of wording was slight, he assured her, and so was the change of meaning. His words of comfort came pouring out of him in a swift stream because the sight of Eunice Pfeiffer's tears made him extremely nervous, and nothing else—least of all his own feelings—seemed as pressing as putting her at ease. He went on consoling her until she got hold of herself and wiped her eyes and insisted on serving him a cup of tea from her hot plate. He remained in the room another half hour or so, chatting and sipping tea and putting her revelation out of his mind until he could be alone and test his reaction. He had learned as a boy never to be emotional in front of Eunice.

Leaving her room, he braced himself for whatever flood of feelings might engulf him, but he needn't have done so. He felt nothing. He crossed the street to the park and stood for a time under the trees. He looked up at the light in Eunice's window and weighed his mother's deathbed message—"I hope Frank will want to be a priest"—against Eunice Pfeiffer's variation of it—"I want Frank to be a priest." It was clear that his mother had allowed him more volition than Eunice, but really, would it have made a difference? Would he have taken his life in a different direction? If so, it was much too late to imagine what that other direction might have been. We are what we are, he told himself. For better or worse I am a priest.

Walking home in the dark, he speculated that a year ago, feeling dislocated and bereft as he moved out of Aquinas valley, Eunice's revelation might have opened an even bigger leak in his spirit, might possibly have changed the course of his life, sending him off in search of the man he wasn't. But now it seemed to mean very little beyond the interesting light it shed on Eunice and the guilt she must have been harboring in her heart since Frank was eleven years old. And the light it shone on himself at forty-four. Surely his lack of emotion was a sign.

Mrs. Tatzig withheld comment when Frank came in during "Hawaii Five-O" with the news that Eunice Pfeiffer had given up trying to coax the monsignor away from the rectory. Her sense of triumph was subdued, overlaid by the melancholy she'd been feeling since Verna moved out. All day the house had been filled with a lonely silence. Ten weeks with a bright, hyperactive girl on your hands and you not only got used to the hubbub, you got so you liked it. No running footsteps up and down the stairs now. No more singing in the bathroom. No girlish chatter at meals. Move a bundle of energy like that out of your house and you're left with very empty rooms.

After the news her priests went up to bed, leaving Mrs. Tatzig sitting pensively before the TV. When at length she got to her feet and put out the lights and retired with the cat to her room at the back of the house, she took the unusual measure of swallowing half a sleeping tablet, for she felt vaguely disoriented and wakeful. She got into bed and listened to the silence. No waterpipe noises from Verna's late-night showers. No disco thump from Verna's radio. No creaking floor in the room overhead.

After twenty minutes of staring into the dark, she got up and busied herself at her dresser, straightening out drawers and dusting the mirror. She went into the kitchen and warmed some milk on the stove. In case the tablet took effect and she needed a few extra minutes of sleep in the morning, she prepared the grapefruit and the coffeemaker and set the table in the breakfast nook. She fed the cat an oatmeal cookie and sat stroking its back while she sipped her cup of Ovaltine. Then she went back to bed and lay listening to sounds she'd disregarded while Verna was living in the house. A car passing in the street. The clock on the mantel marking midnight. The furnace kicking in as the temperature dropped. The phone ringing. Once.

ABOUT THE AUTHOR

JON HASSLER, Regents' Professor of English at St. John's University in Collegeville, Minnesota, is the author of nine novels, most recently *Rookery Blues*, *Dear James*, and *North of Hope*, as well as two books for young adults. He lives with his wife, Gretchen, in Minneapolis, where he is at work on a multivolume series of his memoirs.

JON HASSLER

"A WRITER GOOD ENOUGH TO RESTORE YOUR FAITH IN FICTION."

—*The New York Times*

Published by Ballantine Books.
Available at your local bookstore, or call toll free 1-800-793-BOOK (2665) to order by phone and use your major credit card. Or use this coupon to order by mail.

____ DEAR JAMES	345-41013-0	$12.95
____ GRAND OPENING	345-41017-3	$12.00
____ A GREEN JOURNEY	345-41041-6	$12.00
____ THE LOVE HUNTER	345-41019-X	$12.00
____ NORTH OF HOPE	345-41010-6	$12.95
____ ROOKERY BLUES	345-40641-9	$12.00

Name_____
Address_____
City_____State_____Zip_____

Please send me the Ballantine Books I have checked above.
I am enclosing $_____
          plus
Postage & handling* $_____
Sales tax (where applicable) $_____
Total amount enclosed $_____

*Add $4 for the first book and $1 for each additional book.

Please send check or money order (no cash or CODs) to
Ballantine Mail Sales, 400 Hahn Road, Westminster, MD 21157.

Prices and numbers subject to change without notice.
Valid in the U.S. only.
All orders subject to availability.